### If the Shoe Fits . . .

She drew the slipper from her cloak. Her eyes, adjusting to the thin moonlight, picked out the faintest of shapes on a path between two rows of trees. Could they be . . . footprints?

She positioned the slipper inside one of the prints. It—well, it *seemed* to fit. The problem was, it wasn't a complete print.

"You search for something, *fräulein*?" a gruff voice said behind her.

Ophelia froze. Then, slowly, she straightened and turned.

There was a man a couple of paces off to the side in the shadow of an apple tree. He had a bushy dark beard.

And a long-barreled gun aimed straight at her noggin . . .

# Snow White
# Red-Handed

Maia Chance

**BERKLEY PRIME CRIME, NEW YORK**

*Mystery Chance*

**THE BERKLEY PUBLISHING GROUP**
**Published by the Penguin Group**
**Penguin Group (USA) LLC**
**375 Hudson Street, New York, New York 10014**

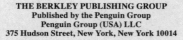

USA • Canada • UK • Ireland • Australia • New Zealand • India • South Africa • China

penguin.com

A Penguin Random House Company

SNOW WHITE RED-HANDED

A Berkley Prime Crime Book / published by arrangement with the author

PUBLISHING HISTORY
Berkley Prime Crime mass-market edition / November 2014

PRINTED IN THE UNITED STATES OF AMERICA

10  9  8  7  6  5  4  3  2  1

Interior text design by Kelly Lipovich.

*For Henry and Aesa, my beloved fairy tale elves.*

*The great deeps of a boundless forest have a beguiling and impressive charm in any country; but German legends and fairy tales have given these an added charm. They have peopled all that region with gnomes, and dwarfs, and all sorts of mysterious and uncanny creatures. At the time I am writing of, I had been reading so much of this literature that sometimes I was not sure but I was beginning to believe in the gnomes and fairies as realities.*

—Mark Twain, *A Tramp Abroad* (1880)

# 1

~~~

Miss Ophelia Flax was neither a professional confidence trickster nor a lady's maid, but she'd played both on the stage. In desperate circumstances like these, that would have to do.

"Who told you that our maid Marie gave notice?" Mrs. Coop said. Her diamond earrings wobbled.

Miss Amaryllis, sitting beside Mrs. Coop on the sofa, sniffed and added, "Uppity French tart."

If ever there were two wicked stepsisters, here they were, taking tea in the SS *Leviathan*'s stuffy first-class stateroom number eighteen: thick-waisted, brassy-haired Mrs. Coop, clutching at her fading bloom in a deshabille gown of pink ribbons and Brussels lace, and her much younger sister Miss Amaryllis, a bony damsel of twenty or so with complexion spots, slumped shoulders, and a green silk gown that resembled a lampshade. They looked up at Ophelia, expectant and hostile.

Ophelia stood before them, tall and plain in the gray woolen traveling dress, black gloves, and prim buttoned boots she'd borrowed—*stolen* was such a rotten word—from the costume trunks of Howard DeLuxe's Varieties in the ship's hold.

"Your maid's abandonment of her post," Ophelia said, "came to my attention during my midday promenade on the first-class deck."

She needn't mention that her own cramped berth was in the bowels of third class, where it stank of sour cabbage and you felt the ship's engines vibrating in your teeth.

"Embarrassing scene." Mrs. Coop pitched herself forward to reach for a cream puff. "The way Marie threw her apron at me! She always did behave as though she were my—my *superior.*"

"It wasn't your fault, ma'am," Ophelia said. "French maids are notoriously fickle. They're not the best for service, I'm afraid."

"But everyone in New York's got one. They're simply mad for them."

"It is my understanding, ma'am, that while a certain . . . class of society cling to the outdated notion that a French lady's maid is the height of elegance, the Van Der Snoots and De Schmeers and"—Ophelia scanned the stateroom's luxurious furnishings—"St. Armoire ladies have of late discovered that a Yankee lady's maid is best."

"Yankee?" Mrs. Coop's bitten cream puff hovered in midair. Yellowish filling oozed from the sides.

"Yes, ma'am. Yankee girls are honest, hardworking, modest, and loyal."

Miss Amaryllis slitted her eyes. "I suppose you're a Yankee girl?"

"Indeed I am. Born and bred on a farmstead in New Hampshire, miss."

That was true. She'd leave out the bits about the textile

mill and the traveling circus. They didn't have the same wholesome ring.

"I'll find a new maid when we reach Germany," Mrs. Coop said. "I've made up my mind. Why, if I had known Marie would quit in the midst of my honeymoon voyage, I'd have left her on the dock in Manhattan!"

"Another virtue of Yankee girls," Ophelia said, "is their ability to arrange coiffures, make cosmetic preparations, and, if needed—although I'm certain ma'am has no need—apply powders and tints with a hand as subtle as nature herself."

A lie, of course. But Ophelia was an actress—or she had been up until four hours ago, when Howard DeLuxe had given Prue the boot and Ophelia had been obliged to quit—and putting on greasepaint was one thing she knew how to do well.

"Yankee girls use face paint?" Mrs. Coop said. "Why, you said it yourself. They're as plain as potatoes."

"But they learned from their grandmothers, ma'am, the arts of medicinal plants. My own gran taught me to whip up an elderflower tincture that returns the skin to snowy youth—"

Another fib. But Mrs. Coop's eyes glimmered with interest.

"—and a *Pomade Victoria* of beeswax and almond oil that makes the hair shine like gold, a salve of *Balsam Peru* that makes complexion spots vanish." Ophelia leaned forward. "I could not help noticing Miss Amaryllis's unfortunate condition."

"Why, the cheek!" Mrs. Coop's bosom heaved.

Miss Amaryllis glared up at Ophelia and bit into a biscuit with a snap.

"And," Ophelia said, "a pleasant-tasting tonic of vinegar that slims a lady's waist without effort."

Mrs. Coop's half-eaten cream puff plopped onto her plate.

Ophelia had hooked her halibut.

"Here," Ophelia said, drawing two sealed envelopes from her pocket, "are my letters of reference. I, and my young acquaintance, Miss Prudence Bright, were traveling to England to work in the employ of Lady Cheshingham at Greyson Hall in Shropshire."

Lady Cheshingham was, in truth, the lead character in the risqué comedy *Lady Cheshingham's Charge*, which Howard DeLuxe's Varieties had performed in May. The letters were forgeries Ophelia had penned an hour earlier.

Mrs. Coop fingered the envelopes. "Ah, yes, yes, Lady Cheshingham."

"While already shipboard, I belatedly read a missive I'd received from Lord Cheshingham on the eve of our voyage, which informed me that the lady had passed away."

"Good heavens."

"Yes. A tragedy. She was so young."

"I had heard so many wonderful things about her."

"Miss Bright and I, then, are in want of employment."

*Want of employment* didn't really pin down the gravity of their circumstances. With the steamship barreling towards Southampton, Ophelia and Prue, with no jobs, only a few dollars, and no acquaintances in England, were well and truly up a stump.

"There are two of you?" Mrs. Coop sounded uncertain. "I—I must ask my husband. We are staying at our castle only until the winter."

*Castle?* Hm. Surely a figure of speech.

"Of course," Ophelia said, and made a show of tearing at the cambric handkerchief she'd plucked from her sleeve.

But she oughtn't get too carried away in her role. Mr. DeLuxe had always complained that she, having once beguiled her audience, tended to careen towards the melodramatic.

She put the hankie away. "Have you, ma'am, tried Russian face powder?"

Mrs. Coop touched her thickly powdered cheek. "I've always used French."

"Russian is the best, used first by the czarina Catherine. It's got crushed pearls in it—pearls from the North Sea, which restore the complexion to a state of infancy. But don't tell anyone. It'll be our little secret."

"Pearls for Mrs. Pearl Coop," Miss Amaryllis said into her teacup. "How poetic."

"It is easier, Amaryllis," Mrs. Coop said through clenched teeth, "to catch flies with honey than with vinegar."

"Whatever would I want with flies?"

"A figure of speech, dear. Perhaps it would be best if you married your *own* fly, rather than straggling along with Homer and me."

"Homer a fly?" Miss Amaryllis smirked. "More of a frog, don't you think?"

"If I may be so bold," Ophelia interrupted, "it would be a privilege to attend to such lovely, refined ladies."

Mrs. Coop blinked, and Miss Amaryllis leaned against the sofa arm and propped her chin sulkily on her hand.

Mrs. Coop sighed and picked up her cream puff. "It seems we've no choice in the matter. When can you start?"

Ophelia held in an exhalation of relief. "Immediately, ma'am," she said.

"Well?" Prue flung herself face-up on her narrow berth. Her cheeks were blotchy and wet with tears.

Ophelia shut the cabin door. "We have jobs."

"That's splendiferous!"

"I am to be a lady's maid—"

Prue's face fell.

"—and you are to be a scullery maid."

"Scullery maid?" Prue struggled to a seated position. Golden ringlets tumbled around her flushed face and her eyes of enamel blue. She was the closest thing to a china doll that a nineteen-year-old American girl could be. Until, that is, she opened her mouth to speak. "I ain't cut out for a scullery maid, Ophelia. I'm clumsy, for starters, but more than that, I ain't got the *concentration* to peel carrots all day."

Ophelia wholeheartedly agreed. "You'll manage," she said. She stripped off the stolen gloves. "It's only a bit of washing pots and scrubbing vegetables."

"Why can't I be a lady's maid, too?"

"Mrs. Coop and Miss Amaryllis desired but one lady's maid between them. We are lucky they agreed to take you on at all. Don't look so weepy. It's only for a few months, until we save up enough to buy passage back to America. Besides, we don't have another plan."

The plan *had* been to perform with Howard DeLuxe's Varieties in its limited engagement at the Pegasus Theater on the Strand. "Limited engagement" meant for however long gin-soaked London gents would pack the seats to watch the troupe's bawdy skits and musical numbers. "The Lusty Whalers of Nantucket" had top billing, alongside a bit about cowgirls and Indians, a romantic scene in which Ophelia played Pocahontas, and "Paul Revere's Bride," featuring a horse that galloped offstage with a scantily clad Puritan wench.

"We could go find my Ma," Prue said. "Nat—you know, the feller who paints the scenery—told me this afternoon he heard she was in Europe."

"We haven't any notion where." Ophelia sank onto the edge of her own berth. "Europe is enormous, not to mention expensive. And she could just as easily be in New York."

"A scullery maid." Prue's tears were spouting again. "What'll become of me? I ain't got anyone. Ma never wanted me—"

"Now you know that isn't true." Ophelia handed over a hankie.

"If she'd hornswoggled a millionaire into marrying her when I was a baby, she would've left me then."

"Nonsense."

Prue noisily blew her nose.

Her mother, Miss Henrietta Bright, had been the star actress in Howard DeLuxe's Varieties, and like so many actresses, she had supplemented her income with—to mince words—additional business endeavors. Last year, she'd run off with one of her admirers. Some said he was a Wall Street tycoon, others that he was a European blue blood. Either way, Prue's mother had abandoned a flighty girl who possessed all the common sense of a tadpole. Ophelia had no living family of her own—a missing brother and a father she'd never met hardly counted—so she'd taken Prue under her wing.

Ophelia bent to unbutton the stolen boots; they were too small, and her toes felt numb. "You know I have a little money saved up, in the bank in New York—"

"For your farm! You've been scrimping for ages."

"I have." A vision of misty green fields, a white barn, and sweet-eyed dairy cows rose up in Ophelia's mind's eye. It was a vision that often lulled her to sleep, that got her through slushy November afternoons and exhausting double matinee performances. "When I buy my farm someday, well, you can come and live with me there."

Prue wrinkled her nose. "Will I have to milk the cows?"

"Certainly not."

"Snatch it, you're just being nice. You're always being too nice. Just because Mr. DeLuxe sent me packing don't mean *you* should've quit."

Ophelia said nothing as she yanked off the boots. But she knew exactly what became of pretty, silly, penniless girls who didn't have a protector, and the idea of Prue alone on the streets of London didn't bear thinking about.

"You could've been a lead actress someday, Ophelia. And now you're just a maid."

"Fiddlesticks. Acting has merely been a way to pay for my daily bread."

"When you filled in as Cleopatra when Flossie broke her arm, you got a standing ovation and enough roses to fill three bathtubs. You were a stunner."

"In a wig and greasepaint," Ophelia said. "Gospel truth, it doesn't concern me in the least that without Cleopatra kohl-lined eyes or Marie Antoinette rouged cheeks, I blend nicely into the backdrop. I'm five and twenty years of age, plenty old enough to have made peace with myself. I'm not saying I'm some mousy thing who gets stepped on—"

"Course not. You're a beanstalk."

"Not as tall as that, perhaps." In truth, Ophelia *was* tall, and she had large feet, and no corset could mold her straight figure into a fashion plate's hourglass. But her oval face, molasses-colored eyes, and light brown hair were presentable enough. "Anyway, since I'm an actress, a knack for blending in is an asset." She wiggled her blissfully freed toes. "Now. If we're ever to get back home in one piece, we ought to prepare ourselves for our new roles as maids."

"Where in tarnation are they taking us?" Prue said three days later. She scrubbed at the grimy coach window with her fist. Their coach creaked and jostled up the mountainous road like a rheumatic mule. "Everything was all right until we got off at that bad railway station—"

"Baden-Baden," Ophelia corrected from the opposite seat. "*Baden* means baths—it's a thermal resort town."

"That in your book?" Ophelia had had her nose stuck in some book she'd borrowed from Miss Amaryllis for the whole of their railway and boat journey between Southampton and Germany. It was called a *Baedeker*, Ophelia had told Prue. Whatever that meant. Prue hadn't bothered to thumb through it. She considered herself a *doing* kind of person. Book learning gave her the jitters.

Besides, Ma had always cautioned that reading gave a lady a scrunched-up forehead and a panoramic derriere.

Baden-Baden, a German town nestled in plush hills, was called the Paris of the summer months. Leastways, that's what the *Baedeker* said. All the cream of Europe's crop, from Polish princes and British nobles to Italian opera stars and Russian novelists, gathered there to socialize, dance, take the waters, and gamble at the races or in the opulent gaming rooms.

But their coach had left Baden-Baden miles behind, and they were headed up into the mountains.

"I reckoned," Prue said, "when we took that boat to Brussels, we were headed to civilization. But this!" She scowled out the window. Mountains reared up into the chambray-colored sky. "This looks worse than Maine."

"We're in the Black Forest, Prue. Haven't you heard of it?"

"Never."

"Your mother didn't read you those fairy stories by the Grimm Brothers?"

"Read me stories?" Prue bit into one of the strawberry jelly sweets she'd spent her last penny on, back at the railway station. "Not her. But I sure know how to tell real diamonds from paste, and if a gentleman's got a walloping bank account or is just trying to dupe a lady." She chewed hard. The topic of Ma made her feel sore somewhere under her ribs. "Looks like the first-class carriage is getting away from us."

"We are servants now," Ophelia said. Her voice was gentle. "We can't expect to ride with the family."

"Can't expect a decent coach, neither."

"I allow, this coach isn't the most comfortable—"

"It's a rickety old rattletrap." Prue eyed the black wood fittings around the window: carved thorny vines. "Or maybe a hearse."

"We are fortunate to have found employment."

"Well, don't that beat all!" Prue exclaimed. "Look at that castle."

"Where?"

"Up there."

Ophelia followed Prue's pointed finger. "That," she murmured, "beats all indeed."

High on a jutting stone outcrop, framed by pine trees, was a castle. It was built of pale stone, with turrets of various sizes, battlements, walls, parapets, and balconies. It glowed like an enchanted wedding cake in the afternoon sun, and hazy mountains stretched endlessly behind it like a painted theater backdrop.

"Ain't got *those* in Maine." Prue popped another strawberry jelly in her mouth.

"I think," Ophelia said, "that's where we're going to live."

# 2

Two weeks later

"Snow White's little house," Professor Winkler said in his thick German accent, "the house, you understand, in the wood wherein she lived with her seven dwarves, has been, according to the telegram, found." He chuckled, holding tight to a hand strap as the carriage bumped up the mountain road. "Such beliefs, of course, are merely fancies of the peasantry. I cannot think how this American millionaire's wife got hold of such a notion, particularly since she has been in Germany only a few weeks."

"Curious indeed," Gabriel Augustus Penrose said. "And I do agree with you, it goes without saying that superstitious stories are the product of debased minds and, I suspect, poor nutrition as well." He tried to stretch his long legs, which were stiff from that morning's fifty-mile railway journey from Heidelberg to Baden-Baden. "We are fortunate that the philological work that began with Wilhelm and Jacob Grimm laid the groundwork for a more enlightened understanding of fairy tales."

"But the folk are wily, Professor Penrose, and ready to defend their backwards beliefs to the death. Why, once, in a dark, *kleine* hamlet in the Brigach River valley, I encountered an old crone who swore that she was the great-great-granddaughter of Gretel."

"Of *'Hansel und Gretel'*?" Gabriel raised an eyebrow as he straightened his spectacles, a bemused, condescending look he'd perfected years ago.

"The same. How I did laugh at the miserable thing. By the sorry appearance of her teeth, I judged she had eaten a fair share of candy windows and cake roofs herself. Now, where is this Schloss Grunewald?" Winkler hunched his aged, oxlike frame to better see out the carriage window. "Mr. Coop's telegram indicated that it was five miles from the Baden-Baden station. Ah. There. I see the towers through the trees. One of those piles the romantics renovated to appear more picturesque."

Gabriel glimpsed the castle, too, floating like a mirage over a half-timbered village in a valley. "I was told," he said, "that the *schloss* retains portions that are ancient, but the greater part was rebuilt in the twenties by the grandfather of the former owner—a certain Count Grunewald—as a summer retreat." He paused to admire the effect of the castle's creamy stones surrounded by emerald mountains. "So, it would seem that it isn't only the peasants who indulge in romantic notions."

Winkler gave him a sharp look. "It is not the same, is it?"

"Mmm," Gabriel said, and pretended to be deep in a study of the passing forest.

Hang it. That had been a slipup.

Gabriel had built his academic career upon a rather snobbish outlook on the origins and significance of folklore. As professor of philology at St. Remigius's College, Oxford, he painstakingly researched archaic texts to expose the deluded—but nonetheless fascinating—imaginations of a pagan folk that still lingered in remote pockets of modern Europe. Fairy tales and myths were nothing but drivel, he and his colleagues insisted.

He was obliged to keep it hidden that he believed quite the opposite. That he had believed in the inexplicable ever since that strange, magical dawn in the Crimea almost thirteen years ago.

"Thank you," he said to Winkler, "for bringing me along, by the way. I'm interested to see how you set these superstitious people to rights."

"I am called upon to do it more than I care to admit. The benefit is that the remote hamlets, where these summons usually bring me, have some of the best food and drink in all of Germany. *Ach*, the bratwurst I dined upon when some fools thought they had found golden straw sealed up in an ancient silo. I must have eaten two hogs' worth! With a kraut to accompany it that—oh!—it was worth all the annoyance." He smacked his lips.

"It was fortuitous that I encountered you at the university last night," Gabriel said. "I usually conduct my evening studies at my rented rooms in the Klingenteichstrasse. I'd only gone in to the university because I'd forgotten a book." Gabriel was spending the summer as a visiting scholar at Heidelberg University in order to examine a crumbling fifteenth-century manuscript.

"I am pleased to have you along."

Gabriel eyed the black bag resembling a doctor's bag on the seat beside Winkler. "What sort of things do you do when you're called upon to investigate so-called fairy tale evidence?"

"It is all strictly scientific, very precise. While I, like you, am a philologist, as a young man, I studied chemistry. In that kit there"—Winkler gestured with his chins towards the bag— "you shall find an array of testing equipment."

"Testing? For—?"

Winkler chuckled again. "Gold, my dear professor. The peasants always believe they have discovered dwarf's gold."

Winkler and Gabriel stepped down from their carriage into Schloss Grunewald's forecourt.

"You the college men?" A middle-aged gentleman gestured towards them with a half-eaten apple.

"Professor Penrose," Gabriel said, extending his deerskin-gloved hand. "And this is my esteemed colleague, Professor Winkler."

"Coop. Homer T. Coop." Coop's handshake was as gruff as his American accent. He had a bristling mustache and side-whiskers, and his head was shrubbed with coppery hair streaked with gray. He was barrel-chested and wearing a well-tailored checked suit and a porkpie hat. His hands were not gloved, and they looked more suited to a railway gang laborer than a railway millionaire. "I want you to know straight off," Coop said, "that I don't have time for this tomfoolery. I telegraphed you on account of my wife, Pearl."

"So you mentioned," Winkler said, "in your telegram."

"Her head's rotted with this storybook nonsense, as if she were a little miss of six. One of the servants told her about the famous fairy tale professor in Heidelberg, and she wouldn't stop buzzing in my ear like a dangnabbed mosquito about it until I agreed to send a telegram." He gnawed his apple. "Never went to college myself. Guess I'm a good example of how you don't need it." He snorted. "I started off on Wall Street, you know. Worked for a Harvard man. He never did manage to get his snotty nose down low enough to sniff out a bad deal. Went bankrupt in forty-nine. That's when I cleared out."

"Shall we have a look at the find?" Gabriel said.

"It's now or never," Coop said. "I mean to raze the house once you've looked it over." He suddenly bellowed, "Smith!" He threw the apple core onto the flagstones. "Smith," he said to Gabriel and Winkler, "is my right hand. I don't cotton to manservants and the like, such as you European fellers have. But for business matters, I've got Smith."

"Mr. Coop?" someone said.

Gabriel and Winkler turned. It was a brilliant summer morning, and sunny where they stood, but half of the forecourt was still in shadow. So when Gabriel followed the meek voice, his sun-dazzled eyes convinced him that one of the crouching stone gargoyles that flanked the steps leading up to the castle doors had come to life and was skulking towards them.

Gabriel's breath caught. There it was, that feeling he'd had a handful of times before. A sense of the bottom quite falling out of reality, and wonderment and magic gusting in.

He blinked. His eyes adjusted to the shadows, and he saw, with combined relief and dismay, that it was only a remarkably short gentleman and that the gargoyles by the stair hadn't moved an inch.

"This here's my secretary," Coop said, "Mr. George Smith."

Smith shook their hands. He had a face like an intelligent pug dog, and graying hair parted and combed like a schoolboy's. He wore a neat suit of flannels and a bowler hat.

"Come on," Coop said to Smith. "Let's take these college boys out to the woods."

They left the castle behind and tramped through rugged, sun-dappled hills for twenty minutes.

"Right through here," Smith called over his shoulder. He led the way up through a dry gully, Gabriel close behind, followed by Winkler and Coop.

All of a sudden, a figure emerged on the path ahead. A sturdy woman, in a dust-colored walking costume, leather belt, and broad-brimmed straw hat. She was all alone. She strode towards them, a leather satchel swinging from her shoulder. She had a large, bland face, a nose like a drawer knob, and pale, nearly invisible eyebrows over lashless gray eyes. Her cheeks were flushed with exertion or, perhaps, sunburn.

The men paused to allow her to pass.

"Fancy meeting anyone out here in this wilderness," she called.

British. The world was simply crawling with British tourists. You could be shipwrecked at the farthest reaches of the globe, wearing mere tatters and chomping coconuts, and look up to see one of the queen's hale subjects striding out of the brush in a safari jacket and a pith helmet.

"Good morning," Gabriel said. He lifted his hat. "Pleasant day for a tramp, isn't it?"

"Oh yes," she said in a hearty voice. "Absolutely ripping. Watch out for the flies," she added over her shoulder. "Horrid little mites. Swarmed like cannibals and made a feast of my apple."

She loped out of sight around a turn in the gully.

"Got to put up some private property signs, Smith," Mr. Coop said.

They continued on their way up the path.

Presently, the gully opened out onto a forest glade filled with wild blueberry bushes and enormous trees.

The four men paused to mop their brows with handkerchiefs.

The glade had an enchanted feeling to it. Insects hummed, the air was spicy-sweet with pinesap and wildflowers, and sunlight mottled the mossy ground.

"The castle woodsman, Herz," Smith said, "will cut these three trees just here"—he gestured with a small gloved hand—"and in preparation yesterday, he was clearing out the undergrowth. To get at the trunks of the trees, see."

"Forgive my impertinence," Gabriel said, "but why would one cut these trees? They must be at least four hundred years old." The pine trees, as big around as barrels, rose cathedral-like into the azure sky. Aloft, their boughs bounced in the breeze.

"Clear the view," Coop said. He propped his thick, booted leg on a boulder, pulled another green apple from his jacket pocket, and bit it. "I was looking out my study window and this here patch lay directly in my line of sight. Couldn't see a consarned thing but trees. Damages the mind."

"Trees do?" Gabriel said.

"They just sit there. No energy to them. That's no way to succeed in life."

"Ah."

"Through here, then?" Winkler called back to them. He

was bustling, black bag in hand, towards the hole in the thicket the woodsman had made. "Shall we proceed? I do not wish to forego luncheon."

"I like that man," Coop said, munching his apple. "Not like a college feller at all. Smith, get out your notebook. I've just had a notion for that St. Louis pickle."

Gabriel followed Winkler into the hole in the thicket, where he found Winkler on his hands and knees.

Gabriel's heart sped up a notch. There, as Coop's telegram had mentioned, was a miniature house with a small door, just high enough for a five-year-old child to pass through. He knelt beside Winkler. "May I?"

"By all means. I have had my fill of such things."

Gabriel pushed aside the tensile brambles that framed the door. The door was made of rough wood planks, and it was soft with decay. It had a small iron handle that felt, as he grasped it, like a toy. He pushed the door inward. Chunks of moss and dirt rained down from the roof, but the door opened. A dank odor of loam and subterranean vegetation swirled out.

Gabriel gasped.

A sliver of daylight illuminated a skeleton lying on the floor, just inside the door. Its bones glimmered whitely. Skull and spine were neatly arranged between short leg bones; one femur was missing. The arm bones were crossed over the ribcage, as in a tomb. Little bones, probably toes and fingers, were scattered about like breadcrumbs.

"What an ingenious hoax," Winkler said. "The German *volk*, Professor Penrose, are perhaps the most enterprising of all the European peasants when it comes to such things. They do so want the rest of the world to believe in their fairy stories as much as they do."

"That's a tiny skeleton," Gabriel said.

"*Ja*. A child's skeleton."

"But the head is the size of a grown man's."

"It would have been but a simple matter to replace the child's skull with an adult's."

"If this is a hoax, you would infer that the house is, what—twenty years old?"

"Fifty at most."

"Then how would you account for the way the roots of that ancient tree have grown quite over the threshold?"

Winkler paused.

Gabriel pointed at the tree root in question, trying not to seem smug. Although he was beginning to believe this find was something very, very important, he could not let Winkler know he cared. "That would date the house to, oh, three or four hundred years, would it not?"

"There are various ways that the roots could have been placed like that, I have no doubt. Let us have a look inside, shall we?" He unbuckled his bag and took out a small gas lantern and a box of matches. Once the lantern was lit, he began to crawl through the door.

For a few seconds, Gabriel feared Winkler's girth would not fit. But after a moment of straining, he popped through. Gabriel followed.

# 3

I t was a one-room cottage, perhaps twenty by thirty feet.
The roof had probably once been thatched, but now
nothing was left but ceiling beams woven with brambles,
which created a roof of green leaves. Splotches of sunlight
fell through the leaves onto the dirt-covered floor. Gabriel
made an exploratory probe in the floor with his penknife,
revealing rotted floorboards.

Puzzling. Everything was coated with rot and loam.
Everything, that is, except the skeleton. That had been laid
out recently.

"Precisely like the Grimm tale," Winkler said, holding up
the lantern. "Little chairs and a table, and seven *kleine* beds
along the wall there. Observe those small pots and kettles by
the fireplace, and spoons and plates"—he lifted a dirt-covered
plate from the table—"of pewter. Our charlatans were certainly faithful to the Grimms' text '*Schneewittchen*.'"

"The style of the spoons"—Gabriel picked up a
begrimed spoon from the table—"is sixteenth century, is it
not? I don't know a great deal about German antiquities,
yet I recall seeing a similar design at a castle in Scotland."

Winkler brought his lantern close and squinted at the spoon. "The peasants tend to reproduce the same styles for century upon century, making their objects difficult to date. They have not the capacity for originality, you see." He crawled away. "What have we here?"

Gabriel looked up. Winkler held the lantern high. The middle ceiling beam glinted behind leafy brambles.

"Gold," Gabriel said, and then recited a line from the Grimms' "Snow White": *"The seven dwarves spent their days mining ore and digging for minerals."*

*"Ach*, you are falling under the spell, Penrose." Winkler moved the lamp along the length of the ceiling beam. Much of it was coated with dirt. But here and there they saw that its surface was carved wooden relief, and flecks of gold leaf and colorful chipped paint still remained.

"We shall have this beam and the skeleton removed and carried to the castle," Winkler said, "and clean and inspect them after luncheon. It must be twelve o'clock already."

"If the images on this beam are still intact," Gabriel said, "they could provide clues to the mystery of this cottage."

It was an effort to sound disinterested. His secret life's obsession was to compile a collection of relics that would at last prove, indisputably, that fairy tales were based upon historical events. Until he did so, however, he needed to keep quiet or become the laughingstock of academe.

"That is all very well and good." Winkler had crawled past the skeleton and was pushing back out through the doorway. "But I am certain," he said over his shoulder, "that what every party is most interested in is whether or not that is real gold leaf."

When Gabriel joined Winkler back out in the forest glade, he saw three ladies and two gentlemen clustered about Coop and Smith. Not wishing to enter the fray, he paced off a distance, leaned against the trunk of a tree, and took the opportunity to write a few lines in the memorandum book that he always carried in his breast pocket.

*Not a hoax*, he wrote with a stub of pencil and underlined it twice.

Feminine titters caused him to lift his eyes. The newcomers were, he assumed, members of the Coop family, their visitors, and their servants. Smith had apprised Gabriel and Winkler of their names during the hike to the cottage.

There was an elegant lady of middle years, petite, brunette, possessing a rose-petal complexion and a refined mien. That was the Russian Princess Verushka, doubtless. The foppish, dark-curled young Adonis who loitered off to the side, smoking a cigarette and looking bored, was probably Mr. Hunt. Smith had said he was British. There was also a bony young lady—Miss Amaryllis, perhaps—with a large nose. She cast her eyes towards Mr. Hunt. He did not seem to notice. The other gentleman was a footman in green livery, holding a parasol over the ladies. He didn't, to be honest, appear as dashing as footmen usually did. He was over fifty years of age, with a small paunch and disheveled gray hair that called to mind the expression *gone to seed*.

A somewhat blowsy-looking woman, yellow-haired and richly attired in a walking costume, was the source of the commotion. Gabriel pegged her as Mrs. Coop. She was pointing to the ground at the entrance of the cottage.

"The soil is sparkling!" Gabriel heard her cry. "It's got gold in it, Homer. Look!"

A hubbub ensued, during which Winkler stooped to open his bag, scrape a sample of soil into a small glass vial, and cork it.

Gabriel suppressed a sigh. The greed and melodramas of the rich and bored were a larger part of his life—at least his life in England—than he'd wish. He longed to roll up his sleeves and begin conducting, inch by inch, an examination and catalogue of the cottage. But it was evident that he'd have to suffer through luncheon with this lot first.

He jotted more notes as Winkler, speaking in his booming voice, led the group into the thicket. Gabriel tried not to think about the damage they could inflict on the house, blundering about in there.

The footman had stayed behind. When he thought he was alone—he did not seem to be aware of Gabriel's presence—he pulled a silver flask from his jacket, unscrewed the cap, and took a long swallow.

Then a small movement across the glade caught Gabriel's eye. There was another young lady, one he hadn't noticed at first, standing in the shade. Evidently there hadn't been room enough for her to go into the thicket with the others, and she was waiting.

She was attired in a charcoal-gray gown with a white collar, and a dark bonnet. A poor relation or a paid companion. Or perhaps a lady's maid. Although there was something graceful about her tall, slim figure, and she held her head so high that it was difficult to imagine she was a servant. Her face was, well, plain. It was a pure oval, very symmetrical, yet somehow, in its very purity, it just missed the pretty mark. Her darting dark eyes reminded him of the centers of poppies.

He hadn't realized he was staring until her eyes riveted on him. A tingle ran down his spine.

She lifted her eyebrows. Gabriel yanked the brim of his hat down over his eyes and scribbled something absurd in his memorandum book.

"I simply must have you at my side this afternoon, Flax," Mrs. Coop said. "I've come down with a sick headache, but I wouldn't miss Professor Winkler's gold test for the world. Tighter!"

"I'm doing my utmost, ma'am," Ophelia said, straining to cinch Mrs. Coop's corset laces.

After luncheon, Mrs. Coop had returned to her cream-and-gold jewel box of a boudoir, high in a turret of the castle, to change into her afternoon gown. She'd been breathless and disheveled, and determined to shrink her waist to a smaller compass.

Mrs. Coop's disarray, and her sudden wish to appear pixielike, resulted, Ophelia suspected, from the presence in the castle of either Princess Verushka or Mr. Royall Hunt.

Mrs. Coop and Miss Amaryllis had made the acquaintance of these two fashionable personages at some point in the last two weeks' frenzy of excursions into Baden-Baden.

"You must," Mrs. Coop said, "stay by my side with my smelling salts, should I need them, and fetch me glasses of water and whatever else I may need. I am not well, Flax—even Mr. Hunt noted that I'm white as a lily—yet this is perhaps the most thrilling day of my life."

"Yes, ma'am," Ophelia said.

"Just think! Snow White's cottage on my own estate. And a dwarf's bones!"

"Mm."

"Do I hear doubt in your tone, Flax?"

"Truth be told, ma'am, it is difficult for me to believe that that house belonged to creatures from a storybook."

"Difficult to believe?"

"Well, ma'am, near impossible."

Ophelia had performed with P. Q. Putnam's Traveling Circus for two years, and she'd known a so-called dwarf. He'd been a shrimp, true, but there hadn't been a thing magical about him. Unless you counted swearing like a sailor and smoking like a house on fire as magic.

"Of course." Mrs. Coop sniffed. "I nearly forgot you're a Yankee."

Ophelia held her tongue; she was stepping out of character. It had to be the result of exhaustion. Mrs. Coop and her stepsister, Amaryllis, kept Ophelia on her feet from dawn to dusk, arranging their hair, pressing their clothing, mixing beauty concoctions, and running up and down the spiraling castle stairs fetching things.

How could anyone past the age of pigtails think Snow White and the seven dwarves had really existed? And it wasn't only Mrs. Coop, who could be counted upon to be frivolous, who was entertaining the notion. Those two university professors were as well. The younger of the two professors, the tall, handsome, bespectacled one with the upper-crust British accent, looked far too intelligent to be taken in by such hogwash.

"There," Ophelia said, tying a seaworthy knot at the end of the corset laces. "That's as tight as I can get it. Will you be wearing the blue silk, ma'am?"

"No, no, the tea gown with the lavender stripes." Mrs. Coop surveyed herself—still in only crinoline, petticoats, and corset—in a tall, gilt-framed mirror. She tipped her head sideways. "Whatever is wrong with this mirror? It's gone all squat."

Mirrors weren't known for lying. But Mrs. Coop wouldn't take kindly to that observation.

"I don't think this corset is strong enough," Mrs. Coop went on. "But it's made of real whalebone, you know. It's not one of those cheap starched things."

Then it had been strong enough for the whale.

"Hurry up, Flax. Professor Winkler shall be starting soon."

"Yes, ma'am."


"The first item I require," Professor Winkler said, once everyone had reassembled in the library, "is a small quantity of washing soda from the castle laundry."

Ophelia watched from the shadows beside the fireplace. Winkler looked like an elderly walrus and had something of the snake oil salesman about him. But everyone else in the lofty, book-lined chamber—Mrs. Coop, Miss Amaryllis, Princess Verushka, Mr. Hunt, Mr. Coop, and Mr. Smith, even Karl the first footman, standing against the wall—was rapt with attention. The lone exception was the younger professor. Ophelia had overheard that he was called Professor Penrose.

While the others stared at Winkler, Penrose was studying their faces. His eyes, behind his spectacles, were hazel, and his eyebrows were straight and dark. His brown hair was as tidy as a professor's ought to be, but how had his complexion come to be so suntanned, and his shoulders so broad, if he spent his days lecturing and reading indoors?

"Washing soda?" Mrs. Coop said. "Whatever for?"

"You do not intend to bore us with housework?" Princess Verushka added in her heavy Russian accent. She was hovering somewhere in her middle years, but she was a marvel of religious preservation, as Ophelia had heard it said of the Sistine Chapel in Rome. Her mahogany hair gleamed, her figure was spry, her fair skin was lustrous, and Ophelia's trained eye could not detect a particle of powder or paint.

"All, my dear ladies," Winkler said, "shall become clear."

Mrs. Coop rose and hurried across the library to yank the velvet bellpull in the corner.

"Luncheon, by the by, was superb," Winkler said to Mr. Coop. "The sautéed liver! Your cook is a sorceress. Did you bring her from America?"

"Came with the castle." It appeared that Mr. Coop had drunk heavily at luncheon. His neck was mottled and his eyes bleary. "Trained in gay Paree, I'm told. Durn well better be, I said to Pearl, for the greengrocer's bills this place runs up."

"It *is* a castle," Mrs. Coop said in a pouting tone, returning to her seat. "You can hardly expect it to run itself."

"Ah, but enchanted castles do," Winkler said. He was taking small objects from a black leather bag and lining them up on a table in the center of the library. "Madam, I am given to understand you are taken with our European fairy stories."

"I've adored them since I was a girl. I always dreamed of being a queen in a castle."

"And now you are," Miss Amaryllis said. She pursed her lips. "Fancy that."

"Enough," Mr. Coop boomed. "Your sister, Amaryllis, has been good enough to give you a roof over your head—begged me to do it, even though I preferred to let you make your own way in the world like everyone else. I gave in, but now you do gad-all but blight our honeymoon with your waspish sniveling."

Ophelia scanned the library. Mrs. Coop's lower lip was tremulous, and her hand was on her husband's arm. Mr. Smith studied the Persian carpet. Princess Verushka fanned herself, nervous as a finch. Mr. Hunt, wearing a bland expression, reached to a side table and took a handful of sugared almonds from a bowl. The footman Karl gazed into space. Professor Penrose watched Mr. Coop.

And Amaryllis glared at Mr. Coop with murderous hatred in her eyes.

"You," Mr. Coop said, wagging a thick finger at Amaryllis, "are a nasty witch—they got those in fairy stories, professor?"

"Homer, *please*," Mrs. Coop hissed.

Amaryllis's hands were trembling in her yellow silk lap. She swiveled her eyes from her brother-in-law to Mr. Hunt.

Mr. Hunt placed a sugared almond between his lips and crunched down.

Tears shimmered in Amaryllis's eyes.

There was a knock on the door. It was a servant—Ophelia couldn't see which one—who Mrs. Coop sent back to the servants' regions to fetch washing powder.

"I do apologize for my sister," Mrs. Coop said, taking her seat once more. "She hasn't been herself as of late. The move from America."

Amaryllis wore the martyred expression of Joan of Arc revolving on a roasting spit.

"Do you intend to stay in Germany permanently?" Penrose asked Mrs. Coop.

He was doing the gentlemanly thing and changing the topic. He did have kind eyes.

"Only through the autumn," Mrs. Coop said. "Schloss Grunewald shall be our summer home, you see. I simply wouldn't want to miss a New York season. Unless, of course"—she glanced out of the corner of her eye at Mr. Hunt, flicked her lashes— "one was to receive an invitation to England."

All that corset-cinching *had* been for Mr. Hunt's benefit, then. And Mrs. Coop a newlywed, too. Scandalous.

Mr. Coop, however, was now in the midst of a hushed conversation with Mr. Smith—the words *St. Louis* and *red cent* reached Ophelia's ears—so he wasn't aware of his wife's flirtations.

Mr. Hunt, however, was. "A London season, Mrs. Coop—"

"Oh!" She toyed with her necklace.

"—would surely surpass any New York season. In New York, can you expect a social invitation from Her Royal Majesty Queen Victoria?"

"You don't mean—"

"It has been known to happen."

Mrs. Coop picked up the bowl of sugared almonds. Her eyes glittered with excitement. "More, Mr. Hunt?"

Penrose shifted in his chair.

Princess Verushka sniggered behind her fan. "Mrs. Pearl T. Coop in Buckingham Palace! *Mon Dieu*!" The princess, like all Russian aristocrats, spoke French.

Mrs. Coop cast the princess a look of loathing mingled, if Ophelia wasn't mistaken, with fear.

# 4

After several minutes, there was another knock on the library door.

"Enter," Mrs. Coop called.

The door swung open and Prue stepped inside.

*Prue?* Ophelia frowned. Prue was a scullery maid. Her duties confined her to the lower recesses of the castle. So what was she doing in an ill-fitting black parlor maid's dress, ruffled apron, and white cap, carrying a bowl of washing powder into the library?

"Here." Winkler pointed to the table.

Prue placed the bowl next to the several odd-looking instruments and vials Winkler had arranged on the tabletop.

Also on the table, Ophelia noticed for the first time, were a long, dirty piece of wood decorated with chipped paint and something underneath a white cloth. An ivory-colored thing extended a few inches beyond the cloth. A finger bone.

Prue turned to go.

"You've got nice, dainty hands," Winkler said.

Prue froze. The room fell silent. She saw Ophelia for the first time.

Uh-oh. Prue had been crying. Her eyes and nostrils were pink.

"Would you," Winkler said, "help us with our experiment?"

Prue clearly wanted to bolt out the door.

"Come now, a pretty girl like you ought to be happy to be the center of notice."

A scowl washed over Prue's features.

Ophelia prayed she wouldn't say anything regrettable.

"Roll up your sleeves," Winkler said. "You shall assist me."

Prue gulped. All eyes were on her. Normally, that wouldn't bother her a bit. She'd first appeared onstage at the age of two, dressed up like a dancing teapot, to the acclaim of all of New York's theatrical critics. Or so Ma claimed.

But Prue had been stuck behind the scenes at the castle for near two weeks. She was dismal in the role of scullery maid; she'd never had what folks called a *domestic education*. Her hands were red from scrubbing the wrong way.

And her hands were still shaking from the shocking thing that had just happened to her.

"Gold," Professor Winkler said, "is the only yellow-colored metal that is not affected by most acids. Therefore, we may test whether this"—he held up a gold-colored flake between metal pincers—"is real gold leaf or merely paint."

Prue kept her eyes on the carpet. He was here, in the library. That lowdown, bullying scallywag. Blood thundered past her eardrums.

"The test is made with a blowpipe"—Winkler displayed a small instrument, like a metal straw that was curved on one end—"and nitric acid." He smiled down at Prue. "You must be very, very careful, *fräulein*. One drop of this acid would corrode your pretty skin into yellow monster's scales."

Prue gaped up at him. She forgot all about the lowdown scallywag for a second.

"Let us begin." Winkler ground the gold-colored flake

into a powder with a mortar and pestle. Then he measured out portions of the gold powder and the washing powder with thimble-sized measuring spoons.

"This commonplace washing powder is also known as sodium carbonate. It removes oils and stains from textiles, but it is also an acid regulator in this test."

He placed a small measure of the powder mixture into a recess in a block of charcoal.

"The candle, *fräulein*."

Prue passed it to him, and he lit it.

The group of observers pressed closer.

Winkler put the metal blowpipe to his fleshy lips and blew the candle flame sideways, over the powders in the recess. The powders melted to liquid.

Winkler stopped blowing and extinguished the candle. "Now we wait."

"May I go?" Prue whispered.

"*Nein*," Winkler said. "We shall wait."

There were several minutes of hushed waiting. Prue lingered at the table while the others chatted. The lowdown scallywag was pretending he didn't even *recognize* her. To soothe herself, she daydreamed about brown Betty pudding and peanut brittle.

Finally, Winkler announced that it was time to conclude the test. He tipped the melted powder into a vial of water. It dissolved in a flurry of golden dust, except for a small lump that sank to the bottom. With his pincers, he removed the lump and held it aloft.

"The nitric acid, *fräulein*."

Prue's hand quivered as she passed it over.

"The cork."

She pried the cork off the bottle.

Winkler dropped the lump into the acid. It gleamed with an unmistakable luster as it sank and hit the bottom with a clink.

"*Mein Gott*," he murmured through his mustaches. "It is real gold."

\* \* \*

Gabriel was quiet as the rest of the party in the library—
except the footman and the tall, serene lady's maid—
erupted into a dither. Unlike Winkler, his hypothesis had
been that the paint from the cottage ceiling beam would
prove to contain gold.

With the help of one of the footmen and the gardener
boy, Gabriel and Winkler had hauled the contents of the
cottage to the castle and placed them in the library alcove.
Seven little wooden beds, seven chairs, and a table, all
delicate with decay, were lined up next to crates of spoons
and pewter vessels, just behind a velvet curtain.

After luncheon, he and Winkler had cleaned the beam
to reveal a carved design of seven little bearded men in
pointed hats, all in a row, with shovels and pickaxes on
their shoulders. Gabriel had struggled to conceal his excitement. Winkler had laughed.

But how would Winkler explain the presence of real
gold in what he'd deemed an elaborate peasant hoax?

Winkler, however, looked as bemused as ever as he
glanced at the clock on the mantelpiece. The old beast was
already getting peckish for tea.


"Test the soil!" Mrs. Coop bounced on her crinoline like a
schoolgirl. "Oh, professor, I'll wager that it's gold, too."

Ophelia frowned. Why was Mrs. Coop so keen on gold?
After all, she was a millionaire's bride.

"Perhaps," Winkler said. "I shall begin by refining a
sample of the soil in question with the mortar, to ensure an
evenly sized particulate."

After he ground a measure of the soil into powder, he
mixed it in a glass bowl with water, producing something
like mud.

"Now for the sodium cyanide," he said. He held up a
vial of clear liquid.

"Cyanide!" Princess Verushka laid a hand over her heart.

"And I thought nitric acid was alarming," Mr. Hunt said. He lit a cigarette.

"This," Winkler said, grinning down at Prue, "is one thing I shall not allow your pretty hands to touch. This is deadly poison—do you understand? This solution of dissolved sodium cyanide crystals is far more toxic even than prussic acid, your common vermin killer. A few drops on the tongue would make you fall down dead."

"Yes, sir," Prue whispered.

Winkler proceeded to pour the cyanide solution into the sludge of soil and water, and mix it with a glass stirring stick.

"Cyanide has," he said, "an affinity for gold—much like dwarves, ha ha. Stirring allows sufficient air into the mixture. Without air, the experiment would not work."

Ophelia refrained from rolling her eyes. The professor's *hot* air was probably responsible for putting countless college boys to sleep.

"Now," Winkler went on, "I filter the mixture using that screen—*fräulein*?"

Prue handed him a small screen of fine metal mesh.

Winkler poured the sludge onto the screen, over a second bowl. A liquid dripped through, leaving the sludge on the screen. He set it aside.

"The final step is zinc powder. That small bottle there."

Prue passed him a corked amber bottle.

"Not poisonous, I hope," Mr. Hunt said in a droll tone.

Winkler tapped white powder into the bowl of liquid. "Quite innocuous. Now—observe."

Everyone crowded close. Tiny flecks of gold winked in the whitish slurry of zinc.

"Is that—?" Mr. Coop said.

"Gold," Winkler said. "The soil about the small house is filled with gold."

In the subsequent commotion, Ophelia saw Prue slink out of the library.

"Ma'am," Ophelia whispered, bending close to Mrs. Coop's ear, "you look pale—shall I bring you a cup of tea?"

"Do I?" Mrs. Coop said distractedly. "No, no, we'll have tea in only an hour."

"You must think of your health."

"Very well, Flax, some cool water, then." Mrs. Coop dove back into excited conversation with the others.

Ophelia slipped away.

She caught up to Prue in the servants' stair.

"What were you doing above stairs?" Ophelia said. "Mrs. Coop will be furious, once she stops to think of it."

Their footsteps echoed off the stone walls.

"Katrina cut her finger on a broken wineglass," Prue said, marching down the steps. "Had to fill in for her."

Ophelia threw her a sharp glance. "What's wrong?"

"Nothing." Prue sniffled.

"Wait." Ophelia touched her arm.

Prue stopped on the stairs.

"Why have you been crying?"

"Haven't." Prue smeared her sleeve across her nose.

*"Prue."*

"It was *awful.*"

Ophelia wrapped her arms around Prue and lowered them both to a seat on the cold steps. Prue cried like a baby against Ophelia's arm. Ophelia waited until the weeping subsided.

"Prue, tell me what happened. Have you been hurt?"

Prue smudged her wet cheeks and shook her head. "I wish we was back in New York."

"It won't be too much longer, now."

"These people are rats!"

*"Shh."* Ophelia pricked her ears. She thought she'd heard a sound, further up the stairwell. She waited a few seconds. Nothing. She lowered her voice. "We oughtn't speak ill of our employers, because if they hand us our walking papers, we'll be in a worse fix than ever. Tell me, what happened to make you so upset?"

"It's all because of Hansel."

"Hansel?" Ophelia frowned, thinking of the smiling-eyed youth who worked in the castle gardens. "He seems pleasant enough."

"Oh, he *is* pleasant." Prue perked up. "Pleasant and helpful and ever so kind to me."

"Lads of nineteen have been known to be kind to pretty girls."

"He's *nice.*"

"Go on."

"Well, after luncheon today the dirty china, silver, and crystal came into the kitchen like a landslide. I was running around like a chicken with its head cut off just trying to keep up—"

The castle was short on servants, since many had left when Count Grunewald had sold the place, and the Coops had yet to hire replacements. Everyone was run off their feet with extra work.

"—and I ran smack into Karl, and he was carrying a half-eaten chocolate cake the size of Pennsylvania, and it went all over me."

"And you cried?"

"Not then," Prue said. "But I almost did, because I looked like I'd been wallowing in a pigpen, and Hansel always comes in after meals to take away the scraps—for his chickens, and they aren't so different than pigs, are they, so he *would* know—and I couldn't bear for him to see me looking like that."

The tale had, so far, all the hallmarks of one of Prue's debacles. She'd been fired from Howard DeLuxe's Varieties, for instance, after she'd clumsily revealed that Mr. DeLuxe was married—to the pretty lady he'd been pursuing around the ship.

"I thought," Prue said, "I'd sneak away and change—I knew Cook would never allow it if I asked her. Only thing was, I couldn't use the servants' stair because I couldn't risk anyone going and tattling to Cook. So I took the other stairs."

"The family stairs?" Prue had not yet caught the spirit of scullery maid decorum.

Prue nodded. "Well, at the top of the stairs, that big corridor with them plushy carpets was empty. So I hurried along, planning to take the grand staircase to the upper chambers." Her voice thickened again. "I'd near made it when someone reached out and grabbed my arm."

Ophelia listened with mounting dread.

"I opened my mouth to scream, see, but he smacked his big, hot hand over my mouth and pulled me into his study."

"Who did?"

"Mr. Coop."

"Mercy."

"He was all big and red-faced, with his hair puffed around his head like a lion—"

"He's pickled today."

"Smelled like a distillery. I said, 'Awful sorry, mister.' He asked me what I was doing above stairs. Said I was just taking a shortcut."

Ophelia's hands had balled into fists.

"I tried to get away," Prue said. "He grabbed my shoulder, rough as can be, and said 'Not so fast.' "

"He touched you?"

"He did! So I said, 'I reckon I'll be obliged to scream soon, mister.' Well, he laughed at that—mean, you know, not funny laughing—and showed his yellow horse teeth. I even saw his two gold molars, way back. Then he shoved his big mug right up into mine and said, 'You reckon so, do you? Well, *I* reckon I'll be obliged to expose every one of you lying harpies in this castle for what you really is.' "

Ophelia tried to swallow, but her throat was too dry. "He knows we're actresses?"

"That's what I thought, but then he said—I remember it clear as day, because it sounded so peculiar—'chippies posing as ladies, and daughters pretending they ain't daughters at all.' "

"What does that mean?"

"Don't know. But I said, '*I* ain't pretending that I ain't a daughter!' I was thinking of Ma, see, and how I wish for the world she hadn't left me. I said, 'I'm perfectly willing to admit to being a daughter. Maybe it's the parents who are pretending they ain't got children.'"

"And?"

"He scratched his head, said something like, 'Then you know?' Well, I hadn't the foggiest what he was going on about, but I was itching to make a getaway, so I said, 'Sure I know. And if you don't leave me alone, Mr, Coop, I'll tell *everyone*.' Well, that did it. He let go my arm. I made a run for it, and I didn't stop till I reached our bedchamber."

There was a clattering above them in the stairwell; someone was coming down. Ophelia and Prue darted to their feet and continued on their way to the kitchens.

# 5

The ground floor of Schloss Grunewald was a honeycomb of low, vaulted stone chambers that housed laundries, pantries, sculleries, storerooms, and even a cider-pressing room. The kitchen had arching stone supports hung with onions and herbs, a yawning fireplace on either end, and scrubbed plank tables heaped with vegetables, bowls, and pots. The kitchen was also equipped with two newfangled stoves, upon which soups and sauces now bubbled. Cook had already begun dinner.

Three servants sat at one of the tables. Freda, a tiny, bug-eyed housemaid, was munching one of Cook's cinnamon pastries called *schnecken*, her eyes glued to a novel. Katrina, a big-boned parlor maid with the listless disposition of a Holstein cow, sipped tea. Her finger was bandaged. She was speaking with the gardener, Hansel. He was a golden youth with curls and shining brown eyes, like Little Boy Blue in Ophelia's girlhood copy of *Mother Goose*.

As Ophelia and Prue neared the table, Prue fixed her eyes on the floor, and her cheeks went pink. When Hansel glanced up to see Prue, his own sun-browned cheeks reddened.

Ah, young love. Not that Ophelia had ever experienced such a malady. She figured she was too practical to be stricken.

The withered, deaf old lady called Matilda hunkered on a stool in the chimney corner, peeling apples with a paring knife at an inchworm's pace.

She glanced up. Her raisin eyes glared.

Ophelia smiled, even though there was no point. Matilda was bent on hating Prue and Ophelia, even though they'd never spoken to her—Matilda communicated by writing in German with the slate and bit of chalk that were always at her side. She was said to be skilled in the arts of herbal medicine, but Ophelia had seen no evidence of this except a dirty little closet cluttered with dried plants, next to one of the pantries.

"High time you returned," Cook said. She cast Prue a sidelong glance while pulling a tray of cakes from the oven. "I thought Madam wanted a bowl of washing powder, not a cozy chat."

Cook—Frau Holder—was a plump and homely lady with a mobcap and jowls. She, like all of the castle servants, spoke perfect English because Count Grunewald had been married to a British lady. The housekeeper had quit after the count sold the castle to the Coops, and until a new one was hired, Cook was acting as household overseer. She had the air of a stern fairy godmother. Maybe it was because she always smelled of nutmeg and sugar.

"Sorry, ma'am." Prue wiped away one last tear. "I'll just get to work on those dirty pots there."

"A fine idea," Cook said. She plopped the tray of cakes on a board to cool. "And you, Miss Flax? I am not accustomed to seeing you down here in the afternoon. *There* you are, Wilhelm."

Wilhelm, the second footman, a pleasant Humpty-Dumptyish fellow of perhaps thirty years, entered the kitchen.

He must've been the one on the servants' stair behind them.

"Fetching water for Madam," Ophelia mumbled to Cook. But Cook had already forgotten her.

She had to pass Matilda's chimney corner on her way back to the servants' stair. The old lady paused once more in her apple paring to fix her hot eyes on Ophelia.

She fancied she felt Matilda's gaze boring into her back all the way up the stairs.

When Ophelia brought Mrs. Coop's glass of water to the library, everyone had gone. Professor Winkler's bottles and instruments, the dirty piece of wood, and the cloth-covered skeleton still lay on the table.

Ophelia returned to Mrs. Coop's boudoir to await her next summons.

She waited for nearly an hour, glad for a moment's peace and a chance to prop up her sore feet. She was still trooping around in the too-small stolen boots, and paying dearly for it.

But mostly, her head was spinning with the strange tale Prue had told her. She was relieved that Mr. Coop hadn't harmed Prue—she'd heard what wealthy masters of households could get away with—but she was still unnerved by Mr. Coop's curious pronouncements. Chippies pretending to be ladies? Daughters pretending they weren't? What could it mean?

One thing was certain: she and Prue had to keep their heads low.

There was a rap on the door. The housemaid Freda poked her head in. She was, as always, eating. This time it was something crunchy. "Madam desires her rose cashmere wrap in the blue salon," she said.

Ophelia heard, from behind the blue salon's door, the hum of chatter, the soft clink of china and teaspoons.

She pushed the door open a few inches. The Coops, Amaryllis, the two professors, Princess Verushka, and Mr. Hunt were scattered about on chairs and sofas. The tea table groaned with a silver service, a large urn of fruits, and several tiered trays of cakes and biscuits. Behind them, a row of French doors opened onto a terrace. A sunlit prospect of mountains and valleys sprawled beyond the terrace, into the distance.

". . . . and I didn't know *what* to say!" Mrs. Coop said to the princess and Hunt, as Amaryllis stared dismally out a window. The princess and Hunt laughed.

". . . ten thousand miles of railroad tracks," Mr. Coop was saying to the professors. "Course, the Irish and Chinamen who lay them down can't be relied on . . . forever demanding higher wages, dirty rascals. . . ."

Professor Penrose lifted his eyes and looked at Ophelia.

Her breath snagged. Why did he have to look at her like he was gazing through a windowpane?

She stepped through the door. Just as she did so, she saw Mr. Coop reach out, select a green apple from the urn of fruits on the tea table, and take a juicy bite. Winkler was rambling on about something even as Mr. Coop emitted an awful retching sound. The bitten apple tumbled to the carpet.

*"Mein Gott!"* Winkler lumbered to his feet. Penrose was already at Mr. Coop's side.

Mr. Coop's fingers scrabbled at his chest; Penrose was attempting to loosen Coop's tie.

At last, Mrs. Coop and the others noticed the commotion.

"Homer!" Mrs. Coop screamed, dashing across the room. But by the time she reached her husband's side, he'd toppled to the carpet.

*"Homer!"* Mrs. Coop sank by his side.

Penrose crouched down, placed two fingers at Coop's neck. Then he touched Mrs. Coop's shoulder. "I'm afraid he's . . . dead."

Ophelia stood just inside the door, as though nailed to the floor. Mrs. Coop's cashmere wrap drooped in her hand.

Penrose looked over to her. "Miss," he said, "please send for the police."

"The police?" Mr. Hunt said. "Surely this is a case of apoplexy—"

"No." Penrose looked grim. "There's a scent of bitter almond on him. He's been poisoned with cyanide."

\* \* \*

"You saw everything," Inspector Schubert said to Ophelia before her rump had even hit the library chair.

Schubert was the inspector fetched from Baden-Baden, a spidery gent of fifty-odd years, with a spare, avid face and the habit of caressing his thin fingers together as he spoke. His black suit of clothes had a shell-like sheen from wear.

It was after one o'clock in the morning. Ophelia felt like a rag that had been sent through the wringer one too many times.

She had been waiting in the kitchen for her turn at police questioning, stealing a bit of shut-eye with her cheek on the tabletop. Prue had been summoned for her interview an hour earlier, and Ophelia hadn't seen her since. Prue was probably curled up asleep somewhere like Rip Van Winkle.

"Yes," Ophelia said to Schubert. "Mrs. Coop had sent for her wrap—I'm her maid, see—and it was only moments after I'd arrived in the salon that Mr. Coop"—she swallowed— "died."

Schubert's assistant, Herr Benjamin, an unkempt young man forever dabbing at his nose with a straggling handkerchief, scribbled in his notebook.

"He was murdered, you understand," Schubert said.

"On purpose?"

"That is generally what murder means."

"The apple?"

Schubert had been pacing, but now he leaned over the table. A hankie was spread over something. He whisked it off with a conjurer's flourish. "Behold."

There was the apple, with a single bite out of it. The exposed flesh was dried and brownish.

"The only apple of its kind," Schubert said, "on the tea table. The other apples were red, perfect, shiny. This apple alone was smaller, green, even—observe—containing a worm hole."

Ophelia studied the apple. "Mr. Coop preferred those orchard apples. He said they reminded him of the pippins from America. And he didn't fancy those the greengrocer delivers to the castle. Said he couldn't tell the difference between those and wax apples."

"So I am told. What I would like to know is, Miss Flax, where is this orchard?"

"Somewhere near the castle, I'd expect. I don't know."

Schubert pressed his wizened face close to hers. His breath smelled of sour coffee. "Are you lying?"

"No." She drew back. "I've been here only two weeks. Besides, I work inside the castle, and I haven't been out-of-doors much."

Schubert straightened. "And Miss Bright—Prue, she is called. She loves the fairy tales, does she not?"

"Prue?" Ophelia's tired, cobwebby mind couldn't piece together what Schubert was angling at. "She's never read a fairy tale in her life."

"Impossible."

"If you think that, then you don't know her."

"And what is it I should know about Miss . . . Bright?"

Ophelia hesitated. Schubert had pronounced Prue's surname with a shade of irony. Could he have already discovered that Prue's mother hadn't been married to her father, the Reverend Arthur Sewall of Brooklyn, New York? Prue didn't confess that to *anyone*.

"It *is* Miss Bright, is it not?"

"Of course."

"Not . . ." Schubert said, wrapping his tentacle-like fingers around the back of a chair, "Miss Coop?"

"Prue? A Coop?"

The assistant had stopped his scribbling to gawp at her. Ophelia felt queasy. "Where is she?"

Schubert ignored the question. "A certain person informed me that they heard a most interesting exchange between Miss Bright and Mr. Coop this afternoon—"

Holy Moses.

"—an exchange that indicated that she is, in fact, the secret daughter of Mr. Homer T. Coop."

"Go along!"

"This appears to come as a surprise to you, Miss Flax."

"You bet it does."

"That is all, then. You are free to go."

"But—"

"And please," Schubert said, "tell everyone to gather here in the library immediately. I have an announcement to make."

Botheration.

Gabriel slapped the magazine shut and tossed it aside. He simply couldn't bear to peruse another issue of *Godey's Lady's Book* or another three-week-old newspaper column about the American stock market. He rose from his chair in the drawing room, where he'd been waiting for the police to finish.

His own questioning had taken all of five minutes. He'd explained to Inspector Schubert that in the hour or so before tea, he'd gone back up to the cottage site alone, partly for a breath of fresh air, but also to examine the cottage more closely. Schubert had seemed satisfied.

Gabriel set off down the corridor.

The best books in the castle would be, of course, in the library, but since that was currently being used by the police, he hoped he would find something to read in the late Mr. Coop's study. He had noticed the study in passing that afternoon.

The study door was slightly ajar. He pushed it inward.

It was dim inside, but a long, clear moonbeam stretched across the center of the room. In the middle of the moonbeam was a desk, and bending over the desk, shuffling through a stack of papers, was Princess Verushka.

Her eyes, luminous in the darkness, flared. She straightened, and a few papers floated to the carpet.

"This is not," she said, "what it may appear to be."

"No? I'd rather thought you were searching for a fresh deck of cards for yourself and Mr. Hunt—I noticed you were playing écarté in the drawing room."

*"Oui, oui."* She patted her sleek coiffure. "Cards. Precisely. But I simply cannot find any." She twitched up her skirts and wafted past Gabriel, out into the corridor and away, trailing civet perfume.

Gabriel paused. It was none of his affair, but . . . He went to the desk, thumbed through the stack of papers the princess had been rifling through. They appeared to be the driest of business documents.

What would a pampered princess want with those?

"Professor Penrose," someone uttered from the doorway.

Hang it.

It was the first footman, the one who'd been tippling that morning in the wood. His eyes were bloodshot and pouched. If he was surprised to see Gabriel going through his late master's things, he didn't show it.

"Inspector Schubert," the footman said, "requests that we all assemble in the library."

Everyone gathered in the library. Everyone, that is, but Inspector Schubert and Prue.

"I see you are all present."

Ophelia turned to see Schubert in the doorway. Prue was just behind him.

Ophelia's belly twisted; Prue's wrists were tied together with rope.

"I have assembled you all here," Schubert said, "to announce that I have found our murderess."

There was a collective gasp. Prue cowered like a fawn.

"You're off your nut!" Ophelia tried to shout. It came out as a croak.

Mrs. Coop lunged at Prue, fingers outstretched like claws. "You little trollop! Murderess!"

Mr. Hunt and Karl rushed forward to restrain her.

"Silence." Schubert turned to his assistant. "Benjamin, the evidence."

Benjamin went to a sideboard, bringing forth a tray with a

few objects on it. He placed it on the table in the center of the library, next to Professor Winkler's gold-testing paraphernalia, the dirty piece of wood, and the covered skeleton.

Schubert circled to stand beside the tray. "This evening, Benjamin and I inspected the bedchamber Miss Bright—or so we shall call her for the moment—shares with the lady's maid. Imagine our surprise when we discovered three curious objects upon the chest of drawers in that chamber."

Ophelia could scarcely breathe.

"First," Schubert said, holding up a small leather book, "a volume of the English translation of *Kinder- und Hausmärchen—Children's and Household Tales*—by Jacob and Wilhelm Grimm."

"That's not hers," Ophelia said.

"Miss Flax, you shall refrain from speaking."

Ophelia pressed her lips together.

"Second"—Schubert held up a small bottle of clear, glittering liquid—"potassium cyanide. The poison that killed Herr Coop, the same bottle used by Professor Winkler in his tests this afternoon. I am told the good professor informed Miss Bright of its lethal dangers."

Winkler nodded.

*Everyone was watching!* Ophelia wanted to scream. *Everyone heard it was poisonous!*

"Third," Schubert said, "a knife." He held up a small paring knife with a green wooden handle, which Ophelia recognized as belonging to the castle kitchens. "The blade of this knife is sticky with what appears and smells to be apple juice, and a sliver of apple seed was found affixed to it as well."

"What are you suggesting?" Professor Penrose said.

"Simply, that Miss Bright, in a duplicitous guise, located the father who had cast her off—"

"Her *father*?" Mrs. Coop screeched. She lunged again in Prue's direction. Mr. Hunt and Karl held her fast.

"—cunningly insinuated herself in his household, and murdered him."

# 6

Murmurs welled up. Inspector Schubert shushed them. Ophelia's tongue went sawdust dry.

"I am saying," Schubert said, "that Miss Prudence Bright, her head turned by the romance of a foreign castle, coupled with an unwholesome fascination with the *kinder* stories of the Grimms, murdered her father, Homer T. Coop, by lacing an apple with potassium cyanide."

"That's the silliest yarn I ever heard," Ophelia said.

"Is it?" Schubert's tone was supercilious. "For the sake of thoroughness, allow me to hypothesize that Miss Bright did not, at first, intend to kill her father. However, when the opportunity presented itself—the lethal poison at her fingertips, the knowledge that only her father ate the orchard apples—she ceased to think clearly."

"Arrest her!" Mrs. Coop shrieked.

"Hold on a tick," Professor Penrose said. "You can't arrest the girl, you know."

"Although she is," Schubert said, "presumably a citizen of the United States of America—she failed to produce identity papers—it is still well within my jurisdiction to arrest her."

"There is no requirement for identity papers when traveling across European borders," Penrose said, "especially for ladies. You know that. The fact is, you haven't enough evidence. Besides which, I assume the Baden-Baden jail is stuffed to the gills with thieving gamblers and members of the demimonde. Your alleged murderess, despite what you believe, is but a girl."

"She shall attempt to flee," Schubert said.

"In a foreign country? Where she does not speak the language?"

"She is clearly desperate and deranged. She must be locked up."

"The tower," Mrs. Coop howled. "Lock her in the tower! Oh, I cannot bear the sight of her!"

"Tower?" Schubert said.

"I believe, sir," the footman Karl said, "Madam is referring to the battlement tower on the far side of the castle courtyard. It has traditionally been used as a fortification in . . . on these sorts of occasions."

How often did people get locked up in this horrible castle, anyway?

"Very well," Schubert said. "The tower must serve for now. Pray show the way." He clutched Prue's arm and pivoted her around.

"Ophelia!" Prue cried over her shoulder.

"This is madness!" Ophelia rushed forward, but Benjamin stepped in her path. She stood in the doorway and, panting, watched them lead Prue away.


"You don't hold it against me," Mrs. Coop said, "do you?" Her words were slow and thick.

Ophelia ran a tortoiseshell hairbrush through Mrs. Coop's frizzled yellow locks, preparing her for bed. Outside the boudoir windows, dawn was beginning to blush. "No, ma'am," she forced herself to say. "If Prue is dangerous, she must be locked away."

She longed to hurl the hairbrush at Mrs. Coop's reflection in the dressing table mirror, to blubber and howl, to rush to Prue's side. But for one thing, Ophelia was a Yankee, and Yankees don't blubber and howl. And for another thing, she was an actress. Right now, everything depended on her acting.

"You're a sensible girl." Mrs. Coop could barely keep her head up. "How did you fall in with a little criminal like that?" The village doctor had come earlier in the evening, and he'd evidently dispensed something for her hysterical grief. Her eyes were as glassy as a stuffed toy's, her pupils mere pinpricks.

Laudanum.

"You never can tell about people," Ophelia said, tying a ribbon in Mrs. Coop's hair. "I knew Miss Bright only a few weeks before we met you on the steamship."

A thumping lie. But Ophelia's gut told her to distance herself from Prue; she needed to stay in Mrs. Coop's good graces in order to get Prue out of this scrape. It was lucky Mrs. Coop hadn't turned on Ophelia yet—but peculiar, too. Was it the laudanum? Or was she pleased that Mr. Coop was dead?

"Now," Ophelia said, "the doctor ordered that you try to rest. You've had a terrible shock." She helped Mrs. Coop to her feet and guided her to bed. "Everything will get put in apple-pie order." She tucked Mrs. Coop's silken quilt around her.

Mrs. Coop's eyelids drooped shut. She began to snore.

Ophelia knocked on Amaryllis's bedchamber door.

*"Go away!"* came the muffled reply.

Ophelia sorely wished she could. Instead, she said, "Allow me to ready you for bed, miss. You've had a trying day."

It *would* be prodigiously trying to murder your brother-in-law and frame the scullery maid all in one crack. And that's exactly what Ophelia figured had happened: Amaryllis, humiliated by Mr. Coop's nasty scolding in the presence of her beloved Mr. Royall Hunt, had taken her vengeance with that bottle of poison.

The door opened. "Go away, Flax."

Ophelia faked a Selfless Servant simper. She'd done it hundreds of times onstage. Never had it felt so difficult. "Allow me to help you."

Amaryllis's lusterless eyes fastened on Ophelia. She said nothing, but Ophelia couldn't look away, even as her heart began to thud. The gaze lasted a smidgen too long.

Uh-oh. She knew what Ophelia suspected.

"I no longer require your assistance," Amaryllis said. She slammed the door.

Finally, Ophelia returned to the bedchamber she'd shared with Prue. It was high up under the eaves, so close to the roof you could hear the clatter of sparrows on the tiles. One tiny, mullioned window admitted pinkish dawn light.

The two narrow iron bedsteads were as neat as she'd left them. The chest of drawers where the police claimed to have found the fairy tale book, poison, and paring knife were empty.

Ophelia's eyes flew to the top of the wardrobe. Yes. It was still there, hidden behind the washing pitcher and Prue's bonnet. The police had missed it.

She stood on tiptoe and brought down a battered leather case. She set it on the floor and knelt beside it.

The brass lock had not been touched.

Phew. Ophelia's shoulders sagged.

She retrieved a key, which she'd wedged between two floorboards under her bed, and opened the case. Inside were tiny glass jars and broken, paper-covered sticks of theatrical greasepaint, pots of glue, false beauty spots and moustaches, powder sifters, paintbrushes, a set of false teeth, soft wax for modeling noses and the like, and a couple of wigs. She'd brought the kit along for sentimental reasons, she supposed; she'd cobbled it together over eight hard years of circus and theater work.

Two envelopes hid at the very bottom of the case.

What if Inspector Schubert were to discover her greasepaint or these forged letters of reference? She ought to hide the case and destroy the letters.

Later. She'd have to do it later.

Ophelia locked the case, stowed the key back between the floorboards, and replaced the case on top of the wardrobe. She wrapped a shawl around her shoulders and hurried out of the bedchamber, down the coiling, bone-cold stairs, and out into the castle courtyard.

Across the courtyard was a tall tower with a lone window at the top. Against the dawn-streaked sky, the tower was a black, menacing silhouette.

How was Prue faring in there? Was she cold? Hungry? Certainly, she'd be scared.

Ophelia had been in the courtyard several times, playing lady-in-waiting to Mrs. Coop. The courtyard was divided from the kitchen gardens by a tall stone wall with a wooden gate. This gate usually stood open. Ophelia had glimpsed, through the gate and across the kitchen gardens, a mysterious barred door. The door was set in the bottom of the long, stone battlement that formed the fourth wall for the gardens, and that connected the tower with the rest of the castle.

Now, common sense hinted that the door might take a person up to the tower. And when common sense hinted, well, wise ladies lent an ear.

Folks figured actresses were flibbertigibbets who did nothing but practice melodramatic faces in the looking glass when they weren't lolling on divans and mowing through boxes of chocolate creams. But the truth was, actresses were some of the hardest-working ladies you could find. Theatrical life had made Ophelia as practical as an iron nail and, some claimed, just as hardheaded.

And she wouldn't stand for this. No, she would *not*. The gumption, the absolute *brass* of that Schubert fellow, tossing Prue in the tower like yesterday's dirty socks!

Ophelia swiped a strand of windblown hair from her eyes and marched along a gravel path towards the kitchen garden gate.

All of a sudden, a movement caught her eye on the far side of the courtyard, along the base of the western castle wing.

Yes. *There.*

Oh, golly.

A person was passing through the courtyard's geometric shrubberies and walks. No, *two* people.

Ophelia dove, palms first, behind a row of big potted shrubs. She crouched, held her breath, and had a look-see through the branches.

Two gentlemen in black clothes and black top hats crept along through the shadows. They carried something long and large, wrapped up in cloth.

*A corpse.*

No—wait. The wrapped thing was too narrow for that and a little too long.

They vanished through the gate in the castle wall that led out to the kitchen gardens.

What in Godfrey's green earth was going *on* around here?

After a minute, to make sure those creepy fellows weren't coming back for a curtain call, Ophelia popped out from behind the shrubs and made a mad dash.

She stopped at the gate and squinted through into the kitchen gardens. The coast was clear—the creepy fellows had vanished.

Ophelia flew between dark rows of vegetables to the mysterious barred door. And—oh, joy—the door opened easily. At the top of a dank flight of steps, she found herself out on top of the windswept battlement and just outside the tower door.

"Prue?" Ophelia made a one-knuckle rap on the door. "Prue, it's me. Ophelia." She joggled the door handle, just in case. Locked tight.

From inside came shuffling sounds, then Prue's stuffy-nosed voice. "Ophelia! Get me the tunkett out of here before I—"

"Prue, try to stay calm. That is the most important thing."

"But it's *freezing* in here, and I—"

"They didn't hurt you, did they?"

"Nope."

"Good. Now, listen. I'll see to it that you have everything you need—food, water. Have you any blankets?"

"Sure. If you call them scratchy burlap things blankets."

"I'll come and check on you as often as I can get away—but I mustn't rouse suspicions. Is there anything in there, something small, that you might place on the windowsill, to work as a signal that you need me to come?"

"Hey! That's what the prisoner did in that play we put on about the—"

"Never mind that. Is there anything you might use?"

"Um . . . there's an earthen water jug."

"That'll do. Now, I'm going to get to the bottom of all this, Prue, and as quickly as I am able."

"How will you do that? It's the *police* we're talking on, Ophelia."

Ophelia jutted her chin. "I'll allow that Inspector Schubert may have a police badge or whatever it is they've got in Germany. But it's pretty obvious he's as blind as a bat. It was Miss Amaryllis who killed Mr. Coop."

"Amaryllis!"

Ophelia glanced over her shoulder. She crouched close to the keyhole and lowered her voice. "I saw Miss Amaryllis making sheep's eyes at Mr. Hunt, the handsome visitor. Then Mr. Coop right humiliated Miss Amaryllis in front of Hunt—in front of *everyone*."

"You reckon Miss Amaryllis croaked him for that?"

"Yes. And I mean to prove it. You can count on me, Prue, but please stay put. As long as you keep in the tower, out of the way and where you're supposed to be, at least I'll know you're safe."

"Don't know about *that*—I wouldn't be staggered if a dragon or a whole mess of ghosts showed up to the party in here."

"*Please*, Prue."

"Oh, all right."

Ophelia returned to her bedchamber. She lay down, fully clothed, on her bed. She hadn't cried in more years than she could count; tears were, she'd learned, nothing but a waste of tuck. But as she stared at Prue's empty pillow and waited for the day, she *did* cogitate a bit on what a relief it might've been to shed a tear or two.

"I admit," Professor Winkler said to Gabriel, "it is a great relief that Mrs. Coop requested we carry on with our study of the house in the wood. I worried her husband's death might dampen her fervor." He took a large bite of hot buttered roll.

Gabriel, across the breakfast table, sipped his coffee. "It is a relief, isn't it?"

As long as the victuals kept coming, Winkler didn't seem to be put off by anything. But tell him the breakfast ham had run out, and well, all operations could screech to a standstill.

Fortunately, Gasthaus Schatz, the Schilltag inn they'd gone to after the police had released them early that morning, served a delicious breakfast in its rustic, pin-neat dining room.

The only other guest, it appeared, was the hearty young British lady they'd come across in the forest yesterday morning. She was alone at a table across the dining room, rhythmically forking up and chewing her repast, at the same time scribbling away with a pencil in a notebook. She wore her dust-colored tramping costume. Her head, without its straw hat, was revealed to be crowned with a massive braided heap of gold hair.

Curious that she was alone. One rarely saw ladies traveling without companions. Although this particular lady could doubtless pass through a Marrakech bazaar at midnight unmolested. She seemed the sort who was adept at parasol whappings and walking-boot kicks.

"I should like," Winkler said, forking up ham, "to begin by having the perimeter of the cottage cleared by the woodsman. We cannot continue to burrow about in the thicket like boars. My lumbar will not stand for it." He chewed vigorously.

"Very well," Gabriel said. "I do wonder why Mrs. Coop asked us to continue, though."

One man was dead, and a young girl who was perhaps innocent was locked up in some dreadful tower. Gabriel kept thinking of the anguish in the dark eyes of the lady's maid. Yet here he and Winkler were, discussing their scholarly work as though they hadn't a care in the world. However, Inspector Schubert had forbidden them to leave the neighborhood, and Gabriel longed to learn more about the cottage and the skeleton. He supposed it wouldn't do any harm.

"Why does Mrs. Coop wish us to continue?" Winkler asked. "Greed." He spooned blueberry jam onto his fourth roll. "Eager to find more gold. They always are."

"She does seem to have a keen interest in Snow White."

"Americans are smitten with European fairy tales. Take that little murderess yesterday! Obsessed. *Mein Gott*."

Gabriel opted not to argue that point. He might give too much away.

The pencil of the British lady across the room had slowed to a crawl. Although she did not lift her eyes from her notebook, Gabriel had the distinct impression she was hanging on to their every word.

"It is," Winkler said, "to compensate for their own nation's sorry lack of history."

"Not because America is a nation of peasants," Gabriel said, "without an aristocracy of its own?"

Winkler liked that. "A nation of peasants. *Ja, ja*."

"Speaking of which," Gabriel said, hoping he hadn't gone too far, "I think I'll poke about the village this morning, while you're having the cottage site cleared. I'd like to learn if there is any local lore we aren't aware of."

"Best of luck. The *volk* will only spout the same tired twaddle."

"Nonetheless, I think it's worth a try."

After Winkler had departed—in, surprisingly, a hired cart, although perhaps he was in danger of having an apoplectic fit if he attempted to haul his bulk up the crag to the castle—Gabriel took more coffee.

"Did you hear about the discovery in Schloss Grunewald's forest?" he said to the innkeeper's wife in German, once the British lady had gone.

The innkeeper's wife set a fresh pitcher of cream on his table.

"Word travels quickly in a village of this size." She smiled, resembling an elf with her bright eyes and white hair.

"What do you make of it?"

"Oh, well, now that is a question." She wiped her wrinkled hands on her apron. "You are one of the scholars from Heidelberg."

"I'm from England, actually, but my companion who just left is from Heidelberg University, yes."

"I suppose you are laughing up your sleeves at we simple village folk."

That was embarrassingly close to the truth. Not that Gabriel could tell her that his own contempt was a sham.

"I suppose," she went on, "you wish for me to say that I believe it is Snow White's cottage that was found out there, and those bones belonged to a magical dwarf."

Gabriel stirred his coffee. "I don't wish for you to say anything in particular, but I allow, I am curious what the villagers think. Has anything like this been found before? In Schilltag, I mean."

She stared past Gabriel, out the window, as though wondering how much to tell him.

Gabriel followed her gaze. At the end of the winding lane, the castle loomed up into the sky, and the clustering pine trees were black.

He found himself gripping his spoon just a bit too hard.

"Odd things have turned up, now and again," she finally said.

"Odd things?" *Things* could mean anything from a relic to a snippet of gossip.

"Not houses or bones, of course. But. . . ." She wiped away a drop of cream from the lip of the pitcher. "It would be best if you went to speak to Herr Horkheimer. He knows more about all this than I do. He owns the cuckoo clock shop down the lane."

Mrs. Coop was snoring like a steam tractor when Ophelia tiptoed into her chamber with a breakfast tray. Ophelia decided not to wake her yet. She placed the tray on a side table and began tidying up the boudoir.

She heard rumbling and hoof clopping, and darted to the window. A carriage rolled to a stop, far below in the shady castle forecourt. Two men climbed out. Inspector Schubert and Herr Benjamin. She saw a flash of Benjamin's trailing hankie.

Back to pry a confession out of Prue, she'd warrant. A pity that Prue was liable to budge about as far as a mule stuck in maple syrup.

Ophelia poked her head back into the bedchamber. Mrs. Coop was still asleep.

Good. Because now that Ophelia had a spare moment, she also had a smidge of business to attend to.

Ophelia hastened back to her own chamber and dragged her battered theatrical case down from the wardrobe. Then she scurried through labyrinthine passages and up and down short flights of stairs, keeping to the highest regions of the castle. There were lots of empty stone chambers and funny nooks and dead ends. But she didn't meet a soul, and she eventually found a cavernous lumber room, right under the roofline, crammed with sagging sofas, trunks, enormous empty picture frames, rolled up carpets, and dusty wardrobes.

She seesawed the case back between two antique iron-girded trunks.

There. She brushed the dust off her hands. Inspector Schubert would never, ever find it.

# 7

Schilltag was a quaint village of crooked half-timbered buildings with reddish tiled roofs. The village was still drowsing as Gabriel made his way to the cuckoo clock shop.

He found it, an antique storefront wedged between the telegraph office and a bakery. He eyed the display of rolls and cakes in the bakery window. Winkler would want to turn somersaults when he saw the place.

As for the cuckoo clock shop, its window was crammed with the intricately carved wooden clocks and bric-a-brac that were requisite purchases for tourists in the *Schwarzwald*— the Black Forest.

Inside, the shop was cool and smelled of wood shavings and, faintly, turpentine and beeswax. The air vibrated with dozens of ticking clocks that were mounted on the walls. All those pendulums swinging back and forth—shaped like pinecones, birds, leaves, and other woodland motifs— were dizzying.

There was a glass display case filled with more carved wooden things, but no one was behind it. Gabriel stepped up to the case and cleared his throat.

*"Guten Morgen,"* a man said, emerging from behind a green baize curtain. He was tall, stooped, and utterly bald. He wore half-moon spectacles and a leather vest over a homespun shirt. *"Kann ich Sie helfen?"*

*"Guten Morgen,"* Gabriel said. "Herr Horkheimer?"

"Ah, you are English," the man said. "Very good. Yes, I am Horkheimer."

Gabriel introduced himself.

"You appear surprised," Horkheimer said, "that I speak English. Most of us in Schilltag do. The English tourists are very good for business, you see. They come up by the cartload from Baden-Baden to picnic and ramble, and to view the famous Schloss Grunewald. And they cannot leave without a curio." He swept his hand around the shop. "Do you see anything you like?"

Gabriel hated to disappoint him. He'd purchase a trinket and then segue into questions. The display case was filled with wooden statuettes of stags, boars, bears, rabbits, and owls, all carved in the finely detailed Black Forest style.

Amid the animals there were also several tiny figurines of what appeared to be little bearded men in pointed hats. There was also a statuette of a girl cowering at the feet of a man, who held a dagger aloft.

"Is that . . . Snow White and the huntsman?"

"You know the tale, then—the Evil Queen bids the Huntsman to cut out the girl's liver."

"Yes, charming story. So wholesome for the little ones."

"Those tales are not for children," Horkheimer said.

"No?" Gabriel already knew this, but he wanted to hear what Horkheimer had to say.

*"Nein.* They are put into children's storybooks because people laugh at we simple *volk,* and think our lore is childish."

How Gabriel wished to heartily shake the man's hand. Instead, he said, "I'd like to purchase this dwarf here. The one holding the pickaxe."

He waited as Horkheimer wrapped the figure and placed it in a small box.

After he'd paid, Gabriel said, "These Snow White figures—why do you sell them?"

"The tourists come to the Black Forest to find an enchanted place. I do not wish to disillusion them."

"But are there not special stories about Schilltag and about Schloss Grunewald in particular?"

Horkheimer paused just a hair too long. "*Nein*." He took up a rag and began wiping the top of the display case.

What was he hiding?

"*Danke schön*," Gabriel said, lifting his hat. He turned to leave.

As he moved towards the door, something caught his eye: a cuckoo clock in the shape, like most cuckoo clocks, of a house, with leaves and branches carved all around. Except this one also had, along its peaked roof line, a relief design of seven little bearded men in pointed hats, marching along with shovels and pickaxes on their shoulders.

It was the same design as that on the ceiling beam they'd taken from the cottage in the wood.

Gabriel's eyes darted to the other clocks on the wall. Several repeated, with exactitude, the design.

He turned.

Horkheimer was watching him. The half lenses of his spectacles glinted.

"This clock," Gabriel said, gesturing. "That design is . . . did you make this clock?"

"I make the clocks with the birds on top—like that one, see?"

"And this one?"

"Made by the wife of the woodsman at Schloss Grunewald," Horkheimer said. "Frau Herz."

Gabriel purchased the clock, and with his two boxes he returned to the inn.

Prue awoke with a yelp. Something warm and wet had splatted on her forehead. She struggled upright and pried her eyes—which were swollen tight as fists—open.

Huh. She wasn't sure what she was looking at. A gray wall. A stone floor. And what was that in the corner? Sweet sister Sally . . . a *chamber pot*?

She touched the warm wetness on her forehead and studied it. White, gray, and smeary. Ugh. Bird's ploppings. She threw a glare towards the sparrow's nest in the rafters. One of the nasty critters looked smugly down.

Then it all came back. Mr. Coop, murdered. Those creepy tests for gold. That policeman Schubert. He'd looked like something the cat dragged in from a cemetery for social misfits.

The worst part was, Prue was hungry. She always had trouble thinking clearly when she was hungry. Whenever things got bleak, she liked to have some crisp slices of bacon or a toasted muffin or maybe a couple penny jujubes. That always put life into perspective.

A scraping sound outside interrupted her gloom-and-doom ponderings. She took off her apron, wiped her forehead clean, balled up the apron, and threw it in the corner. Then she went to the window. It was just a tall rectangle cut out from the stone wall. No glass. They did things old-fashioned here at Schloss Grunewald. She leaned out.

Down below, maybe two stories, were the walled kitchen gardens with leafy vegetable beds and gravel walkways. The scraping sound came from a hoe, and the hoe was held by Hansel.

Crackers.

There he was, splendiferous in his white peasant shirt. His sleeves were rolled up to show sun-brown forearms, and his golden curls shone in the morning sun. Meanwhile, *she* was got up in an ugly brown dress with straw stuck all over, her nose and chin felt greasy, and there wasn't a mirror or hairbrush in sight.

Well. Ma sure wouldn't approve of her talking to a fellow when she was so messy. But Ma wasn't here, was she?

"Psst," Prue whispered.

Hansel went on hoeing.

She surveyed the garden. No one else was around,

unless you counted the pecking hens in the yard by the wall.

"Hey!" she whispered, louder this time.

Hansel paused and straightened, wiped his forehead with his arm, and went back to hoeing.

Prue turned and scanned the dim tower room. Her eyes fell on a tray by the door, which she hadn't noticed before. On the tray were an earthen jug and a plate of—she went and crouched beside it—pastries. Three of them. Frau Holder's scrumptious kind with the buttery apple on the inside. And cinnamon. Still crouching, Prue gobbled one up. Heaven. She washed it down with water from the jug. Then she ate a second pastry. She'd have to sacrifice the third.

She took it to the window, aimed, and pelted it. Her lessons backstage in New York with the baseball-mad boys paid off. The pastry hit Hansel square on the back of the head.

He spun around.

Prue smiled and waved with just her fingers, like Ma had shown her.

Hansel dropped his hoe and came to the base of the tower. He shaded his eyes with his hand. "I will not tell Frau Holder you are squandering her pastries."

"She'd never believe you, anyway. She knows them apple ones are my especial favorites." Prue batted her lashes, something else Ma had taught her early on. "Won't you let me out of this dump? It's a sparrow hotel in here. I know you could go and fetch the key from Frau Holder and—"

"Let you out? I ought not even be speaking to you. Not after last night."

"How could you even *suggest* I killed that old boiler? After—"

"Not that, Prue. You know I—you know that we are friends. I would not betray you."

"You didn't say anything about me being an actress to the police, you mean?" She'd accidentally spilled the beans to Hansel about that last week, but she was fair certain she could trust him.

"No. We are friends."

"Then who's going to tattle if you let me out for a little leg stretch? Them chickens over there?"

He scratched his head. "Truly, Prue, it would be delightful to stroll with you awhile, but—"

"I was intending on asking you. How come you didn't tell that horrible police feller that I was with *you* before tea yesterday? So I couldn't have gone up to my chamber and poisoned that apple like he said?"

Hansel glanced away.

Prue watched him. He was a looker and mighty gentlemanly for a gardener. But he was still just a servant. Ma would never approve. Ma had always claimed that a gent's best feature was his bank account.

"I did tell Schubert," Hansel finally said. "He did not believe me."

"But why would he think you'd lie?"

"He suspects that I helped you."

"Helped me?"

"Helped you kill Mr. Coop."

"Carry me home! Why would you ever do that?"

"Because we are friends."

Prue sighed. "I'm sorry, Hansel, truly I am."

"So you can see, it would not be wise for me to let you out."

Something told Prue that no amount of eyelash fluttering or lower lip wobbling was going to change his mind. "Will you at least tell me what's happening in the castle? Surely they ain't going to keep me locked up in this tower once they learn more about who really done in Mr. Coop." Miss Amaryllis had done it, Ophelia had insisted last night. And Ophelia was almost always right. But Prue also knew she'd deserve a dunce cap if she trumpeted Ophelia's suspicions to Hansel.

"I shall tell you every new thing that I learn."

"And maybe bring me some more pastries, too?"

Hansel grinned and sauntered back to his vegetable patch.

Ophelia looked left and right. The long castle corridor was empty. She let herself into Amaryllis's bedchamber.

Inside, the drapes were drawn, and the air was choked with lilac eau de toilette. The bed was unmade and clothing littered the carpet.

Interesting. Amaryllis hadn't allowed *any* of the servants into her chamber that morning, then. That explained why she was taking her breakfast downstairs, instead of on her usual tray in bed.

Ophelia got started with the dressing table.

She'd find proof, somehow, that Amaryllis had poisoned Mr. Coop and fixed things so that Prue would take the blame.

The dressing table held only a couple of boxes and bottles, since Amaryllis used few cosmetic preparations. Still, Ophelia did a thorough rummage of the dressing table drawers and even felt—recalling a pivotal scene in *The Terrors of Swansdon Hall*—along the underside of the table, in case an incriminating letter had been hidden there.

Nothing.

Next, she checked the tables on either side of the bed but came up with only a dog-eared volume of Lord Byron and a dented tin of anise pastilles.

She looked under the bed, behind the drapes, and beneath the pictures on the walls.

She was about to shuffle off—Amaryllis had surely finished crunching toast—when it hit her: the wardrobe. She hadn't checked there.

The wardrobe was big as a barn, painted white and gold, and bursting with gowns. Even though Ophelia had tidied it just yesterday morning, it was already higgledy-piggledy.

She knelt to feel along the sides and back. No thick envelopes, no diaries.

She stood. Her knee bumped the boots and slippers piled on the bottom, and a shoe tumbled out onto the floor.

It was one of Amaryllis's pale yellow silk slippers. The fragile material was blotched with dirt, the suede sole grass-stained and embedded with pebbles.

Hang on to your hat.

Yesterday, when they'd all gone out to the woods to

view the cottage, Amaryllis had been attired in a walking costume and sturdy leather boots. Before luncheon, Ophelia had helped her change into the yellow silk gown and slippers that she'd worn for the rest of the day.

If this slipper was soiled, then Amaryllis had gone outside at some point *after* luncheon. At some point, as a matter of fact, in the window of time that Mr. Coop's murderer had fetched an orchard apple and laced it with poison.

If Ophelia could match the soil and pebbles on the slipper to those in the orchard, or even find matching footprints, well, that was proof of Amaryllis's guilt, wasn't it? Ophelia could go straight to Inspector Schubert with the evidence, Prue would be freed, and they could stir their stumps as fast as they could back to New York.

She bundled the slipper in her apron pocket, closed the wardrobe, and hurried out of the room.

"What do you mean, gone?" Gabriel said to Professor Winkler. The woodsman, Herz, was chopping away at the thicket around the cottage, and Gabriel had to speak over the noise.

"I cannot put it more simply," Winkler said, blotting his forehead with a handkerchief. It was almost midday, and the sun was growing hot, even in the forest glade. "When I went to the castle library to view the skeleton, just after we had breakfasted together—with the view of drawing and measuring it, you see—it was no longer there."

"Did you ask the servants—"

"Of course. No one claimed to know anything."

"What about the ceiling beam?"

"Gone as well."

"But that," Gabriel said, "could've been the key to verifying the significance of the cottage." It was a struggle to sound disinterested. "What about the furnishings from inside the house—the beds and dishes and such that we placed in the library alcove?"

"Alas, also gone."

"What a terrible loss to science."

"Science? My dear Penrose, this cottage shall prove to be a hoax, mark my words. I fancy whichever peasant dug up a child's grave to obtain that skeleton began to grow anxious about vengeful spirits or the like, and decided to rebury it."

Gabriel set his jaw. Thank God he'd found that cuckoo clock with the same design as the ceiling beam. Not all was lost.

# 8

"Perhaps," Winkler called to the woodsman, Herz, "you ought to find some village men to assist you. At this rate, the thicket will have grown back by the time you are finished."

Herz paused, panting, and wiped the sweat from his brow. The look he gave Winkler could've withered grapes on the vine.

"I wished to ask you," Gabriel said to Herz, "when you first began to clear the brambles from about the cottage, were there any signs of recent entry?"

Herz glared out at him from the shade of his brow. Then he licked his lips. "No."

Winkler swiveled his chins to regard Gabriel quizzically. "Recent entry?"

"The skeleton had been positioned there more recently than the rest of the contents of the cottage. It hadn't the same coating of dirt."

Winkler treated Gabriel's shoulder to a hearty slap. "You have come round then—you agree that it is a hoax. I must say, I am relieved."

Herz was still staring at them with the sort of expression a cook might've worn while observing a plump goose's neck. Unnerving, considering the chap was brandishing an axe.

"Well then," Winkler said to him. "What are you waiting for? Go away and fetch some men to assist you."

"I," Herz said, swinging the axe over his brawny shoulder, "go to village now." He slouched away.

"Well then," Winkler said to Gabriel, "surely, despite the unfortunate death yesterday, they shall put something out for luncheon in the castle. Perhaps some of that delicious liver. Shall we go eat?"

Herz the woodsman, Gabriel learned from the castle's first footman after luncheon, lived with his wife and an indeterminate number of offspring in the castle's rear gatehouse.

"Not," Karl said, "the main gatehouse above the road from the village, mind. There's another, at the back, below the castle orchard. This gatehouse is built over a road that leads far, far back into the forest."

"Thank you," Gabriel said, slipping a coin into Karl's hand.

The coin disappeared beneath Karl's wine-stained cuff.

Mrs. Coop dozed and thrashed against her pillows all day. Her glazed eyes and half-conscious yelps reminded Ophelia of Dolly, the trained seal in P. Q. Putnam's Traveling Circus.

It was not until late afternoon that Ophelia, as she was tidying up the water glasses, crumpled handkerchiefs, and smelling salts on the table beside Mrs. Coop's bed, noticed the brown glass bottle.

She picked it up, keeping one eye on Mrs. Coop. Mrs. Coop's eyes were shut and her mouth was open, but like Dolly, she was proving herself disposed to sudden fits of snarling.

The label was not, as Ophelia had expected, in handwritten apothecary's script. Nor was it in German. The label displayed an etching of a girl's plump-cheeked face surrounded by rose blossoms, and it read:

### Dr. Alcott's Celebrated Hysteria Drops

*For the cure of hysteria and all*
*manner of feminine complaints*
*Dose: A teaspoon full in a little water,*
*to be taken every three to four hours*

*Theodosius Alcott, Pharmacist*
*Rochester, NY*

Rochester, New York? These drops hadn't been dispensed by the village doctor, after all. Mrs. Coop must've brought them from America. The only thing was, Ophelia had never noticed Mrs. Coop under the influence of strong medicine before that morning.

Peculiar.

Ophelia replaced the bottle on the table, put the empty water glasses on a tray, and left for the kitchen.

The kitchen was silent.

Freda the housemaid sat alone. The flowered cotton sleeves of her housemaid's dress were rolled up, and it appeared she had been tasked with shelling a pile of peas. But the peas and a bowl lay forgotten on the table. She was munching some kind of chocolate biscuit, and her eyes were riveted on the pages of a book.

"Freda?" Ophelia said.

"Miss Flax! You made me jump near out of my skin!" Freda pressed a palm against her cheek. "You should not go sneaking up on a body when there has been a murder in the house. And with me reading Mr. Poe, too."

"I beg your pardon. I thought you'd heard me come in." Ophelia took Mrs. Coop's dirty water glasses to the sink. "Has Prue been brought everything she needs, Freda? Food? Water?"

Freda's expression closed. She'd remembered who she was talking to.

"Why are you asking me about Prue?" Freda said. "With her locked up in the tower, I have to do all her work *and* mine."

"Might I help you? With those peas, perhaps?"

Freda scowled, slapped her open book facedown on the tabletop, and started shelling peas.

"The police were here again today," Ophelia said, "weren't they?"

"Seems you already know the answer."

"They spoke to Prue?"

"To Prue and to a few others as well. Trying to build up a case against her, I suppose. They did not get far, by the sound of it. Prue did not say a word."

*That* was a relief.

Suddenly, Cook swung into the kitchen with clattering boot heels and puffing breath. "You two! Gossiping like queen bees when we have enough work for a staff of thirty."

"No one but that fat professor is eating what we cook," Freda said. Peas plinked into her bowl.

"Why are you bothering Freda, Miss Flax?"

"She has been asking," Freda said, with a devious glance at Ophelia, "where the orchard is. The *apple* orchard."

The little liar! But . . . perhaps an opportunity had been plumped in Ophelia's lap.

"The orchard?" Cook placed her hands on her hips. "Now why would you want to go there? That place has caused more than enough mischief."

"It's only," Ophelia said, "Inspector Schubert asked me where it was, and I couldn't say."

"You are not poking about on Prue's behalf, are you?" Cook's voice was softer.

"Not—"

"Orchard's on the slope behind the castle. Past the courtyard, through the kitchen gardens. Behind a green wooden door in the wall."

"Thank you. I—"

"I do not wish to hear a thing about it."

\* \* \*

The sun was sinking by the time Gabriel rapped on the knotty door of the rear gatehouse. From inside came the playful screams of children, the yaps of a dog, crashing crockery.

The gatehouse hadn't been easy to find. He'd followed a road that began at an old mill on the edge of Schilltag, led around the base of the castle bluff, and meandered through a somber stretch of forest before he'd found the overgrown cart track leading to the gatehouse. The gatehouse had a moldering, forgotten air. Clearly, it hadn't been remodeled at any point in the last three centuries.

Gabriel rapped again.

The door swung open. A plump woman, perhaps thirty years old, with a rosy baby on her hip, appeared.

*"Ja?"* She sounded impatient and looked suspicious.

"Good evening," Gabriel said in German with a slight bow. He introduced himself as a professor who was visiting the castle.

Frau Herz's eyes narrowed. "There was a murder up there. What do you mean, coming unannounced to a private home like this, when there has been a murder! Why, *you* could be the murderer."

"I beg your pardon, madam—"

"Mina!" Frau Herz yelled over her shoulder. "Put the kitten down this instant!"

There was a feline yowl, more crashing, then a chorus of giggles. Gabriel allowed his eyes to drift past Frau Herz into the gatehouse interior. It was shabby and smelled of fried onions.

"Get a good look?"

"I came here," Gabriel said, "only to make the briefest of inquiries, after which I shall beat a hasty departure and leave you and your cherubs in peace."

"What is it?" Frau Herz wiped snot from the baby's nose with the corner of her apron.

"It is a matter of a clock—a cuckoo clock, which I

purchased from Herr Horkheimer's shop this morning. He informed me that you made it. A beautiful thing it is, too."

"Well"—Frau Herz was joggling the baby on her hip, but her countenance had relaxed somewhat—"it may be difficult to believe, but when these brats are not driving me mad, I do make carved pieces, mainly for Horkheimer's shop."

"Is it not, traditionally, a man's trade?"

"It was my father's trade, and my grandfather's and great-grandfather's before that. Papa trained my brother, but Joachim was never very strong, and he died young. I had always been watching and learning, too, ever since I was a wee one. With his only son dead, Papa agreed to let me train, too."

"I've come to ask—the design of the clock, along the roofline, has a rather fascinating design. Seven little men, with shovels and pickaxes over their shoulders, marching in a line."

"Never heard of Snow White, then? A fancy scholar-man like you?"

"No, no—I identified the figures as Snow White's seven dwarves. But the exact design—is it your own?"

Something drifted across Frau Herz's eyes.

The baby whimpered. Inside the gatehouse, a child yelled, "Mama! Mama! Peter hit me!"

Frau Herz sighed. "I must go."

"Is it your own design?"

She paused, then looked him straight in the eye. "I will tell you if you go away."

"All right."

"It is not my own design. I copied it, years ago, from a tapestry in the castle. A tapestry that belongs to the old deaf woman who . . . who works in the kitchens."

"A servant owns a tapestry?" Gabriel frowned. Tapestries, at least real ones, not the machine-made copies that were beginning to be produced, were immensely valuable.

"You said you'd go away." Frau Herz slammed the door shut.

* * *

Prue's tower had two windows. One overlooked the kitchen gardens, and the other faced west. The westward one had iron bars, and it was a good thing, too, because the sheer drop outside was enough to make you lose your vittles.

Around sunset, light in every shade of fruit punch came pouring through that iron-barred window.

Prue dragged the three-legged stool over. Maybe a little perusing of the scenery would take her thoughts from her face-off with Inspector Schubert that afternoon. He and his faucet-nosed assistant had come to the tower and tried to make her confess to killing Mr. Coop. Seeing as blabbing had never gotten her anything but in the suds, she had decided not to make a peep. Schubert had been hopping mad by the time he left.

Nothing but hills and pointy treetops outside the tower, and sparrows flitting around in the lit-up air. Far down below was a sort of rockslide at the base of the castle wall.

Prue blinked. There was a person down there, too, hustling along. Prue made out the dun-colored blur of a lady's walking skirt, a flash of a yellow hat. Straw. A satchel, swinging on a strap.

The figure disappeared under the trees.

Prue chewed her lip. She was new to these parts, true. But that was castle property down there. And that lady, well, Prue had never laid eyes on her before. Not once.


Gabriel hiked along the dark, wooded track towards Schilltag, thinking.

Perhaps the tapestry had been a gift from the old servant woman's employer. He had learned yesterday that some of the castle servants had stayed on after Count Grunewald had left.

Or perhaps the old woman had stolen the tapestry. That would account for Frau Herz's reticence. But there he was, thinking like one of those awful nobs who suspected the servants were forever after the silver teaspoons—

There was a snap of twigs.

Fancy running into a bear when he hadn't got his gun.

He caught a movement in the trees, a metallic glimmer. Silently, he stepped behind a tree trunk.

It wasn't a bear. It was the woodsman, Herz, prowling through the undergrowth.

Odd. He hadn't a torch to light his way, and he wasn't on the track.

And—Gabriel observed him a few seconds more—he wasn't heading home, towards the rear gatehouse. No, he was traipsing deeper into the wood, and he had a rifle on his shoulder.

Gabriel decided to follow him. Perhaps Herz would lead him to the secret that the Schilltag folk were so eager to keep hidden.

Gabriel had been a lieutenant in the cavalry during the Crimean War. He'd led scouting missions many times. So creeping through an ink-shadowed forest in pursuit of an armed and disgruntled man did not faze him quite as much as it ought to have.

He didn't dwell upon that, however, as he was led deeper and deeper into the trees. He was too intent on keeping sight of Herz, and on keeping his own footfalls silent.

Herz was nothing more than a black shape up ahead, blending in and out of still blacker shadows. Now and then, the steel barrel of his rifle flashed.

After about twenty minutes, Gabriel stepped on a rotten log. It collapsed under his weight. The undergrowth crackled.

Up ahead, Herz froze.

Gabriel held his breath, watching as Herz turned his head from side to side, listening.

Presently, Herz set forth again.

After a few heartbeats, Gabriel followed.

They were passing a stream that gurgled alongside a

vertical, fern-covered bluff. By Gabriel's calculations, they were heading to the northwest, away from the castle and Schilltag. The cottage was directly west of the castle, and Gabriel estimated that they had passed it already. Where was Herz going, then?

And, for that matter—where was Herz?

Gabriel stopped. He'd lost sight of the woodsman, and he couldn't hear anything but the splashing stream and the sighing tree branches. He took a step, towards an opening in the trees, and another and another.

Something clamped his leg with shocking force. He cried out, collapsing sideways into a damp cluster of ferns.

His left calf was caged inside a steel trap.

Thank God he was wearing tall stovepipe boots. And the trap did not, like most bear traps, have steel teeth; its jaws were padded with leather.

Which suggested—Gabriel gritted his teeth against blinding bursts of pain—that the trap was not for animals at all.

It was a man trap.

The shadowy undergrowth parted. His gaze traveled up the barrel of Herz's rifle.

# 9

∽⤬∾

"*P*rue."

Prue jerked her head up. She was sprawled face-down on the lumpy ticking mattress, dozing. It wasn't late, but she only had a candle, and anyway, she sure didn't intend to peruse the Bible someone had put in the tower. It didn't have a single picture, even.

"*Prue.*"

Hansel! Her heart pitter-pattered. She scrambled to her feet and dashed to the window.

"Hello," she whispered into the darkness.

Hansel was just a smudge of gray in the garden. "Did you enjoy the pastries I sent along on your tray with Freda?"

"Yes. And the biscuits, too, and the sausages. Oh—and the Turkish delight." Ma would be shocked. She always said a lady should give the impression of watching her figure in front of a gentleman, even if it meant stuffing her face like a carpetbag later on. But then, Hansel wasn't really a gentleman.

"I have come," he whispered, "to tell you what I have learned."

"They going to let me out?"

"Not yet. But something strange has occurred. All of those things that were removed from the house in the wood yesterday by the two professors and taken to the castle library—all of those things have gone missing."

"Missing?"

"Someone stole them. The skeleton, the furniture, the cups and plates. The painted ceiling beam with the gold leaf. Gone."

"How's that going to let me out?" Prue tapped her fingernails on the stone sill. She was starting to feel like a monkey in a cage. A wild monkey. Not the melancholic kind in the zoological gardens who'd given up on life.

"I suspect," Hansel said, "that Mr. Coop was killed because of something to do with the house in the wood, and the things taken from the house. It is too much of a coincidence that they were stolen just after he was killed."

"But I don't see—"

"Listen." He lowered his voice. "I observed the skeleton, when it was laid out in the library yesterday."

"And?"

"It had soil on it. Fresh soil, of a different sort than that found about the cottage."

Prue rolled her eyes. These kinds of details were dull as, well, dirt. She hankered for something to *happen*.

"Which means," Hansel said, "that the skeleton was placed in the cottage quite recently, and it was taken from the ground elsewhere. And"—Now his whisper was almost lost in the night—"and I believe I know where it came from. I am going there, tonight, to learn if I am correct."

"Wait. You're headed somewhere? Tonight?"

"Now."

Prue's heart leapt. Something was happening! "Take me along."

"It is not—"

"Oh, please, Hansel! *Pretty* please. I'm coming down with cabin fever in here. I swear you can lock me up again as soon as we're back."

"If anyone were to see you—"

"Who's going to see me?" If Ophelia saw her, of course, she'd be furious. But Prue couldn't bring herself to worry about that. She just needed *out*.

Prue wasn't sure how much Hansel could make out in the moonshine, but she pulled her best *Romeo and Juliet* face.

Maybe Hansel saw her Juliet face, maybe he didn't. But he sighed, paused, and then said, "All right. I will go and attempt to fetch the key. It is kept on a hook in the kitchen."

Mrs. Coop rallied from her stupor not long after sunset. She demanded that Ophelia help her bathe and fetch her beef broth and toast. It was after dark when she finally dissolved once more into snores on her bed, and Ophelia was able to sneak off.

She made her way, in a dark hooded cloak and with Amaryllis's yellow silk slipper tucked away in a pocket, down a spiral stair and out into the fresh-scented night. She hurried through the courtyard garden. White blossoms glowed and nodded like phantasms.

She cast an anxious glance up at Prue's dark tower. She'd sent Prue a note of encouragement earlier, and she'd heard from the second footman, Wilhelm, that Prue was warm and well fed in there, and equipped with an English Bible. Katrina and Freda had been enlisted to take Prue trays of food and remove her chamber pot. Poor hapless Prue.

Ophelia's heart thumped as she neared the gate in the wall, the same gate those two black-clad gentlemen had vanished behind at dawn. Or *had* they?

Ophelia gave her head a brisk shake.

Surely her mind hadn't cooked those fellows up. It wasn't like her to see things that weren't there. The world was like a theater stage set, as far as she could figure. If you went peeping around the back of things, you were likely to find rope pulleys, wooden supports, and some frowny fellow smoking a cigarette. No magic. Just bare facts.

She let herself through into the kitchen gardens. They smelled of earth and tangy tomato leaves. She picked her way between the vegetable beds, spying what had to be the chicken yard, off to one side. Feathery rustles and soft clucks came from inside the henhouse.

And there it was: the wooden door Cook had spoken of, in the far wall. In the moonlight it looked gray, not green, but that had to be it. Ophelia pushed it open.

On the other side, rows of gnarled fruit trees fanned down a steep slope. Their branches stood out like black claws against the moon-sheened sky. A breeze shuffled their leaves.

She scanned the jagged black perimeter of forest at the bottom of the slope. Somewhere, an owl hooted. Goosebumps prickled her arms.

Merciful heavens! Ophelia Flax. You aren't one to quiver like a Christmas jelly. Get *on* with it.

She drew the slipper from her cloak.

It was too dark to see the exact tint of the grass stains or the size of the pebbles embedded in the leather.

To be sure, there was grass out here, and pebbles, plenty of them. Piles of leaves and rotten apples, too.

What had she been thinking? That she'd just waltz out here, find—

Her eyes, adjusting to the thin moonlight, picked out the faintest of shapes on a path between two rows of trees. Could they be . . . footprints?

She dropped to her knees and positioned the slipper inside one of the prints. It—well, it *seemed* to fit. The problem was, it wasn't a complete print.

She got back on her feet and walked slowly down the slope, bending to peer at the path.

"You search for something, *fräulein*?" a gruff voice said behind her.

Ophelia froze. Then, slowly, she straightened and turned.

There was a man a couple of paces off to the side in the shadow of an apple tree. He had a bushy dark beard.

And a long-barreled gun aimed straight at her noggin.

He stalked closer.

She couldn't move; it was as though her feet had become tree roots. She could only stare, a sob of terror swelling her throat, as he approached. He produced from somewhere a sack and threw it over her head. The silk slipper fell as she tried to tear the sack off, to blindly run.

But he'd hoisted her over his shoulder as easy as a bag of barley, and with his arm hooked around the backs of her knees, he loped off with her down the orchard slope.

She kicked and wriggled, screamed and berated him, but none of it slowed him down. He muttered and cursed in German—they *sounded* like curses, anyway—and tightened his sweaty hold on her knees.

They went like that for twenty minutes, maybe more, over terrain that felt rocky and through brambles that dragged against her body like longing fingers.

Then there was the sound of a door slamming open, and they were inside—light shone through the sack on her head—and he flung her down on a chair.

Ophelia had a split second of freedom, which she used to rip the sack off her head. They were in a big stone chamber, nearly empty. There was a massive fireplace, unlit, gaping like a hungry mouth, and the furry heads of bears, deer, boars, and a wolf mounted on the walls. A chandelier made of bronze and antlers held two dripping tapers. Their flames shuddered in the wind from the open door.

No sooner had she glanced around than the man was binding her arms behind her with a rope.

"For mercy's sake!" she said. "I'm a lady, not a ship's barrel. That hurts!"

He jerked the rope even tighter.

"You won't get away with this." Ophelia kicked at his arm.

"You will find," someone else said, directly behind Ophelia, "that Herr Herz doesn't take kindly to threats." Whoever the man was, he had a British accent, and his voice was familiar. "Tried it myself."

Ophelia realized for the first time that her shoulders were pressed up against something more solid and warm than a chair back. She tried, out of some hazy sense of modesty, to lean forward, but Herz had tied her fast. "You're the professor," she said, twisting her neck. "The young one." She glimpsed only a square, woolen-clad shoulder.

"Young? Well, for the moment, I daresay."

"You're laughing? Can't you *do* something?"

"I'm trussed up as tightly as a roast goose, I'm afraid."

"You"—she addressed the bearded man—"are Herz? Why, I've heard of you!" He was crouched down, tying her booted ankle to the chair leg. "You're the woodsman at Schloss Grunewald." She made a half-relieved, half-anxious laugh. "This is a misunderstanding—I work at the castle, you see. I'm not a—"

"*Nein*, big feet." Herz grabbed her other ankle. "No misunderstanding."

Big feet?

Ophelia tried to kick him again, but his hands were like clamps.

He bound her ankle and stood, picked up his gun, and strode towards the door. "You stay here. I find out what to do with you." He stepped out into the night.

"He's leaving us?" Ophelia said.

"You'd rather he stayed? I don't know if you noticed, but he isn't one for light conversation."

"Who knows how long he'll be gone. We could freeze. We could starve!"

"Perhaps this isn't the proper moment, then, to inquire how it is that an American lady's maid finds herself in the Black Forest after nightfall, tied to a chair in an abandoned hunting lodge?"

"That's what this is? A hunting lodge?" Ophelia looked around. The glass eyes of all those dead, stuffed critters looked right back. "What are *you*, a college professor, doing out in the woods after midnight? Strolling around composing sonnets in your head? Odes to the moon?"

"Sonnets and odes are not quite the same thing—"

"Kindly answer the question."

"I asked you first, you may recall."

Ophelia felt as steamed as a forgotten teakettle. Worse,

she was painfully aware of the way their shoulders were pressed together, and that the feel of his body, the faint scent of his shaving soap were . . . comforting.

"Listen," she said, "Professor—Professor What's-Your-Name—"

"Penrose."

"Professor Penrose. Let's not waste time splitting hairs but decide how we're going to get out of this scrape before that mad woodsman comes back. I didn't like the look in his eye one bit, and goodness knows who he'll bring back with him."

"How do I know I can trust you?"

"Trust me? With what?"

"Well, in order to get ourselves unfixed from these chairs, we must work together. I don't wish to risk you leaving me high and dry."

"I'm a Yankee. We're a dependable sort."

"Ah. Like one of those severe ladies in black bonnets you see in old portraits from the colonies. Ladies who could churn butter with one hand, burp a baby with the other, and read a psalm book with the other?"

"Exactly." Ophelia had an itchy suspicion he was teasing her. Yes. He was. "Three hands!"

"Three? Forgive me. I must've lost count. But, pray tell, how did such an upright young Yankee lady find herself in such a compromising position?"

Ophelia chewed her lip. "All right. I'll tell you. But only because I'm—well, as a matter of fact, I'm most grateful to you for sticking up for Prue like you did. If it weren't for you, she'd be in jail in Baden-Baden this minute."

"Don't mention it."

"Well," Ophelia said, "it's like this: I was out in the castle orchard when Herz caught me."

"Searching for an apple, like the one that was poisoned? You do realize that that apple needn't have been picked just before tea yesterday—could it not have been sitting in a pantry in the castle for days, even weeks?"

He *was* a highfalutin tinhorn, wasn't he?

"I think," Ophelia said, "Mr. Coop usually picked those apples himself. He always seemed to have some in his pockets. None of the servants got them for him, not that I know of, anyway. As a matter of fact, I was in the orchard looking for footprints to match a—a suspicious shoe I found."

"Ah. Taking matters into your own hands, then?"

"Prue wouldn't hurt a fly. I've got to get her out of that tower before—" She snapped her mouth shut. She'd almost said, *Before Inspector Schubert finds out we're really actresses.* "And you? What were you doing?"

"Following Herz."

"But why?"

"Scholarly pursuits." He fell silent.

"Now listen here, professor. You're clamming up on me, and after I told you everything." Well, *almost* everything. "It's not fair."

"I study folklore," he said.

"Everyone in the castle knows that, and let me tell you, if I'd known you could study fairy tales at college, I would've gone a long time ago."

"Fairy tales aren't for children, and they aren't trivial."

Ophelia rolled her eyes in the direction of a stuffed bear's head. "No?"

"Their careful study takes one to the very heart of how language works. How it is transmitted from generation to generation, how it evolves through the centuries. These tales even allow scholars to track the migration of ancient peoples across Europe."

Ophelia felt out of her depth. It wasn't a familiar or pleasant feeling. "But why follow Herz?"

"I had hoped—foolishly, I suppose—that he would lead me to a clue about the cottage and skeleton that were found."

"Did he?"

"I had the misfortune of stepping into a steel-jawed trap before I could find out."

Ophelia gasped. "Are you all right?"

"My leg will be bruised." He paused. "Miss Flax. Your intention is to unmask Homer Coop's killer."

"I'm getting Prue out of that tower. And then we're going straight back to New York."

"We may be of some benefit to each other."

Ophelia jiggled her foot, trying to make the pins and needles stop. The ropes were far too tight. "What're you angling at?"

"I'll be blunt: you have, in the capacity of a castle servant, access to certain persons and places that I do not. If you agree to ask a few discreet questions of persons in the castle, I shall, in return, do my utmost to aid you in your search for Homer Coop's murderer."

"Just ask a few questions?"

"Very simple."

"And then you'll help me?"

"To the best of my ability."

Ophelia mulled it over. Professor Penrose was clever. Very clever. And he seemed trustworthy, even if he was a stuffed-shirted, high-muck-a-mucking—

"Do you," he asked, "accept?"

She sighed. She needed help. "You've got yourself a deal."

"Splendid."

She felt him bump around behind her for several moments. The next thing she knew, his shoulders were no longer pressed against hers.

"What are you—?" She tried to crane her neck to see what he was doing. She heard a faint, rhythmic, sawing sound—

"You sneak!" she cried. He had somehow freed himself, and he was crouched at her feet, cutting at ropes around her ankles with a small knife.

He glanced up at her, a lopsided smile on his lips. His hazel eyes shone behind his spectacles.

"You could've freed us sooner," she said.

"Is that all the thanks I get?" He cut her other ankle loose.

# 10

⊱—❦—⊰

Miss Flax hurtled to her feet and rubbed her wrists. "Is that the only way you're able to converse with a lady?" Her dark eyes flashed. "Keep her tied up?"

"Until Herz inadvertently loosened my ropes while he was tying yours," Gabriel said, folding his penknife and slipping it into his breast pocket, "I wasn't able to reach my knife."

"Wasn't able to, my eye." She started for the door.

"Wait." He held her shoulder. "You can't go out there."

"Can't I?"

"Alone?"

"Would it blow you sideways to hear that I'm capable of looking after myself, without being herded around—and tied up—like an especially dull-witted sheep?" She shook her shoulder free.

"This isn't a matter of wits. Herz is armed, the wood is laid with traps, and, as you noted yourself, we don't know who he may be bringing back."

Her mouth softened, and she knit her eyebrows.

They were lovely eyebrows, he noticed, finely sketched and tapering.

"What do you think he's doing," she said, "patrolling the forest like that?"

"He's clearly working in the capacity of some sort of night watchman. Perhaps he is overzealous, or perhaps he has been instructed by whomever he is reporting back to, to detain anyone he finds on the estate at night."

"But what's out here, that he's so affrighted someone might find?" Miss Flax drew her cloak close.

"It doesn't seem to be a simple matter of keeping poachers at bay." He paused. "You don't think he could be reporting back to Mrs. Coop, do you?"

"She's. . . ." Miss Flax pressed her lips together, as though wondering how much to tell.

"Mrs. Coop," Gabriel said, "despite her recent, tragic loss, is quite taken with the idea of the cottage in the wood—perhaps she wishes to safeguard the site?"

"Maybe."

He lifted an eyebrow.

"Oh, very well." She sighed. "Last night—or, really, early this morning, at dawn—I happened to see two gentlemen, all in black, carrying a bundle through the courtyard garden."

Gabriel's heart quickened. "Go on."

"They disappeared behind the gate."

"Did you recognize them?"

"No."

"And the bundle—what did it look like?"

"Long. Long and narrow."

"The ceiling beam—you do know it's gone missing, along with all the relics from the cottage?"

"Yes. The whole castle's humming with the news."

"So it's possible," Gabriel said, "that Herz is not reporting to Mrs. Coop, but to whomever those mysterious gentlemen were."

"Or maybe Herz and those two gentlemen are in the employ of the same person."

"Perhaps."

Miss Flax narrowed her eyes. "My notion's just as much of a dinger as yours."

Gabriel had been under the obviously mistaken impression that Miss Flax was a quiet, rather regal young lady. Yet she was, evidently, loquacious, a bit hotheaded, and the proud owner of a steely will.

And what had possessed him to say that he'd do his utmost to help her find Coop's killer? Gabriel had always made a point of steering well clear of human entanglements. They only got in the way of his work.

But that was just it: he'd agreed to help her, not for her sake, but for the sake of those missing relics and the mystery of their origins. She could easily inquire as to the whereabouts of the tapestry Frau Herz had mentioned.

His fingertips tingled in anticipation of touching that dwarf's skeleton again, of caressing the hand-carved shapes in the ceiling beam.

He'd just have to humor Miss Flax a short while longer.

"Your notion was, indeed, a dinger," he said. "Shall we venture forth?"

Hansel and Prue sneaked away from the castle grounds and trooped up into the mountains. Hansel lugged a knapsack on his back. He'd said there was a lantern and matches inside.

The night was as deep and dark as a pot of coffee. The forest rustled in a way that made Prue's skin creep. But she wasn't about to complain about that or about the blister popping up on her heel or how the sleeves of the ugly brown dress were chafing her elbows. She was out of the tower. That's what counted.

"When I was a boy," Hansel said, "I loved to play in the forest all about here."

"You grew up in the castle?"

"I did." Hansel paused to lift a bramble so Prue could pass underneath. "My family has been living at Schloss Grunewald for many, many years. As servants. I had a little playmate, just my age, named Franz. We would come out here with my dog, Wolfgang, and romp and fish, practice with our slingshots on the poor birds—"

"On the sparrows?"

"Poor little creatures. I regret it now."

"Oh, you shouldn't be too sore. Sparrows ain't as nice as they're made out to be." Prue shuddered at the thought of those sharing her tower.

"Well, one day—I have never forgotten this—we were playing up here, on a cliff. Wolfgang was digging about and barking, as he often did. He dragged a bone to us and laid it at our feet. He had done this sort of thing before, having found the bones of deer or rabbits and once, the skull of a boar. But this bone. . . ." Hansel fell silent.

"What?"

Hansel turned to help her up a slick boulder. The path had grown steep as a staircase, and the brush hunkered over like it was trying to cover a secret. But Hansel's hand was strong and warm. So Prue probably didn't need to pay mind to the feeling that something with horns and teeth might bound out of the darkness at any second.

They paused, panting, on top of the boulder.

"It was a human bone," Hansel said. "A radius—a bone of the forearm."

Prue licked her lips and drew closer to him. In a vague sort of way, she wondered how a servant knew the word *radius*.

"Yet," he said, "an exceptionally small radius, although not delicate enough to be that of a child. When we looked about we discovered, up on the top of the cliff, a grave, marked by a stone. The stone was covered in moss. It could have passed for one of the other mossy stones up there. Except this stone was marked."

Prue stared up into Hansel's shadowed face. The sky behind his head swirled with moon-milky clouds and a few lonesome stars. "What was the mark?"

"The Roman numeral four." He lifted his finger and traced the sky. *IV.*

"That where we're headed now?"

Hansel cocked his head towards the steep, gloomy path. "We are nearly there."


Ophelia and Professor Penrose crept through the rustling forest. It had grown cool, and wind rocked the black branches and sent clouds coursing across the moon.

"I don't know how to get back," Ophelia said. Her voice was extra firm. Something about Professor Penrose bubbled all the fight in her right up to the surface.

"I've a good idea," he said. "Stay close, try not to make a sound, and watch where you put your feet. Thank heavens the moon is so bright."

They set off.

As they tramped through the trees, Ophelia saw that the professor was limping. But it was still reassuring—more than she liked to admit—to be close to his tall, sportsmanlike form.

After several minutes, they began walking alongside a stream in the shadow of some sort of cliff. Ferns dragged at the hem of her cloak, drenching it with dew, and the heels of her boots sank in the spongy earth. But Penrose moved, despite his limp, easily through the terrain.

You'd think that a bespectacled scholar wouldn't be so sure of himself in the nighttime forest.

Ophelia eyed his back. He could be leading her straight to the gates of Tartarus. What reason did she have to trust him?

Just then, Penrose froze.

Ophelia's heart set off at a gallop. She didn't even mind the way his big hand wrapped around her wrist, because there was a rustling coming from the opposite side of the stream.

Penrose pulled her down to a crouch beside him.

They watched through the ferns as a form—a human form—skulked along the streambed, heading in the direction of the hunting lodge. It was Herz.

Ophelia's palms started to sweat. She would've rather seen Mr. Wolf all dressed up like Granny.

They waited, frozen, as Herz passed. The professor's fingers were still around her wrist, and she was pressed up against his big, tweedy body in an unseemly fashion. Even as her eyes followed Herz, and as her blood thundered past her eardrums, she noticed, again, the professor's mild scent of shaving soap.

Her ears went hot.

After a minute or two more, Penrose released his grip on her wrist. "I think," he whispered, "it's safe to go. But we must travel quickly, because once he reaches the lodge and realizes we've gone, he'll be tracking us like a foxhound."

They set off again, following the stream, and after several minutes they turned away from the streambed, into the trees. When Ophelia caught a glimpse of the castle through the branches, she sighed in relief.

They passed through the trees and found themselves on some kind of unused cart track. Tall grasses and wildflowers swayed, silver in the darkness.

"This track leads into Schilltag," Penrose said. "I took it earlier this evening."

"Is that—" Ophelia squinted. "Are those lights up ahead from the village?"

The professor stopped so suddenly that Ophelia bumped into his back. "No. Those are lanterns, just round the bend. Quick—behind the trees." They scurried off the track and waited.

The two yellow splotches of light didn't move.

Ophelia and the professor picked their way closer, staying inside the trees, to find a coach standing on the track. It was large, elegant, raven-black, with two horses and two lamps. A coachman hunched on the driver's box with his face buried deep in his collar. He was asleep. There was a crest on the coach door, and the curtains were drawn.

"Do you recognize the crest?" Penrose whispered.

"Well, it's not the Schloss Grunewald crest, and that's the only crest I've ever seen."

The only *real* one, anyway; Ophelia had seen plenty of fake ones painted on stage props.

One of the horses swiveled an ear in their direction. Ophelia and Penrose sank back into deeper shadow.

"Let's stay right here," Ophelia whispered, "and see who the coach is waiting for—I'd wager it's to do with Herz and whoever he's working for."

"I must return you to the castle."

"You make me sound like a princess." She perched on a fallen log. "Either that or an express mail parcel. I don't need beauty sleep, and no one will notice I'm gone. I'm staying."

The professor straightened his spectacles. Ophelia could tell that's what he did when he was nettled.

But he kept quiet, and after a few minutes, he sat down next to her on the log to wait.

Prue and Hansel reached the top of the ladder-steep path. Prue tried her best to wheeze in a ladylike way. Didn't work. She sounded like she was auditioning for the part of a bellows.

They had arrived on a cliff that was about the size of a theater stage, jutting out like an open dresser drawer on the side of the mountain. The cliff was littered with rocks of different sizes, probably tumbled down from above.

"Be careful," Hansel said, pointing. "That is a very steep precipice over there."

Beyond the cliff, the whole black-and-gray world opened out, with rolling hills stretching back and back under a starry sky. "Never been out in the countryside at night," Prue whispered.

"Never?"

"Nope. I feel like I might just—just disappear or something."

Hansel was eyeballing Prue through the dark. But not in the way she was used to having men eyeball her, like she was a picture hanging on a wall or a bauble for sale in a shop window. He only looked . . . curious. She wasn't sure she liked it. He could probably see the knots in her hair.

"Well?" she said, rubbing her nose. "What're we going to do?"

Hansel knelt and drew the lantern from his knapsack. The first two matches died in the wind, but the third one caught. Yellow light swelled. He slammed the lantern's little door shut, and stood. "We are going to confirm my suspicion that the skeleton that was placed in the cottage was dug up here." He lifted the lantern and climbed over the jumbly rocks.

Prue followed. The rocks were fuzzy with moss, in every size from shooter marble to steamer trunk. "How are we going to find a rock with something carved in it?" She bent to study a stone.

"We do not need to find the stone." Hansel turned and beckoned. "Because we have found the grave."

"Grave?" Her boots didn't seem to want to go any farther.

Hansel hopped down from the rock he'd been on. The lantern swung to and fro, creaking. Its light was too puny for such a big, dark night.

Prue looked down at her boots. They started to move. She crept to Hansel's side.

At their feet was a big, dark, damp hole.

"It's empty," he said.

"Whoever dug it did it all sloppy, like." Prue pointed to the edges of the hole. "See?"

"Perhaps they were in a hurry."

"Nope. Not in a hurry. Just drunk." She gestured to the far side of the hole. There was a pile of dirt over there, and on top of the dirt were two shining bottles.

# 11

⤜⤛

Prue and Hansel circled around and picked up the bottles. Both were empty. Prue gave one a sniff. "Brandy." She wrinkled her nose and tossed the bottle back into the dirt. It landed with a clunk.

Hansel held the other bottle up. "It is still wet inside. This was left here quite recently."

"A couple weeks?"

"Perhaps even in the last few days."

They stared at each other through the gloom.

"Someone came up here to get fuddled up," Prue said.

"And to dig up the grave. Which they must have intended to do in advance, because they would have needed a shovel."

"Then, for some reason, they went to all the trouble of hauling the skeleton to the cottage and leaving it there."

Hansel held up the lantern and bent over the dirt pile. "There are footprints."

Prue hitched up her hem and crouched next to him. "That's a man's boot print," she said. "And so is that one—that one's a different size."

"There were at least two men, then."

"Should hope so, considering they polished off two bottles of popskull. Wait." Prue squinted, then poked at the dirt. "Now this is not a feller's print at all. It's a lady's." She swiveled to face Hansel. "What in tarnation were these folks doing, drinking out here and digging up skeletons? It's downright ghoulish."

"I agree." Hansel helped Prue to her feet. "Are you frightened? You are shaking."

"No, I ain't," she fibbed.

"We should go back." He still had her hands. "We have learned what we needed to know. However, I should like to have a look about before we go. Do you wish to sit here on this rock for a moment? Here." He shrugged his jacket from his shoulders and folded it around her.

Prue quirked her lips. Him being so nice made her want to cry for some reason. "All right." She sure as Sheboygan didn't want him to see her boohooing. "Go ahead. I'll wait."

He went off with the lantern, bending to see the ground.

Prue didn't sit, but she hugged the jacket close. It was homespun wool and scratchy. It smelled like Hansel, sort of fresh and leafy.

She'd have to tell Ophelia about this, after all. Sigh. Because this jaunt had turned into something serious, something to do, just maybe, with Mr. Coop's murder. Prue mentally crossed her fingers that Ophelia wouldn't be too sore.

She glanced into the black pit of the grave. Instinctively, she edged away, backwards into the dirt pile.

Something crunched under her boot heel.

She gulped away the nasty notion that she'd just crushed some half-pint skull, and lifted her foot.

Something glittery was down there. She scooped it up, scraped away the earth clumped over it.

A little comb. It was heavy for its size, and there were designs along its spine and some kind of dirt-crusted stones inlaid. Her heel had bent some of the teeth, but it was still intact. It could still be useful for fixing her hair in the tower, once she cleaned it up. Then she wouldn't have to be such a Medusa in front of Hansel. She flicked away a few more particles of dirt, and slid the comb inside her bodice.

A few moments later, Hansel returned to her side. "I did not see anything else," he said. "Did you?"

"Nope."

"Are you ready?"

Prue nodded.


Ophelia and the professor had been waiting for what felt like an hour. The moon arced across the sky. Ophelia rested her elbows on her knees and propped her chin in her hand. She watched the horses' restless treading, the breeze-blown treetops. She peered through the under-growth, up and down the track—

"I see someone," she whispered.

It wasn't Herz. It was a slighter person, flitting through the tall flowers and grasses of the track towards the coach. There was something familiar about the person's uncertain step. "Miss Amaryllis!"

"So it is," Penrose whispered.

Amaryllis wore a billowing cloak and a bonnet. She minced her way, now and then pausing to chipmunk-glance around, before proceeding forward again.

The coachman lifted his head.

Amaryllis reached the coach. A door swung open. An arm—a fellow's arm, in a dark coat—extended to help her inside.

The door slammed shut, and the coachman cracked his whip. The coach rumbled away towards Schilltag and was enfolded into the night.

"Miss Amaryllis, abroad in the wee hours?" Penrose got up from the log and helped Ophelia to her feet.

"I can't think who she'd be meeting at this hour, or, for that matter, at all. But I'm fair certain she killed Mr. Coop, and now it looks as though she might've had help."

They stepped onto the track and started in the direction of the village. They spoke in undertones and searched the edges of the trees for signs of Herz.

"Miss Amaryllis a murderess?" Penrose said.

"For revenge, see. You saw how Mr. Coop belittled her."

"I did."

"And did you notice the way she regarded Mr. Hunt?"

"I do recall some languishing stares, yes."

"Well, she could have killed Mr. Coop and fixed things up for Prue to take the blame."

"Have you any proof?"

"Well, that's what I was looking for." Ophelia told him all about the soiled slipper. "She'd only go out in good slippers like those if she was up to something."

Penrose was silent, but Ophelia could almost hear him thinking, like gears and cogs whirring along.

"Perhaps," he said, "her slippers bear marks of having been in the out of doors because she wore them on past occasions for a rendezvous, like the one we just witnessed. When did you discover the slipper?"

"This morning."

"Then they could have been soiled on the afternoon of the murder or yesterday evening."

Why did he have to be so dratted *logical*?

"The dilemma," he said, "is that nearly everyone in the castle had the opportunity to plant a poisoned apple in the urn before tea."

"Everyone? Even you?"

"During the hour in question, between the conclusion of Winkler's tests and tea, I returned to the cottage for another look round. Hunt and the ladies went off somewhere—I know not where—Winkler remained in the library to record the results of his tests, and Coop's secretary, Smith, was holed up with him in the study, working. However, I have no firsthand knowledge of any of this. And then, of course, there are all the servants to be accounted for." He cast her a glance.

"You don't suppose I—"

"No." He paused. "Where is the slipper now?"

"Dropped it in my tussle with Herz."

Penrose stopped walking. "We ought to fetch it. No sense in leaving a trail of breadcrumbs, so to speak." He turned on the track. "We'll return to the castle by way of the orchard—it is at the rear, is it not?"

"Yes." Ophelia dreaded revisiting the scene of her recent kidnapping, but the professor had a point. She caught up to him. "Maybe that was Mr. Hunt in the coach."

"Hunt? I never noticed him so much as glance in Miss Amaryllis's direction. Could it not have been one—or both—of the mysterious gentlemen you saw in the courtyard? If Miss Amaryllis is meeting with the same gentlemen who stole the relics from the cottage, and she is indeed the murderess, it resolves the rather untenable theory that the thefts and Mr. Coop's death are not related."

"But what would Miss Amaryllis want with a parcel of bones and a dirty old beam?" They walked in silence for a few moments. "If," Ophelia said, "Miss Amaryllis has her heart set on Mr. Hunt, maybe she had the relics stolen for *him*."

"Forgive me, but is it not a bit far-fetched to assume that Hunt returns Miss Amaryllis's regard?"

"You can't conceive of a plain girl being loved by someone as handsome as Mr. Hunt? Plain girls have the same sort of hearts as pretty girls. Maybe even more tender."

"I would not venture to challenge that point, having neither the inclination nor the knowledge, except to say that Miss Amaryllis, if she indeed harbors a tender heart, keeps it remarkably well hidden."

"Well, who else could it have been? Don't forget we arrived in Germany only a fortnight ago. Miss Amaryllis has very few acquaintances here."

"We must learn more of Mr. Hunt. That much is clear."

Because of the castle hulking above them, they easily found the bottom of the orchard. Ophelia led the way to the spot where Herz had captured her.

The slipper was nowhere to be found.

"Are you certain," Penrose said, "this is the place?"

"I'm not liable to forget the greatest fright of my life. Someone's taken the slipper." Ophelia stared down the slope into the pointed black wall of trees. Herz could be there, at the edge of the wood, watching them right now. She shivered.

Penrose took her elbow and steered her farther up the slope to the gate in the wall.

"Tomorrow morning," he said, "I shall go to Baden-Baden and attempt to learn more of Hunt. It is, at least, a place to begin. You, in the meantime, must exercise the utmost caution. Stay inside the castle, and if you see Herz, stay well clear. We don't know who he's working for or what he might do next. As for Hunt—do you know how Mrs. Coop made his acquaintance?"

"I don't." Ophelia tugged her elbow free of Penrose's hand. "I'll go with you to town."

"Nonsense."

"You said we'd work together."

"I said nothing of the sort. Are all American maids so high-handed?"

"A bargain's a bargain."

"You seem to have acquired your lady's maid training aboard one of those famed gambling boats on the Mississippi River."

"Americans aren't the only ones who don't like being double-crossed. And are you suggesting I'm not a proper lady's maid?"

"Now that you mention it—"

She shot him a dark look. "I *am* going with you. Where are you staying?"

"At Gasthaus Schatz. In the village. But you really mustn't—"

"*Mustn't* isn't a word I fancy."

"That doesn't come as an immense surprise."

"I'll meet you at your inn at ten o'clock in the morning. If I can't get away, I'll send word. But I mean to be there." Ophelia pushed the gate open.

"I don't doubt it for an instant," Penrose said.

She slipped through the gate.

\*   \*   \*

Ophelia closed the gate behind her and set forth across the kitchen gardens.

Hmph. That Professor Penrose was as bossy as a—

Her eyes lifted to Prue's tower window.

Uh-oh.

Ophelia could just discern the silhouette of a jug, sitting on the windowsill. The signal!

She hitched her skirts and broke into a jog. She thrust through the barred door at the bottom of the battlement, flew up the dank stairs, and thudded her fist on the tower door. "Prue! Prue, are you all right?"

"Keep your bonnet on!" came the muted reply. "I'm just dandy."

"What was—the jug—did you—"

"Ophelia." Prue's voice was closer now. "I've got a sort of, um, confession to make."

Ophelia frowned at the door. "Oh?"

Ophelia listened in silence as Prue described her outing with Hansel. A cliff in the forest. A tale about a dwarf's bone. A dug-up grave on a cliff. Empty brandy bottles and footprints—multiple men's and at least one lady's.

"Ophelia?" Prue said, when she'd finished. "Are you awful steamed?"

"Steamed doesn't even—Prue! You're placing yourself in unnecessary danger, and all for—for what?"

"Them things on the cliff could have something to do with Mr. Coop's murder!"

"Perhaps. But if Inspector Schubert—"

"Aw, to Timbuktu with Inspector Schubert!"

Well, Ophelia couldn't argue with *that* sentiment.

"Hansel thinks," Prue said, "that the dwarf bones that were in the cottage came from that grave on the cliff. So that means—well, I'm not so sure."

Ophelia turned it over in her mind. "It means," she finally said, "that since the skeleton was stolen from the castle, along with the other relics—did you hear about that?"

"Hansel told me."

"All right—so it means that the folks who stole the skeleton and the relics might be the same folks who dug them up in the first place."

"Makes sense."

"But there is nothing to suggest that the skeleton and the relics had anything to do with Mr. Coop's murder. It's only a case of two different—and I'll admit, peculiar—events happening around the same time."

"A mighty big coincidence."

"True. But stranger things have happened. Now listen here, Prue. Don't leave the tower again, because I—"

"No."

Ophelia rolled her eyes at the keyhole.

"It's *my* freedom we're talking on," Prue said. "Not yours. I have a right to take a fair crack at helping myself—why, you'd say the same thing yourself, Ophelia Flax."

Once again, Ophelia couldn't rightly argue. "Fine," she said. "But we've got to work together on this, understand? No more sneaking behind my back. If I've got one leg and you've got the other, we need to share what we learn so we can put the thing together again. Promise?"

"Pinky swear."


When Gabriel entered his chamber at the inn that night, the air pulsated with a sense of intrusion.

He struck a match and lit a lamp.

It was a small, neat room with sloped ceilings and worn, rustic furnishings. The window was open, and a cold wind fluttered the embroidered white curtains.

He'd left that window shut.

The one piece of luggage he'd brought, a brown leather valise that he'd hastily packed in Heidelberg, sat on a chair in the corner. It gaped open, and upon closer inspection he saw that it had been rifled through. Nothing, however, seemed to be missing. Not even his pair of Webley Longspur revolvers in their felt-lined case.

He closed the window, drew the curtains, and sank onto the bed. He pulled off his boots and inspected the nasty, raised welt that Herz's man-trap had left on his shin. Then he crawled beneath the eiderdown and fell instantly to sleep.

"Ma'am," Ophelia said to Mrs. Coop in the morning, "might you be wanting mourning things?" She winched Mrs. Coop to a seated position in bed, plumped up the pillows behind her, and handed her a steaming cup of Darjeeling.

"Mourning things?" Mrs. Coop sipped her tea.

There was no telltale glimmer in her eye to suggest she knew anything about Ophelia's run-in with Herz the night before. Her hair was like a scarecrow's, and her eyes had a rabbity, red appearance.

Ophelia glanced at the bedside table. The bottle of hysteria drops was already half empty.

"I know," Ophelia said, bustling across the chamber to open the drapes, "you've some black gowns to wear—once you're up and about—but there are certain fashionable things a lady ought to have when in mourning."

"Please!" Mrs. Coop raised her arm to shield her eyes. "Please, leave the drapes drawn. I cannot bear to see the sunlight yet. It reminds me so of poor Homer and the sunlit life we led together."

Sunlit life? Golly, how memory did play tricks.

Ophelia pulled the drapes shut.

"What is this," Mrs. Coop said, "about mourning things? Do you mean black fans and reticules? Because I have those."

"Those things, yes. But all of the choicest ladies of fashion—I read this in a Paris magazine, see—also wear brooches of jet beads, made to look like flowers."

"Black flowers?"

"That's right," Ophelia fibbed. "And you'll need a likeness of poor Mr. Coop, rest his soul, painted up in a nice locket for you to wear." This last bit wasn't a lie, although the smartness of such an item was questionable. Ophelia had only seen dreary old dames wearing the things. Old dames with hair parted like two lank beaver pelts. "After your bath, ma'am, I will be happy to go into Baden-Baden and purchase these things for you."

"Well, if you say they're fashionable. . . ."

"You simply couldn't leave the castle without them. Or receive visitors. I understand the funeral is set for tomorrow?"

"Oh!" Mrs. Coop flung her head back against her pillows. Her tea sloshed. "How my heart shall ache to see Homer sent to his final rest."

"Will Princess Verushka attend the funeral, ma'am?" Ophelia tidied the bric-a-brac on the mantelpiece. "And . . . Mr. Hunt?"

"The princess?" Mrs. Coop's voice was suddenly shrill. "Why ever would I invite *her*?"

"I beg your pardon, ma'am. I was given to understand she was—"

"She is only the most casual of acquaintances. You wouldn't know it by the way she clings to me like a leech. She's a guest for the season at the Hotel Europa in Baden-Baden, you see, and I met her purely by happenstance. Why, the poor thing grasped at me as though I were her first-class ticket." Mrs. Coop fiercely slurped her tea. "It positively makes me cringe that she told that officer of the police—what was his name?"

"Inspector Schubert?" Ophelia was rearranging a vase of roses on the mantel, but she was all ears.

"Yes, Schubert—well, Princess Verushka told him that she was with me during the hour before tea that—that afternoon."

Ophelia turned to face Mrs. Coop. "Wasn't she with you?"

"Oh, she was. But the way she *announced* it to everyone, as though to suggest we were the closest of friends. She is desperate to create the appearance of intimacy with me. To elevate her own position, you see."

Elegant Princess Verushka using Mrs. Coop in a game of society leapfrog? Not likely.

"But Mr. Hunt will attend the funeral," Ophelia said. "He is surely a closer acquaintance."

"That dear, dear gentleman. I hadn't thought to ask him. He was ever so solicitous to me the day Homer died."

Mr. Hunt hadn't seemed concerned about anything beyond sugared almonds, the contents of his cigarette case, and the arrangement of his Grecian curls. Should she ask how Mrs. Coop had made his acquaintance? No. Better not press her luck.

"I shall write Mr. Hunt," Mrs. Coop said, "and request his presence at the funeral. And Flax—"

"Yes, ma'am?" Ophelia knew exactly what Mrs. Coop would say next.

"I simply must have one of those jet flower brooches. And a locket. You are to order the coachman to take you shopping in Baden-Baden this morning."

"Yes, ma'am."

On her way down to the kitchens with Mrs. Coop's tray, Ophelia took a circuitous route in order to pass by the breakfast room.

The door was ajar, and she caught a glimpse of Amaryllis, sitting at the big table all alone, nipping into a triangle of toast.

She'd returned from her nocturnal rendezvous, then.

# 12

When Prue woke up, she felt brittle, chilled, and hungry enough to take fork and knife to Moby-Dick. Straw from the mattress was stuck to her cheek. She picked the straw off, with beady-eyed sparrows looking down. Whippersnappers.

She polished off two of the raisin buns, four sausages, one pear, and the entire pot of tea that someone had left for her on a tray inside the door. Then she felt a little less like kicking the wall. She washed herself with cold water in the basin in the corner and set about cleaning the comb she'd found on the cliff last night.

It was a pretty trinket—or it had been, once. It was made of tarnished metal, all carved with frail vines and flowers. Tiny red stones were inlaid to look like berries.

Ma had taught Prue a lot of things, some of them more useful than others. One thing Prue knew was how to spot real gems. These were genuine rubies. Not glass.

She'd forgotten to mention the comb to Ophelia last night. Well, *almost* forgotten. Surely Ophelia didn't need to know that Prue had reached the rank of grave robber.

Prue's hair was a tangly mess and it was going greasy at the roots, so she set to work.

She was just fastening her hair into a complicated plait that hid the greasy bits when she heard a faint crunching sound. She dragged the stool to the iron-barred window and looked down.

It was that lady again, the one with the dun-colored walking costume and the straw hat. She was directly below and the brim of her hat was wide, so Prue couldn't see her face. But Prue recognized her purposeful stride, girthy middle, and swinging satchel before she disappeared into the trees.

Downright peculiar.

Prue picked up the earthen water jug. She scurried to the tower's other window and plunked the jug on the sill.

"Girthy?" Ophelia said. "Straw hat?" She was out of breath after the sprint from her bedchamber. She'd seen the jug in Prue's window from her window and had skedaddled as fast as she could to the tower door.

"That's right," Prue said through the keyhole. "It's the second time I've seen her, now, and it seems a sight suspicious."

A lady. In the woods. "I wonder," Ophelia said slowly, "if she might be the lady whose shoe prints you spied at the graveside last night."

"Could be!"

"And what might she be doing in the wood? I had supposed, until now, that the suspicious folks were limited to those we already know—to persons residing in the castle. But what if. . .?"

"You giving me your blessing to have another sneak out of this dump?"

Ophelia sighed. "I fancy I sound like a door hinge that wants oiling, but please, *do* take care."

At a quarter past ten, Gabriel paced back and forth in front of the inn.

He'd told Professor Winkler that he had a few items of business to attend to, so Winkler had gone up to the castle without him. First, Gabriel had walked down to the telegraph office and sent a message to his landlady in Heidelberg requesting that his clothing trunk be sent. Then he'd arranged for a hired carriage.

Now the carriage stood waiting, but Miss Flax hadn't turned up.

He took one last look up and down the village lane. Two small boys romped with a yipping dog in front of the butcher's shop, and a few women strolled with wicker baskets on their arms, doing the day's shopping. A wiry chap of middle years strode down the lane in a woolen walking costume and bowler hat.

Another British tourist, no doubt. Gabriel pushed the brim of his hat further down, not wishing to engage in pleasantries.

No go.

The chap slowed as he drew near. "Lovely morning, isn't it?" he said in a crisp British accent, lifting his bowler.

"Indeed."

The chap stopped.

Bother.

He wore gold-rimmed spectacles, and his side-whiskers were graying. "Have you," he said, "hired a carriage?"

"I beg your pardon. I'm not certain we've met."

The chap waggled one of his bushy eyebrows.

"Now see here," Gabriel said, "I don't—" He paused. He'd noticed that, behind his spectacles, the chap had rather beautiful dark brown eyes.

"Miss Flax," Gabriel said, straightening his tie and gazing past her shoulder. "Good morning."

She tossed him a toothy, triumphant smile that was out of keeping with her side-whiskers.

Miss Flax's smile was, admittedly, charming. But Gabriel didn't wish to find Coop's killer for Miss Flax; he wished to find the killer in order to get those stolen relics back.

And then, of course, there was the matter of someone searching his chamber last night. Gabriel had, albeit reluctantly, entered the fray.

"You didn't think," Miss Flax said, "I could go dressed as myself, did you? What would people think, seeing an unmarried lady sashaying around with a gentleman?"

"Are we to sashay?"

"Undoubtedly."

"Well, then, I am ashamed to admit I hadn't given the matter a thought." He studied her. The transformation was remarkable. "Didn't anyone in the castle notice that something was amiss?"

"Sneaked out."

"Naturally." He led the way to the waiting carriage. He was no longer limping. "No sign of Herz, I trust?"

"None."

"Good. And I am almost frightened to ask—how is it that you were able to put together such a cunning disguise?"

"I found this suit of clothes in a storeroom of the castle—they're a decade out of mode. I reckoned you wouldn't mind."

"And your face? You seem to have aged forty years."

"I'm a lady's maid. It's my business to be clever with cosmetics. You don't think all those rich ladies happen to be more lovely than poor ladies by coincidence, now do you?"

"I never once thought that rich ladies *were* more lovely than poor ladies." He moved to hand her into the carriage but stopped himself just in time.

"Well, they are." She stepped up into the carriage and took a seat.

Gabriel seated himself across from her, shut the door, and the carriage creaked into motion.

"It's because," she said, "rich ladies have got more time and money to spend on pulling the wool over everyone's eyes."

"Then their beauty is a put-up job? A confidence game?"

"You could say that."

"What about your British accent? I must concede it's convincing."

She paused just a tick too long. "I was practically raised by an English lady."

Gabriel tried to read the expression in her eyes, but she'd turned her face away.


Ophelia concentrated on the scenery. It was time to shut her mouth about her disguise before she gave too much away.

"Prue's been doing a little sleuth hounding," Ophelia said.

"You don't mean—"

"Sneaking out of the tower. Yes. With Hansel, the castle gardener."

"Ah. Hansel seemed a good lad, at least—helped carry the relics out of the wood and to the castle."

Ophelia told Penrose about the bone, the cliff, the grave, the footprints, and the brandy bottles.

Penrose's eyes gleamed. "An uncommonly small bone, you say?"

"Oh criminy—you don't think it's really a *dwarf's*—"

"I merely wished for verification with regards to its purported dimensions."

There he went again: wheeling out the fancy terminology to cover up the fact that he was a grown man who believed in fairy stories. "He said it was small. Oh, and there's more." Ophelia told Penrose about the straw-hatted lady Prue had seen in the forest.

Penrose knitted his brows. "I have seen that lady."

"Indeed!"

"Once on the path leading up to the cottage, the day that Coop died. And again just this morning—she is staying at the Schilltag inn."

"Wonder what she's about."

"Simply another British tourist, from what I gather. Surely she has nothing to do with anything."

Their carriage followed the winding road down through the valley. They passed more and more houses, and then they were in Baden-Baden.

The town was built of meandering streets and filled with sparkling walled villas and hoity-toity hotels, shops, and restaurants. The sidewalks bustled with smartly dressed people, and the streets were crowded with rich carriages, many of them open. There were flowers everywhere—in window boxes, on balconies, in public gardens.

They even passed, in one of the public gardens, an orchestra playing in an outdoor pavilion. Ophelia's ear caught a few snatches of *La traviata*. Howard DeLuxe's Varieties had performed an abridged—and distinctly saucy—version of the opera a few years ago.

"This is," Ophelia said, "one of the prettiest places I've ever seen." The green mountains of the Black Forest reminded her a little of New England, but New England's sleepy hamlets and simple wooden buildings didn't hold a candle to this.

"They call it Europe's summer capital," Penrose said. "It's been quite the most fashionable town on the Continent ever since the gaming rooms opened up ten years ago. The czar banned gambling, you see, and gambling is illegal in France as well, so the Russians and French flock here. Invalids come here to take the waters and bathe, too. Sadly, countless people have ruined themselves and their families in the gaming rooms and at the races in Iffezheim. And some of these ladies parading about . . . well, they aren't the sort of ladies you were acquainted with in New York."

Oh, if he only knew.

"Let's alight here." Penrose rapped on the ceiling.

The carriage rolled to stop on a street marked *Küferstrasse*.


"I thought we'd have a good chance of sighting Hunt here," Penrose said a little later. They were seated in an outdoor café that was shaded by a large tree. "This is one of the more fashionable streets. He's a gallant, you understand."

"Right. A dandy." Ophelia surveyed the promenaders on the sidewalk and the other patrons in the café. All the ladies were got up like bonbons in pastel summer walking gowns and hats with flowers, and the gentlemen wore tailored suits. There was a lot of laughter and animated chatter, mostly in French.

"Hunt is not *only* a dandy."

"No?"

"Do you remember," Penrose said, "how Hunt insinuated that it was within his power to obtain an invitation for Mrs. Coop to be presented at court in England?"

"It isn't?" Ophelia straightened her cufflinks.

The professor's eyebrows twitched.

"You've *got*," she whispered, "to look at me as though I were a gentleman. Not the bearded lady in the circus."

"I beg your pardon. Your disguise is somewhat . . . disconcerting." Penrose *ahem*ed. "As I was saying, the odd thing is, I've never heard of Hunt."

"Do you know everyone in England, then?"

He adjusted his spectacles.

Annoying him was far too easy.

"He's pretending," he said, "to be something he's not."

Ophelia glanced away. *Not* a welcome topic of conversation.

The waiter brought thimble-sized coffees. They watched and waited.

Ophelia was broiling beneath the wig and bowler. Worse, her left muttonchop was coming unglued from her cheek. She twiddled her spoon on the tablecloth.

"There," Penrose murmured eventually, "is our man."

"Where?"

"Across the street. Walking arm-in-arm with the lady in pink."

Ophelia squinted through her false spectacles. Mr. Hunt was strolling with a rather plump lady who appeared, at least from this distance, to be approaching her middle years. Madam Pink wore a beautifully cut walking gown of seashell pink and a big hat piled with white roses, and she carried a parasol. "She looks mighty pleased to be with him."

"And he appears pleased with himself." Penrose was on his feet, placing some coins on the tablecloth. "Shall we follow?"

When Hansel turned up in the garden after lunchtime and started hoeing, Prue pelted him with the raisin bun she'd saved from her breakfast tray. It had gone nice and hard.

He sauntered over, hoe in hand, rubbing his crown where the bun had hit. "I intended to come over," he called up to her.

She leaned over the sill. "Why'd you start hoeing, then?"

He glanced over at the door in the wall. "I did not wish to arouse suspicions. Speaking to prisoners is frowned upon in some circles."

Prue's cheeks flamed. *Prisoner.* She stuck out her tongue to hide her shame.

He grinned.

Prue told him about the girthy woman in the dun-colored walking costume and the straw hat. "That's two times I've seen her so far. Ophelia said we ought to investigate."

"Miss Flax said that?" Hansel's eyebrows drew together.

"Ophelia's looking into things. She's going to get me out of here. So. Who is the lady in the walking costume?"

Hansel scratched his ear. "I do not know anyone in Schilltag who matches that description. She is most likely a tourist, staying at the inn. I will go ask the innkeeper's wife if she knows. But first I must finish hoeing those beans, or Frau Holder will wring my neck."

Ophelia and Professor Penrose trailed Madam Pink at a discreet distance. They passed grand hotels, cafés and restaurants, jewelers, haberdashers, and tourists' trinket shops.

"Easy enough to keep sight of them," Ophelia said, "with her wearing that enormous hat."

"Rather. Like tracking an animated flowerpot."

A block later, Ophelia noticed an advertisement hung on

the side of a building, with French lettering in gold and col-orful pictures of fairy tale queens, frogs, geese, and drag-ons. "What does that say?"

Penrose stopped to read the advertisement. "There is to be a masquerade ball tomorrow evening in the public dan-cing rooms—in the *Conversationshaus*—and the guests are to dress as fairy tale characters."

"Everyone here is mad for fairy tales!"

"It's the Black Forest. Come on. We'll lose sight of Hunt."

They followed for a few more blocks.

"What have we here?" Penrose pulled Ophelia into the doorway of a building. Slowly, they both poked their heads around the corner to see Mr. Hunt and Madam Pink ascend the white stone steps of a splendid hotel and disappear through the doors.

Ophelia became aware of the professor's hand on her arm, and she tensed.

He dropped his hand.

She pretended to adjust the brim of her bowler hat. Wait. *What* was she doing gallivanting with this strange gentleman?

Oh, right: Prue. Prue was locked up in a tower, accused of murder.

"Presumably that is Hunt's hotel," Penrose said, "or else it is the . . . lady's." He *ahem*ed again.

Mercy. If Penrose knew Ophelia was an actress, he wouldn't have to be so *delicate* all the time. She knew exactly the sorts of things ladies and gentlemen got up to in hotels. Never mind that she'd never done any of those things herself.

On the other hand, if he knew she was an actress, he wouldn't trust her as far as he could—well, the professor surely didn't spit.

"Hotel Europa?" Ophelia said, noticing the elegant sign above the hotel's doors. "Mrs. Coop told me that's where Princess Verushka is residing."

"Did she? Then we'll kill two birds with one stone.

Let's wait until they come out. Then we'll go inside and ask the hotel workers about both the princess and Hunt."

Ophelia pushed her bowler down more firmly on her head. "I've got a better idea." She was already setting off towards the hotel. "Let's follow them and find out where they go."

Penrose gained her side in a few strides. "Are you mad?"

"No. Bold."

"How would we profit from this? Aside from being recognized by Hunt, that is?"

"And I thought you were logical." Ophelia tut-tutted. "If it's the lady's chamber, then if we know its number, we may easily discover her name, and who she is, and perhaps what Hunt could be doing with her." They trotted up the steps to the hotel doors. "And if it's Mr. Hunt's chamber. . . ."

"You can't be serious," Penrose said through gritted teeth. "*Danke schön*," he said in a louder voice to the doorman, who bowed and held the door.

The lobby had pillowy carpets, fat velvet chairs, potted palms, and chandeliers dripping crystals.

Ophelia spied the hem of a seashell pink gown as it twitched around the landing of the grand marble staircase. "There they go," she whispered.

They tried to appear nonchalant as they hurried to the stair. At the top, they craned their necks left—the wide, carpeted corridor was empty—and right.

"Ah," Penrose whispered.

Hunt was unlocking a door halfway down the corridor. Madam Pink hovered at his side.

Penrose jerked his neck, and Ophelia followed him back down to the staircase landing. They waited until they heard the sound of a door closing shut, and then returned to the upper corridor.

Hunt and the lady, they swiftly figured, had disappeared into room number seven.

From behind the polished door came the faint sound of Madam Pink's kittenish giggles.

Ophelia lifted her eyes to Penrose's and fought the urge to giggle herself when she saw his embarrassed grimace.

Poor fellow. Trying to shield her maidenly purity.

"Perhaps"—Penrose was ushering her back towards the staircase— "that is Mr. Hunt's sister. Or cousin."

# 13

In the lobby, Gabriel cornered a bellboy behind a potted palm while Miss Flax waited with a newspaper on one of the velvet chairs.

"*Entschuldigen Sie bitte*," he said to the spotty lad, who wore a red suit decorated with brass buttons and a visored cap. "Could I trouble you with a few questions about two of the guests of this establishment?"

"We do not speak of our guests," the bellboy said in a nervous warble.

"*Nein?*" Gabriel pressed a coin into the boy's gloved palm.

"Well. Er." The bellboy gawked through the palm fronds towards the reception desk. "You must be quick. Herr Lipsett will be looking for me."

"Room number seven. A certain Mr. Royall Hunt is in residence?"

"That is correct."

"For how long has he been staying here?"

"Since the start of the season."

"This must be a very costly establishment. Is he current on his account?"

The bellboy ran a finger beneath his collar. "I do not handle accounts. I only carry luggage to and fro."

Gabriel slid another coin in his hand.

"Now that I think of it"—the bellboy gawked again through the palm fronds—"I did hear Herr Schmidt, who manages the billing in the back office, say that Herr Hunt has not paid a thaler for several weeks past."

"Indeed."

"But that is all I know."

"Is it?"

"Er. . . ."

"What of the lady he went upstairs with only minutes ago? A wealthy-looking lady, in pink."

"Sir, you must know what sort of place Baden-Baden is. The gamblers. . . ."

"Hunt is a gambler? Perhaps in debt?"

"N-not that sort of gambler."

"I see. And is there a Princess Verushka in residence as well?"

The bellboy frowned. "No."

"Are you certain?"

The bellboy puffed his chest. "I always know every single guest, and there is no Princess Verushka at the Hotel Europa." He emitted a yelp, and his chest deflated. "I beg your pardon, but I must go." He skittered off in the direction of the reception desk, before which a portly, managerial-looking gentleman had begun to pace.

Gabriel didn't tell Miss Flax what he'd learned from the bellboy until they were back outside on the sunny sidewalk strolling away from the hotel.

"Well?" she said, breathless.

"There is no Princess Verushka in residence at the Hotel Europa."

"I'm certain that's what Mrs. Coop said."

"She was lying to you. Or Princess Verushka lied to Mrs. Coop about where she was lodging."

"Or Princess Verushka is not her real name. Or she's booked into the hotel under an alias."

"You've a diabolical imagination, Miss Flax. How ever do you think of such things?"

She was silent.

His conscience gave a twinge. The poor girl was only trying to help.

"It is," Gabriel said, "rather interesting, because this would not be the first instance of Princess Verushka being caught in a lie." He told Miss Flax about how he'd encountered the princess rifling through Coop's desk. "I also learned from the bellboy," he said, "that it seems our Mr. Royall Hunt is a fortune hunter."

Miss Flax frowned.

"That is," Gabriel said, interpreting her frown—despite the whiskers and spectacles—as one of naiveté, "a gentleman who hopes, like a debutante, to make his fortune through a good match, but who in the meantime supports himself with the . . . attentions of wealthy ladies."

He hated discussing this with her. True, Miss Flax wasn't exactly a debutante herself, but there was an innocent air about her.

"If ladies may do it," she said, "gentlemen should be able to as well."

Gabriel quirked up a corner of his mouth. "The important thing is, this explains how Mrs. Coop and Miss Amaryllis made Hunt's acquaintance so quickly after their arrival in the neighborhood: he is presumably on the lookout for wealthy ladies. He knows how to flatter and charm his way into their good graces."

"But he couldn't have fancied that Miss Amaryllis possesses a fortune, could he? And he couldn't marry Mrs. Coop because she's already. . . ." Miss Flax's voice trailed off, and she came to a standstill. Pedestrians flowed around them as she stared up at Gabriel. "She's not. She's free."

"Free as a lark, and very, very wealthy. That's what we might call a rather good motive for murder, isn't it?"

"Let's go back to the hotel," Ophelia said.

"Whatever for? And shouldn't you be returning to the castle soon? Surely Mrs. Coop shall be expecting—"

"We've got to look around Mr. Hunt's chamber. If we are to convince Inspector Schubert to stop thinking of Prue as the murderer, we must show him something that'll convince him once and for all."

Penrose set his teeth.

"You know I'm right."

"This is harebrained."

"It's necessary."

He sighed. "Very well. Shall we sit in that café across from the hotel and watch for them to come back outside?"

Prue paced, twiddled her thumbs, and dodged sparrow ploppings for eternity and a day. At last, she heard Hansel's voice in the garden.

She hurried to the window.

He was flushed, tipping his head to see her. "That woman you saw is indeed a tourist. Staying at Gasthaus Schatz, in the village. British. Her name is Miss Gertie Darling. She has been tramping about the forest for days, and she will not tell the innkeeper's wife what she is about. She has just eaten her luncheon at the inn and is returning to the forest. I mean to follow her."

"Throw me the key! I want to come, too." The key opened the tower door from either side.

"Someone will see. It is daylight."

"Not in the forest it ain't. Besides, I saw her first." Prue batted her lashes, just in case Hansel needed more convincing. Hopefully he could see her eyelashes from down there, and her pretty new plaits. Not her shiny nose and chin.

Hansel heaved a sigh, pulled the key from his vest pocket, and tossed it up through the tower window.

The clank of the brass key hitting the stone floor was the sweetest sound Prue had heard all day.

A coiled stair connected the battlement outside the

tower door with the kitchen gardens below. Prue scurried down the stair and burst out into the sunlight.

"Hurry," Hansel said. He was already jogging towards the door in the garden's outer wall. "She was going in the direction of the orchard."

No sooner had they passed through the door than they saw Miss Darling's ample, biscuit-colored backside sway into the dark of the pine trees at the bottom of the orchard. They hurried after her.

The orchard was hot and bright, but the forest, when they stepped across its leafy edge, was all coolness and shifting shadows. Sun mottled the floor, illuminating orange-and-white toadstools, flitting butterflies, wafting ferns, and moss-fluffy tree trunks.

They paused to listen. Snapping and crunching up ahead.

Miss Gertie didn't tread silently like a fur trapper.

Prue and Hansel minced their way around crackly things on the forest floor. They came to a walloping big tree that had fallen slantwise. Side by side, they peeked over it.

Gertie crouched many paces ahead, half obscured by a clump of thicket. She was staring through a pair of binoculars. She balanced a notebook on her squatted knees, spread open across her skirt.

Something in the green shadows had snagged Gertie's attention. The binoculars were glued to her eyes. Her shoulders were hunched, her mouth slightly ajar. From time to time, she paused to scribble in her notebook, and then she'd press the binoculars back to her eyes.

One of those scientific ladies. Prue had heard of them. They liked to pin beetles to cork boards, stalk zebras, collect rocks in jars, wade into ponds after tortoises—

Hansel poked her.

Gertie was on the move.

They crept after her, keeping to the deepest pockets of shadow. A few minutes later, they saw her again, this time ogling through her binoculars at—

Prue clapped her hand over her mouth to keep in a guffaw—

At Mr. Smith, Homer T. Coop's secretary.

Mr. Smith was far off enough to resemble a mantelpiece figurine. He perched on a large rock, swinging his stumpy legs and doing something with his shotgun. Loading it up with bullets, maybe.

"He enjoys hunting," Hansel whispered. "Fowl, I believe."

"Poor Mr. Smith's just minding his own business." Mr. Smith had always been kind to Prue. "That Miss Gertie, she's a—a peeping tom. It's downright rude."

Hansel's eyes twinkled. "But *we* are spying on Miss Gertie."

There came the tinny sound of Mr. Smith whistling. He laid his shotgun over his shoulder, hopped down from the rock, and marched further into the trees.

Gertie jammed her binoculars and notebook into her satchel and went after him. She hadn't gone three paces when she screamed. Then she crashed, flailing, to the ground.


"Λaaaaaah!" Miss Gertie wailed into the treetops. Startled birds flapped away.

"We must help her," Hansel said, springing forward.

Hansel and Prue hurried to Gertie's side. Gertie was a pile of rumpled beige linen and snarled satchel straps. Her straw hat was askew, and one long, blond braid dangled over an ear. Her eyes were screwed up, and her face was the exact shade of lobster bisque.

"What's the matter?" Prue said, out of breath.

"Where did *you* come from?" Gertie unscrewed her eyes. They were small, a silvery color, and eerie without eyelashes. "What are you waiting for, you silly little ninny! Get this bloody thing off my leg!" She had a British accent, just like Prue had used sometimes in Howard DeLuxe's Varieties. Well, sort of like it.

"Your leg?" Prue stared down at Gertie's tangle of large leather boots and wrinkly skirts. Mixed in the jumble were two green apples. The kind from the orchard, with the pinky streaks.

The kind, as matter of fact, that Mr. Coop had been killed with.

Gertie met Prue's eyes. Gertie swallowed.

Hansel knelt beside Gertie. He gingerly drew back the hem of her skirt to reveal a leg like a jumbo bowling pin in a white woolen stocking. It was sandwiched between the jaws of a rusty iron trap. Prue gasped; red wetness seeped through the white stocking.

"Get it off, lad!" Gertie yelled.

"Be patient, miss," Hansel said. "These traps are meant only to be opened with a special key belonging to the woodsman."

"You are *not* bloody saying," Gertie roared, "that you're going to go toddling off after a key while I—"

"No." Hansel's voice was firm. "I know how to open these traps without a key. But you must be still, or you will only hurt yourself."

Gertie gnashed her teeth while Hansel fiddled with the springs on the trap.

Meanwhile, a thought hit Prue: funny that Mr. Smith hadn't come running, too. Gertie had sure made enough racket. Maybe he'd just chalked up all the yelping to some wild critter.

There was a clink and a twang of the springs. Hansel pried open the jaws of the trap.

Gertie staggered to her feet and gathered up her satchel. "Damn and blast and botheration times ten thousand!"

"Allow us to help you to the castle," Hansel said. "That wound needs tending to."

Gertie cast a wistful glance towards the fold of trees where Mr. Smith had disappeared. Then she winced and took her weight off her injured leg. "I'd just as soon go back down to the village inn. Gasthaus Schatz. Do you know it?"

"Indeed I do." Hansel glanced at Prue. "Although Miss Prue must return to the castle."

Shucks. Prue had hoped he'd forgotten about the prisoner song and dance. "I'll help as far as the orchard," she said. She was itching to figure out what Miss Gertie was up to.

They limped along, over logs and around rocks. Gertie leaned her weight on Hansel's and Prue's shoulders.

Good thing Prue had eaten a hearty breakfast.

Prue licked her lips. "You known Mr. Smith long?"

Hansel shot her a *have you lost your marbles?* look.

Gertie said, "Mister who?"

"Smith," Prue said. "The feller with the shotgun."

"I hadn't noticed," Gertie said in an airy tone, "any fellows with shotguns."

Was Gertie really expecting them to buy that clunker? "What're you doing in the forest, then?" Prue said.

"This and that." Gertie winced again, and paused to bend and touch her leg. "I adore viewing the birds and whatnot."

Prue and Hansel traded a look over Gertie's bent back. Those binoculars of hers hadn't once strayed to bird-level.

"Are you enjoying your stay in Schilltag?" Hansel said. They were wobbling along again.

"Nice enough place, I suppose," Gertie said. "Bit dull. I suppose you natives are used to that." She glanced sideways at Prue. "You're not a native, what? One of the American family that's been getting bumped off, I assume?"

"Not me," Prue said. "Staying much longer in Schilltag?"

"No," Gertie said.

She was clamming up.

"Them apples you dropped back at the trap," Prue said. "Were they tasty?"

Gertie's gaze kept forward. But her cheeks went from lobster bisque to fire brigade red.

"It's funny, see," Prue went on, "because they're the same apples that done in Mr. Coop up at the castle. With a little poison mixed in, of course."

Gertie stopped in her tracks and tore her arm from Prue's shoulder. "What precisely are you insinuating, you ill-spoken little muttonhead? That I had something to do with that appalling crime? Why, I've only been in Schilltag for three days. I have every right to be here and not to be accused of—of murder!" She stuck her schnozzle in the air. "I'm on a little holiday from the *Hermannschen Hei-*

*lanstalt für Lungenkranke* in Baden-Baden, if you insist on prying."

Prue didn't have an inkling what that gibberish meant. But it sure had startled Hansel; his eyebrows had shot up. She'd have to ask him about it later.

"I," Gertie said, waggling a kid-gloved finger an inch from Prue's nose, "have never even laid eyes on Homer T. Coop." She didn't meet Prue's eye.

She was blowing smoke.

"Then what're you up to," Prue said, "tracking his secretary, Mr. Smith, like he's a rhinoceros on the plains of Australia?"

"Australia?" Gertie spluttered. "The rhinoceros, of the family *Rhinocerotidae*, is not found in—hold on a tick. Did you say *secretary*?" She tipped her head back, opened her mouth to reveal teeth as big and square as dice, and laughed.

"What's so funny?" Prue said.

Hansel, who was still supporting Gertie's entire weight on his shoulder, looked like he was about to crumple to the ground with fatigue.

"Oh, ho!" Gertie wiped a tear of glee from her lashless eye. "Secretary!"

"Shall we continue on?" Hansel suggested in a wheezing voice.

# 14

❧⁓❧

Ophelia and Penrose had been waiting forty minutes over untouched coffees and unread newspapers, when they saw Madam Pink descend the hotel steps. She was alone, and she sailed away down the sidewalk. Hunt emerged a few minutes later in a fresh suit of flannels and set off in the opposite direction.

Penrose placed a few coins on the table. "Shall we?"

It wasn't until they reached the door of room number seven that Ophelia realized they hadn't had a confab about getting inside. But before she could pipe up, Penrose had wiggled his penknife—the same one he'd used to cut the ropes in the hunting lodge the night before—into the lock.

"You seem," she whispered, "to have criminal tendencies."

"Not tendencies." There was a small click as the lock gave way. Penrose pushed the door inward. "Merely abilities."

Ophelia followed him into the chamber. "Do professors usually have need for picking locks, then?" They were in a sitting room with flocked green wallpaper, high ceilings surmounted by rich moldings, and plenty of gilt clocks, marble busts, and beveled mirrors. Double doors opened onto a bedchamber. "I thought your sort read books all day."

Penrose was picking things up, pulling open drawers, looking under sofa cushions. "What a stodgy lot you must think us."

"I'm not the only one." She watched him search. He was efficient and unruffled.

Almost, truth be told, as though he'd done this sort of thing before.

Suspicion washed darkly over Ophelia. How did she know if he was really a professor at—what had Mrs. Coop said?—Oxford University? Or that he was a professor at *all*?

He glanced over his shoulder as he pushed open the doors to the bedchamber. "We must be quick about it."

"Right. Sorry."

The bedchamber drapes were drawn, but a slice of sunlight illuminated the rumpled bedclothes.

Madam Pink had been tickled all right.

Ophelia moved to the chest of drawers, which was scattered with silver brushes and combs, colorful silk neckties, bottles of scented Macassar hair oil, and cologne water. There was also a handsome mahogany dressing box. She pried it open. Inside was a jumble of handkerchiefs, cuff links, a fingernail buffer, several loose cigarettes, and a gold matchbox inscribed—she held it up in the shaft of light—*For my divine Eros—L. B.*

"Know of anyone with the initials L. B.?" she called to the professor, who was pawing through the wardrobe.

"L. B.? No." He glanced over. "He's got mounds of trinkets from ladies—gold toothpicks, diamond tie pins, and the like—in a box here. It's part of his profession, but I must hand it to him, he's careful to keep them out of sight."

"I wonder how he makes ends meet? He can't live on pawned cigarette cases."

"Not by the looks of his clothing. He's got a Bond Street tailor."

"Well, I reckon he must look the part," Ophelia said. "He is, in a way, an actor. All those rich ladies wouldn't traipse around with a gentleman in a second-rate getup, now would they?"

"An actor," Penrose said. "That's remarkably astute, Miss Flax."

He shot her a look that was, itself, just a smidge too astute.

Ophelia gulped.

She nestled the matchbox where she'd found it in the dressing case.

She was about to close the lid when something caught her eye. "Professor . . . I think I've found something." She pulled a folded hankie from the bottom of the box. "This belongs to Miss Amaryllis."

Penrose was beside her. "Are you certain?"

"See the lilacs embroidered on the corner? She's got a whole set of these. Lilacs are her favorite." She sniffed it. "It smells like lilac eau de toilette, too—this handkerchief has been scented."

"Miss Amaryllis wears lilac toilette water?"

"Nothing else."

"Don't say it."

"Say what?"

"Oh, you know what I mean—I told you so."

"I thought that went without saying. Now, if Mr. Hunt kept her hankie—"

"It would appear that he prized the token."

"Which means that maybe that *was* him last night, waiting in the coach."

"It would seem so. The troubling thing is, if Hunt is indeed a fortune hunter—and it appears that he is—it is highly unlikely that he would be inclined to return Miss Amaryllis's regard. She is penniless, is she not?"

"The very definition of a poor relation. Mr. Coop never let her forget it, either."

"So, then. The dove-like hearts of plain girls aside, I would propose that perhaps Hunt could be using Miss Amaryllis as part of a larger plan."

"You think Mr. Hunt is the murderer?" Ophelia chewed

her lip. All signs seemed, to her, to point straight at Amaryllis. Not Hunt.

"Who better to suspect, than a fortune hunter in close proximity to a colossal fortune?"

"But if Mr. Hunt wished to claim Mr. Coop's fortune as his prize by marrying Amaryllis, Mrs. Coop would need to . . . die."

Oh, lorks—that bottle of laudanum drops!

"Yes—if it is indeed the case that Miss Amaryllis would inherit her elder sister's fortune, in the event of her demise."

"Then Mrs. Coop could be in danger! And to think that I encouraged her to invite Mr. Hunt to the funeral tomorrow."

"Let's not get ahead of ourselves. The next step is to observe Hunt and Miss Amaryllis together, and attempt to discern the true nature of their acquaintance."

At that moment, there was the *click-clack-click* of a key in a lock.

They dove under the bed.

Ophelia's left knee throbbed where it had hit the floorboards. She was crushed like a kipper against the professor, and her bowler hat was smashed down on her forehead.

They listened to the sound of footsteps in the outer sitting room.

Penrose lifted the bed skirt a few inches.

A woman's black, buckled shoes moved to and fro, below a swinging black hem and the edge of an apron. A maid.

Penrose corkscrewed his neck.

There wasn't much light beneath the bed, but she could've sworn he had a, well, a *peculiar* look in his eye.

The top of her bowler was stuck tight against the bed slats. She couldn't turn away.

Ophelia's palms sweated. She'd never been so close to a gentleman. Last night, when they'd been tied to the chairs and when they'd hidden in the ferns, they hadn't been nose to nose. Even when she'd performed romantic scenes on the stage, the actors hadn't had their thighs and shoulders shoehorned against hers. And those actors had reeked of greasepaint, overripe costumes, and stale cigars. The professor smelled like soap and pine needles.

And that look in his eye. It was at once gentle and a bit . . . surprised.

Well, of *course* he was surprised. She was wearing false spectacles, muttonchops, a wig, and she'd made her skin look like parchment. Professor Penrose was squashed under the bed with a scrivener out of a Charles Dickens novel.

Ophelia's ears blazed. With effort, she turned her head away.

"She's going to clean the washroom," he whispered.

They watched as the maid plunked a bucket, mop, and a basket of rags on the floor. Then she took up the mop, stepped inside the washroom, and shut the door, all the while humming to herself.

"Come on," Penrose said softly.

They edged out from under the bed and stole away.

Ophelia and Penrose didn't speak as they left the hotel.

They managed to find, after poking through three jewelers' shops, a floral brooch of jet beads for Mrs. Coop. Then they left the photograph of Homer—scowling and tuft-headed—that Mrs. Coop had given Ophelia for the jeweler to copy into a mourning locket.

All the while, Ophelia felt jumpy, and she hankered to get away from the professor.

*He* seemed distracted and aloof.

They found the hired carriage waiting in the *Küferstrasse* where they'd left it hours earlier, and Ophelia clambered inside.

Penrose didn't join her. "I shall return to Schilltag later," he said. "I'll instruct the coachman to deposit you back at Gasthaus Schatz, since I presume you would not wish to be seen at the castle in disguise." His eyes gave nothing away.

Something had changed when they'd been underneath the bed. She couldn't put her finger on what it was, exactly.

"I didn't ask you," he said. "Did anyone in the castle give any indication that they knew about what happened last night? With the woodsman, I mean."

She shook her head.

"And no one said they'd discovered that slipper in the orchard?"

"No."

"Then perhaps it's safe—would you ask for me, of the old woman Matilda who works in the castle kitchens, if she knows of a tapestry with a design of seven miners?"

Dried fruit Matilda and her resentful stares. Ugh. "Snow White's little men?"

He nodded. "I was told that the design on this tapestry is the same as that on the stolen ceiling beam. I am hoping that by studying it—if it indeed exists—I might unearth a clue as to why the beam was stolen. If Matilda does know of the tapestry, find out where it's kept."

"All right," Ophelia said. "I'll ask her. Fair's fair."

"What does that mean?" Penrose straightened his spectacles.

"It's my turn to uphold the terms of our bargain. You've helped me out all day, after all. I'll bet you have more important things to do."

Now what had made her say *that*?

Penrose simply bowed his head as he shut the door.

Ophelia didn't look out the window as the carriage pulled away from the curb.

In Schilltag, the hired carriage left Ophelia at the inn.

That morning she'd discovered an overgrown stone staircase zigzagging down the castle bluff, into the village. She'd spied it from a window—it started on the far end of a terraced side lawn—and had decided it'd be a better way to sneak than going through the orchard.

She walked up the lane from the inn and found the bottom of the stair behind a scraggly patch of bushes. She started up the steps.

There were probably hundreds of steps. The castle was almost overhead as she trudged upwards and the afternoon sun beat down. It was rough going, because of all the loose stones and crumbling bits of mortar, and she began to sweat beneath her woolen suit. She paused at one of the hairpin turns, in the shade of an overhanging juniper bush, to catch her breath.

From down below came the sound of steady footfalls and scattering pebbles.

If someone got a gander of her in this disguise—

She scampered into the bushes off to one side. She wasn't completely covered there, but it was shady.

She tried to hold her breath.

The footfalls grew louder and louder.

And then there was little Mr. Smith, the secretary, hiking up the steps in a hunting jacket, tall boots, and a deerstalker hat. There was a knapsack on his back, a rifle strapped to his shoulder, and he was whistling "The Arkansas Traveler."

He passed without seeing her and disappeared up the steps.

She allowed herself to breathe.

Only Mr. Smith. Returning from bird hunting by the looks of it. Well, the poor fellow deserved a holiday after the way he'd slaved away for Mr. Coop.

Ophelia waited five minutes, and then hastened up the steps, too.


"Miss Flax. I wonder if I might have a word?" Inspector Schubert crawled out of the shadows of the corridor.

Ophelia nearly screamed. "You'll make a person fair turn up their toes in fright, sneaking like that!"

She'd made it up to her chamber unseen—as far as she knew—cleaned off her greasepaint, and dressed in her lady's maid gown. But Inspector Schubert had been lying in wait for her just outside Mrs. Coop's bedchamber door.

"I did not intend to frighten you." Schubert massaged his fingertips together. "I was merely waiting, these many, *many* minutes past, to speak with you."

"Yes. Well. Madam keeps me busy."

"So I see." Schubert paused.

Had she scrubbed off all the greasepaint by her ears? Sometimes she missed that spot.

"Mrs. Coop," Schubert said, "informed me that you only recently made the acquaintance of Miss Bright."

"That's right." Ophelia tried to remember exactly what she'd told Mrs. Coop. "We met in New York, only a few days before we sailed for Europe. At an agency. A domestic service agency."

"Ah. And you were traveling to England to work in a grand household, I understand?"

"Lady Cheshingham's."

"Cheshingham," Schubert murmured, as though committing the name to memory.

This called for a change of subject. A quick one.

"I wished," Ophelia said, "to ask *you* a question, Inspector Schubert."

He flared his nostrils. "*Did* you?"

"Has the American consulate been told about all this?"

"The consul shall be abroad for another week." Schubert drew his thin lips back.

She'd have to ignore his anger. She might not get another chance to speak with him. "Who was it that overheard Prue conversing with Mr. Coop?"

"You are under the mistaken impression, Miss Flax, that it is your place to interrogate the police."

"I only—"

"Impertinent, are you not? It is I who shall ask questions. Now. I wish to learn more about Miss Bright's past, and you are the only person who knows anything about her."

"Like I said, I haven't known her long. I reckon you're looking for evidence against her, but I really haven't got anything to say. Now, if you'll excuse me, Madam will be wanting me."

Ophelia slipped through the door and shut it behind her.

At least Inspector Schubert seemed to know nothing about last night's incident in the forest. Not yet.

# 15

Mrs. Coop was at the dressing table in her boudoir, her face buried in her arms. She was bawling.

"Ma'am?" Ophelia hurried to her side.

Had she found out that Mr. Hunt wished to kill her and marry Amaryllis?

"Are you hurt, ma'am?" Ophelia said.

"Hurt?" Mrs. Coop lifted her puffy, pink face. "Don't be a fool! I'm heartbroken. Where have you been?"

Ophelia found her a hankie. "Your sorrow is very fresh," she said, "but it'll pass in time. When my mother died, I thought I'd never—"

"Not Homer!" Mrs. Coop's tone was raspy.

"Not—?"

"This!" Mrs. Coop pointed a plump, trembling finger at her own face. "I look an absolute fright, and Mr. Hunt is coming to the funeral tomorrow. Can't you *do* something?"

When Gabriel returned by hired carriage to Schilltag, he sent a brief note up to the castle, addressed to the gardener boy, Hansel. The note requested that Hansel pay Gabriel a visit at the inn, at the boy's leisure.

Gabriel wished to quiz the lad about how to access the gravesite on the cliff. The Grunewald woods were such a tangle of paths and undergrowth, Gabriel was not certain where to begin.

He could scarcely keep still for the crackling anticipation. Because, if that cliff and that grave were what he suspected they were, well, what a stupendous find.

But Hansel did not come, and he did not send a reply.

Ophelia saw Hansel in the kitchen, when she was waiting for Cook to finish assembling Mrs. Coop's dinner tray. Hansel was, it seemed, the only cheery person in the castle. Mrs. Coop lay like a log upstairs, her face covered in the mask of French green clay and honey that Ophelia had mixed up for her. Amaryllis was holed up in her own chamber, Mr. Smith had gone out hunting again, and all the other servants were crotchety.

Probably on account of the funeral tomorrow.

Ophelia took Hansel aside.

"Poking around with Prue, are you?" she whispered.

Hansel blushed. "I—I am sorry, I do not know what came over me. She is quite persuasive, so I—"

"No matter. Every soul is at liberty to save their own skin. Only, Hansel, *please* take care of her, and I'd also be most obliged if you kept me informed of your discoveries."

"Oh, yes. Prue told me that you are doing a bit of sleuthing, Miss Flax."

Ophelia lifted her chin. "Merely making judicious inquiries."

"We did learn about the lady in the straw hat this afternoon. She is a British tourist, called Miss Gertie Darling, staying in Schilltag—"

Penrose had hit that one on the nose, then.

"—and when we followed her into the woods, we discovered her, by all appearances, spying upon Mr. Smith."

"Mr. Smith?"

"With binoculars. And taking notes."

Odder and odder. Ophelia shook her head. Well. It took all sorts to make a world. Bunking in a circus wagon with the Fat Lady and a girl who could sit her own feet on her shoulders while walking on her hands had cemented *that* notion. And if some tourist had set Mr. Smith in her sights, who was Ophelia to judge?

"Miss Darling lied about why she is here," Hansel said. "She told Prue and me that she had been staying in Baden-Baden at the *Hermannschen Heilanstalt für Lungenkranke*."

"The what?"

"It is a sanatorium—a sort of long-term hospital. For invalids. There are several in Baden-Baden, because the thermal springs there are thought to have curative powers."

"She is an invalid?"

"That is the trouble—she appeared healthy as a horse. And her claims are particularly strange because the *Hermannschen* sanatorium is for those afflicted with diseases of the lungs."

"Consumption?"

Hansel nodded.

"Lying," Ophelia murmured. "Perhaps she had nothing to do with Mr. Coop's death. All the same, she has been snooping around the castle forest."

"And spying upon Mr. Smith."

"Yes. And there were lady's footprints at the cliff gravesite that may have been hers. I cannot fathom how, exactly, this Miss Gertie Darling could be involved in the murder and those missing things. Yet she appears to be suspicious." Ophelia considered. "Only one thing to do, then."

Hansel nodded. "I shall go to the sanatorium this evening, and discover if she is truly in residence there." He ran a finger under his collar. "I shall ask Prue to stay behind this time."

"Thank you, Hansel." Ophelia turned to go. She stopped. "Oh—I near forgot. Would you do me a great favor and ask Matilda a question?"

"Certainly, Miss Flax."

The thought of Professor Penrose made Ophelia feel unaccountably jittery and distracted all-overish. Something to do with his gleaming eyes under the bed in that hotel. . . . All the same, she'd agreed to hold up her end of the deal. She'd find out about the tapestry.

Hansel and Ophelia went to the chimney corner.

Matilda huddled on her customary stool, peeling potatoes with a green-handled paring knife.

Hansel crouched and embraced her. Matilda's withered-apple face remained blank.

"What would you like to ask her?" Hansel said to Ophelia. He took up the slate and chalk from the flagstones, and rubbed the slate clear with his cuff.

"Ask her . . . ask her if she knows of a tapestry that has a design of seven men on it. Little mining men, like Snow White's."

Hansel jerked his head. His brows were furrowed. "Why do you want to know this?"

"Um." Ophelia swallowed. "It might be the same design that was on the ceiling beam taken from the house in the forest."

Hansel's usually pleasant face had taken on a hardness. "The *stolen* ceiling beam."

"Um. Yes."

"Who told you about the tapestry?"

"So there *is* a tapestry?"

He ran a hand through his blond hair. "*Ja*, there is a tapestry. Matilda told me about it once."

"Would you ask her where it's kept?"

"Very well." Hansel printed in German on the slate. The chalk clicked and screeched.

Matilda's eyes smoldered as she read the question. She snatched the chalk and scrawled something over Hansel's neat handwriting. Then she thrust the slate back into his hands, muttering, and resumed peeling the potato.

"What does it say?"

"She writes, T*he tapestry was lost a long time ago.* And, *Maidservants should keep to their places.*"

"Yes, well, thank you." Ophelia fetched Mrs. Coop's dinner tray and hastened out of the kitchen before Hansel could ask any more questions.

Ophelia was uneasy about Prue snooping with Hansel. Hansel was a good fellow—a little guarded at times, but a good fellow all the same. Still, Prue was a prisoner, if not exactly under arrest. If Inspector Schubert got wind of her doings, who knew what might come about?

And yet, the way Ophelia was thinking, this predicament was like any other sprawling, disheartening piece of work—a field to be plowed, a circus tent to be erected, a whole pantomime's worth of costumes to be stitched. No matter the task at hand, the more people pulled together, the faster the job got done.

And, by gum, Ophelia was going to dig in and get this job done.

"You're going to town *without* me?" Prue whispered to Hansel out the tower window. The dregs of sunset lingered in the sky. "Now you're confabulating with Ophelia and leaving me out of things? Hey! I suppose Ophelia gave you a stern lecture about how you ought to leave me behind? That it?"

"Oh. I—well. . . ."

"Come on! Throw me that key!" Prue struck her wistful Juliet pose in the tower window frame. Assuming Juliet ever had a pimple brewing on her left nostril.

Hansel scratched his head. "Oh, all right."

Prue and Hansel rumbled into Baden-Baden in a farmer's hay cart that Hansel had borrowed. It was dragged by a mule. Between the rattletrap, the ugly brown dress, and the suspicion that her left nostril was starting to resemble a gumdrop, Prue felt like a yokel. At least her oily hair was neatly braided and covered with a kerchief.

They clip-clopped through winding streets, weaving

towards what Hansel said was the town center. The buildings got fancier, and there was more hustle and bustle, more light and music spilling out of hotels and restaurants. Then they turned up a steep street. It was strung with grand stone villas that were surrounded by lush trees and spiked walls. Light beamed from their tall windows. Piano music and the scent of honeysuckle drifted on the air.

"Here it is," Hansel said presently. "The sanatorium."

They had turned a corner. A large ivory building, a mix of grand hotel and hospital, nestled back against the hillside. All the windows were lit up, pooling gaslight on the circular front drive. The drive was lined with crisp trimmed shrubbery. Grecian urns of roses flanked the double doors at the top of wide steps.

Hansel stopped the cart.

"Now what?" Prue said.

"I had supposed we would sneak in through the back somewhere. Attired in this fashion, no one will believe we are visitors. This is a costly sanatorium."

"How about we take a look through the windows and size things up?"

They left the mule and cart on the shadowy side of the street. Prue hoped some prince wouldn't look out the window of his villa and notice it. They slunk around the side of the sanatorium and burrowed through a boxwood hedge to a lit-up window. They peeked through.

A dining room. All filled with pale, trembly ladies and gents hunched over bowls of soup.

"Isn't this a late suppertime for sickies?" Prue whispered.

"They are wealthy. Perhaps they wish to keep up their aristocratic routines."

They did look rich, despite all the crunched-over spines and dribbling soup. Their clothes weren't festive, but there was a lot of sheened black silk and elegant cashmere wraps. And all their consumptive hacking was directed into hankies of delicate linen and lace.

Waiters sprinted around on the Turkish carpet, refilling

water glasses and picking up soup spoons dropped by quivering fingers.

"Must be horrible, having consumption," Prue said. "I just can't picture Miss Gertie here."

They watched for about half an hour. Prue had been ravenous during the ride in the hay cart. But the sight of this bunch was enough to put her off her feed for a week.

"There she is." Hansel prodded a fingertip against the windowpane.

"That's her all right."

Miss Gertie posed like one of those Viking ladies at the opera, all blond braids and magnificent bosom, in an arched doorway at the far end of the dining room. All that was missing was one of those helmets with horns. She gripped the handles of a wicker wheelchair, which was occupied by what appeared to be a heap of black wool with a white wig.

"That's why Miss Gertie is staying here at the sanatorium," Prue said. "She's a nurse or companion to that shrively old lady."

Gertie wheeled the old lady to a table and arranged everything just so before seating herself.

"She was not lying, then," Hansel said. He turned and slid down from the window into a crouch, leaning against the foundation stones. "She truly is staying here."

Prue slid down next to him. "I still think she's mighty suspicious. So will Ophelia, I'd wager. Hey!" She elbowed Hansel. "Seeing as she's occupied with dinner, why don't we sneak into her room? Maybe we'll find that notebook she was scribbling in."

"Now?"

"Sure."

"How? Besides, if we were caught, they would summon the police. You are an escaped prisoner."

"You're making me sound like a criminal."

"I do not wish for you to be taken to the jail here in town. There are rough people there."

"All the more reason to get to the bottom of what Miss Gertie is doing with her spying."

Hansel thought about it. "That makes sense," he said at last.

They elbowed out of the boxwood and circled around to the back of the sanatorium. They approached what seemed like a workers' door. As they drew closer, they saw the door led to a bustling kitchen, jam-packed with waiters and cooks.

"We'll be about as sneaky as a brass band in a funeral parlor if we go in there," Prue said.

Just then, the kitchen door burst open and a dough-faced man in white cook's coat emerged. He brandished a whopping knife.

Prue and Hansel stepped backwards.

The cook yelled something to Hansel, swinging the knife in a way that Prue wouldn't have called hospitable.

Hansel said nothing. He just grabbed Prue's hand, and they piked off.

"What did he say?" Prue panted, once they had reached the hay cart.

"He called us beggars and said that we should go to the soup kitchens if we were hungry." Hansel helped her up into the seat. "Or he would send for the police."


Hansel did something odd as they creaked their way back through the streets of Baden-Baden in the hay cart.

It happened when they passed by a shop. Prue couldn't read the German sign, but it had the look of a pawnbroker's shop. There was an accordion in the window and a pair of high-heeled shoes with jeweled buckles, a bone fan, oil paintings and enameled snuffboxes, a revolver in a pink satin-lined case, and a whole set of silver cutlery.

Prue knew a pawnbroker's shop when she saw one. Ma had squeaked them through the lean times, between bene-factors, by selling off jewelry, fancy clothes, and furniture that she'd been given by some gentleman or other in the first flush of his ardor. Which, Prue knew, never lasted. Just like a pastry, you had to make the most of a man's lovesickness when it was fresh and hot.

Well, when they rolled by the pawnbroker's shop, Hansel slowed the mule to a crawl. He stared into the display window like he was searching for something. His expression was sort of yearning and bleak all at once. His eyes landed on something—Prue thought it was maybe one of the snuffboxes, one with a gold lid—and his cheeks went red. Then he urged the mule faster.

"Looks like you saw a ghost in that window back there," Prue said.

"You might say that." Hansel's voice was a growl. Sort of like a wounded dog.

Maybe it was better not to talk.

A few moments later, someone called, "Hansel."

They were trying to get through a clog of pedestrians and carriages in front of a drinking establishment. Traffic had stalled. Coarse laughter and clanking beer glasses sailed out on a tide of tobacco smoke and stinky whale-oil lamp fumes.

Hansel's shoulders hitched and something—what? Pain? Anger?—washed over his features. Whatever it was, he recognized the voice. He turned.

"Good evening, Franz," he said.

Franz. Why did that name ring a bell?

Franz was a handsome young man—in a smallish, dark, dapper sort of way—standing on the busy sidewalk. He reminded Prue of a magician. Or maybe an otter. He was about twenty, trim in a black swallowtail coat and crisp white shirt. His black silk stovepipe hat tilted at a rakish angle, and his tie was undone.

Liquored up. No doubt about it.

"Good evening," Franz said to Hansel. He stepped into the street, close to the hay cart. "Are we speaking English on account of that pretty little thing?"

Prue tilted her chin and gazed past his shoulder. Although it was a relief to learn that two days in the tower hadn't completely spoiled her looks.

Hansel introduced Prue as his American cousin, Lottie.

Franz—his last name was Lind—sidled even closer. "I

had no notion"—he snatched up Prue's hand and kissed it—"that you had a beautiful little American cousin hidden away somewhere. How positively modern of you." His accented voice was custard smooth.

"Yes, well," Hansel said. "Second cousin, actually. She is here paying a visit."

"Well, Hansel, my man, what are you doing in town?"

"An errand. For the castle mistress."

A smile spread over Franz's face. "Oh? Keeps you busy, does she?"

Why was this was such a mirthful topic of conversation for Franz? And such a sore one for Hansel?

"And you, Franz?" Hansel inspected Franz's fancy duds. "Are you still employed as a croupier in the gaming rooms?"

Something dark flickered across Franz's face. "No. I am a student now at Heidelberg."

Hansel tensed.

Something weird was going on between these two.

"Come into the inn here, and have a drink with me," Franz said. "Surely the mistress of the castle does not have you on *such* a short leash."

Prue noticed that Hansel's fists were clenched around the mule reins. But he said, "All right."

# 16

⚜

Hansel helped Prue down from the cart and left the mule under the supervision of a small boy. They entered the stuffy, smoky inn. They found an empty table, and Franz wiggled his fingers for the barmaid.

As they sank into their rough wood chairs, Franz flipped his evening coat so as not to squash his swallow-tail. Prue glimpsed a bit of ribbon folded over his belt at his hip. A ribbon striped red, black, and white.

Prue considered herself an authority on fashion. Ladies' fashions, mostly, but she knew plenty about gents', too. Ma had subscribed to *Godey's Lady's Book*, *Le Salon de la Mode*, and *Peterson's Magazine*, and Prue had learned the alphabet on their fashion plates. Yet she had never seen anyone wear a bit of colored ribbon over their belt like that.

"If you are studying at Heidelberg, what brings you to Baden-Baden?" Hansel said to Franz, once they had three glasses of beer before them.

"I do, of course, make my home in Heidelberg now. But Baden-Baden has its allures."

Hansel stared at him coolly over the edge of his beer glass. "You have been gambling."

Franz shrugged. "This, that, and the other, as they say." He swigged his beer. His movements were loose and jerky, like he'd been drinking for hours.

"Is that," Hansel said, leaning forward, "how you are paying for university? And for these fine clothes? With winnings from the gaming rooms?"

Franz ignored the question. "What *I* would like to hear about is the murder at Schloss Grunewald. It has been plastered all over the newspapers and on every serving wench's wagging tongue."

Hansel and Prue described what they knew, leaving out the tidbits about Miss Gertie. Oh, and the fact that Prue was not really Hansel's American cousin Lottie, but the accused murderess herself.

"The objects from the cottage were taken?" Franz repeated, when they got to that part. He lurched forward, sloshing his beer. "Even the skeleton?"

"Even the skeleton," Hansel said. He leaned in, lowered his voice. "Do you remember, when we were boys, finding that small bone up on the cliff? With my dog?"

*That's* where Prue had heard about Franz. That story.

"Of course," Franz said. "That little bone gave me nightmares for years. I was frightened that it belonged to a diabolical elf hiding under my bed."

"It was a dwarf's bone," Prue blurted. "Snow White's dwarf."

Hansel bugged his eyes at her.

Crackers. Was she not supposed to have said that?

"A dwarf's bone!" Franz reached over and chucked Prue's chin. "Fancy that."

She recoiled.

"Do you mean to suggest," Franz said, "that the skeleton in that cottage was dug up from the place where we found that bone when we were boys?"

"Yes," Hansel said. He seemed reluctant to fess up to it.

"How fascinating." Franz's eyes glittered.

He wasn't really drunk. Prue saw it now. He was play-acting.

What if some of those boot prints in the dirt, up at the cliff gravesite, had been Franz's? *That* would give him something to hide.

"Listen here, Lottie." Franz scooted his chair next to hers and put his mouth so close she felt his moist breath on her earlobe. "What say you about having a bit of fun while you are here on your visit? I am told you American chits are game for a laugh."

"Now see here," Hansel said, his voice hot.

"There is," Franz went on, ignoring Hansel's warning and Prue's wrinkled nose, "a masquerade ball here in Baden-Baden tomorrow evening. Fairy tale costumes. Meet me there, and I shall give you an evening you shall never forget."

"Never." Prue scooted her chair away.

"No? Not even if I said that I know who you really are?"

Prue's eyes flew to Hansel. He looked like he'd just tippled an entire bottle of cod liver oil.

"You are that murderess," Franz said. "Not cousin Lottie."

"I'm *not* a murderess. That's slander."

"Oh, no? Then prove it. Say you shall meet me at the ball tomorrow evening."

Prue narrowed her eyes. "That's blackmail."

"Is that what it is called?" Franz stood and slapped a few coins on the tabletop. "I would be curious to hear how the police would characterize it." He smiled down at her, revealing too-small teeth and red gums.

Prue suppressed a shudder. "Fine." She'd go to the ball with him all right. And she'd squeeze his secrets out of him like she was a juicer and he was the last lemon in the world.

But one thing was firm: Prue couldn't breathe a word of Franz or the ball to Ophelia. If Ophelia knew about Franz, she'd sniff out the risks. She'd put her foot down about

Prue taking any more sneak-outs. She'd have reason to look slantwise at Hansel, too.

Prue didn't give a fig about risks, though. There was no way in creation she was going to miss going on Hansel's arm to that fairy tale ball.

"So, Miss Gertie Darling wasn't fibbing," Prue said, summing up her excursion to Baden-Baden to Ophelia through the keyhole. "She ain't an invalid, but she *is* staying at the sanatorium."

Ophelia nodded, crouched in the cold shadows outside the tower door. What a relief. This would put an end to Prue's excursions. "I reckon she had nothing to do with it. A dead end. Which means, Prue, you should sit tight in the tower from now on."

Dead silence on the other side of the door.

"Prue?"

"Yes ma'am," Prue said. "I'll sit tight till the cows come home."

Ophelia stood and headed back towards the main castle. Why did she have the suspicion that Prue was holding something back?

Directly after breakfast the next morning, Gabriel walked up to Schloss Grunewald. The funeral was scheduled for later, Gabriel had heard, and he had no wish to attend. But the gardener boy, Hansel, had never replied to his note, and Gabriel desired to investigate the gravesite on the cliff with such fierceness his every muscle was taut.

Gabriel discovered Hansel hoeing a long, lush row of beans in the kitchen gardens.

"Hello there, lad," Gabriel said.

Hansel froze and turned. "Professor Penrose, is it not? You sent that note."

"Yes. I won't beat around the bush, Hansel. I see you've

work to do. Miss Flax apprised me of the existence—the possible existence—of a gravesite on a cliff in the woods about here. Of your suspicion that the skeleton found in the cottage was, in fact, dug up from that cliff."

Hansel leaned on his hoe. His expression was pleasant yet closed. "Yes."

"Would you tell me how I might reach that cliff? I wish to examine it myself."

Hansel shrugged. "Very well." He gave Gabriel directions, starting from the bottom of the orchard.

"Seems simple enough," Gabriel said. "I am most obliged."

"No trouble," Hansel said, hoisting his hoe. "No trouble at all."

Homer T. Coop's funeral was held in Schloss Grunewald's dim, vaulted chapel. Reddish light bled through the stained-glass windows, and the tapers on the altar sputtered. Spiders scurried across the flagstone floor.

Ophelia's skin crawled as she watched yet another eight-legged mite dart behind a hymnal. What a pity Inspector Schubert wasn't here to frolic with his kin.

She sat with the other servants and Mr. Smith in a rear pew.

In the pulpit, a robed priest with a big sniffer and hooded eyes droned on in Latin.

Mr. Coop had not, as far as Ophelia knew, been a pious man. He probably would've never guessed his funeral would be conducted by a German Catholic priest, or that he'd be laid to rest in the ancestral crypt of a fizzled-out aristocratic family. But Mrs. Coop had insisted on these arrangements. It seemed she was bent on staying in the castle indefinitely, now that her husband's business ventures would no longer require her to return home.

But Ophelia wasn't paying much attention to the funeral mass. When she wasn't dodging spiders, she was watching the back of Mr. Hunt, who sat between Mrs. Coop and Amaryllis in the first pew.

If Mr. Hunt had killed Mr. Coop, and if he planned to kill Mrs. Coop next and then marry Amaryllis for her money, there had to be some sign of it.

Ophelia scrutinized them with eagle eyes.

Mrs. Coop wore a black crepe gown and a complicated black veiled hat, and her plump shoulders heaved with silent sobs. Now and then, she stole a sidelong glance at Hunt—gauging, by the looks of it, what effect her display of grief had on him.

Amaryllis, in a nun-like gown of black wool, a plain black shawl, and a close, spinsterly hat, now and then cast vitriolic glances at her elder sister. Ophelia saw, in profile, her carrot-like nose and curled upper lip.

Hunt, dressed to crisp perfection in a dark suit, merely seemed bored and paid neither lady any heed.

Yet he had accepted Miss Amaryllis's scented hankie and Mrs. Coop's invitation to the funeral. Why would he have done those things, if not to further his sinister plot?

Karl and Wilhelm, the two footmen, with the aid of Hansel and a burly gent from Schilltag, hauled Mr. Coop's coffin down the stone stairs to the crypt beneath the chapel.

Everyone followed.

The stairwell was covered with lacework patches of lichen, and the air smelled of cold minerals.

Inside the crypt, with its arched ceiling and marble pillars, there were rows of carved stone sarcophagi with the blank eyes and crossed hands of generations of Grunewalds.

Ophelia tasted in the back of her throat, rather than smelled, decay. She drew closer to Cook and Freda.

The men slid the coffin onto a stone dais. Mrs. Coop launched into a fresh bout of weeping, and the priest started up with more Latin.

Ophelia had a better view of Hunt now, which was only somewhat obstructed by short Mr. Smith just in front of her.

Hunt stood partially behind one of the marble pillars, and his sculpted features were as empty as those of the sarcophagi. Yet he seemed to be fidgeting with something inside his breast pocket.

Ophelia's heart squeezed. He wouldn't dare murder Mrs. Coop in front of all these people, would he?

She stood on tiptoe, straining to see better. That would foil his carefully laid plans, and—

"*Ach*," Cook hissed in Ophelia's ear. "You trod on my toe, clumsy girl."

Ophelia gave her a sheepish smile. "Sorry," she whispered.

Cook sniffed, and Katrina threw her the evil eye.

Mr. Smith glanced back with a sharpness in his usually mild blue eyes. Ophelia saw that his eyes were reddened. She gave him an apologetic smile.

When she looked over to Hunt again, he was no longer fidgeting with his pocket.

But—she glimpsed a flash of white a few steps from Hunt—Amaryllis was furtively edging an envelope beneath her black shawl.

Gabriel hiked with Winkler to the site in the wood.

Gabriel was in an ill temper, and hot, and furious with Hansel. The lad's directions had sent Gabriel on a wild goose chase that led him right back to where he had started, at the bottom of the orchard. Hansel did not, it seemed, wish for Gabriel to go anywhere near that cliff. Like every other local resident, Hansel was hiding something.

The thicket around the cottage had been almost completely cleared, leaving the cottage exposed to the late morning sunlight. From behind the house, echoes of chopping rose up.

"Herz is still cutting away," Winkler said in response to Gabriel's quizzical look. "He claims that he shall finish today, although he seemed reluctant to be done with it."

"That is . . . all he said?"

"He did mutter something about payment, too—these

peasants are always begging for handouts, are they not?—
but I suggested he take that up with the lady of the castle."

Good. Gabriel tossed his knapsack onto the mossy
ground. Herz had not thought it fit to mention having captured Gabriel in a steel man-trap in the wood the night before last. Perhaps whomever Herz was working for had
thought it best to simply watch and wait.

They approached the cottage. It was of half-timbered
construction, and the spaces between the wooden beams
were filled in with what appeared to be wattle and daub, a
substance of slats, straw, and clay. Flecks of gold winked
in the clay.

The cottage could be very, very old. Wattle and daub
was a building technique that had been used for eons.

The chopping noise stopped. Herz emerged from behind
the house, beetle-browed and perspiring, with his sleeves
rolled back.

Gabriel met his stare. Herz's lips peeled back.

"Good morning," Gabriel said to him in a genial tone.
"Splendid work on clearing the place."

Herz said nothing in response but turned to Winkler. "I
am finished."

Then he looked back at Gabriel as he swung his axe,
with rather more force than necessary, over his shoulder.

"I shall just go look it over," Winkler said, toddling
round the corner of the cottage.

As soon as Winkler was out of earshot, Gabriel said
softly, "Not especially gallant of you, Herz, to have hauled
a lady about like you did two nights ago. And Miss Flax is,
if you weren't aware, Mrs. Coop's maid. She could have
your head for that."

"The *fräulein* will not say anything, if she is not stupid."

"Who are you working for?"

Herz sneered. "Ha! You think *I* am stupid?"

"Not at all. But it's clear you are patrolling the castle
estate for someone, and I'd like to know who."

"Someone," Herz said, "who has forbidden me to do

what I would like to you." His calloused fist squeezed the axe handle as though he were snapping a rabbit's neck.

"Ah," Gabriel said. "I see."

Just then, Winkler emerged from behind the cottage. "It is," he said, "quite as good as may be expected, Herz. You may go."

Herz gave Gabriel one last sneer before he strutted away into the trees.

"What an unpleasant specimen," Winkler said. He was unrolling a bundle of paper. "Shall we draw and measure the house, then?"

Hansel delivered a ball gown to Prue in the tower around midday. It was stuffed in a sack. He said he'd found it in a storeroom in the castle.

"Wish I didn't have to meet Franz tonight," Prue said to Hansel, taking the sack off his hands. Guilt smacked her, but she ignored it. It was none of Ophelia's beeswax if she was going to the ball with Hansel. "I've never been to a ball before, and he'll be like an ant at my picnic. Annoying and small. And crawly." She studied Hansel. "Seemed like there was something funny between you two last night."

"Funny?" Hansel scratched an eyebrow. "No. It is only that we were such friends as boys, and we have grown distant. Such circumstances are always awkward."

Prue wished she could believe him.

"Meeting Franz at the ball," Hansel said, "is an opportunity to learn if he had anything to do with Mr. Coop's death or the thefts. You must not forget that Franz told us he remembered discovering that bone with me when we were younger. And last night, I could tell he was quite interested in the skeleton and the cottage—"

"But he was trying to hide it. I know. What if them boot prints up by that cliff grave were his?"

"They very well might have been. Though there were the footprints of other people there, as well. Of at least one other man."

"And a lady. Maybe even Miss Gertie."

Hansel nodded. "I thought we might stop again at the sanatorium, before we go to the ball, and make another attempt to enter her chamber. Whatever she was writing in her notebook will doubtless shed light on her motives for spying on Mr. Smith."

Prue spent the afternoon primping for the ball the best she could. First, she laboriously washed her hair in the basin with cold water and a cake of castile soap. After that, she spent all afternoon drying individual locks with a linen towel that gave off more moisture than it took in. Then she combed her hair out, strand by strand, with the ruby comb she'd found on the cliff. There had been porridge on her breakfast tray, and since Ophelia always said oatmeal was good for the complexion, Prue dabbed some on her percolating pimple. It seemed to help. Tough to be certain when your only mirror was the back of a spoon.

The ball gown made up for all that. It was a princess getup of apricot brocade and whipped cream lace. It was a hundred years out of fashion with a square neckline, deep V waist, drapey bits at the elbows, and big poofs on the hips. But it fit pretty well, and so did the matching Louis-heeled slippers.

Whose gown was it? Not, hopefully, one of those Coop shrews. The very thought made Prue's skin itch. Although she would've been willing to wear burlap from the Bible days if it meant getting out of the ugly brown dress.

# 17

⁓⚬⁓

Ophelia had to get hold of that envelope Mr. Hunt had passed to Amaryllis. It could contain, in plain writing, the evidence she needed to convince Inspector Schubert that the murderer was not Prue, but Mr. Hunt.

The hitch was, Amaryllis no longer allowed Ophelia in her bedchamber, and it was risky to sneak in. And what if Amaryllis chose to carry the envelope around rather than hide it?

When Mrs. Coop sent Ophelia to fetch smelling salts and bring them to the drawing room, she saw her chance.

Mrs. Coop, Amaryllis, Hunt, and Smith were draped drearily on the furniture. No one appeared to be speaking. Hunt was smoking, and Smith stared bleakly out the window.

The servants had set out a cold collation in lieu of luncheon, but the meats, cheeses, fruits, and goose liver pie were untouched. A fly buzzed over the table.

Ophelia crept in.

"What took you so long?" Mrs. Coop said.

Ophelia passed her the vial of smelling salts, which

she'd carried on a small silver tray. "Sorry, ma'am." Her eyes stole to Amaryllis.

"It's terribly warm in here," Mrs. Coop complained.

Amaryllis was staring at the wainscoting—doing a mighty convincing job of ignoring her beloved Mr. Hunt—and her black shawl was draped loosely around her waist.

Ophelia spotted the corner of the envelope. Amaryllis must've been holding it, but in her state of melancholy it lay, forgotten, on her lap.

"It is indeed warm," Ophelia murmured. She swooped close to Amaryllis with her tray. "Allow me, miss, to take your shawl."

Before Amaryllis could respond, Ophelia had tugged the shawl free of her waist and pretended to drop it on the floor. The envelope tumbled down beside it, just as Ophelia said, "Oh! What a peculiar bird outside the window!"

"You clumsy fool!" Amaryllis's eyes were on the window as she sprang to her feet.

"I beg your pardon." Ophelia knelt, placed the silver tray on top of the envelope, and gathered up the shawl. "Here, miss. Forgive me for my clumsiness."

Amaryllis snatched the shawl and slumped away to the windows.

Ophelia picked up the tray, holding the envelope tight against its underside, and glided out of the drawing room.

She opened the envelope—the wax seal had already been broken—in the servants' stair.

There was a handwritten note inside. The script was elegant but masculine.

*My Tender Little Swallow:*

*My heart palpitates in joy, anticipating the delights in store for us tonight! I shall wait in the coach for you this evening at nine o'clock. Pray do not forget your mask!*

*Your H.*

Mask? Ophelia frowned.

Then she remembered the colorful advertisement she'd seen in Baden-Baden yesterday. The downtrodden stepsister was off to the fairy tale ball. And, it appeared, with none other than the handsome prince Hunt himself.

She slid the note back in the envelope.

After the ladies, Hunt, and Smith had left the drawing room, Ophelia tiptoed back in and wedged the envelope behind a cushion of the sofa Amaryllis had been sitting on.

The innkeeper's wife brought Gabriel a note early in the afternoon, moments after he'd returned from the cottage site. He and Winkler had spent hours mapping and making pencil drawings of the cottage. It wasn't the same as having the missing relics in hand, but at least they wouldn't return to Heidelberg empty-handed when all this was done.

The note was from Miss Flax.

> *They plan to attend ball in B-B tonight. Am going with you. Please advise regarding transport.*

Gabriel went downstairs to speak with the innkeeper's wife. She told him his trunk had arrived from Heidelberg, and she assisted him in hiring a carriage for the evening. Then he sent a handwritten note up to the castle with the lad who worked in the Schilltag telegraph office, which read:

> *Did not doubt for a moment you would come. Have hired a carriage. Shall be waiting at the inn at ten o'clock.*

Gabriel knew it was all very scandalous, arranging meetings like this with a maidservant. To an outsider, it wouldn't appear any different from the sort of thing the more unconscionable gentlemen of his class had dragged pretty serving girls into since time immemorial. It had taken him two hours of blind wandering about Baden-Baden yesterday to come to the conclusion that he must be far more cautious in his dealings with Miss Flax.

Yet now, he couldn't help but feel that it was she who was doing most of the dragging.

Prue and Hansel rode the farmer's hay cart into Baden-Baden again. The scene at the sanatorium was the same as the evening before: the consumptive tremblies were all at their soup in the grand dining room, and at the rear of the building, the kitchens were going full chisel.

Prue and Hansel talked things over behind some flowery shrubs.

"I'm thinking," Prue said, "that we ought to just waltz in through the front doors like we own the place." Acting like she owned the place had worked a couple of times in the past. Course, it had gotten her thrown out on her rump a couple of other times, too. "How about it?"

"I cannot think of another way to enter Miss Darling's chamber, short of scaling the vines."

"There ain't any vines."

"Precisely."

They started jostling out from the shrubs, and Prue's poufy left hip caught on a branch. She lost her balance and took Hansel down with her. He landed on his back with Prue piled on top of him.

"Good evening," he said, half whisper and half croak. His eyes were inches from hers, and their noses nearly touched.

She hoped to horseradish he couldn't see the pimple.

His eyes were coffee-bean black in the shadows. She felt the puff of his breath right on her lips, saw the fine golden stubble on his chin.

She didn't want to leave.

She could just picture Ma's mouth-pucker. Hansel had calloused gardener's hands. Probably kept his life savings under the mattress.

But Hansel was, despite all that, so confounded *interesting*.

"We should go," Hansel murmured. He didn't move a muscle. He was fixing on Prue's eyes like he was curious what was stacked up inside her brains.

Funny. Nobody had ever wondered that before. It made something kind of unspool in her chest.

She wiggled her waist away from his nice, warm hands and clambered to her feet. She shook out her layers of skirts, trying to hide her consternation. "Got two left feet tonight. Me, I mean. Not you."

Hansel was brushing leaves off his tailcoat. He didn't look her way. And suddenly, his profile was the most beautiful, heart-wrenching sight Prue had ever laid eyes on.

Was there a word for that?

A minute later, they burst right through the sanatorium's front doors, into the foyer. They were very majestic, at least to Prue's way of thinking, in their ball togs.

A squirrelly man with a moustache like a charcoal smudge came rushing at them from behind a desk.

Hansel said something to him in German, in the snootiest voice Prue had ever heard. The squirrelly gent wrung his fingers, made a wheedling reply, and backed off.

Hansel led Prue up the stairs, which had a bannister polished to a spit shine, into an upper corridor that was all soothing floral wallpaper and carpet like quicksand.

"What did you say to that feller down there?" Prue whispered.

"I told him I am a prince of Prussia, and we are here to collect Miss Darling for the ball at the *Conversationshaus*."

"Worked like a charm."

"Perhaps. But we must hurry. I believe this is Miss Darling's door. The gentleman downstairs said it was number twenty-one." Hansel tried the knob. The door swished inward.

Miss Darling and her old trout lived well, in a medicinal sort of way. There were two mahogany beds, with a table in between. The table had lots of tonic bottles—brown, blue, and clear glass, with labels in English and German—along with smelling salts and an ample stack of clean hankies. For all that coughing. The wardrobe was filled with thick crocheted shawls and bombazine gowns. Everything was of the first quality, but plain. Nothing seemed out of keeping with what Prue knew about Gertie, though she wouldn't have been surprised to see a gnarled walking stick or maybe a meerschaum pipe.

Hansel was flicking though the opened mail on the desk. Prue looked around his shoulder. "Anything?"

"Letters to the old lady—her name is Miss Abigail Upton—from doting nieces in England. Accounts are all tidy. They have been staying here at the sanatorium for some two weeks. It appears that before that, they were in Switzerland."

"What's this?" Prue had opened a desk drawer, and she pulled out a book. It had a leather cover worn soft with use. "Ain't this what Miss Gertie was writing in when she was spying on Mr. Smith with her binoculars?"

Prue flipped through the pages. The notebook was half filled with scribbly, cramped writing in pencil. There were rough sketches sprinkled in, too. The second half of the notebook was still blank.

She stopped on a page near the front. It had a date: May 25, 1864.

"What is that?" Hansel poked his fingertip on a funny little picture. "It looks like a doll. Or a child."

Prue's mouth tasted funny. "That thing has got wings. I think it's supposed to be a fairy. See them flowers?"

"A fairy?" Hansel leaned closer. "Perhaps she fancies herself an authoress of children's storybooks."

Prue squinted. *"I attempted to lure them with sugar lumps,"* she read aloud, *"but alas, it would seem they prefer natural nectars. Little blighters. Spoiling my research precisely when I had boasted to Sir Lionel about my scientific progress on the Wee Folk."*

Prue swiveled her eyes to Hansel's. His eyebrows were lifted in disbelief.

Prue thumbed to a page closer to the end of the entries.

*"July 29th, 1867. Miss Upton has informed me we shall be moving on from Switzerland in a fortnight, to a sanatorium in Baden-Baden. At last, I shall have the opportunity to try my*

*hand at hunting Wee Folk in the Black Forest! I hid my delight from Miss Upton, as she always seems to have a fit of coughing whenever I am pleased. Miserable old biddy."*

"Miss Darling," Hansel said, "would seem to be, well, mad."

"Hasn't got all her buttons, for certain." Prue turned to the last entry in the book. "Look. This one's dated two days ago. There's a sketch of Mr. Smith working on his shotgun, sitting on a log."

"It is not a log," an imperious voice said behind them. "It is a stump. Any fool can discern the difference."

Prue jumped. She twisted around to face Miss Gertie.

"What do you mean by this, you impudent children," Miss Gertie said, "nosing about in my research? The front desk clerk notified me that I might discover intruders in my chamber."

"Um." Prue said. She adjusted a lace ruffle on her bodice.

"There has been a murder," Hansel said in his hoity-toity voice. "We have taken it upon ourselves to investigate."

Gertie emitted a bark of laughter. "And you are investigating me? Oh, for pity's sake, why don't you two go back to playing Ring Around the Rosie and leave me alone?"

"Because," Hansel said, "you have been spying upon members of the castle household. That seems to connect you to the crime."

"Oh, indeed?"

"Sneaking around after Mr. Smith," Prue said. "Who's to say he's not going to be the next one bumped off in your—your wicked plot?"

"I haven't any *plot*." Gertie drew herself up.

"What about this notebook?" Prue said. "All about wee folk. Why, Mr. Smith's no more a wee folk than I'm the president of the United States. How did you meet him, anyway?"

Two salmon pink spots glowed on Gertie's cheeks. "We were never formally introduced. Although that is none of your affair."

"How," Hansel said, "did you encounter him?"

"I simply came upon him in the wood."

"Bunkum," Prue said. "You're keen on wee folk, you

think Mr. Smith's a wee folk, and you just happened upon him? A mighty big coincidence that would be."

Gertie snorted. "You are an uneducated bumpkin."

"Lived in New York City all my born days." Why did everyone think she came from the sticks? Ophelia was the bumpkin. Not her.

"Very well," Gertie said. "You are an uneducated guttersnipe. You know nothing of the natural sciences."

"Wee folk," Hansel said, "are not scientific. They are myth."

"How *dare* you?" The cords on Gertie's neck popped out like harp strings. "That is my life's work you are speaking of!" She lunged forward and snatched the notebook from Prue. She cradled it against her bosom. "If you must know—because I can perfectly envision you pair scampering off to the police if I don't tell you this—if you must know, I learned of the discovery of Snow White's house and the dwarf skeleton, and decided to look into it myself."

"Where did you learn of it?" Prue said.

"Everyone in Baden-Baden knows. Gossip. The newspapers. I took a few days' leave from Miss Upton to stay at Gasthaus Schatz in Schilltag to conduct my research. I happened upon Smith one day."

Prue scrunched her lips. "And decided he was one of them storybook dwarves?"

Gertie pointed a shaking finger to the doorway. "Leave. Before I notify the staff."

Prue and Hansel legged it out of there like the place was on fire.


"Now that I see you in the light," Professor Penrose said to Ophelia, "I'm not certain I can say your disguise this evening is a decided improvement over yesterday's."

Ophelia took his hand and hopped down from the carriage outside the *Conversationshaus* in Baden-Baden. "Well, that would depend," she said, "on what you mean by improvement, I reckon." She looped her arm through his.

They started up the steps.

The *Conversationshaus* was a long, palatial building of creamy stone with tall pillars, fronted by a white gravel drive. It housed the town's infamous gaming rooms, a concert hall, dining rooms, and a grand ballroom. The drive was filled with carriages and glossy horses, and music and light poured down the wide steps.

"You are," Penrose said, "as unrecognizable this evening as you were yesterday."

"Today, at the least, I am dressed as a lady."

"Indeed." His tone was dubious.

Ophelia had cobbled together a costume from things she'd found in the castle lumber room. Since it was a fairy tale ball, she'd outfitted herself as an old crone, like the one in "Hansel and Gretel," with a faded, voluminous cotton gown and apron, a peasant bonnet, a homespun shawl, and even a wooden crutch made from a piece of a broken chair. Then she'd made her face wrinkly and slightly greenish with her greasepaint, and given herself a couple of warts and a hooked nose made of wax. The crowning touch, however, was her hunchback, made of an old pillow pinned beneath the gown.

After examining herself in a tarnished wardrobe mirror, she'd decided the effect was perfect. She'd been so elated she'd nearly tripped with her crutch on a trunk and a big rolled-up carpet as she left the lumber room.

But now, seeing the other ladies flowing up the *Conversationshaus* steps, her heart sank.

True, the other ladies were dressed as fairy tale characters, too. But the beautiful ones. Cinderella, Rapunzel, and various beauties all made appearances, alongside several pretty little cats in satin trousers and high-heeled boots, flocks of fairies, charming goose girls, and herds of queens and princesses. Their gowns were exquisite, and they were all bedecked in real jewels.

Oh, well. At least no one would see how red her cheeks were underneath all that green greasepaint.

# 18

❧

"I must confess," Ophelia said, casting Penrose a side-long glance, "that I am mystified by *your* costume."

"Oh?" Penrose wasn't, in fact, costumed at all; he wore an impeccable suit of evening clothes. "I thought I'd rather gone out on a limb, parting my hair on the opposite side."

They paused outside the open doors. Penrose removed his spectacles, drew a small black half mask from his breast pocket, and affixed it across his eyes with a ribbon. "Is that at all better?"

"I see. You're a burglar. To go with the lock picking."

"You're rather flippant for a young lady who's sneaked out on borrowed time."

Ophelia ignored him and took in the brilliantly lit foyer. A gorgeous chandelier was suspended from an ornate ceiling, and the floor was marble. Along the walls, gilded niches sported classical statuary.

Penrose led her along with the crowd, through a red velvet-swagged doorway, and into the ballroom. A Strauss waltz rippled out, and crowds of gentlemen and ladies twirled around the parquet floor. The ceiling was ablaze with more sparkling chandeliers, and the perimeter of the floor was a hive of swirling motion, laughter, and tinkling champagne glasses.

But on closer inspection, the ball had a grotesque effect: amid all the gorgeous ladies were men wearing hedgehog masks, beast's heads, and wolf's tails.

"We must only catch sight of Miss Amaryllis in the company of Hunt," Penrose said. "If we are able to confirm that they are indeed—as all evidence seems to suggest—paramours, then we may have a better understanding of how to proceed."

Ophelia nodded, feeling dizzy. She leaned on her crone's crutch. "But if they are here, how will we spot them? This looks like a fever dream." She watched a gentleman in evening clothes and a large papier-mâché pig's head. He held a glass of wine aloft and swayed to the music.

"'The Pig King,' I gather," Penrose said. "A fairy tale collected by the sixteenth-century Italian Straparola."

"It's downright eerie."

Ophelia refused to admit to Penrose that she'd never been to a ball before. Theirs was merely an acquaintance of mutual benefit. She'd told him in the carriage what Hansel and Matilda had said about the tapestry, to show her good faith in keeping up their bargain. Whatever discomfort that lingered from their excursion under the bed in the Hotel Europa was of no account.

"Let's make the rounds of the ballroom," Penrose said. "While we cannot see people's faces clearly, we are familiar enough with Miss Amaryllis and Hunt to recognize their voices, and even the way they comport themselves."

"And if we spot them?"

"We'll worry over that when the time comes."

Ophelia and Penrose, arm in arm, made their way around the perimeter of the ballroom. It wasn't easy. The general air was edging towards wanton gaiety, it was growing hot, and despite their elegant appearances, folks were pushing.

It wasn't a far cry from the unruly crowds that lined up to ogle the sideshows in P. Q. Putnam's Traveling Circus.

Ophelia was grateful for Penrose's arm. Yankee ladies didn't cling to gentlemen like starfish to rocks, of course. They were too self-reliant. But his solid form *was* helpful for keeping her balance. Her pillow hunchback was beginning to shift from side to side, and people were stumbling on her crutch.

"Is that Miss Amaryllis?" Ophelia whispered. "See? The lady in white, standing against the wall, with the peacock feather mask."

Penrose glanced over. "No. See, she's lowered her mask."

They pressed further into the ballroom and came to a standstill beside a table heaped with petits fours. Ophelia plucked one up and bit into it. Lemon meringue. Scrumptious. She polished it off and reached for another.

Her hand bumped the outstretched arm of a portly gentleman, who was reaching for the same raspberry tartlet she was.

"I beg your pardon," he said in a British accent. He eyed Ophelia. "Rather fitting, Hansel and Gretel's old crone having a jolly go at the sweets table."

Penrose hadn't heard him; he was busy scanning the crowd.

Instead of tossing the British gent a retort, Ophelia took the raspberry tartlet and bit into it.

As she chewed, she caught a glimpse of Princess Verushka in a crimson gown, sailing around the dance floor. She was in the arms of a gentleman in evening dress, a frog mask, and a golden crown.

"Look!" She jabbed Penrose with her elbow. "The princess."

"So it is."

"She's a bit long in the tooth," the gentleman said on her other side, "to be Little Red Riding Hood, don't you think?" He was shiny and jowly, like a porcelain baby doll.

"Are you acquainted with Princess Verushka?" Ophelia said.

"I know everyone in Baden-Baden."

"She is Polish, is she not? Or is it Russian?"

"Russian. Widow of that decrepit prince from St. Petersburg."

"The . . . the really rich one?"

"Mm. Rich as Midas." The British gent popped one last petit four into his chops and wandered away.

"Did you hear that?" Ophelia whispered to Penrose.

"I did. She's a real princess."

"And rich, too. But why did she lie to Mrs. Coop about staying at the Hotel Europa?"

"Presumably Mrs. Coop misheard her. Or Mrs. Coop could have misspoken. There is no reason for us to suspect the princess of murder."

"Except that she was searching through Mr. Coop's desk."

"There is that."

Prue was dazzled by the ball. She and Hansel were both hidden behind the masks Hansel had brought, but no one would have noticed them, anyway. It was like a carnival. The flashes of rubies, emeralds, and diamonds in the crazy swirl of China silk, embroidery, and tulle made her woozy. She caught whiffs of fine French perfumes like Ma used to hoard: amber and musk, vanilla and bergamot. And dancing with Hansel, polonaises, waltzes, mazurkas, and polkas, amid the lavish throng—well, she felt like she'd arrived smack-dab in the center of the world.

For once, Prue figured Ma would approve of her doings. Supposing, that is, Ma didn't know Hansel was just a gardener. Anyway, tonight Hansel really did call to mind a prince, though Prue found it tough to look straight at him. The sight of him made her chest go all loopy inside.

They were taking a breather by the champagne table when Prue felt a tap on her shoulder.

"You have been hiding from me," Franz said. Same as last time, he looked like either an otter or a magician with his black evening clothes and Macassar-oiled dark hair. He didn't wear a mask.

"I ain't hiding from you," Prue said. "It's a masquerade ball."

"But I wish to see your lovely face."

"You ain't keen on ladies of mystery?"

"There is nothing mysterious about you," Franz said, trapping Prue in his wiry arms, "aside from your grammar. Come, give me a waltz, or I shall make good on my threat to notify the police that their murderess has escaped for an evening's entertainment."

Prue swallowed. Franz tugged Prue out on the glittering dance floor. Prue caught one last glimpse of Hansel, hot-eyed, gulping the rest of his champagne.

"Holy mackerel," Prue said, a few dances in. She craned her neck as Franz whisked her by the refreshments table. She'd caught sight of Miss Gertie Darling.

"Mackerel," Franz said in her ear, "is a fish, you gorgeous little dimwit."

Prue stomped his foot.

"Ow!" he yelped.

"Begging your pardon, sir." Her tone was treacly.

They thundered to a stop, right by Gertie.

Handy.

Franz bent to nurse his trodden toe.

Gertie stood at the helm of the wicker wheelchair again. Miss Upton, the old lady, was shriveled inside folds of black gown and shawl, scowling out from under her white bun. Her humped back sprouted two small fairy wings. Gertie was also dressed as a fairy. Her seafoam gossamer gown billowed, and her fairy wings could've been ship sails.

"Oh," Gertie said over the music to Prue. "It's you."

Prue touched her mask; it was still in place. Gertie must have recognized her gown.

Franz stood. He and Gertie sized each other up. Gertie looked like she'd enjoy picking Franz up and tossing him out the window. Franz eyed Gertie with cool dismissal.

Prue introduced them, watching for any sign that they knew each other.

If they *did* know each other, they were splendiferous actors.

"What brings you to Baden-Baden?" Franz said to Gertie in a bored voice.

Gertie gave the wheelchair handles a shake. "Is it not obvious?"

The old lady made a grunt and smacked one of the wheels.

"Miss Darling is keen on wee folk and fairy tales and such," Prue said to Gertie. "Didn't you say, Mr. Lind, you thought all that fairy tale hocus-pocus was—what was the word you used? Fascinating?" Maybe he needed a little nudge in the direction of the murder and thefts.

A vein throbbed on Franz's temple. "I believe I expressed a polite interest."

"But," Prue said, "you said you remembered finding that dwarf's bone in the forest when you was an ankle biter."

Gertie had stopped blinking. "Dwarf's bone?"

"I did not claim that it was a dwarf's bone," Franz said. "That is merely one rather childish theory."

He was playacting again, pretending he didn't care.

"It is a perfectly sound theory," Gertie said. "I understand that the skeleton in question is exceedingly uncommon in its dimensions."

"Hoaxes, my dear lady. At my own university, there is a professor who specializes in the study of fairy tales, and it seems he is continually barraged by fairy tale hoaxes put on by locals who wish to drum up a tourist trade."

"Oh. Him," Gertie said. "Yes, I've heard of him. Professor Winkler. Bit of a bore, insisting everything's a hoax and whatnot."

"Heidelberg University's library," Franz said, "houses rare fairy tale books. If one were to examine them, it would become apparent that they are merely the product of excessive fancy."

Franz was only being a clever clogs, trying to show up Miss Gertie.

"Rare fairy tale books?" Gertie clutched the wheelchair handles so hard that the chair was starting to tip backwards. The old lady smacked one of the wheels again, and Gertie lowered the chair with a jolt.

"Indeed," Franz said. Then he slithered away, dragging Prue with him. "Insane creature," he muttered.

After one more dance, Prue pried herself from Franz's moist clutches. Hopefully she'd danced with him enough to keep him from reporting her to the police.

She found Hansel leaning on a wall by a gaggle of wallflowers. The wallflowers were all glancing sidelong at Hansel. But Hansel's glum gaze was directed out into the sea of dancers.

"You look like someone nicked your hot-cross-bun money," Prue said.

"Did you learn anything?"

"Only that Franz and Gertie have never laid eyes on each other before. And that he likes to boast." She frowned. Hansel was still searching the dance floor. "What's the matter?"

"It is . . . would you like to view the gaming rooms?" He offered his arm.

"All right."

Ophelia was beginning to despair of spotting Amaryllis and Mr. Hunt.

"Miss Flax," Penrose said suddenly, "if you would be so kind as to direct your gaze in the direction of the orchestra."

Ophelia squinted over the swaying mob of dancers. "Oh! That's her."

Miss Amaryllis, her frail form bedecked in a lavish—although rather ill-fitting—gown of robin's egg blue, fanned herself near the orchestra. She wore a mask, which she'd pushed up over her coif, and a pair of feathery wings.

"That's one of her sister's gowns," Ophelia said. "She must've taken it in herself. No wonder she didn't leave her chamber last night. And she's dressed her own hair, too."

Penrose was staring intently. "Here is a gentleman, bringing her something to drink."

Ophelia followed his gaze. "Mr. Hunt." He wore a furry beast's mask and a red martial costume, complete with medals, epaulets, gold braid, and tall, shiny boots.

Amaryllis accepted the glass with a dazzling smile.

"I've never," Ophelia said, "seen her so . . . happy. She's transformed."

"We've only to wait for Hunt to unmask himself—surely he'll need some fresh air—"

"Or to smoke a cigarette."

"Yes, I hadn't thought of that—and our task is complete."

This, however, proved less simple than Ophelia had hoped. She and Penrose loitered and strolled, even had glasses of champagne, all the while keeping Amaryllis and her beastly squire in sight. But although Amaryllis and Hunt danced waltz after waltz and went out onto the terrace for a breath of air, Hunt never removed his mask.

Ophelia was getting antsy. "We can't wait all night," she said. Amaryllis and Hunt were chatting and laughing just inside the terrace doors. "And what if he never removes his mask?" Before Penrose could respond, she handed him her empty champagne glass. "I've had a notion."

"*Miss Flax*," Penrose warned.

But Ophelia was already limping her way through the throng with her crutch, in the direction of Amaryllis and Hunt. Her hunchback leaned perilously to one side, but she didn't slow down.

When she reached them, she moved as though to dodge past Hunt, through the doors, and out onto the terrace. It was more crowded than ever, so it was simple enough to run into him, as though she'd tripped or been shoved.

Amaryllis squealed.

Hunt gasped as Ophelia, pretending to be off balance, caught at his arm. This threw *him* off balance. As he stumbled forward, she grabbed the edge of his beast's mask and pulled.

He landed on the floor with a thud. Ophelia held the mask in her hands.

"Darling!" Amaryllis cried, hurling herself down at his side.

Ophelia looked at the mask in her hand. Then she looked down at the gentleman she'd been so certain was Hunt.

She blinked. She was looking at none other than the first footman, Karl.

"You poor poppet," Miss Amaryllis said, helping Karl to his feet. She threw Ophelia a grimace that could've curdled milk. "*You*. Flax. What are you doing here? Did my— did Mrs. Coop send you to spy on me?"

Ophelia touched her face. She'd lost her wax nose in the scrimmage.

Then Penrose was at her side, still wearing his mask. "A mere coincidence. It is Miss Flax's evening off, and I thought I'd bring her to see the famous social whirl of Baden-Baden. Terribly sorry for the accident." He attempted to edge Ophelia away.

"Wait a moment," Amaryllis said. "You're that professor, aren't you? What are you doing with my maid?"

"Little swallow," Karl said in Amaryllis's ear. His sparse gray hair had tufted up, and he was smoothing it over his balding dome. "There is no need for a scene." He scanned the ballroom, looking twitchy. However, no one was paying them the least bit of attention anymore.

Amaryllis ignored Karl. "Well? Explain yourself."

"I was," Penrose said, "most gratified to make Miss Flax's acquaintance and, as I already mentioned, I wished for her to see the sights."

"But her horrid little friend is locked up for murder."

"I wished to take her mind off things."

"But she ought to be at the castle. In mourning."

"As," Penrose said, "should you. Now. I'm certain we may all agree not to mention this unfortunate incident to anyone."

"You mean"—Amaryllis narrowed her eyes—"to Inspector Schubert?"

"As much as that good officer of the police would, doubtless, be interested to hear that the young lady of the castle has taken up with the footman—what an intriguing turn of events—"

"Of course, of course, no need for that." Karl swabbed his brow with a handkerchief. "Come, little swallow. Let us go for some air."

"Quite right." Amaryllis straightened her feathery wings. "I won't allow a wretched maidservant and a moldy professor to spoil my evening." She hooked her arm through Karl's. They made for the doors that led to the foyer.

# 19

⁓

"Bold move, Miss Flax," Penrose said. His eyes glittered behind his mask. "Admittedly, it had all the grace of elephants dancing a pas de deux."

"I've always been one to rise to the occasion."

"And rise you did. Although I can't say the same for your hunchback." He gestured with his chin to her middle.

Ophelia looked down. The hunchback had come unfastened and had migrated to the front of her bodice. She appeared to have a ponderous belly.

She sighed. "Nothing to do about it now."

"I admire your fortitude. Many ladies would dissolve into a mortified puddle."

"I'm not prone to dissolving."

"True enough. Miss Amaryllis and the footman—I must confess, I am surprised."

"We've been blind. All those times I thought she was staring moon-eyed after Mr. Hunt, she was really staring at Karl. He's always just standing in the background, see. When Mr. Hunt was fiddling with his waistcoat pocket in the crypt this morning, he must've been checking for his cigarette case. Meanwhile, I didn't even notice Karl pass Amaryllis the note."

"I wonder how Hunt came to have her handkerchief in his hotel chamber. Are you certain it was hers?"

"Yes. There must be some explanation."

"Did you observe," he said, "the way Karl was looking about so anxiously just now?"

Ophelia nodded. "As soon as I removed his mask—"

"Removed. What a delicate way to put it."

"—he got as jumpy as a cricket."

"His eyes were rather as big and wary as a cricket's, too. I suspect he's afraid of being spotted by someone. Let's follow them."

In the foyer, it was blessedly cooler and far less crowded. Ophelia and Penrose spotted Amaryllis and Karl behind one of the huge pillars. They were bickering.

Ophelia and Penrose darted behind another pillar. They strained their ears.

"—*you said you'd stop*—" Amaryllis's voice was squeaky.

Karl's deeper voice rumbled something unintelligible, but his tone was not as placating as it had sounded inside the ballroom.

"—*and they'll find you and*—" Amaryllis said.

There was a clatter of heels.

Ophelia peeked around the pillar. "They're leaving," she whispered.

Karl was stalking away across the expanse of marble floor. Amaryllis scurried after him.

"That didn't sound like a lover's quarrel," Ophelia said.

"And Karl isn't going outside. He's headed for the gaming rooms."

"Judging from the way Miss Amaryllis was protesting, gambling seems to be a sore point."

"I agree. And not only between Miss Amaryllis and Karl. Look."

Ophelia saw a towering gentleman in black evening

clothes watching Karl as he passed through the gaming room doors. Amaryllis trailed after Karl. Then the black-clad gentleman smoothly followed.

Ophelia frowned. "Do you reckon Karl owes that gentleman money?"

"I suspect that Karl owes not that gentleman but the gaming establishment a great deal of money." Penrose removed his mask and placed his spectacles on his nose. "That gentleman has the look of a guard. Shall we?" He proffered his arm.


The gaming room was, like the ballroom, large and crowded with richly dressed ladies and gentlemen. The walls were hung with scarlet damask, and the ceiling was all gold moldings and tubby cherubs.

But unlike the ballroom, the gaming room was hushed, and the atmosphere, punctuated by nervous or relieved bursts of laughter, was charged. Croupiers murmured in French, and ivory balls bounced with fragile clicks in the spinning roulette wheels. Coins jingled and cash rustled.

Ophelia held Penrose's arm as they wound their way between the gaming tables, searching for Amaryllis and Karl.

Ophelia made a point of ignoring all the furtive glances at her crutch and belly.

Through the phantasmagoric swirl of tobacco smoke, she saw faces clustered around the roulette tables in all species of ecstasy and torment: a plump gentleman in Russian officer's clothes dabbed his streaming forehead with a hankie; a lady in a scandalously décolleté gown giggled as she ran her fingers through a mound of gold coins; a threadbare gentleman laid down a thick stack of paper notes before a croupier; a handsome youth in evening clothes plucked a glass of brandy from a passing waiter's tray—

Ophelia gasped.

Penrose glanced down. "Do you see them?"

"No, but"—Ophelia steered him behind a crowded roulette table—"that's Hansel, the castle gardener, over there. I nearly didn't recognize him in those evening clothes."

"Has the entire castle staff decided to duck off to Baden-Baden this evening?"

"It's not funny! I can't be seen by him. If Cook—or, heaven forbid, Mrs. Coop—finds out I've been here, I'll be out on my ear."

Penrose's smile evaporated.

"What is it?"

"It seems Miss Bright has accompanied Hansel."

*"Prue?"* Ophelia's belly plummeted. "Prue didn't tell me she was coming here tonight! Why, anyone might see her. Even Inspector Schubert could be here!"

Ophelia no longer cared who saw her. She tucked her crutch under her arm, held fast to the pillow at her waist, and marched around the crowded roulette table.

And there was Prue, decked out in an antique-looking gown of apricot-colored brocade. Her golden hair fell in cascading ringlets, and she clung to Hansel's arm.

Neither Hansel nor Prue noticed Ophelia, so absorbed were they in the roulette game.

Almost everyone around the table cheered as the ball fell home. Hansel, however, was grim.

Ophelia followed Hansel's eyes. They were locked on Karl, who was in the thick of the crowd, Amaryllis at his side. While everyone else at the table was jubilant, Karl was misery itself, and Amaryllis looked like she could bite through a ten-penny nail.

But Ophelia couldn't get in a lather over Karl and Amaryllis. Not now. She reached Prue's side. "If it isn't," she said through the din, "Cinderella herself."

"Ophelia!"

"Where'd you get that gown?"

"Hansel dug it up in some old storeroom in the castle attic."

Ophelia's breath caught. She wasn't the only one rooting around up there, then. What if Hansel found her theatrical case?

Hansel disengaged his arm from Prue's and gulped.

"Prudence Deliverance Bright," Ophelia said, "what are you doing here? You're supposed to be in the tower! Don't you remember"—she glanced around and lowered her voice—"you've been accused of murder?"

"You can't think what it's like in that old tower." Prue's lower lip quivered. "It's chock-full of bird droppings, it's as cold as the Antarctic, and—"

"I'm not saying it's the Astor House Hotel, but you need to stay put in that tower for a little while longer while I sort things out, or we shall have the mischief to pay."

Prue's eyes welled up.

"Miss Bright only wished to get out for an evening," Hansel said. He sounded distracted; he was still watching Karl.

Karl reached into his pockets for money to place a fresh stake.

"Get out for an evening!" Ophelia said. "Why, Prue's been more *out* than *in*."

At that moment, Hansel stepped forward and tapped Karl's shoulder. Karl turned. When he saw who it was, he made a grimace that was part smile, part guilty cringe. Ophelia couldn't understand what Hansel was saying, but he appeared to be dead earnest.

"What's happening?" Ophelia asked Prue.

"I—I don't know."

Now Hansel was speaking to Karl more emphatically, and people were beginning to stare. Amaryllis fanned herself in nervous bursts. Her feathery wings were askew. Hansel placed a hand on Karl's sloping shoulder.

Karl shook it off, suddenly angry. The hairs he'd so carefully arranged over his balding pate came loose. "*Nein, nein, nein!*" he said.

Then the gentleman in black, the one who'd followed Karl in from the foyer, appeared. A second black-clad gentleman was with him.

Ophelia gasped. The two guards were heart-stoppingly familiar. They were the same gentlemen she'd seen skulking across the castle courtyard with the ceiling beam. She was sure of it. One of them had a chin like an anvil, and the other had a single black eyebrow sprawled across his forehead.

One of the guards pushed Hansel aside. They each grabbed one of Karl's arms and drew him away from the roulette table.

"Darling!" Amaryllis wailed.

The room erupted in gasps and chatter as Karl was ushered to the doors. Amaryllis skittered at his heels, snarling imprecations at the two guards. Hansel strode just behind, with Ophelia, Prue, and Penrose not far after.

The guards dragged Karl through the foyer and out the front doors, down the *Conversationshaus* steps, and thrust him out onto the gravel drive.

"*Gehen Sie aus, Graf Grunewald*," one of them said, "*oder Sie werden ausweisen von Baden sein!*" They climbed up the steps and disappeared through the doors.

Karl, his hair and clothing in disarray, made a show of tidying his cuffs.

"I told you," Amaryllis said to him, "you oughtn't go in there."

Karl smoothed one of his epaulettes.

"Father," Hansel said. "I did not believe it when they told me you had been coming back here—"

"Father?" Ophelia said.

"Be quiet!" Amaryllis said to Hansel.

"Hansel," Ophelia said, "Karl is your father?"

Hansel sighed. "Yes."

"I'm rather more curious, Karl," Penrose said, "as to why those guards addressed you as Count Grunewald."

Karl suddenly seemed shabby and defeated. Moonlight bounced off his bald head. He parted his lips as if to speak, but before he could utter a word, Amaryllis turned him around and they marched off across the gravel, disappearing behind a row of waiting carriages.


"Your pa is the count?" Prue said to Hansel. "Don't that mean you're a prince or something?"

Hansel jammed his hands in his trouser pockets. "I am

able to explain all of this—well, I cannot explain why my father was accompanied by Miss Amaryllis. But for the rest, there is a rational explanation."

"Go on," Penrose said.

"My father, Heinrich von Förster, Count Grunewald, was the owner of Schloss Grunewald until he sold it to Homer T. Coop four months ago."

Ophelia thought hard. *Heinrich*. That explained the *H.* on the note to Amaryllis.

"I am sorry"—Hansel looked softly at Prue—"that I deceived you, Miss Bright. He is my father. I shall inherit his title."

"What about your mother?" Prue asked.

"She died years ago."

"How come you're only a gardener?"

"I was forced to discontinue my studies at Heidelberg University when"—he stared down at the ground—"when funding ran out." He lifted his chin again. "But I plan to return, as soon as I find a way, and study medicine."

"Gambling," Ophelia said. "Count Grunewald lost everything here in the gaming rooms?"

"At first, he played with his aristocratic friends. When they refused to play anymore, out of conscience or, more usually, because Father owed them too much, they disappeared like smoke. Then he turned to the gaming rooms."

That had to be why those two guards stole the ceiling beam and the skeleton—probably as some sort of debt collection for the gaming establishment.

"Slowly," Hansel said, "everything drained away. My mother's jewels, the silver plate, the valuable pieces of furniture, carpets, tapestries."

Ophelia and Penrose exchanged a glance. *Tapestries.*

"Finally," Hansel said, "he sold the castle to that upstart Coop."

"It is remarkable," Penrose said, "to say the least, that a count and his son stayed on as servants in the castle they were forced to sell."

"That was part of the agreement. Father sold the castle

to Coop only on the condition that he and I, and Grandmother, could stay on as long as we wished as domestic
servants in our ancestral home."

"Grandmother?" Ophelia said. But she'd already guessed
the answer.

"Matilda." Hansel shook his head. "To think that a *gräfin*—
a countess—should be reduced to peeling apples in a chimney
corner."

Ophelia glanced again at Penrose. His eyes glowed.

He was thinking of the tapestry.

"Homer T. Coop," Hansel said, kicking the gravel,
"cheated us. Schloss Grunewald is worth far more than he
paid for it, but he took advantage of my father's desperate
circumstances to strike a scoundrel's bargain. I can easily
understand how Coop amassed such a fortune. He doubtless cheated and tricked for every penny of it." Hansel's
boyishly handsome face was suddenly altered. Maybe it
was a trick of the moonlight, but his eyes were too bright,
his lips tight, as he said, "Homer T. Coop deserved to die."
He dug something from his waistcoat pocket. A key. He
placed it in Prue's hand.

Then, hands still in his trouser pockets, he slouched off
into the night without even saying good-bye.

Ophelia and Penrose herded Prue towards their hired
carriage, which was waiting at the far end of the *Conversationshaus* drive.

"You ought not speak to Hansel again," Ophelia said to
her. "He could be dangerous."

"Don't be a looney. He's about as dangerous as a new-
hatched chick."

"A chick? He could have killed Mr. Coop!"

Prue spun to face her. "How could you?"

"How could I? I'll tell you how. If Karl is Count
Grunewald and Hansel is his heir, then they were both, at
least the way Hansel tells it, cheated by Mr. Coop."

"Making a deal for yourself ain't the same as straight-up

fleecing. Hansel and his pa wouldn't kill Mr. Coop over that."

"Perhaps," Penrose said, "the count did not foresee the humiliation entailed in performing the duties of a domestic in one's own ancestral home." He paused. "At this juncture I should mention that young Hansel has been unaccountably obstructive with regard to the location of the cliff gravesite. Now I understand, at least in part, why: he wished to protect his family's estate from further investigation by outsiders. The question remains, however, what precisely is he protecting?"

"He wouldn't tell you where the cliff is?" Ophelia said. "Sent me off in quite the wrong direction, I'm afraid."

"Maybe it's only that *you* ain't too good with your geographies, professor," Prue said. She twisted her lips. "Is that Hansel's fault? Anyway, Miss Amaryllis is a sight more suspicious than Hansel or Karl. I'll bet *she* killed Mr. Coop. To get at the castle and money."

"Mrs. Coop inherited her husband's castle and money," Ophelia reminded her. "Not Miss Amaryllis."

"Unless," Prue said darkly, "Mrs. Coop was to kick the bucket."

That's exactly what Ophelia was afraid of.

# 20

They'd reached the carriage. Ophelia climbed inside—
no easy feat with her pillow belly and crutch. Prue, still
standing on the drive, hesitated.

"Miss Bright," Penrose said, just behind her. "Be reason-
able. If you attempt to bolt now, the entire Baden-Baden police force will be after you. You are an accused murderess."

Prue burst into tears. "I'm ever so fond of Hansel! I
don't mind he's a count. I've got to go find him."

Ophelia met Penrose's eyes.

"Come, now," Penrose said. He helped Prue into the
carriage.

As the carriage left the lights of Baden-Baden behind
and began its ascent into the dark mountains, Prue's weeping faded to sniffs and hiccups.

"Prue," Ophelia said, "you've got to listen to me. I'm not
saying Hansel did anything wrong—but he *could* have."

Prue gave her a sullen look through the shadows.

"We're caught in a mess," Ophelia said, "and the only
way to get out is to be very careful."

"What"—Prue gestured towards Penrose—"does he
know?"

"Know?" Penrose's voice was pleasant, but the glance he threw at Ophelia was thorn-sharp.

"Only," Ophelia said quickly to Prue, "that we are servants, professional servants, with very little money to our names." She swallowed. "What does Hansel know?"

Prue hesitated. "About the same."

Ophelia felt Penrose's eyes on her. She tried to ignore them.

"If Hansel would only tell the police that he is Count Grunewald's son," Ophelia said, "maybe they'd believe him."

"I wouldn't," Penrose said, "be too confident of that. If the police knew that the count, his mother, and his son were all still in residence at the castle—all of them bearing, mind you, a sizeable grudge—it could cause suspicion to fall still more heavily on Prue."

Both Ophelia and Prue stared at him in surprise.

"Inspector Schubert," Penrose said, "believes Prue is a gullible creature—"

"Thinks I'm a numskull," Prue said.

"—and so he might surmise that Prue, taken with the handsome young son of the disgraced count, was working in tandem with him. Or even. . . ." He paused.

"Yes?" Ophelia said.

"Or even covering his tracks."

"You mean to say I'm lying about something?" Prue said.

Was Prue really capable of lying for Hansel? That was difficult to believe. But then, she'd said she was ever so fond of him.

"Hansel is hiding something," Penrose said. "He is hiding the location of the cliff gravesite—"

"Not from me!" Prue swung to face Ophelia. "You're buying this claptrap?" She was crying again, but she sounded angry. "Maybe you are a wicked old witch, just like your costume."

A lump like a goose egg filled Ophelia's throat. "Let's just get you back to the tower," she said, "before anything else happens." She kept her spine as straight as a broomstick and stared out the carriage window, into the night.

*   *   *

Prue went with Ophelia willingly, although silently, back to the tower.

Off to the side, the battlement plunged down into a tar pit of darkness. A cold night wind whipped their hair.

Prue unlocked the door with the key Hansel had given her. Through the open door, Ophelia saw the outlines of a stool, a chamber pot, a mattress.

It really was a dungeon.

"Prue," Ophelia said. "I'm sorry. Don't—"

"I thought we was friends, but I guess not. I reckon you want this?" Prue passed over the key and shut the door right in Ophelia's nose.


Ophelia hurried up to her chamber, changed out of her crone's costume, and cleaned off the greasepaint.

Prue being so angry pained Ophelia to be sure. But she couldn't dwell on that just now. Everyone seemed to be lying about *everything*. This puzzle was beginning to have too many threads flapping in the breeze, like a sweater come unraveled. She must do things with great care now, and one thing at a time, or . . . well, what might happen next didn't bear contemplation. She only hoped Prue would have the sense to stay away from Hansel.

Ophelia replaced the tower key on its hook in the kitchen, so the maids could bring Prue her breakfast in the morning. Then she went to check on Mrs. Coop.

No lights burned in her bedchamber, but the drapes hung open and moonlight leaked through. Mrs. Coop was a snoring mound, sprawled diagonally across the twisted bedclothes. Her face seemed oddly radiant. Ophelia crept closer.

*Eek!* She recoiled.

Mrs. Coop's face was paper white, her lips unnaturally dark. She'd used powder and paint to make her face as white as snow and her lips cherry red. Surely the intent had been Snow White, but it was verging on Parisian mime.

The lip paint had smudged across her cheek, giving her the look of some bloodsucking ghoul.

And the bottle of hysteria drops on the table—Ophelia picked it up—was empty.

That was the last of those, then.

But until they wore off, if anyone felt inclined to do Mrs. Coop in, she'd have no way of defending herself.

Ophelia pulled an extra quilt from a cupboard in the boudoir and curled up on the sofa by Mrs. Coop's fireplace.

Just as Ophelia dropped into a black, restless sleep, she thought of Prue, of Hansel. Of fierce Amaryllis, and of Karl's tragic eyes.

"Did you really sleep on that sofa like a pet poodle?" Mrs. Coop said.

Ophelia's eyes flew open, and she struggled upright beneath the quilt. "I beg your pardon, ma'am. I wished to watch over you last night. You did not seem quite well."

Mrs. Coop was sitting up in bed. Her face was a disaster of caked powder and smeared red paint, and her hair was a haystack. "I can't think why that would cause you to hole up in my chamber as though we were Irish piled in a tenement."

Ophelia was on her feet and folding the quilt. "Forgive me, ma'am. Shall I fetch your breakfast?"

"Well, of course! Professor Winkler said he would pay me a visit this morning to apprise me of the progress of his investigation of Snow White's cottage. And Princess Verushka is calling on me this morning, too, the silly cow. Said it was to pay her respects, but it's more likely another of her attempts to cultivate a friendship that is quite out of her league. I must bathe and dress." Mrs. Coop smeared her fingertips across her cheek. "What *is* this on my face?"

While Mrs. Coop received her visitors in the morning room, Ophelia stripped the linens from Mrs. Coop's bed. They were damp and sour smelling with perspiration, and streaked with red face paint. Changing the linens was, strictly speaking, the chore of a chambermaid, but there was no chambermaid at the castle, and Freda had been engrossed in a lurid-looking novel and hazelnut breakfast buns in the kitchen.

Ophelia stuffed the linens into a basket and set off for the laundry.

She was nearing the bottom of the servants' stair when she heard, a long way off, a marrow-chilling scream.

She froze, listening. Another scream, coming from somewhere in the upper rooms. She dropped the basket and tore up the stairs.

She burst out of the door that led from the servants' stair to the family chambers. There were pounding footsteps.

Katrina was running down the corridor. Her face was a mask of fright, and she clutched at her apron bodice like it was choking her. "*Mein Gott, mein Gott im Himmel!* I cannot go back in there!"

"In where? What is it?"

Katrina stopped, panting through her mouth like a sick animal. "I went to the smoking room to brush the carpets— Frau Holder said I ought to—and—and—*ach*, I am afraid he is dead."

Ophelia felt dizzy. "Who?"

"Karl."

Ophelia stared at her. "In the smoking room?"

"*Ja*—but I cannot go back!" Katrina's hand, still clasping her bodice, shook. Her finger was still wrapped in gauze.

"Go to the kitchens and send someone for the doctor."

"He shall not need a doctor. Not ever again."

"Well, then, send for the police."

Ophelia went to the smoking room by herself. Her spine prickled. But what if Karl was only ill? He'd need help.

The door was ajar. Karl was seated, slumped over a table with his face on his arm. He wore his green footman's livery, and the balding back of his head was neatly combed.

Ophelia forced herself to approach.

She couldn't see his face, but one touch at his wrist assured her that he was dead as a doornail.

A delicate, gold-rimmed teacup sat on the table at his elbow. Inside the teacup was a deep brown liquid. It was too reddish to be coffee, too murky looking to be tea.

Ophelia leaned forward and sniffed it. It smelled of twigs and dirt, and also of mold.

She frowned, took another sniff.

It smelled like nothing so much as . . . mushrooms.

"I heard a scream," a man said.

Ophelia jumped back from the teacup. Wilhelm, the second footman, stood in the doorway. His eyes were as big as dinner plates.

"I think he's been poisoned," Ophelia said.


There were a few minutes of calm. Then the castle burst into a tizzy like an overturned wasp's nest.

Ophelia lingered by the bells in the corridor outside the kitchen, waiting for Mrs. Coop to ring for her and trying to stay out of the way. A weeping Katrina was being consoled by Freda in the kitchen, Cook was searching for Hansel out in the gardens, and Wilhelm had gone to break the news to Mrs. Coop, Smith, and Amaryllis. Old Matilda was missing from her customary chimney corner.

The village doctor came and went, and then the village constable.

Mrs. Coop never rang. Ophelia loitered in the kitchen. She thought of making herself some tea but, remembering the weird mushroom brew in Karl's cup, changed her mind.

Presently, Hansel, pale and stricken, sprinted through the kitchen.

He'd be heading to his dead father's side. How terrible that she had suspected him! He was innocent, a victim. Surely.

Ophelia hugged her own elbows. This storybook castle was starting to feel like one of Freda's gothic horror novels.

* * *

Prue lay curled up on her mattress in the tower. Cherry pies and gingersnaps cavorted with flapjacks and bacon in her head.

No one had come with her breakfast tray today. She didn't know why. No one had come to haul her chamber pot away, either. She'd thought about dumping its contents overboard, out the window. Instead, she'd settled on covering it with the washbasin and pushing it to the farthest corner of the tower. And, to take the cake, Freda had carried away Prue's earthen water jug, so she couldn't even send a signal to Ophelia for help.

It was impossible for Prue to sort out all she'd learned about Hansel last night with an empty belly and a sandpaper throat.

What she *did* know was that him being a—what was it?—right, a future count, explained a bundle. The hoity-toity voice, the gentleman's manners, the way he'd gazed so bleakly into that pawnbroker's window. It also explained why he'd been so bent on figuring out who had dug up that skeleton and who had stolen the cottage furnishings. Those things, after a fashion, belonged to him. Or, they had once. What she didn't understand was the scary look in his eyes when he'd said that Mr. Coop had deserved to die.

Or the way she still yearned to see him, despite that scary look.

Around teatime, the police arrived and set up shop in the library.

"Unlock Miss Bright?" Inspector Schubert said, after Ophelia had been shown into the library and demanded that Prue be released. "What a fine joke."

"But she couldn't have killed Karl. She has been locked up in the tower all this time."

"That does not negate the possibility—and, indeed, the probability—that she killed Mr. Coop."

"It's not likely," Ophelia said, "that there are two different murderers stalking the corridors of this castle."

"You shall leave considerations of likelihood to my professional judgment."

Ophelia's shoulders wilted. She'd been sure, in the light of Karl's death, that Prue would be released from suspicion. Especially since Schubert didn't seem to know about Prue's escape to the ball last night or that Karl had really been Count Grunewald.

"Until I have communicated with the crew of the *Leviathan*," Schubert said, "I shall not release her."

Benjamin sneezed into his hankie.

"The crew?" Ophelia asked. "Of the *Leviathan*?"

"The steamship in which you sailed from New York to Southampton. Surely you have not forgotten it."

Forgetting wasn't the problem. If Schubert spoke with the ship's crew, he'd figure out pretty quickly that Prue and Ophelia had been traveling as actresses in Howard DeLuxe's Varieties. That they were liars. Confidence tricksters.

"When I telegraphed the shipping company's offices in England," Schubert said, "they confirmed that you and Miss Bright were indeed on the voyage from New York. But I was not able to ask questions of the crew as the ship had already sailed on a new passage back to New York."

"When"—Ophelia's throat was scratchy—"when will it land?"

"Is that a concern?"

"I merely wish to know when Miss Bright will be released from her unjust bondage."

"I would not, if I were you, Miss Flax, be very certain of her release. Indeed, you might do well to prepare yourself for joining Miss Bright in her tower."

Ophelia's chest felt too tight.

"Miss Flax," Schubert said in a musing tone to Benjamin, "appears worried, does she not?"

"Why should I be worried?" Ophelia was holding on to the table's edge so hard her fingernails went white. "I haven't got a thing to hide."

"No? Mrs. Coop informed me that she took you and Miss Bright on as domestics solely upon the written recommendations addressed to one Lady Cheshingham of Shropshire, England."

"That's correct."

"Yet, oddly, a perusal of Burke's Peerage indicates that there is no such lady. Oh, my, Herr Benjamin. Miss Flax looks as though she's seen a ghost."

Benjamin smirked as he dabbed his pink nose.

"You must've made a mistake." Ophelia stood, but her knees felt like corn puddings. "You ought to check again. Is there anything else?"

"No." Schubert dismissed her with a flicking motion. But as she was walking out the library door, he called after her, "Prepare yourself, Miss Flax. The *Leviathan* shall land in New York in two days' time."

Ophelia trudged up the spiraling stair to Mrs. Coop's chamber. Stony determination settled around her heart. She would *not* let Inspector Schubert get the better of her. She'd find a way to crowbar herself out of this corner if it was the last thing she did.

However: double drat! She'd been so certain Schubert would let Prue out of the tower. In her head she'd already had Prue and herself buttoned into their traveling dresses and their trunks all packed up, even though they hadn't a penny to pay for the train out of Baden-Baden.

But things had gone from bad to worse. When the *Leviathan* anchored in New York and Schubert was able to telegraph its crew, it'd be curtains for Ophelia and Prue. Never mind that they'd had no reason to kill Karl. And did Schubert even know it was probably poisonous mushroom tea that had done Karl in? Because—

Ophelia froze on the stair. Her heart jigged forward.

*Mushrooms.* Of course.

# 21

Ophelia spun around and flew down the stairs to the ground floor of the castle.

She poked her head into the kitchen. Cook and Freda talked softly as they kneaded bread dough at one of the tables. They didn't notice Ophelia.

Good.

She stole down the corridor in the opposite direction, past the scullery and the pantries, and, after a glance over her shoulder, she darted into old Matilda's herb closet.

Late afternoon light seeped through a slitted window. The cramped space was lined from floor to ceiling with shelves, which were cluttered with bottles and earthen jars in all shapes and sizes. Dry plants were strung from the ceiling, and the table that took up all the floor space was strewn with bottles, jars, and loose herbs.

Where to begin? The place was a pigsty.

She closed the door and started rummaging through the shelves.

Nothing was labeled. Matilda probably knew each leaf and twig by sight and smell, and where to forage for them in the woods and hedges. Everything was dusty, though. There were even delicate cobwebs woven into the bunches of hanging flowers and roots.

Ophelia's fingers shook as she squinted and sniffed through bottles and jars, and her ears were pricked for sounds out in the corridor. Dried mushrooms would be easy enough to spot, but if they had been ground into a powder—

Hold your horses.

One corner of the worktable had been cleared of clutter. There, shining in the dim light, was an ornate silver tea strainer, one of those used for tea service upstairs.

The strainer was filled with a brown, mushy substance that—Ophelia leaned her nose close—smelled exactly like the tea Karl had drunk. Twiggy and moldy. It was still wet.

A small, corked glass bottle next to the tea strainer was full of what had to be dried mushrooms.

Ophelia slipped the bottle into the pocket of her gown and tiptoed out of the closet.


"What's this?" Professor Penrose said. He stood in the doorway of his chamber at the inn, staring down at the bottle Ophelia had thrust into his hand. He looked up. "And what are you doing here?"

"Know anything about mushrooms?" Ophelia had had all the puff taken out of her, trotting down the steps from the castle. "Besides that elves use them for umbrellas."

Penrose glanced down the corridor, and then said, "Perhaps you ought to come in. I'll leave the door ajar."

For the first time since Ophelia had bolted from Matilda's herb closet, she realized how crackpot this was. Then again, she was about to become a confirmed confidence slicker and maybe an accused murderess in the bargain. She had bigger fish to fry than a tarnished reputation and an unexplained absence from the castle.

"Thank you," she said. She followed him into the chamber. She also noticed for the first time that Penrose was barefoot, that his white shirt was rumpled, untucked, and open at the throat, and that his hair was tousled.

Her ears scorched.

He closed the door all but a few inches. Then he drew his spectacles from his shirt pocket, put them on, and studied the bottle again. "I assume this has to do with Count Grunewald's death?"

"You've heard."

"Winkler told me. He was at the castle this morning to speak with Mrs. Coop, evidently. Said the count had died."

"Murdered. With mushroom tea." Ophelia told him how she'd discovered the mysterious brew beside Karl, how it had smelled like mushrooms, and how she'd gone to Matilda's herb closet to find evidence.

Penrose frowned. "You suspect Matilda?"

"Maybe. The paring knife that was used to doctor the poisoned apple was just like the one Matilda uses."

"It is within the realm of possibility that Matilda might've wished to kill Coop. But would a mother kill her own son?"

"She was displaced and humiliated by a wastrel son who squandered the ancestral fortune. Besides, she isn't exactly a darling old granny, not as far as I can make out."

"What about Hansel?"

"It's possible. But these are Matilda's mushrooms."

"If it was Matilda, then why today of all days?"

"Maybe she discovered that Karl had taken up with Miss Amaryllis. Hansel could've told her. Hansel just found out about that last night, remember."

"Miss Amaryllis would not make the most appealing of daughters-in-law, true."

"I came here for you to help me. Not laugh at me."

"Miss Flax, I assure you, I am not laughing."

"Your eyes have always got this—this infernal *gleam* to them. Course, you're not the one who's locked up in the tower, like Prue, and you're not the one who's been threatened by the police that you might get locked up, too."

"Schubert said that?"

"Yes."

"He said you killed Count Grunewald?"

"Hinted at it."

"That's absurd." Penrose sank into a flower-painted, ladder-back chair. "It is also more serious than I thought. Did he say why?"

She waited too long to respond.

His mouth tightened.

"No," she said. "He's just bent on Prue and me being murderers for, I suppose, the sake of convenience."

He rolled the bottle of mushrooms thoughtfully between his palms. "You didn't happen to see a tapestry rolled up in the corner of Matilda's little room, did you?" One corner of his mouth twitched north.

"The tapestry? Is that all you care about? Your everlasting moldy old storybook relics?"

It was all starting to fall into place. The mad glint in Penrose's eye whenever the topic of fairy tales came up. The way he so easily did things like pick locks and creep around in the forest. He was some sort of criminal. An antiquities thief, maybe.

"They are not," he said, "all I care about." He paused, watching her. Then he stretched his long legs in front of him, crossed his bare ankles, and clasped his hands behind his head.

He was infuriating.

"But, yes," he said, "I do care about the tapestry, and the relics from the cottage, and the skeleton. I thought I had made that perfectly clear from the outset. And the fact that they have all gone missing seems to indicate that I am not the only one who cares about them."

Ophelia smacked a palm across her mouth.

"What is it?" he said.

"I nearly forgot. Last night, in the gaming rooms— remember those two guards who threw Karl out?"

"Yes."

"Those are the gentlemen I saw stealing the ceiling beam."

Penrose dropped his arms and leaned forward tensely in his chair. "Are you certain?"

"Fair certain. I wouldn't swear on a stack of Bibles about it, but that's more on account of an aversion to swearing."

"Very funny. Miss Flax, don't you see? There is some connection between the gaming establishment and the murders. Herz may be linked to that establishment, too. That would explain why no one at the castle seems to know anything about how he caught us in the wood or about that slipper you dropped in the orchard. And Count Grunewald could've been killed by those guards." Penrose was on his feet.

"What're you going to do—go take them on? I don't know if you noticed, but they were built like brick barns."

Penrose was pulling on boots. "Do you doubt my vigor and brawn?"

"Let's just say I'll include you in my prayers tonight." Ophelia paused. "Wait a minute. You're only keen because you think you're going to get those relics back."

"I admit the idea does considerably brighten the prospect of a run-in with two professional thugs."

"Then I'm going with you."

"Don't be ridiculous."

"I don't trust you to find out about the murders. All you care about are those relics."

"That's a dagger to my heart."

"You'll need help with those two hooligans."

Penrose laughed. "I suppose you could take swings at their kneecaps with your reticule. As a matter of fact, I thought I'd go have a word with the owner of the gaming establishment."

"That's all? Why, that's as safe as Sunday school. It's decided, then." Ophelia opened the door. "I'll go with you. But I won't be able to devise a way to sneak out again until tomorrow morning. Ten o'clock?"

Penrose sighed and sank back down in the chair. "Has anyone ever said no to you?"

She smiled over her shoulder as she left. "Not successfully."

Ophelia went straight back to Mrs. Coop's chamber. The climb up the castle bluff had made her perspire right through her linen chemise, and her bun was coming unraveled.

Mrs. Coop didn't seem to notice. She was slumped at her dressing table in the boudoir.

"Flax. You naughty girl. Naughty. Sneaking off when I need you most." Her words were clumsy, as though her tongue was too big for her mouth.

She'd been at the face paint again, and she wore, instead of mourning black, a girlish afternoon gown of white muslin.

"Allow me, ma'am," Ophelia said, "to assist you with your toilette."

"Ass-assist me? If you'd only whiten my complexion the way you'd promised, I wouldn't have to use this powder. I'd have the real thing. Lovely, young, white skin." She dragged her fingers down her cheeks. "Why are you looking at my gown like that? I'm out of mourning. I've decided. We can't have two of us sulking. Amaryllis is soured by the death of that footman. He wasn't even young. Not handsome." She leaned close to her reflection, her face screwed up. "My complexion is as—as earthy as a bit of shoe leather. Isn't it? Isn't it?"

"Of course it isn't, ma'am. You are ever so careful to avoid the sun—why, you almost never set a foot out of doors, and when you do, well, you've always got your sunbonnet, gloves, a parasol, and—"

"Don't lie to me, Flax! Fix my hair."

Funny. She usually liked to be lied to.

Ophelia reached for the tortoiseshell hairbrush. There was a brown glass bottle beside it.

Dr. Alcott's Celebrated Hysteria Drops.

The bottle was almost full.

"Did the doctor give you some more medicine?" Ophelia began to untangle Mrs. Coop's yellow hair.

"Doctor? That doctor's useless."

"I suppose that's all very well, if one had the foresight to bring medicine with them from America, and—"

"Quit prattling. My complexion is too dark. Fix it. Concoct me one of your preparations with the juice of a lemon or whatever it is you use. And I wish you to make my hair the color of ebony. You are capable of that, aren't you?"

This was as good an opportunity as she was going to get.

"Yes, ma'am," Ophelia said. "I can surely dye your hair. If you'll give me leave to travel to the apothecary's shop in Baden-Baden in the morning, I'll mix you up something nice and strong."

The day came and went in the tower. By the time evening rolled in, Prue was near frantic with hunger and thirst. She tried pacing, to get her mind off things, and talking to the sparrows. She pounded on the door and shouted out the windows. No one came.

She huddled down on the mattress in the dark. She was too hungry and parched to cry, even.

There was a thud on the door.

Prue bolted upright.

"Who is it?" she called.

"Hansel," came the muffled reply.

Crackers. "Just a minute!" She nudged the chamber pot further into the shadows. There was nothing to do about the straw in her hair, the shine on her chin, or the way the ugly brown dress was starting to smell a little ripe.

"What's happening?" she said through the keyhole. "Thought everyone forgot about me."

"May I come in?"

She swallowed. "Course."

Hansel unlocked the door and stepped inside. In the darkness, he seemed bigger than she remembered, and something ferocious thrummed in the air around him. His hair stuck out like a lion's mane.

He shut the door behind him. "Here." He passed her a

jug and a plate of—oh heavenly!—hazelnut buns and sausages. "I was told you were forgotten today."

She grabbed the plate and jug and sank to the stone floor. To heck with Ma's lectures about ladies pretending they hadn't got appetites. She uncorked the jug and took several gulps of cool water.

"We are leaving in the morning," Hansel said.

Prue sputtered on water. "Leaving! What's the matter? Where?"

"My father is dead."

"What?" Prue's first thought was the booze. Maybe Karl drank himself under the daisies after the humiliations of last night.

"Poisoned."

"Like Mr. Coop?"

"Not precisely." Hansel began pacing back and forth, making the tower feel even more like a cage. He described how Katrina had discovered Karl collapsed beside a teacup.

Prue sat still on the floor, the buns and sausages forgotten. Her heart was pumping fast.

"I went through my father's things," Hansel said. He stopped to stare out the iron-barred window. "To see if I might find some clue as to why anyone would kill him. I suspected it might have something to do with his gambling debts. Instead, I found a letter. Addressed to me."

Prue waited.

"He wrote that he feared he might be killed soon, although he did not say by whom. And that he wished to relay to me important knowledge, in the event that he was killed."

Prue licked her lips. "Knowledge?"

"The Grunewalds—my family—are directly descended from Snow White." Hansel turned to face Prue. "I have heard fanciful stories about this since I was a baby. That the original Schloss Grunewald was Snow White's childhood home, and that her son returned here as the first Count Grunewald."

"Snow White was your . . . ancestor?"

"Yes."

"Does your gran know? Matilda?"

"It was from her, I think, that I first heard the stories. She is very distraught. Father was her only child—" Hansel's voice broke up. "In the letter, there was more that I did not know. Father beseeched me to find Snow White's burial place. He wrote that he did not wish to relay, in the letter, precisely why, because he feared his letter would fall into the wrong hands. Only that I should find her tomb before the thieving Americans did. And that if I found her tomb, it would somehow change everything for me and for Grandmother."

Prue considered for a long moment. "So you're heading out to search for . . . Snow White."

"*We* are. You shall come with me."

# 22

❧

"I ain't going anywhere until you explain things out, Hansel," Prue said.

"Very well. Snow White lived in the days of the Holy Roman Empire—"

Prue blinked.

"In the middle ages. Knights in armor and castles and so on."

"Dragons?"

For the first time, Hansel smiled a little. Or maybe it was just a trick of the moonlight. "Sometimes. Snow White's prince was the youngest son of one of the electors of the Rhine Palatinate."

"Pala-what?"

"The elector was a grand nobleman who oversaw a region called a palatine. A bit like a duke in England nowadays. What this means is that Snow White's prince—whatever his name truly was—would have lived in Heidelberg, where I attended university up until last year."

"Heidelberg. That's where Franz is going to college, too."

"Yes. It is about fifty miles from here."

"I still don't know what you're slanting at."

"If Snow White's prince belonged to a powerful Heidelberg family, there is a good possibility that he is buried in Heidelberg, in the Church of the Holy Spirit. Snow White would be buried beside her husband. We must go there to search the tombs. I will take you with me. I do not believe it is safe for you to stay here. Two people have been murdered. More may follow. You are unprotected. Vulnerable."

"Horsefeathers," Prue said. Inside, she was shaking like a leaf. Because of the two murders, yes. But also because Hansel seemed . . . dangerous. Just like Ophelia had said.

And because, notwithstanding Hansel's lion-in-a-cage routine, Prue knew she'd follow him to the ends of creation.

"Why are you doing this?" she whispered.

"I must honor my father's wishes. And if I were to find the tomb, it would point the way to his killer."

"They'll notice I'm gone. Katrina and Freda. When they come with my tray."

"I shall pay Katrina and Freda to keep silent. They will be only too happy to oblige. They are greedy girls, and idle."

Prue had never heard Hansel speak ill of anyone before. He'd changed.

He strode over to her and crouched down. She shrank back. He took her chin between his thumb and forefinger, and lifted her face so he could see into her eyes. "Gather your things together," he said. He stood, opened the door. "I will arrange for us to ride in the greengrocer's cart into Baden-Baden in the morning. We will take the railway from there. I will come for you when the way is clear."

Then he was gone.

As soon as Hansel was gone, Prue polished off the jug of water. She set the empty jug on the windowsill and roosted down to wait for Ophelia.


Ophelia saw the jug. As soon as she was able to peel herself away from Mrs. Coop, she made slam-bang for the tower.

"I know about Karl," Prue said through the door. "Dead."

"Are you—you aren't still cross about last night, are you?"

A pause. "You can't still think Hansel's a murderer, can you?"

Ophelia *could*. A little. Anyone could be a murderer, it seemed.

"Well, this'll go down like medicine," Prue said, "but I'm going to Heidelberg in the morning. With Hansel."

*"What?"*

Prue, breathless and taking lots of hairpins and forks in the road, told Ophelia about Hansel's claims: Karl's letter, the Grunewalds' supposed ancestry, and Hansel's conviction that Snow White lay buried in a church in Heidelberg.

Ophelia rubbed her temples. "Hold it. First of all—Snow White was the Grunewalds' ancestress? You aren't going to start believing this—"

"What if it's true?" Prue's voice was shrill. "Ever stopped to consider that?"

Ophelia thought about it. "No. I haven't."

"Well, why not? Believing Snow White was a real lady, back in them knights-and-castles times, don't mean you need to believe in *magic*."

"Perhaps not magic. But I'd have to believe in the seven dwarves."

"You've *seen* the dwarf bones, Ophelia. With your own eyes. What more do you want?"

What more *did* she want?

Ophelia was suddenly afflicted with unfamiliar—and shockingly impractical—notions creeping into the back of her mind. Unwelcome, these notions were, like tiny intruders sneaking in through a rusted trapdoor. Maybe Professor Penrose was right. Maybe fairy tales were real. Ophelia gave her head a shake.

"Karl's letter," Prue said, "made it out that he was killed because of this tomb of Snow White's. And he mentioned thieving Americans—"

"So, *Mr. Coop's* death had something to do with this tomb, as well," Ophelia said. "According, anyway, to Karl's letter."

"According to common sense!"

Ophelia pressed her lips tight. She didn't wish to give Prue's trip to Heidelberg her stamp of approval. No, she most assuredly did not. But that unraveling-sweater feeling was getting stronger by the hour.

And if Ophelia admitted to herself that maybe, just *maybe*, there was a twinkle of truth to the notion of Snow White being a real lady, well, one thing was blindingly obvious: finding Snow White's tomb, and whatever secrets it held, just might lever Prue and her out of this mess.

"It isn't proper," Ophelia finally said. "You going about with a gentleman without a chaperone." The hypocrisy of that statement made her cheeks warm up.

"Know what *else* isn't proper?" Prue said. "Going to prison."

True enough. True enough.

"Hurry," was all Ophelia could say.


"Have a look at these," Gabriel said to Winkler in the morning. "But you'd better wear gloves." He placed the bottle of mushrooms beside Winkler's coffee cup and lowered himself into the opposite chair in the inn's dining room.

"Allow me to guess," Winkler said. "It is another specimen of fool's gold." He took an enormous bite of a roll that dribbled blueberry jam.

Gabriel poured cream into his coffee. "If I recall rightly, the last specimens of fool's gold proved to be genuine."

Winkler twiddled sausage-like fingers. "A rarity, professor, a rarity."

"Those," Gabriel said, "are dried mushrooms. I wonder if you could—since you are, after all, a trained chemist—determine if they are a poisonous variety."

"Easily done. I know all the wild mushrooms in the *Schwarzwald*."

And every edible one, too, no doubt.

"Speaking of poison," Winkler said, "Inspector Schubert

told me that the footman who died in the castle yesterday was poisoned. I had my money on apoplexy. The man was red in the face."

"As a matter of fact, that's what intrigues me so about these mushrooms. I wish to know if they could have been used to poison him."

Winkler guffawed. "Poisoned by mushrooms! *Mein Gott*, what a folkloric way to die! These peasants are true to the woodland soil to the end, are they not?"

Evidently, Winkler didn't know that Karl had been the disgraced Count Grunewald. Gabriel wouldn't tell him just yet.

Winkler forked up a rasher of bacon. "I shall examine your mushrooms with pleasure," he said.

Ophelia helped Mrs. Coop breakfast and bathe—she'd had another difficult night under the influence of the hysteria drops—and then dashed up to the lumber room to put on her disguise in preparation for her trip to Baden-Baden with the professor. True, Mrs. Coop had given her leave to go to the apothecary's shop, but a disguise would come in handy should she cross paths with Inspector Schubert.

Ophelia fretted as she buttoned up her gentleman's shirt. Had she erred, allowing Prue to go off with Hansel? No. Life was like a trapeze act: you had to take risks or the show never got off the ground. Only thing was—Ophelia shrugged on her waistcoat—in this case there was no safety net below. Only the prospect of prison. Or worse.

She crouched on the rolled-up rug and inspected herself in the tarnished wardrobe mirror. She'd use a double helping of glue on her muttonchops today. The strain of them threatening to come undone last time had been awful.

As she bent to rummage in her theatrical case for the glue, something shiny caught her eye. It was the corner of the rolled-up rug, just barely jutting out. It appeared to be woven with gold thread.

She hadn't noticed *that* before.

She stood up and, with great effort, because the rug was enormously long and heavy, pushed it like a log to unroll it.

Holy Moses.

The Baden-Baden railway station was all abuzz. Folks with harried faces dashed hither and thither; peddlers yelled about rolls, fruits, and newspapers; and everyone chattered too quickly in German, Russian, English, and Italian. A black train hulked and hissed alongside the platform, ready to go.

Prue and Hansel slipped through the crowd. Neither of them carried a bag or a bundle. Prue had brought nothing but the clothes on her back and the ruby comb, stuffed in her bodice. She reckoned they looked like a couple of servants on their day off, him in his shabby clothes and her in her brown dress, knitted shawl, and the close straw bonnet Hansel had given her to hide her face.

Maybe they even looked like sweethearts, with her shoulder pressed tight against his. Prue's belly was full of knots, though. Probably on account of the fact that she was traipsing off to unknown parts with a handsome count who had a barbarous glint in his eye.

Still, it felt good to be out of the tower again. Maybe if she left the castle and Baden-Baden behind, all the trouble she was in might vanish in a puff of smoke.

They plowed their way across the platform, towards their railway carriage.

All of a sudden, something caught Prue's eye. A dark suit of clothes, shiny shoes, a black bowler hat. Her heart tripped over itself.

*"It's Franz."* She elbowed Hansel.

Hansel didn't hear. He was too busy trying to squeeze between a man with a push-broom moustache and a girl holding a basket of apples.

Prue craned her neck around the girl's apple basket. It was Franz, all right. He didn't appear to have seen them. He bent to flick something off his trouser leg. As he did so, his jacket fell open and there was a flash of red, black, and white. That striped bit of ribbon again, wrapped around his belt. Then the crowd closed, and he disappeared from view.

Prue had not once mentioned Franz to Ophelia. Explaining things about Franz would surely have made Hansel seem bad in Ophelia's eyes. But . . . what if Franz had something to do with the murders?

Hansel helped Prue up into the railway carriage. It was bursting with babies, wicker cages of ducks, and roly-poly women in kerchiefs. Third class.

Soon, the train was chugging along through picture-postcard hills, and Prue was munching on the shelled walnuts Hansel had bought for her at the station. She asked him about the ribbon on Franz's belt. "Is it some kind of German fashion? Because American men don't ever wear ribbon, unless they're soldiers or something. Or somebody died."

Hansel's brow furrowed. "You are certain you saw this ribbon?"

"Saw it twice, clear as day."

"With three stripes."

"Red, white, and black."

Hansel stared out the window, still scrunching his brow. "It sounds like one of the symbols used to identify a member of a *Studentverbindung*."

"What's that?"

"About fifty years ago, many student societies were formed at European universities. Secret societies, with membership oaths, intricate—even occult—rituals, and such. They still exist to this day. Mostly they are, I suspect, an excuse for young men to enjoy glass after glass of beer. Still, they are quite secretive, and one must be initiated into them."

"Did you belong to one? When you were studying at college?"

"No. I was too occupied with my books."

Since Hansel was being loose-lipped, Prue went on and asked, "Why is Franz always going on about you being reduced in circumstances?"

Hansel rubbed his eye sockets and sighed. "Franz's family were servants at the castle—at Schloss Grunewald. Franz's father was my father's valet, and even though Franz was my boyhood playmate, he was also in training to become *my* valet. But when Father ruined our fortune and so many servants were forced to leave, Franz went to make his way in the world."

"You traded places, then."

Hansel nodded. "After Franz left the castle, he started out working as a croupier in the gaming rooms in Baden-Baden. That is when he began to take on those gentlemanly airs."

"There's nothing wrong with coming up in the world," Prue said, "but Franz carries on about it. Never can resist a dig at you. There's something just not—not *right* about him."

"I agree. Little remains of the gentle boy I used to play with. I worry what he has done to fund his gentleman's habits."

Prue paused her walnut chewing. There it was again. That haunted gleam in Hansel's eyes.

Did he think Franz had something to do with his pa's death?

"I cannot," Hansel said, "envision Franz as a member of a *Studentverbindung*. He is not really the sort that is attracted to those societies. Although he did seem rather drunk when we encountered him that evening in Baden-Baden."

"Funny you say that, because I didn't reckon he was really, truly soaked that night. He was only playacting."

Hansel met her eyes. "For what purpose?"

"Don't know. To cover something up, I'd wager." Prue crunched down on another walnut.

"I found the tapestry," Ophelia told Professor Penrose, just as soon as she'd hopped into the hired carriage in front of the inn.

"You found it! Where?"

"In a sort of attic lumber room, all rolled up. You didn't tell me what a whopper it'd be."

"And you saw the design? Of the seven dwarves marching with their shovels and pickaxes?"

"That's just the border—the same group of seven dwarves goes around and around the edge—at least, where it isn't so faded you can't tell what's there."

"And the middle?"

"It's a beauty, and colorful." The tapestry had reminded Ophelia of the fanciful theatrical set of Howard DeLuxe's Varieties' *A Damsel in Distress*. But she couldn't tell Penrose that. He had already thrown her too many suspicious, penetrating glances. "Green-wooded mountains, a river, a castle, men on horseback, and hunting dogs. Deer and bears."

"Typical medieval motifs." Penrose slouched back against the carriage seat.

"Don't look so disappointed. There was storybook gimcrackery, too."

He lifted an eyebrow.

"You're hiding your excitement," she said, "about as well as a little boy on Christmas morning."

"Tell me."

"Fairies," she said. "A dragon." She paused for dramatic effect.

"Enjoying yourself?"

"Very much." She smiled. "Snow White's cottage in the trees. Snow White herself."

"On the tapestry?"

"Yes."

"I must examine it," Penrose said, almost to himself.

"There was also something much more peculiar. In the background, behind the castle, the cottage, and the trees was something, well, I couldn't make out if it was a mountain or a sort of man's face. Near the top, to the left of the castle. It looked more like a face the more I backed away, but seeing as it was spread out on the floor, and all wrinkled, I couldn't be exactly sure."

"A face or a mountain?"

"That's the thing. I couldn't say."

They rolled along for a few minutes. Ophelia had been

chewing over whether or not to tell Professor Penrose about Prue and Hansel going off searching for Snow White's tomb. She knew the professor would be intrigued. That was the problem—he'd be *too* intrigued. And she also dreaded anyone telling her *I told you so*. Still, he was helping her out. She ought to come clean.

"Professor," she said. "There's something else. Something about a tomb." She told him all she knew.

"Of course," Penrose said, when she'd finished. His eyes glowed in that special way. "The Church of the Holy Spirit. It is a wonder I did not think of it before. She must have married one of the electors of the Rhine Palatinate."

How did he *know* these things? It was too annoying by half. "Don't tell me you're itching to traipse off to Heidelberg now," Ophelia said.

Penrose quirked a corner of his lips. "I'd be lying if I said no. But we've somewhat more pressing business to attend to today."

"I meant to tell you," Gabriel said to Miss Flax, once they were seated in the tearoom at the *Conversationshaus*, "your British gentleman's disguise is, if possible, still more convincing than the last time. Your side-whiskers seem . . . fuller. Grayer."

She laughed. "I'm most obliged."

Jesting helped to take Gabriel's mind off all that Miss Flax had told him in the carriage. The tapestry, found. Snow White's burial place, perhaps identified. He burned to simply *go*. To see for himself, to touch. But discerning whether or not the gaming establishment was tied to the murders was, at this point, essential to proving Miss Flax's and Miss Bright's innocence.

The tearoom was filled with swaying palms, tall hat plumes, and tinkling china. After they ordered coffee, they asked their waiter where they might find the owner of the gaming establishment.

The waiter's eyes bulged. "The owner? Herr Ghent?"

"Yes," Gabriel said. "You are surprised."

The waiter's gaze shifted. "I have never met him. He does not—we do not speak to him directly. I am not certain that even the manager has made his acquaintance."

"And where is the manager?"

The waiter cringed, as though Gabriel were waving dentist's pliers before his nose.

Gabriel slipped a coin onto his tray. "For your trouble."

The waiter jerked his head towards the corner of the tearoom, where a man in a waistcoat and glossy moustache hovered over a table of ladies. "There." He rushed away.

When the manager drew near, Gabriel signaled to him.

"Is everything to your satisfaction, sir?" the manager said. He wrung his gloved hands.

"Everything except, well, a rather delicate matter has emerged, which involves the gaming rooms."

The manager's face froze in a humorless grin. "Yes?"

"And I wished to speak with Herr Ghent of the matter."

"Herr Ghent does not speak to public persons regarding"—he cleared his throat—"*accounts*."

"It is not a matter of debt."

"One of Herr Ghent's famous wagers, then?"

Intriguing. He'd have to bluff his way through this.

Gabriel scratched his temple. "I wasn't aware that Herr Ghent's wagers were famous. I was under the impression that only I knew of them."

"Only you? No, no, no. Last week, sir, he forgave a Florentine viscount an immense debt on a single round of roulette. The gentleman stood to lose his ancestral villa."

"Indeed."

"Herr Ghent enjoys the excitement, you see, and he can afford to lose. I suspect"—the manager lowered his voice, leaned forward—"it might afford him pleasure at times, too."

"Pleasure?"

The manager's eyes were steely, now. "To see desperate people lose everything."

"Ah." This explained, perhaps, how Count Grunewald

had become so mired in debt to the gaming establishment. "Well, at any rate, I must speak with him."

The manager straightened, all business again. "I simply cannot—"

"Perhaps this"—Gabriel extracted a small card from a case in his breast pocket—"will vouch for my sincerity."

The manager took the card between his thumb and fore-finger, as though it were soiled. But as he read the card, his face wreathed into smiles. "I apologize, sir. I was not aware. Please forgive me."

"Herr Ghent's office is on the premises?"

"Indeed, indeed. On the third floor—there is a long corridor at the top of the stair. At the end, go left, and follow that corridor to the end, where there is a set of doors. That is where you should knock." He reverently placed the card back in Gabriel's hand.

# 23

*ﾟﾟﾟ∞ﾟﾟﾟ*

"Allow me to take a gander at your magical card," Ophelia said.

"I'm afraid not." Gabriel withdrew the card case from his jacket.

Before he could put the card away, Ophelia leaned across the tea table and plucked it from his fingers.

"Not very gentleman-like of you," he said.

"It's awful easy to slip out of character."

The card's elegant script read, *Gabriel Augustus Penrose, Fifth Earl of Harrington.*

"Well, aren't you grand," Ophelia said. "Is this a forgery?"

Penrose sipped his tea.

"It's not?" Ophelia stared down at the card and then back at Gabriel. "Earl of Harrington? You've been lying about being a professor? I knew you were a sham! As soon as—"

"I am a professor. And an earl. I prefer the former occupation immensely, however, and I'm more than a little embarrassed to have wheeled out my title. But we must see Ghent, and a title does come in handy in a pinch."

Ophelia was deflating like a squashed sofa cushion. It had been one thing to go gadding around with a professor of crinkumcrankumology. But it was quite another to gad around with an earl.

Poppycock, Ophelia Flax. When did a Yankee ever quiver before an English blue blood? He was still just a man. She'd seen his bare feet, too.

"We've not a moment to lose," Penrose said. He paid for their tea.

They made their way out to the foyer and up a grand staircase.

The third floor's wide, carpeted corridor was hushed. No one was about. They found the set of doors the manager had mentioned, and Gabriel rapped twice.

There was a long silence. Then, a rustling. At last, a man opened the doors just a crack. He was small and papery-looking, and the eye he put up to the crack was blue and watery, with a purplish pouch beneath.

"What is it?" he said in German. His voice was creaky.

"Good afternoon," Gabriel said. "I am Lord Harrington, and this is my assistant, Mr. Beals. I wonder if I might have a brief word with Herr Ghent?"

The eye bulged. "Who sent you here?" He now spoke English.

"I come of my own accord."

"But who told you where to find this door?"

The manager in the tearoom would be out on his ear if he were betrayed. "I deduced it."

"Deduced?" The eye bulged still more. "Herr Ghent does not accept visitors."

"You are his—secretary?"

"Correct. But he does not accept visitors."

Gabriel tried to peer over the secretary's head, through the crack. "He's here, then?"

"No. No, he is not here. He is afflicted with rheumatism. He visits the thermal baths every afternoon for his cure."

There were footsteps behind them. Ophelia glanced over her shoulder; Gabriel heard her gasp. He turned.

The two guards. They drew closer. He saw the one's heavy cleft chin, the other's black slash of eyebrow.

His belly clenched for battle.

But the guards' faces remained impassive as they arrived at the door.

They didn't recognize them from two evenings ago, then.

The papery little secretary opened the door to admit the guards. "Go away," he said to Gabriel and Ophelia. "Do not come back."


"If Herr Ghent is at the thermal baths," Ophelia said, once they were outside on the steps of the *Conversationshaus*, "you might go there and speak to him directly."

"That'd be more efficient, I agree, than attempting to circumvent those guards."

They crossed the white gravel drive, towards the promenade. The colorful gowns and parasols of the strolling ladies stood out like airy confections against a rich green backdrop of shade.

"I believe," Penrose said, "if we follow the promenade to the end, and then climb one of those cobbled streets that go up the hillside, we'll find the baths."


The newly constructed Friederichsbad was a stately stone building halfway up the hill, with large, arching windows and Romanesque caryatids. Miss Flax stayed behind on a bench on the expanse of lawn in front of the baths, and Gabriel went inside.

In the lofty foyer, a porter greeted him with a bow. He was ushered to a table at which sat a fat lady whom Gabriel paid for a ticket. He was led by a serving man down a long marble corridor to a private chamber. There was a red sofa, a washstand, a gilt mirror, and a velvet curtain.

"Bath's behind the curtain," the serving man said. He turned to leave.

"I beg your pardon—"

The man turned back. "Yes?"

"Have you any idea if Herr Ghent is here at the baths?"

Something unreadable flickered across the man's eyes.

Good lord. Was every last soul in Baden-Baden tasked with protecting Ghent's privacy? Perhaps that wasn't surprising. Ghent was surely one of the most powerful men in a town clogged with the titled, the influential, and the wealthy.

"I know," Gabriel said, "that Herr Ghent suffers from rheumatism, and I am a sufferer myself."

"Not a very bad case," the man said. His eyes traveled with unmasked suspicion up and down Gabriel's frame.

"It's worse than it looks. I am particularly pained in my knees. My doctor, who once treated Herr Ghent in London, suggested I speak to him in person about the efficacy of the waters here."

"Everyone here has rheumatism. That is why they come."

"My doctor said Herr Ghent was the man to speak to."

"Very well." The serving man's face was unreadable. "I shall make inquiries and return presently."

Gabriel investigated behind the velvet curtains while he waited. There was a large white bathtub sunk into the marble floor, filled with steaming water. Snowy towels were stacked beside it.

Several minutes later, there was a thud on the door.

Gabriel swung the door wide, expecting to see the serving man again. Instead, there stood an enormous gentleman, built rather like a prizefighter, with a neck as wide as his bald head and a water barrel of a chest. He wore a tailored black suit of capacious dimensions.

"Yes?" Gabriel ignored the menacing look in the man's eye.

By way of answering, the man pushed into the chamber. He slammed the door behind him and thrust his face right into Gabriel's. His breath stank of rancid meat; it was all Gabriel could do to stand his ground.

"I suspect," Gabriel said, "you have the wrong chamber. This is—"

"You have been asking for Herr Ghent."

"Well, yes. I desired to converse with him briefly regarding a matter of mutual interest. You aren't Ghent, are you?"

"Do not be coy." The man rammed his smashed nose still closer—if that was possible—to Gabriel's. "If you ask about Herr Ghent again, or enter his gaming rooms, or even speak his name, you will regret it."

What was so important about protecting this Ghent fellow?

"Do you understand?" the man said.

"Quite. Although one might inquire why."

"You know why."

"Do I?"

"Prying where you do not belong." He grabbed Gabriel's lapel, twisted. "Meddling in business that you do not understand." He shoved Gabriel against the wall.

Gabriel resisted the urge to free himself. The man had an ogre's strength, and going about with a broken arm or a black eye was not a savory prospect.

He needed to keep him talking. Perhaps bluffing would do the trick.

"I don't understand the connection between the murders at the castle and the gaming establishment."

*"What do you know?"* the ogre roared.

Ah. So that *was* it. This was all, somehow, about the castle, rather than simply having to do with the lately departed Count Grunewald and his gambling debts.

He only needed the ogre to give him some clue.

"I confess I do not know very much," Gabriel said, "but I shall soon enough."

"You must not! Herr Ghent will have our heads!"

"Your heads," Gabriel said, eyeing the ogre's massive bald dome. "No simple task."

The ogre's hand fell from Gabriel's lapel.

What sort of monster was Ghent, if the thought of his displeasure could make *this* one kowtow?

"The head." The ogre clenched and unclenched his teeth. "Do you know where the head is?"

He'd gone off his onion. Dangerous in a gentleman of those proportions.

"I don't," Gabriel said, "know about any heads."

"You do not?" The ogre appeared, for a second, as relieved as a child who'd been reassured of a biscuit. But he abruptly reassumed his menacing air. "If you search for Herr Ghent again or poke your nose in business that is not yours, I will kill you."

"I don't doubt it," Gabriel said, adjusting his spectacles.

The ogre crashed out of the bathing chamber.

"I don't know if Herr Ghent was really in there, steeping his rheumatism away," Penrose said to Ophelia, as they hurried away from the Friederichsbad, "or if being sent there was a setup."

"It had to be a setup," Ophelia said. "The two guards at the *Conversationshaus* must've recognized us. Otherwise, how would that roughneck have known you were a meddler?"

"You say that as though it were a fact."

"You *are* a meddler—and he threatened you. He threatened to kill you."

"Whoever Ghent is, he's got his henchmen cowed. Although I must say this particular specimen wasn't up to scratch in the intellect department. In fact, I suspect he was a bit mad. Said something about finding heads or some such rot."

Ophelia stopped on the steep, cobbled street in front of a florist's shop. "What did you say?"

"You're quite rosy under your whiskers."

She gave him a stern look.

Penrose smiled. "He said, 'Do you know where the head is?' or something to that effect—after, mind you, we'd been discussing Ghent having *his* head if he—"

"But don't you see? The head! They're looking for the head!"

"I fail to see your point."

"On the tapestry. Remember I told you about the peculiar thing that looked a little like a mountain but also like a man's face?"

"Good God." Gabriel shook his head. "That's it. For some reason, Ghent's guards are searching for that head."

"You mean, they're searching for the tapestry."

"Perhaps." His eyes shone. "But if the castle depicted on that tapestry were a representation of Schloss Grunewald and its surrounding environs, would it be unreasonable to surmise that there is also an actual mountain, somewhere out there in the woods, that resembles in some way a man's face?"

"But the castle on the tapestry didn't look like Schloss Grunewald. It looked more, well, square. Plainer."

"The *schloss* was rebuilt about fifty years ago. That tapestry is much, much older."

"Are you saying that the tapestry is some kind of . . . map?"

"Precisely."

"Herz," Ophelia said.

Penrose met her eyes. "Yes. He's guarding that mountain."

"Maybe he works for Herr Ghent. What do you reckon is out there?"

"That I cannot say, although my suspicion would be some sort of site or relic that solves the puzzle of the cottage and the skeleton."

"Not," Ophelia said, "Snow White's favorite picnicking spot?"

He lifted a shoulder.

She pursed her lips. Was she, Ophelia Flax, practical to her marrow, really entertaining the notion that that cottage had belonged to Snow White? That the skeleton was not some hoax, but an important relic?

She pictured the *Leviathan* foaming across the Atlantic towards New York. Inspector Schubert's slippery sneers. Prue—now ranging heaven only knew where, doing who knew what.

Beggars couldn't be choosers.

"Let's go find the mountain," she said. "I saw the tapestry, and Herr Ghent's guards haven't, so we've got a head start."

"Gone are the days when you thought relic-hunting was a waste of time, then?"

"Mrs. Coop gave me leave today. She sent me to purchase ingredients for black hair coloring at the apothecary's shop."

"She means to dye her hair black?"

Ophelia told him about the hysteria drops and how Mrs. Coop seemed to fancy, at least when she was under the influence of the medicine, that she was Snow White. "For once," she said, starting off down the street, "I'm not sneaking around, and I mean to make the most of it."

"I suspect," Gabriel said, having gained her side in a few strides, "I ought to save my breath regarding the matter of you not participating in risky excursions? We must go into the wood, you understand. I assume you haven't forgotten Herz's rifle? His traps?"

"Nightmares of them every night." Miss Flax nestled her bowler down on her head.

"And we needn't discuss the impropriety of a young, delicate lady elbowing through the brush?"

"I'm not delicate. And you may have noticed that I've got on a pair of sturdy tweed britches and a pair of boots that would be equal to an expedition in deepest Africa."

"Yes. I won't inquire where you got those."

"Good."

She tossed him what he would've sworn, under any other circumstances, was a coquettish smile.

For God's sake. Why must she always be got up like a gentleman pheasant-shooter? He had the disconcerting urge to rip off her wig and whiskers. Perhaps tear off that cravat for good measure.

\* \* \*

By the time Prue and Hansel's train puffed and squealed into Heidelberg, it was afternoon. Prue's spine felt like a clothespin bent the wrong way.

They stepped down onto the mobbed platform in a swirl of steam. The sky had gone pewter-colored, threatening rain. Everyone was shoving, and Prue stumbled. Hansel caught her hand to steady her. Then he didn't let go.

It felt nice. But her palm was sweaty, the pimple on her nostril was starting to throb again, and she was still in the ugly brown dress. She glanced up at Hansel. He didn't seem to give a fig about how she looked. In fact, it didn't seem like he was thinking about her at *all*. His dark brows, under his woolen cap, were drawn together; his gold-stubbled jaw was locked; and his eyes were fixed on the pavement. Even though he was in his gardener's clothes—work boots, brown trousers, loose white shirt, and a patched homespun jacket—he strode along with an air of grandeur, Prue's hand fast in his grip.

They walked like that all the way out of the station and into the streets of the town.

Heidelberg was snug in a steep gorge that billowed with greenery. It stretched along a river in a network of streets and stone buildings with tile roofs. A huge, ruined castle sprawled above the town. The ruin looked haunted, with empty arch-ways and crumbly towers, especially under the roily sky.

They followed a twisting main street, bustling with shoppers and carts and, several blocks in, college boys with knapsacks and books tucked under their arms. The rain started with a few fat drops.

The only thing amiss, if you forgot for a minute about pimples and greasy hair and sweaty hands, was the tickle between Prue's shoulder blades.

Just like someone was following them.

# 24

After a brief stop at an apothecary's shop in Baden-Baden, Ophelia and Professor Penrose rode the hired carriage back to Schilltag under a glowering gray sky. By the time they reached Gasthaus Schatz, a misty sideways rain had started. They left the carriage at the inn's stables, made their way on foot to the old mill track, and plunged into the forest.

It was still afternoon, but by the time they had turned off the forest track and onto a footpath, a dense gloom had settled under the trees. They went carefully, keeping an eye out for traps and keeping their eyes and ears open for signs of Herz.

It was raining harder, too. Drops fell from the brim of Ophelia's bowler, making it hard to see.

Maybe that accounted for her tingling unease.

"I recall," Penrose said over his shoulder, "that this path opens out, presently. This is the same way I came when I followed Herz. We're gaining elevation, and the trees will thin out when we near the top. It was dark then, but I expect we'll have a vista of sorts today, despite the rain."

Ophelia staunchly followed. The rain pounded harder, and water seeped through the seams of her tweed jacket.

A sizzle of lightning made the forest white. There was a boom of thunder.

Ophelia jumped. She lost her footing on the muddy path and was about to pitch face-first into the brush, when Penrose grabbed her arm and steadied her.

"Are you all right?" Penrose said. His voice sounded far away. Now the rain was coming down in blinding buckets.

"I think so," she called.

"We ought to turn back."

"It's just a cloudburst. It'll let up soon."

"We could return tomorrow."

She shook her head. Tomorrow would be too late. The *Leviathan* was scheduled to anchor then.

She caught a flash of motion out of the corner of her eye. She turned her head. First, she saw nothing but huge, black fern fronds bobbing under raindrops.

It had only been a bird. Or a squirrel.

She was about to turn back to Penrose when she saw the white, shining orb of an eye, just between two fern fronds, ten paces away.

The eyeball was staring back.

Her heart, she was fair certain, stopped beating.

"Professor," she whispered. "*Look.*" She couldn't move her neck—it seemed to have seized up like a piece of rusty machinery—so she gestured with her eyes.

Penrose's eyes widened—he'd seen the eyeball—and his entire body stiffened.

There was an electric pause. Gabriel's heart made two mallet strokes against his ribs. He reached into his breast pocket, wrapped his fingers around the cold handle of his revolver.

Yellow light exploded from the ferns, accompanied by a sharp crack. Then the *thunk* of a bullet lodging itself in the tree trunk just behind his left ear.

"*Run,*" he hissed.

Miss Flax stood stupefied. He grabbed her hand and pulled her across the path and into the trees on the other side. They stumbled forward, wading through shadows, wet branches clinging to their legs.

There was another crack of gunfire behind them and a searing splatter through the bushes to their right. Gabriel pushed Miss Flax behind a wide tree trunk and stepped beside her. He held his revolver up beside his face.

"Where did that gun come from?" she whispered.

He made a one-eyed glance round the tree trunk. "You sound put out. Oughtn't you be relieved?"

"*Relieved?* Relieved to be caught in the middle of some kind of Wild West shoot-out?"

Gabriel strained his eyes for any hint of motion in the streaming shadows. "Better in the midst of a shoot-out than trembling like a doomed hare, don't you think?"

"You could've told me you were armed."

Gabriel spied the black forms of two men, dashing from tree trunk to tree trunk, several yards away.

"Ghent's guards," he said.

"What? I thought it was Herz, come back for a second helping. This is even worse. Let's get out of here." She turned.

He turned her back round. "Don't do anything impulsive. They're watching for us. If you break into a run, I don't doubt they'd shoot you in the back."

Just then, a bullet slammed his shoulder. He doubled forward, crouching in pain at the roots of the tree.


Ophelia gasped and dropped down beside him. "What happened?"

"I've been shot." His voice was taut with agony. "Hurry. They're coming." He was crawling into the dripping underbrush.

"But—"

"For God's sake, no arguing this time!"

Ophelia shut her mouth and crawled after him. They were inside a tangle of some kind of berry bushes. Thorns ripped her sleeves, and fallen branches pierced her knees.

Deeper and deeper they went.

Crawling through a thicket. In the Black Forest. *How* had she gotten here? She couldn't exactly remember.

After a few minutes of crawling, the brambles opened out again. Penrose stopped, touched his shoulder, and winced.

"You're bleeding!" Ophelia said. The shoulder of his jacket had a spreading dark stain.

"Only a flesh wound."

"That's a lot of blood."

He gazed out into the clearing. "Can you ride?"

"Ride?" Was he delirious from his wound?

"A horse."

She poked her head around his shoulder. Out in the clearing were two saddled horses tethered to a bush. "It's too good to be true."

"They must belong to the guards."

"I don't care who they belong to." Ophelia was already scrambling to her feet.

"I take it that means you know how to ride?"

"Course I do."

They crept towards the horses.

"Those aren't ladies' saddles," Penrose said.

"Never did like those silly contraptions."

The horses eyed them. One of them snorted.

"Hi there, girl," Ophelia said to the black horse. "Pretty girl." She untied the bridle from the bush and mounted, throwing her leg over like a boy. The horse began to prance.

"You American girls," Penrose said, "are flush with talent." He mounted, grimacing with pain.

"Which way should we go?"

"Back to the village. This way." He rode towards the far edge of the clearing.

Another gunshot rang out, just behind them. Ophelia's horse whinnied and reared up. She struggled to keep her seat, leaning forward against the saddle horn. The horse took off.

Everything was a blur of black branches and tree trunks as the horses streaked through the forest. Icy raindrops slashed her cheeks.

Penrose was somewhere off to the side—she could hear his horse's hoofbeats, the crashing brush.

Then, with a sickening chill creeping over her, Ophelia realized that there were other hoofbeats, other crashing sounds, somewhere behind her.

She stole a peep over her shoulder.

She saw a horse charging up. The black outline of a man. A thumping big chin. A gun.

That guard was going to kill her.

Her horse was beginning to tire. Its flanks were hot and frothy, its motions less elastic.

"Come on, girl," she yelped, nudging the horse with her boot heels.

It was now or never. Soon the guard would be too close for her to give him the slip.

Ophelia had been a trick rider in her circus days. She and two other girls had paraded around in frilly pink tutus and satin slippers, standing on the backs of horses that had big bows around their necks. She'd never decided if all the applause had been for the balancing feat or for the view of the girls' stems.

She made her horse careen to the right. Up ahead, she spied a low-hanging branch. She pulled her feet from the stirrups and made her way to a crouch, still clinging to the saddle horn.

As the horse neared the low-hanging branch, she stood shakily. Just before she lost her balance and pitched sideways, she grabbed the branch.

The horse galloped away without her.

Up ahead, beyond the retreating horse, Penrose rode by. He turned his head, saw her dangling from the branch. His face registered utter disbelief before he disappeared.

Ophelia didn't have time to laugh. Using her last fragments of energy, she managed to drag herself up into the crook of the tree. She clung to the wet trunk and held her breath as the guard raced past beneath her in pursuit of her horse.

It had worked.

Penrose could fend for himself.

* * *

Ophelia huddled in the tree, panting, for ten minutes or so before Penrose returned on foot. He held his bloodstained shoulder.

He stopped at the base of her tree. "Are you quite all right up there, Miss Flax?"

What a scream she must look, crouched in a tree in a three-piece suit. Like an organ grinder's monkey.

"Oh, yes, I'm fine." She tried to sound nonchalant.

"Good."

"And you? Your shoulder, I mean."

"I'll survive." He scratched his temple. "I won't ask how you learned to leap from the back of a galloping horse into a tree, by the way. I'm under the distinct impression that such questions won't get me anywhere."

"They won't."

"Right. Well. If we can make it down to that stream-bed"—he pointed—"we might be able to take shelter beneath the cliff on the opposite side before the guards find us again."

Ophelia squinted through the sheets of rain. She saw a long, jagged crack, half hidden by ferns, on the side of a cliff.

She edged down the tree trunk. Thank the heavens she was wearing trousers.

She made it to the bottom.

He grinned.

Her bushy eyebrows and both of her muttonchops had come unglued in the rain—she felt them dangling—and the greasepaint she'd applied to make herself middle-aged and manly was streaming down her face.

She smeared it out of her eyes and followed Penrose down the slope, across the stream, and up a slippery bank. They entered the mouth of the cave.

Inside the cave, the rain was muted. It was dark and icebox cold, but at least it was dry. It smelled of earth and tree roots.

Ophelia tore off her soaked bowler hat and wig, loosened the drenched cravat, and undid her top shirt button to get the wet fabric away from her throat. Her hair, which had been pinned up beneath her wig, tumbled down around her shoulders.

Penrose was watching her.

Wondering, probably, what he was doing in such close quarters with a clown.

Her eyes adjusted to the dimness. The cave was widest at its mouth, and the rock ceiling sloped back to meet, somewhere in the shadows, the floor. There were a few pieces of rubble in the corners, sticks and leaves were scattered around, and—

"What's that?" She pointed to a shadowy lump.

Penrose moved across the cave, crouched down. "A knapsack."

She joined him at his side and watched as he opened it. It was the sort of knapsack military men carried, made of canvas, with leather straps and brass buckles.

Penrose pulled out a folded bundle.

"Papers?" she said.

He held the bundle up to the light seeping in from outside. "Maps." He unfolded one. "Or, rather, a map in progress. It's graphing paper, see? Someone has been charting territory. I used to do this myself, when I was in the cavalry."

Cavalry?

Aha. *That* explained a bundle. Because even with his steamed-up spectacles and scholarly frown, Penrose didn't look like a professor *or* an earl. Ophelia chalked it up to his broad shoulders. Or maybe it was the tattered, blood-stained jacket.

At that moment, she realized how awfully alone they were in this secret cave. Her heart kicked up a notch. She drew away.

It wasn't fear. Not of *him*, anyway. She was frightened of herself, of this tugging towards him. She held her elbows.

"This appears to be a chart of the terrain just about here," Penrose said, still studying the map. "I see the stream"—he traced a fingertip along the paper—"and this very cave. No writing, however."

"Mm."

He glanced up. "Are you quite all right, Miss Flax?"

"Oh, yes." She forced a cheery smile.

"But you're shivering." He folded the map and nestled it in the knapsack, but he didn't buckle the straps. He stood.

Ophelia swallowed. "I'm all right."

He moved closer.

Ophelia glanced out the mouth of the cave. "Oh," she said. "Is the rain letting up?"

He didn't look out.

She felt rather than saw his presence: tall, dark, humming with life. He took another step closer. Then he was reaching up to her face.

"Let me help you," he said. His voice had gone rough.

She gazed up into his face.

He peeled her right muttonchop from her cheek, dropped it.

Oh.

A half smile curled his lips as he, very gently, removed the other muttonchop and both her bushy eyebrows, too. "That's better," he said. His eyes, behind his spectacles, held a lamp-like intensity.

Ophelia's lips parted in a breathless gesture she'd pretended hundreds of times onstage but that she'd never had need for in her real life.

His hand went to her cravat and yanked it free.

Her eyelids drooped. Her body, all on its own, drew closer to his chest.

His face was coming closer. She saw the sandy texture of his jaw, his now serious-looking mouth.

There was a flash of motion in the corner of her eye. She turned her head and saw the hulking silhouette of a man. She screamed.

# 25

❧❈❧

"Hold your ground!" Penrose yelled. His hand was on his breast, over his revolver.

The person held up his hands. "Smith here."

"*Mr. Smith?*" Ophelia said.

Smith stepped into the cave, looking much smaller than he'd seemed at first. Water streamed from his deerstalker hat, and his shooting jacket was soaked. A rifle was slung across his back.

"Out hunting?" Penrose said. He'd stepped away from Ophelia.

"Got caught in this downpour." Smith appeared to have tobacco in his cheek. His eyes fell on the knapsack. "Reckon I oughtn't ask what the two of you are doing out here."

Ophelia's cheeks smoldered as she fastened the top button of her shirt.

"It would, perhaps," Penrose said, "be a superfluous question." He shifted so his bloodied shoulder was in shadow. "May I be so bold as to ask, why are *you* here?"

"Birding. Castle's a wretched place these days." Smith moved to the knapsack, knelt beside it.

Ophelia and Penrose exchanged a glance.

The knapsack and the maps were his.

"The place is filled with the despair of women." Smith stuffed the maps into the knapsack. "Chews at a man's soul like termites." He tightened the straps with a jerk, buckled them. "I've spent most of my life in the out-of-doors. Wasn't made for parlors and paperwork. But I did it for Homer. He was my greatest friend." His face—at least in the dim light—appeared to crumple.

"What will you do next?" Penrose said. "Now that Coop is gone."

"It's back to Nevada for me, or California, maybe. Haven't been out to the territories for more than a dozen years past. Lately I've been fired up with a longing for the wilderness—too much fancy food and piped-in hot water at that castle for my constitution."

"What about this forest—the *Schwarzwald*?" Penrose said. "Is it not at all like California?"

"Like California? Haw! It's about as much like California as one of them Arabian racehorses is like a Mexico donkey. Oh, that's a hoot! No, one thing's certain, and it's that I've got to get myself back to some real wilderness. That durned policeman, Schubert, has forbidden us all to leave until he gets to the bottom of the murders, but I figure that'll take about as much time as for him to learn to be a ballerina."

"Who," Penrose said, "do you believe killed Coop?"

Smith worked the plug of tobacco in his cheek. "Who did it? You want to know who did it?"

"Yes."

"I'll tell you who. That vixen Princess Verushka."

"Princess Verushka?" Penrose said. "But she only met Coop for the first time the day he was killed."

"That's what I thought—that's what everyone thought. But there's something mighty strange about that one, mark my words." Smith's eyes suddenly flashed with malice. "You just take yourself down to Baden-Baden and have a squint at what's she's up to, flitting around in that there conversation-what's-it."

"The *Conversationshaus*?"

"That's what I said. Go and have a look-see for yourself. She's not who she says she is, that's for dang sure."

"Not a princess?"

"Oh, I reckon she's a princess. But she ain't a lady. I hear tell she's taken up with the owner of that gambling joint. Rich as a king, they say he is. Bet that'd suit a little frippet like her just fine."

"Herr Ghent?" Ophelia said.

"Don't know what his name is. All I know is, that princess has got rich fellers on the brain. And don't you forget, Homer was real rich." Smith glanced out the mouth of the cave. "Now look at that. Rain's letting up." He slung his knapsack over his shoulder. "Afternoon to you both. And don't worry about me finding you two here. I know how young folks got to have their fun." He winked, ducked out from under the rock ledge, and was gone.

"If Princess Verushka is Herr Ghent's mistress—" Miss Flax said.

*Mistress.* Gabriel frowned. Were proper young ladies acquainted with such terms?

"—then she might've killed Mr. Coop. Maybe she's somehow mixed up with, well, whatever Ghent and his thugs are doing."

"She was there when Coop died, true."

"She could've been sent to the castle to kill him and to ferret around in Coop's study. She was also in the castle yesterday morning, calling on Mrs. Coop. When Karl died."

Miss Flax had knotted her loose hair and buttoned her shirt. The change did nothing to assuage Gabriel's preposterous urge to drag her into his arms. Thank God Smith had shown up when he did. Gabriel had rather not have the sullied innocence of a maidservant on his conscience.

Miss Flax was worrying her lower lip.

Gabriel forced himself to look away—the sight was a bit much under the circumstances—as he said, "You've thought of something else."

"Yes, well, remember I told you about those laudanum drops Mrs. Coop has been guzzling?"

"Yes."

"Well, Princess Verushka has been in the castle"—she tipped her head, thinking—"yes, she's been in the castle both times the new bottles of drops appeared."

"Are you suggesting—?"

"What if Princess Verushka is the one who's keeping Mrs. Coop in that state?"

"I must go back to Baden-Baden and try to discover what Smith was referring to." Gabriel looked out of the cave. The rain had indeed let up. "I think we ought to wait for a while here. Those guards could be searching for us still."

They settled down to wait inside the cave. Yellow sunbeams poured through the steamy greenery, and the birds gradually started twittering again.

They didn't speak. Gabriel didn't trust himself to. And he could tell Miss Flax was embarrassed by their encounter. As well she ought to be. He'd been a cad.


Prue and Hansel marched a long while down Heidelberg's main street. They arrived, presently, in a big market square. The rain was splatting down harder, and the market vendors were packing up their carts and stands. Vegetable scraps littered the paving stones. An enormous funny-shaped church, like a big loaf pan, loomed over the square.

Prue tipped her neck to see the top of the steeple. It looked like a jumbo black handbell.

"The Church of the Holy Spirit," Hansel said. He shoved the brim of his cap down to keep the rain out of his eyes.

"Where Snow White's buried?"

"Perhaps."

That feeling of being followed clung to Prue all across the market square and into the church.

Inside, it was cool and dim, but dry. It smelled of burned beeswax and spicy incense. The ceiling was sky-high and obscured by shadows. A few figures in black knelt in pews way up by the altar, but the church was mostly empty.

She and Hansel poked around the edges of the sanctuary, searching for the entrance to the crypts, trickling rainwater behind them. They found the choir robe closet, confessional booths behind curtains, a broom cupboard, and what looked to be the organist's secret supply of schnapps. But no crypts.

The whole time, that sense of being watched stuck around.

Hansel dragged open a big, iron-girded door that they'd discovered in a chamber behind the baptismal font. "Ah," he said.

Prue joined him. Candles in black iron holders lit a shuddering path down the stairs. Looked like the entrance to Fire and Brimstone Town. "Maybe I'll keep watch up here," Prue said. "Make sure no one follows you."

"I may need your help."

"Doing what?"

"Moving sarcophagus lids."

Sweet sister Sally.

"Do you even know her real name?" Prue said. "Snow White's, I mean? Because surely that ain't written on her tombstone."

"I do not. However, last night I examined a history of the region, taken from my—from the castle library. I believe I know the name of the man Snow White possibly wed."

"Her prince?"

"In a manner of speaking, yes."

The crypt was bone-cold, but not smelly and slimy like Prue had feared. It was filled with stone coffins with chiseled human figures lying on their lids.

She hung close to Hansel as he inspected the coffins, one by one, holding the candle that he'd brought down. Each coffin had a name carved in its lid. Hansel's eyes were eager, his mouth rigid, as he searched.

Prue eyed the staircase, half expecting the door at the top to slam shut. She was sure she heard mouse squeaks somewhere.

"Look at this," Hansel said, after going over about a dozen coffins. He rubbed at the carved letters with his cuff. Cobwebs balled up. "This is the sarcophagus I was searching for."

Prue sidestepped some mouse dribbles. "Snow White's old man?" The carved figure on the lid was a bearded fellow in robes, holding a sword.

"Perhaps. Kunibert Odovacar. The third son of one of the electors palatine in the fifteenth century. He is the youngest son of an elector palatine in that era, so I deduced it was he that Snow White married." Hansel checked the name on the coffin next to Kunibert's. "But there is no wife buried beside him."

"No Snow White." Prue had reckoned it would be simple: they'd go to the crypts and find a coded message explaining who was the murderer and why, and then all their problems would be solved. Her shoulders sagged. "What'll we do next?"

"Yes," someone said behind them, "what *will* you do? First a railway journey to Heidelberg, then an antiquarian expedition in a crypt—what next? A sojourn to the moon?"

Prue and Hansel whirled around.

"Franz," Hansel said.

She *knew* it. "You been following us since the train station?"

Franz removed his bowler hat and flicked raindrops off of it. "Ever since I saw you on the platform in Baden-Baden."

"Following us." Hansel said. "Why?"

Franz shrugged. "Boredom. Mind you, I was returning to Heidelberg anyway. When I saw an escaped convict and a castle gardener out for a secret gallivant, perhaps my curiosity got the better of me."

"You will not," Hansel said, "tell anyone you saw Miss Bright out, will you?"

"I have never seen her anywhere *but* out." Franz's eyes fell on the coffin behind them. "What is more intriguing than an escaped murderess is that you claim to have located the tomb of Snow White's prince. Perhaps, Hansel, completing your university education would do you a world of good. Believing in fairy stories! Tsk, tsk."

Hansel scowled.

"Why," Franz went on, "are you attempting to find the tomb of a lesser character from the murk of mythology? *Do* tell. I find the beliefs of servants so fascinating. Perhaps it is a notion gleaned from your wretched grandmother?"

"See here, Franz," Prue said. She felt hot, despite the crypt's clammy air. "There's no need to be so stuck-up about Hansel just because he's come down in the world. He's finer and grander than you'll ever be, and matter of fact, his pa wrote him a letter that said everything's going to go back to the way it used to be, just as soon as we figure out where Snow White is buried."

Hansel winced.

Crackers. Was that letter supposed to be a secret?

Franz wormed closer, around a couple coffins. He moistened his skinny lips. "There is something buried with Snow White?"

"Not necessarily," Hansel said. He picked up the candle.

Franz edged still closer. His shoes crunched on the gritty floor. "I do not believe you." He leaned around Hansel and read the inscription on the coffin lid. "Kunibert Odovacar. Your fairy tale prince, I presume?" He snickered. "Come, dear Hansel. You need a drink. Join me at the beer hall, and we shall show your sweet little murderess a splendid time. And you"—he reached out and straightened the placket of Hansel's homespun jacket—"shall tell me all about that letter."

Hansel and Prue exchanged a glance.

"We do need to eat," Hansel said, "but there is nothing more to say about the letter." He pushed Franz's fingers away from his jacket and led the way out of the crypts.

* * *

After an hour of waiting inside the cave, Gabriel and Miss Flax made their way back through the forest without seeing a soul. When Gabriel left her at the foot of the orchard slope, he passed her his revolver.

She stared down at it, and then up at his bloodied shoulder.

"You may require it," he said.

"I don't know how to use it."

"No? You know how to do so many other things."

She frowned.

He took the gun. "It's loaded. Six bullets. You need only cock it—like this—"

She winced.

"—and pull the trigger. After a shot, hold up the gun, like so, when you cock it again, to allow the spent caps to fall out."

"I really don't think—"

"Those guards meant to kill us."

She set her lips, took the gun, and slipped it into her trousers pocket in silence. She started up the slope.

"And Miss Flax."

She turned.

"Be careful."

When Gabriel returned to the inn, bone-tired and soaking wet, Winkler was ensconced before the sitting room fire with a newspaper, some kind of steaming drink, and a plate piled high with biscuits.

Gabriel tried to slip past the open sitting room door unseen. He intended to go directly up to his chamber, peel off his wet clothes, pour himself a large brandy, and see to his shoulder.

"Penrose," Winkler called.

Hang it.

"Good evening." Gabriel poked only his head round the doorframe, so Winkler wouldn't see his bloodstained jacket.

Winkler lowered his newspaper. "I inspected those mushrooms."

"And?"

"Innocuous. Completely. Used by the *volk* in a broth for treating headaches and such. Utter quackery, needless to say."

"Well, thank you."

Once in his chamber, Gabriel removed his jacket and shirt. Luckily, all that rainwater had prevented the bloody fabric from crusting to the wound.

It was, thank God, but a flesh wound. A deep one, yes, but nothing serious. No embedded bullet. He'd suffered worse.

He cleaned it with a wet cloth, doused it with brandy, and bandaged it as best he could with a few shreds of linen nightshirt.

He stretched out on his bed, shirtless, with the brandy bottle in one hand and his second Webley revolver in the other.

There. Comfort and safety. The two guiding ideals of the British Empire. Although he rather doubted those guards would have the audacity to try to murder him in his bed. Surely Ghent, whoever he was, wished to cover his tracks.

He took a deep swallow from the bottle.

A wet evening sank over Heidelberg. Prue and Hansel followed Franz through twisting, turning streets, dodging around puddles and dripping roofs. Franz quizzed them about Karl's letter. Prue buttoned her lips, and Hansel was vague.

The student's beer hall that Franz took them to was the frolicsome kind. The wooden sign above the door had red lettering and a picture of a jumping pig. Someone was playing an accordion inside, badly enough to make your ears curl up and die. Prue could barely hear the accordion anyway, through all the clattering beer glasses and boyish hooting. The rowdiness rolled, along with light, cigarette smoke, and puffs of stale beer, out into the dark, narrow street.

Prue wriggled her fingers into Hansel's. He gave them a squeeze. Good. He wasn't too mad about how she'd spilled the beans to Franz about the letter, then.

"Come meet my friends," Franz said over the uproar inside. "The fine student gentlemen of number seventeen, the castle stairs."

Number seventeen, the castle stairs? Was that really an address?

"I'm awful hungry," Prue whispered to Hansel. That was the truth. But she also couldn't bear to meet new folks dressed in the ugly brown dress, with her hair under a milkmaid's straw bonnet, and in a rain-drenched knitted shawl the color of mold.

"Miss Bright desires something to eat," Hansel said. "We shall have a meal, and then we shall go."

"I suppose it must be trying for you, Hansel," Franz said, "seeing your old classmates in your . . . reduced circumstances."

Hansel met Franz's eyes coolly. Then he led Prue to a table in the corner.

# 26

After they sat down, the barmaid came to ask what they wished to eat and drink.

The barmaid wore a sapphire blue cotton dress with a tight bodice, puffy white sleeves, and a white swath of apron. She had shining raven-colored hair piled on her head. Her skin was a rare porcelain, without any sun coloring or pink. Her lips were red, her eyes onyx and darting.

In fact—Prue felt an unfamiliar pang—she was prettier than Prue.

Prue was accustomed to fellows of all ages walking into walls and tripping on their own bootlaces when they saw her. But these days, for the first time in her life, Prue wouldn't describe herself as pretty. Ma had taught her that her beauty was her greatest prize and her meal ticket. Without it, Prue felt near invisible.

Even Hansel, who in the first few weeks after Prue's arrival at the castle had seemed enchanted, no longer looked at her the same way. The problem was, Prue realized, she'd fallen in love with him, right when the only thing she had to offer—her beauty—had vanished.

She wiped the tears from the corners of her eyes so Hansel wouldn't see them. *He* was the one who ought to be crying, anyway. His pa was dead.

Prue and Hansel studied Franz and his friends, who were crowded at a table on the other side of the beer hall.

Franz was the runt of the litter. His friends were all strapping. When they whacked Franz's back in jest, Prue reckoned it was with a mite more vigor than necessary. But Franz played along, even as the other young men seemed to be jeering at him.

When the barmaid came around with more beer, the men all fell silent and stared after her like they were plants and she was the sun. Then, as soon as the barmaid was out of earshot, they stood to raise a toast. Almost like they were toasting . . . the barmaid. Prue saw flashes of red, white, and black ribbons wrapped around belts, hidden beneath jackets.

"Look," Prue whispered to Hansel. "Them secret society ribbons."

Hansel stole a look. "So they are."

After a while, the barmaid brought Hansel and Prue plates of oily noodles with cheese and bits of sausage. Prue dug in like a coal miner.

Hansel forked noodles into his mouth, chewed. "I am not certain where to search for Snow White next. Perhaps we might visit my former history professor. Although. . . ."

"You're afraid he might laugh at you?"

"Yes." Hansel prodded noodles with his fork. "But my father was adamant that Snow White was a real lady. So, perhaps there is something in a dusty book somewhere. I do not know."

"A book?" Prue's eyes fell on Franz, pretending to carouse with his fellows. He must've felt her looking, because his gaze slanted in her direction. His eyes were beady. "Franz said something about books to Miss Gertie at the ball the other night. Said there are some kind of old fairy tale books at the library."

Hansel hunched forward. "Which library? In Schloss Grunewald?"

"No. He said they were in the one here, in Heidelberg."

Hansel slumped back in his chair. "The university library closed at five o'clock. We shall go there first thing in the morning."

They finished eating and paid. Without saying good-bye to Franz—he was in the middle of singing, beer glass aloft, with his student friends—they wandered out into the soggy night.

Prue hugged her ratty shawl around her arms. "Where will we go?" Despite the ups and downs of her childhood, she'd never actually slept in a gutter. Yet.

Hansel took her hand. "I know a safe place."

He led her to a row of houses facing the river. They stopped at a door painted dark blue. There was a white oval sign hanging above the door that Prue couldn't read. It had a painted sprig of violets, though. That was reassuring. Prue was pretty sure dens of sin didn't have painted violets on their signs.

"Frau Bohm was my nursemaid at the castle when I was small." Hansel knocked on the door. "After I was grown, she cared for some children at an estate outside of Mannheim. Now she runs this little boarding house. She will not turn us away."

The door swung open. A lofty lady with jutting bones like a scarecrow stood there. She wore a dove gray cotton gown, an immaculate white apron, and a white mobcap on her dark, gray-streaked hair. "Hansel!" She clasped her long fingers and said more things that Prue couldn't understand. Then she looked at Prue, wearing an expression that was kind but inquisitive.

Prue wanted to turn tail and jump into the river. She felt so grimy and crumpled. And she was fair certain there was a bit of dinner stuck between her two front teeth.

Hansel drew her forward and introduced her. Frau Bohm smiled and led them inside, through to the back of the house and into a kitchen.

Ma had never done a scrap of cooking, unless you counted cracking oysters and pouring champagne as cooking. Prue had somehow grown to young womanhood nourished by gingersnaps, pretzels, roasted peanuts, and fried dough purchased for pennies from New York street vendors. So Frau Bohm's pristine little kitchen seemed like a wonderland of cross-stitched dish towels and shining copper pots.

Hansel and Frau Bohm spoke softly in German for a bit, and they all drank chamomile tea. Frau Bohm cast a few maternal looks in Prue's direction. Prue tried to dissolve into her periwinkle-painted chair.

It seemed to work, because Hansel didn't look her way. Not once.

Then Frau Bohm led them upstairs, carrying two milky-globed hurricane lamps. Prue's chamber was on one side of the corridor, and Hansel's was on the other. Prue whispered good night, took one of the lamps, and shut herself in her chamber. She untied her bonnet strings, listening to Frau Bohm's footsteps going back downstairs, and to the creak of Hansel's door swinging closed.

Impulsively, she tossed aside her bonnet and pushed open her door. "Hansel!" she whispered.

He regarded her through the door crack. "What is it?"

She paused. What *was* it? She wasn't sure. Only that she felt like crying, and she wanted one last glimpse of him before she went to sleep, and—

He crossed the corridor in a stride and took her face in his hands. His chest rose and fell, and his eyebrows were drawn together in fierce concentration as he gazed down at her.

Prue couldn't breathe, and she wasn't sure if her kneecaps were jiggling from fright or something else altogether. "Do you . . . do you see me?" she whispered.

Surprise flickered over his features. "See you? Of course I see you, Prue. How could I see anything else?"

A lump gathered in her throat. She squeezed her eyes shut, trying to make it last, him holding her head, his palms rough and warm against her cheeks. "But I'm so ugly now. How can you bear it?"

He paused. He stroked a thumb over her cheekbone. "There are many ways to be beautiful," he finally said.

Then he turned and went back into his chamber.

Prue held her eyes shut. Her body whirred with his touch. But she didn't understand what he had meant.

Schloss Grunewald was quiet that night.

The servants kept to themselves. Miss Amaryllis refused all admittance to her chamber and lay sobbing in the dark.

Mrs. Coop was abed, thrashing and muttering, under the effects of the hysteria drops.

Ophelia stashed the revolver Penrose had given her under a sofa cushion in Mrs. Coop's chamber. Then she went to the window, pulled the drapes aside, and stared out at Prue's desolate tower. No jug in the window. Which likely meant Prue had not yet returned from Heidelberg.

Ophelia hoped to hickory that Prue was all right, wherever she was.

She curled up on the sofa and watched over Mrs. Coop until she nodded off, too.

In the morning, Ophelia realized she wouldn't be able to sneak away to Baden-Baden again. Mrs. Coop was up and about, and making demands. It was all Ophelia could do to transport the revolver from under the sofa cushion up into her own chamber unseen.

When she spied the greengrocer's delivery lorry outside the kitchen door, she dashed off a note to Professor Penrose and entrusted it to the deliveryman.

Gabriel was relieved that Miss Flax couldn't accompany him. She'd be safer at the castle.

After breakfast, he took a hired carriage into Baden-Baden and went directly to the *Conversationshaus*.

It was probably madness to go there after what had happened yesterday in the wood. But even if Ghent's guards were bent on killing Gabriel, they surely wouldn't do it here. It'd be bad for business, for one thing.

He checked the tearoom and the gaming rooms. They were nearly empty since it was before luncheon. Many of the town's denizens were surely still abed, sleeping off the effects of last night's revelries.

No sign of Princess Verushka.

He crossed the marble foyer. He'd nearly made it to the doors that led outside when two looming forms appeared from behind one of the great pillars.

The guards.

"Good morning," Gabriel said, lifting his hat. He didn't stop walking.

One of the guards, the one with the black caterpillar of an eyebrow, stepped in his path. "Have a pleasant ride yesterday?" he growled.

"Yes, thanks awfully. Despite the weather and"—Gabriel's shoulder, bandaged beneath his shirt and jacket, throbbed—"a bit more excitement than we'd planned for."

"We know what you are searching for—"

"Do you? Because I'm not certain that *I* know—"

"—and if you enter the wood again, you and that strange woman who wears gentlemen's clothes will die."

"Thank you for the suggestion." Gabriel lifted his hat again and dodged by the guards.

They didn't follow.


Across the gravel drive from the *Conversationshaus* was a long, tree-shaded avenue. Fashionable ladies and gentlemen sauntered up and down the white gravel. Birds chirped and the sun sparkled. The only traces of yesterday's rainstorm were the puddles shimmering on the gravel.

Gabriel took a seat at one of the many green-painted benches along the avenue and pretended to read a newspaper.

Now and then he glanced up to see society matrons thrusting their daughters at gentlemen, blushing debutantes casting shy looks at Russian officers, matrons flirting with gentlemen who were not, perhaps, their husbands. It was rather like an aviary during mating season. Some of the birds were gorgeously plumed, but—he watched a corpulent old fossil strolling with a damsel one-third his age—others resembled overfed vultures.

It was difficult to picture Mr. Smith here. What business could he have in Baden-Baden's most fashionable spot? And why, for that matter, was he mapping the forest about Schloss Grunewald?

Gabriel had finished one newspaper and was halfway through a second by the time he finally sighted Princess Verushka.

She was as lovely as he remembered, with her leaf green, flounced walking gown, parasol, and a smart little hat. She was tripping along beside a dignified-looking gentleman in a dark suit, silk hat, and a waxed white moustache.

Gabriel buried his nose in his newspaper as they came closer.

The princess emitted a tinkling laugh. "How you flatter me, baron," she said in French, with her rich Russian accent. "Calling me a debutante! Why, you know I am, sadly, a widow."

"The loss of the prince was indeed a tragedy," the gentleman said, "but now at last the rest of the world may enjoy the exquisite charms of the bride he kept so jealously locked away."

Gabriel peered over the top of the newspaper as the princess and her squire passed. She looked smug. As well she might; Gabriel recognized the gentleman as a high-ranking French politician and wealthy aristocrat.

If Princess Verushka were Ghent's mistress, perhaps it was her task to socialize with Baden-Baden's elite. Although Ghent, if he had red blood in his veins, wouldn't be too pleased about the way she was flirting.

Gabriel followed their retreating forms with his eyes. Another gentleman strode up to them. They were out of earshot, but the second gentleman—also in the prime of life—appeared to be having words with the baron. The princess

watched fretfully. Then the second man thrust something—
a letter—into the princess's hands and marched away.

The baron appeared to quiz the princess; she was tearful.
The baron made a cold bow before he, too, stalked away.

Gabriel folded his newspapers.

Smith had been mistaken. The princess was not Ghent's
mistress. She was on the hunt for a wealthy husband. And,
evidently, she'd been overfilling her dance card.

She hurried away, in the opposite direction the baron
had gone.

Gabriel followed.


Princess Verushka, as soon as she'd turned onto a side
street, no longer took mincing steps. Her stride was purposeful.

She walked for fifteen minutes, Gabriel trailing a block
behind. She left the central district, with its magnificent
hotels and shops, and entered a cramped quarter where
everyday people lived. The streets were tighter, packed up
against a hillside, and the windows fluttered with washing
hung out to dry. Grubby children romped in the streets,
bony cats slunk along gutters.

Presently, she turned into a side alley. Gabriel stopped
at the corner and poked his head round the building.

She slowed as she neared a door. A faded wooden sign
read *Pension Schmidt*.

A boardinghouse.

Two little girls in pinafores and caps perched on the
doorstep, chattering in German and playing with dolls.

"Oh, get out of my way," the princess said, pushing by
them. She disappeared into the boardinghouse.

Gabriel pulled his head back around the corner, stunned.

Princess Verushka had spoken in English to the little girls.
With what was quite unmistakably an American accent.

# 27

⚬❦⚬

Ophelia colored Mrs. Coop's hair a deep ebony, using ingredients she'd purchased in the apothecary's shop: four grains nitrate of silver dissolved into a bottle of rosewater and half a dram of aqua ammonia. The effect, against Mrs. Coop's powder-white skin and painted lips, was enough to make your hair stand on end. But Mrs. Coop was pleased and spent the remainder of the morning trying on gowns and preening in front of the boudoir mirrors.

When she finally collapsed on her bed to rest, Ophelia went to Mr. Coop's study.

The study was dim and already musty-smelling. She locked herself inside and pulled open the velvet drapes.

First, she flipped through the stacks of papers on the desk and in its drawers. Business documents from America—one pile was all about the Oregon Territory Railway Company and another concerned land parcels in St. Louis.

What could Princess Verushka have wanted with those?

The opposite wall was filled, floor to ceiling, with a bookcase. Now there was a notion: stage plays were chockablock with papers hidden in the pages of books.

Ophelia hurried over and plucked a volume off the shelf, opened it, and shook the pages. Nothing fell out.

She braced herself. There had to be hundreds upon hundreds of books. But she intended to shake as many as it took.

She began to shake the books, one by one. They were all old, gilt-stamped volumes in German. Dust billowed up.

After a few dozen books, she flopped into a chair for a breather. Her eyes and nose itched from the dust.

Her gaze drifted to the ornate brass fire screen, then to the mantelpiece. There was a blue Chinese jar up there and a framed photograph of Mrs. Coop, all creamy shoulders, gleaming hair, and dewy eyes, wearing a rich necklace and furs.

But there was something strange about it.

Yes—she stood and picked up the frame—the photograph was crooked.

She turned the frame over and unfastened the back.

There, between the frame and the photograph, was an envelope. Unmarked. She pried it out.

There was a clatter of horse hooves down in the forecourt.

She dashed to the window. A carriage had pulled to a stop. Two men jumped out. Inspector Schubert and Herr Benjamin. They marched towards the castle doors.

The *Leviathan* had landed.

Ophelia stuffed the envelope into her bodice and ran.


Gabriel paused on the street corner and weighed his options. He could take the information of Princess Verushka's charade to the police, or he could confront her himself, right now.

He thought of Schubert's derisive face and decided on the latter option.

But just as he was about to go round the corner into the alley where the boardinghouse was, Princess Verushka sailed right past him—she didn't see him—and hailed a carriage in the street.

"Schilltag," he heard her say to the driver. "Schloss Grunewald."

There wasn't time to return to his own carriage, waiting in the town center. He found another—it cost him several precious minutes—ordered the driver to take him to Schloss Grunewald, and leapt inside.

Princess Verushka was an impostor and, apparently, hard up. She'd just been jilted by two suitors in one morning.

Hence, she couldn't be up to any good.

When Gabriel's carriage rumbled through Schilltag, heading towards the castle road, he glimpsed a woman's tall, slim form, a white face, a charcoal gray gown, outside the inn.

Miss Flax.

He pounded on the roof, and the carriage jolted to a stop. He jumped out.

When Miss Flax saw him, her face registered relief. She dashed over. "I've found it," she said.

"Are you well, Miss Flax? I—"

"I found what the princess was searching for in Mr. Coop's study."

He stared down at her. She appeared pale and strained. She hadn't even a bonnet on.

"You'd better come inside the inn," he said.

He ordered the driver to wait, and they shut themselves up in the inn's sitting room.

Miss Flax handed him an envelope. Inside was a single handwritten page.

*My Dearest Pearl,*

*Goodness, I've heard of pearls before swine, but I never fancied how frightfully amusing a Pearl in a chicken coop might be! Imagine my delight when I learned that you had wed the New York millionaire Homer T. Coop. A millionaire! Just as we both swore we'd do when we were girls in that milliner's shop in Berkeley Street. How well you have done for yourself.*

*Imagine, too, my delight in seeing your daughter Amaryllis so grown-up. Takes after her father—a dog catcher, wasn't he? Or was it a fishmonger? Something to do with little beasts.*

*Now, dear Pearl, as your oldest friend, I'm certain you will take pity on me when I say that I have not managed to snare a fresh millionaire. Not even an old one. Although I am called Princess Verushka now, fate has not been kind. But I am certain you will be able to help. If not, perhaps Homer T. Coop will help me—of course, that might entail revealing to him a few tidbits that you may have neglected to tell him yourself. But what, possibly, could be the harm in that?*

*I am staying at Pension Schmidt in Baden-Baden. I eagerly await your response.*

*—Lily*

"Daughter?" Penrose said. "Miss Amaryllis is Mrs. Coop's *daughter*?"

"I wonder we didn't see it before. Mrs. Coop is certainly old enough. But it's difficult to understand a mother being so cruel to her own child."

"We moderns detest the idea of cruel mothers. Even the Grimms edited out all the nasty mamas in the original tales and replaced them with stepmothers. Sits better." He paused. "It's clear that Coop knew nothing of Mrs. Coop's true relationship to Miss Amaryllis until he saw this note."

"Well, he must've known he hadn't gone to the chapel with a spring chicken."

"In order to appear attractive to Coop, doubtless Pearl had to pretend to a more ingénue role than she was accustomed. To admit to being a mother, well, that changes things in a gentleman's eyes. Far better to pass the daughter off as a clinging sister." Penrose told Ophelia what he'd unearthed about Princess Verushka that morning. "Now we know why the princess was searching through Coop's desk. This is a blackmail note. And it's addressed to Pearl, not Coop. Which means that at some point before he died, Coop got hold of this note—"

"And learned his wife's secret."

"No wonder he seemed so furious the day he died, and no wonder he was drinking heavily. He'd been disillusioned about his new bride."

Ophelia considered. That's what Mr. Coop must've meant when he said those things to Prue. Chippies posing as ladies and daughters pretending they weren't daughters, and all that. She'd never told Penrose that part, for fear he'd figure out they were actresses.

"Wait," she said. "Mrs. Coop and the princess were together when that apple was poisoned and put on the tea table. What if the princess got Mrs. Coop to lie for her as part of her blackmail plot?"

"If she merely wanted money from Mrs. Coop, then she hadn't any reason to kill. However, Coop may have threatened divorce. I understand you Americans are mad for it. Divorce would mean, for Mrs. Coop, losing all the wealth she had so recently attained, so it wouldn't have been in the princess's best interest. However, after Coop was killed, she would've swiftly realized that it *was* in her interest if Mrs. Coop didn't take the blame. After all, it's difficult to extract money from someone in prison."

"You're saying the princess didn't kill Coop?"

"Correct."

"And that Mrs. Coop did."

"Perhaps."

"But that the princess knew about it and helped her to cover it up."

"We've got to speak to the princess. If we tell her we've found the blackmail note, she'll talk. She's gone up to the castle. Come on."

Ophelia tensed. "No."

"For heaven's sake, Miss Flax. You've spent the last several days insisting on coming along on every excursion, and now when—"

"I can't go back to the castle."

"May I ask why not?"

She swallowed. "Let me wait for you here."

"Very well."


The Heidelberg University library was built of pinky-brown stones and fronted by lush green gardens. It had big rectangular windows, sharp spires, and bulging, carved stone fruits and ladies' heads all around the front doors.

Prue and Hansel mounted the steps. Hansel didn't seem to want to talk, which was fine with Prue. Just the thought of whatever it was that had happened in Frau Bohm's corridor last night made her break into a cold sweat.

Inside, the library was like a church. If a church had carved wood shelves filled with books instead of pews and smelled like papery mold instead of incense. They went to a desk occupied by a sour little man with a few hairs combed over his head and spectacle lenses of paperweight thickness. He was stamping books with violence.

A malcontent librarian. Prue had heard stories. She'd never actually been inside a library before.

The librarian glanced up. His eyes skimmed their seedy getups, but when Hansel said something to him in German, the librarian's sour expression sweetened up a little.

The librarian scurried out from behind his desk and led them through the shelves.

"He said," Franz whispered to Prue, "that there is a very old manuscript about the life of Snow White in this library. It is housed in a special room where they keep the rarest books."

"He's going to let the likes of us paw it over?"

"I told him who I am. And I said we were members of the university dramatic society and that we are wearing costumes for a rehearsal."

Prue smiled for the first time all day. "Smart aleck."

The special book room had a churchy hush. Prue could practically hear the dust motes whispering as they twirled through sunbeams.

No one else was in the room. The librarian unlocked a glass-fronted bookcase and slid out a large, thin, leather-bound volume. He set it on the table and left them to it.

The book's cover was green, stamped with golden curlicues. The pages inside were intricate and colorful, with fancy hand lettering in black ink. The words were surrounded by borders filled with colorful pictures touched with gold.

"It is an illuminated manuscript," Hansel said.

They inspected the first few pages.

"The pictures look like a fairy story, for certain," Prue said. "A castle, a girl with dark hair and red lips, a forest filled with animals. Lots of spotted toadstools. A nasty queen with a mirror."

Hansel nodded. "The text is very much in keeping with the versions of the Snow White stories that I know. Here is the cottage."

Prue studied the picture. Seven short fellows standing in front of a little house. "Does it look like the one they found in the forest by Castle Grunewald?"

"It is difficult to say. The one the woodsman found was overgrown and decayed, and surrounded by large trees. The trees in this picture are mere saplings."

"But they'd be old as the dickens by now."

"True."

They kept on thumbing through the book. There was a part about an old peddler crone, a poisoned apple, and Snow White in a glass casket. Then the prince showed up and gave poor, dead Snow White a miraculous smooch.

"Is it Kunibert?" Prue said.

"It is." Hansel pointed to the text. *Kunibert Odovacar.*

The next page showed Kunibert on a white horse riding off with Snow White towards the setting sun. "There is nothing unusual about this story. No mention of her burial. Nothing different from the story everyone knows."

"But it ain't over," Prue said. She turned to the next page. "There's more."

The next page showed Snow White holding a baby in

swaddling cloths and Kunibert, his back turned, staring out a castle window.

"What does it say?" Prue said.

"That Kunibert was not as charming as Snow White had believed. That he grew cold and distant."

Ma would've seen *that* part coming.

Prue flipped the page. "Snow White don't look too happy here, either. I guess Kunibert didn't come round?" Snow White was in a chair, looking lonesome. She was gussied up in colorful jewels, and she was combing her hair.

Prue's breath caught. Snow White's comb looked a lot like the one Prue had found on the cliff. Dark gold with little red stones. The comb that was, this very minute, pinched between Prue's chemise and corset.

She should tell Hansel. She knew that. But then she'd have to fess up to keeping the comb for the sake of vanity. After what Hansel had said to her last night, about there being lots of different ways to be beautiful, well, she couldn't bear it. Not yet.

"Snow White," Hansel said, "grew melancholy. Her happiest times had been in the dwarves' cottage in the wood, and she longed for those days. The dwarves made her jewelry, crafted from ore and gemstones they mined themselves, and gave it to her as gifts when they came to visit and cheer her." He turned the page.

But there was nothing there. Just the blank inside cover. And, along the inner binding, a jagged strip of paper.

Prue gasped. "Some rapscallion tore out the last page. I'd wager it said exactly where she's buried."

"The librarian will have a log of everyone who has viewed this book."

They legged it back to the librarian's desk. He was book stamping again.

Hansel and the librarian held a brief exchange in German.

Hansel's eyes flashed. "Franz," he said to Prue. "Franz was the last one to have viewed that book, only an hour ago. He was so eager to view it, in fact, he was waiting on the library steps before it opened this morning, and he had a tussle with a lady over it, too."

"That milk-livered measle spot! He's looking for Snow White's tomb, just because we said *we* was. We've got to go and see him, face to face. Make him show us the torn-out page."

"Where did he say he and his student society fellows lived?"

"On the castle stairs. Number seventeen."

Hansel was already headed for the door.

# 28

❦

"There isn't much to tell," Princess Verushka said to Gabriel.

Gabriel had found her in the castle drawing room. Mrs. Coop had been detained by Inspector Schubert somewhere. When Gabriel had repeated Smith's accusations and shown her the blackmail note, she'd sighed and begun speaking with an American accent.

"But," Gabriel said, "your note indicates that you knew her in girlhood."

"Oh, I did. We were both employed in a milliner's shop in New York. Decorating hats with ribbons and feathers and wax cherries, that sort of thing. We became friends. We both had aspirations to get out of that squalor. And we both succeeded, although I must say, she far better than I. There was always something so *gritty* in her, you see. She stopped at nothing. Even the distressing appearance of that sickly infant didn't stop her. Amaryllis called to mind a blind, hairless baby possum when she was born. But perhaps Pearl loved her, in her own way, since she dragged her all the way here to Europe."

"Or perhaps Miss Amaryllis secured a home for herself by threatening—like you—to expose her mother's secrets to Coop."

"I hadn't thought of that. What a clever gentleman you are! A university professor. And so *young*."

"Clever, I'm told, and clinging to the remains of youth, perhaps, but penniless," Gabriel lied.

"Am I that obvious?"

"You are forgetting I've read your blackmail note."

The princess's smile drooped.

"Why," Gabriel said to Princess Verushka, "put on the Russian accent?"

"Oh, I don't know. For glamor, I suppose. European aristocrats can't fall in love with American ladies with their homespun accents, can they? And I *was* married to a Russian prince for six years. He left me with nothing except a horrid, muddy farm where nothing will grow but beets, and where bears roam the woods, and the serfs are forever on strike. The dreadful creatures are hungry."

The bears? Or the serfs?

"And you come to Baden-Baden," Gabriel said, "searching for—another prince?"

"*Mais oui*, darling."

"You realize that if Coop had learned of his wife's true past, on the very day he was poisoned, it makes things look rather bad for her. I'll put it bluntly. Do you think she's capable of murder?"

"Murder? Pearl? Well, of *course*."

Gabriel lifted an eyebrow.

"However," the princess said, "you really ought to investigate that nasty man."

"Who?"

"Why, Smith! The little insect lied about me only to distract you from himself. Perhaps he feared you were getting too near the truth."

"What is the truth?"

"Why, his name."

"And what, pray tell, is his name?"

"I wish for no further involvement in this affair." The princess stood. "You must, as in the story 'Rumpelstiltskin,' guess."

"You are too coy, madam. This is a matter of the utmost gravity."

She shrugged. "Perhaps you might contrive to have Herr Ghent tell you. Something tells me he might know, and they say he simply *adores* wagers. Now, I've a train to catch."

"Train?"

"I only came here to bid farewell to Pearl."

"Did the police not forbid you to leave the neighborhood?"

"That's why Inspector Schubert is here. Haven't you heard? I left my lodgings as soon as he sent word. He's making an arrest."

"Who is it?"

"The maidservants. The Americans. Both of them. Turns out they aren't really maids at all. They're variety hall actresses! And, it seems, confidence tricksters, too. Horrid creatures. Good afternoon." She floated out of the drawing room.

Gabriel stared at the empty doorway.

The sun worked up to a sizzle over Heidelberg, burning through the river mist. Hansel and Prue trooped up the castle stairs. The steps went crookedly up the hill, and foliage clustered over them. Funny old houses with pointy turrets and mossy gargoyles perched just off to the sides.

Prue had counted fifty-three steps when Hansel suddenly stopped. A skinny, sinister building rose up from the trees behind a black iron gate. The gate was decorated with little iron gnomes.

"I believe this is Franz's student society house," Hansel said. He pushed aside an overgrown rose bush. A green-coated plaque said *17.*

They went through the gate to the front door and rang the bell. A steward answered, and Hansel exchanged words with him that Prue couldn't understand. What she *could* understand was the steward's snooty look as he surveyed their peasants' duds.

"He says Franz is here," Hansel whispered to Prue.

From somewhere behind the steward came male shouting, metallic clattering, the crash of glass.

The steward sighed. He led them into the dim interior of the house.

The house was magnificent. Or, it *would* have been, if it hadn't been for the trousers slung over the carved wooden banister, the wine bottles on the checkered marble floor, and the lady's bonnet dangling from a chandelier. And if it hadn't smelled of cigarettes, spilled brandy, and boy sweat.

The steward led them down a passage, towards the shouting and crashing.

"Lucifer's lollipops," Prue said, when she spied the source of the noise. "They're going to kill each other!"

The steward rolled his eyes and slipped away.

Two young fellows in shirtsleeves were sword fighting in a big parlor sort of room. They leapt on sofas and flew backwards and forwards across the bunched-up carpet.

"Hansel," Prue whispered. "Stop them!"

"It is only sport," Hansel said. "They are dueling. The students of Heidelberg are mad for it."

One of the fellows made a slash in the crimson drapes before he noticed Prue and Hansel. His sword fell to his side. Prue recalled his face from the beer hall last night. It was stubbly and crisscrossed with thin scars. Probably from sword fighting.

"Ah, the bedraggled baby birds Franz dragged in yesterday," Stubbly said in English. "I was told the girl is American? Welcome. Please, sit." He used the tip of his sword to shove two empty wine bottles off a settee. They smashed to the floor.

"The steward told me that Franz is at home," Hansel said. He and Prue sat. Good thing Prue's dress was already ruined, because otherwise the cigarette ash and damp wine on the settee cushions would've done the job.

"Oh, he is at home," the other young man said. He slumped into an armchair and slung one leg over the side. Prue remembered him from the beer hall, too. He was shaped like a pencil, and he had one long scar across his cheek. "Little Franzie takes hours at his toilette."

Both fellows snorted with unkind laughter. The bits of red, white, and black ribbon at their belts flashed.

"The steward will fetch him," Stubbly said. He ambled to the fireplace. "He will have to drag him away from his hairbrushes and cologne water. Drink?" He laid his sword across the cluttered mantel and picked up a wine bottle.

"No, thank you," Hansel said.

Prue shook her head. She took in the room. There were bottles everywhere, and the marble fireplace was carved with . . . dwarves in hats.

She frowned. The wallpaper? Red apples and thorny vines. The mirror above the fireplace? Framed in shining black wood. And above the bottle-cluttered sideboard was a portrait of a girl combing her hair, framed up in fancy gilt. The girl had a pasty complexion and black hair. Her ruby lips had a victim's pout. The comb in her fingers was gold, with little red stones.

Prue's chest, where the comb was hidden, started to feel all rashy and hot.

Hansel was looking around the room, too. Was he thinking what Prue was thinking?

Pencil lit a cigarette. Stubbly guzzled like a nursling calf from the upended wine bottle. He came up for air and wiped his lips on his sleeve.

"What, precisely," Hansel said slowly, "is the name of your student society?"

"The Order of Blood and Ebony," Pencil said. He blew a perfect smoke ring.

Prue's eyes met Hansel's.

"Blood," Hansel said. "Ebony." His eyes were latched

on the girl's portrait by the sideboard. "Do those symbolize anything in particular?"

Prue stared at Stubbly's belt and the striped ribbon there. Red for blood, black for ebony. White for . . . a girl's snowy skin?

Stubbly was swishing the bottles on the mantel, one by one, searching for more tiddly. "It is a secret society, in theory, but I thought everyone had heard of us. The Order of Blood and Ebony was founded at Heidelberg University in 1820. Ah." He'd found a bottle that made a sloshing sound. He took a swig.

"To preserve the sacred memory of the princess in the wood." Pencil said in a chanting voice, like he was reciting an oath. He flicked ash on the carpet. "To protect the memory of her ideal womanhood. To let it never be forgotten that Prince Kunibert was an arse."

"That," Stubbly said, "and to give us the excuse for a good carouse."

Pencil nodded. "And so we do not seem overly lecherous when we adore girls with black hair and white skin."

Prue's skin was creepy-crawly. These fellows had built a whole society—a religion, almost—around the notion of a certain type of pretty girl. She shrank back against the settee cushion. Then she winced. Something behind the cushion was poking her. She swiveled around and dug it out.

"*Mein Gott*," Hansel muttered, staring down at what she held in her hand.

It was a short, stubby bone. Ivory-colored and streaky, chipped away on the ends where it must have once attached to a knee and a hip.

Bile prickled Prue's tongue. She wanted to toss the disgusting thing across the room. Trouble was, she couldn't pry her fingers loose.

Stubbly and Pencil were staring, too.

"Where did you find this femur?" Hansel said.

Stubbly said, "I don't know."

At the exact same time, Pencil said, "What femur?"

Liars. "It was *you*," Prue said, still unable to let go of the bone. "Those were your footprints up on the cliff. You dug up the dwarf skeleton. And the women's prints—those were the black-haired barmaid's."

"Kathy," Stubbly said. "Yes. She consents to playing the part of Snow White in our rituals, provided she is well paid."

"What in tarnation were you doing up there on the cliff?"

"Initiation rite. You do realize this is supposed to be secret? Franzie led us up there to prove his worthiness. We would not have admitted him into the Order if it had not been that he somehow seems to possess tidbits of Snow White lore that the Order was not aware of."

"You laid out the skeleton in the cottage," Hansel said.

Stubbly swallowed more wine. "It seemed to make sense at the time. Mind you, we had drunk a trifle too much brandy."

"Did Franz show you the cottage, too?"

"Yes. He has proved to be quite the most resourceful little initiate the Order has ever seen."

"Hansel." Franz stood in the doorway, neatly combed, hair-oiled, and suited. His smile twitched. "To what do I owe the pleasure of your visit?"

Hansel surged to his feet. "What were you doing, Franz, digging up that grave on the cliff? Why did you pretend you knew nothing of it? And where is the final page of the Snow White story that you tore out of the library manuscript?"

"All of you are so earnest about this fairy story business," Franz said. "I would find it tiresome if it weren't so amusing."

"Is that so?" Prue flung the dwarf's bone to the other end of the settee. "If you don't believe any of this Snow White business, like you say, then how come you stole the page from that book?"

"Book?" Pencil said, as he lit a fresh cigarette. "You don't mean the illuminated Snow White manuscript in the university library, do you? Franz, didn't your mother ever teach you not to rip books?"

"I am," Franz said, "unaware of any Snow White manuscripts, illuminated or otherwise."

Prue had had it up to her earlobes with Franz's lying. Besides, she was getting hungry, and her disposition was taking a tumble. She marched right up to Franz. She was all ruffled and messy, but she didn't care. "Where's that missing page? I know you tore it out."

"I did not tear it out." A muscle under Franz's left eye jumped.

"Sure you did. The librarian said you were the last one to get his dirty little mitts on that book."

"I *was* the last one. But someone else had already torn out the page before I viewed the book. A rather unladylike female engaged me in what could have been described as a Greek wrestling match in order to get to the librarian's desk first. I was forced to withdraw."

Oh. That's right. The librarian had said there'd been a tussle for the book.

"I believe," Franz said, "you are acquainted with the female in question. You introduced us at the ball in Baden-Baden."

"Gertie Darling?" Prue said.

"Yes." Franz's gaze had come to rest in the region of Prue's bodice.

Prue glanced down. A few inches of the ruby comb had wiggled out from the edge of her neckline.

"I had intended," Franz said, "to intercept that vile woman in her hotel at luncheon and extract the page from her fat clutches. However, now I suspect that I need not bother."


"You're an actress," Professor Penrose said to Ophelia. He closed the door of Gasthaus Schatz's sitting room behind him.

Ophelia darted to her feet. She'd been fretting on the edge of a chair before the cold fireplace. "Who told you that?"

"Is it true?"

She held her head high. "Yes. It's true."

"That explains the disguises," he said. "The accent. What about leaping from running horses into trees? Surely one doesn't perform such feats on the stage."

"I've been an actress for nearly six years. Before that I worked in. . . ."

This was silly. He wasn't the Grand Turk. And what did she care if he knew, anyway?

"I was employed by P. Q. Putnam's Traveling Circus in New England," Ophelia said. "Then there was the war, and the circus folded. I found work as an actress in a variety theater troupe—that's where I met Prue. Before the circus, I had a job in a woolen mill. But that was for only six months or so. I've been making my own way since I was seventeen years old. You must understand, I only did all this for Prue."

"Only did all what?"

"You don't think I—"

"No, I don't think you and Miss Bright are murderesses. I simply wish to know what, precisely, you mean."

"Prue got herself fired on our way to England, see. On the steamship. The little mumchance made a mess of telling the lady our theater troupe owner was chasing that he was really married."

"Ah. Well, Schubert is up at the castle now, you understand. He means to arrest both of you."

"What am I to do?"

"The princess suggested that Smith is the one we want."

"We can't keep chasing after our tails like this!"

"Have you a better suggestion?"

Ophelia jutted her chin. "Give me a minute or two."

"Listen," Penrose said. "Smith lied to us about the princess—we know that now. But when he did so, it occurs to me that he made a small error."

"Error?"

"He connected the princess to Ghent and to the gaming establishment in his efforts to mislead us. That means he knows, somehow, that the gaming establishment is linked to the murders."

"We ought to find Smith, then."

"I searched for him at the castle. He's nowhere to be found. No, I've got to try to speak to Ghent again."

"He'll kill us!"

"Not necessarily. Do you recall the manager in the tea-room saying Ghent enjoys risky wagers?"

Ophelia nodded.

"Well, Princess Verushka said something similar. So, I suggest we give Ghent an invitation he'll find difficult to turn down."

# 29

❧⟳❧

Prue and Hansel hoofed it down the fifty-three castle steps, back to Heidelberg's streets.

"If we return to the library," Hansel said, "we might ask if anyone has seen Miss Gertie Darling, and attempt to track her movements."

"She could be anywhere." Prue wiped sweat from under the edge of her straw bonnet. "Supposing that the last page of the book really does say where Snow White is buried, and supposing Miss Gertie wants to find the tomb as much as we do, well, she could be headed to a churchyard or the railway station or, for all we know, to kingdom come."

"It is worth attempting. We have nothing else."

They started with the librarian, who wasn't amused to see them again. He told Hansel that Gertie had gone out the side door.

Outside the side door was a walkway. Students and learned-looking gents walked to and fro.

"There," Prue said. "A gardener." He was old and bent, sweeping the pavement. "He's sweeping slow enough to have been there for an age."

Hansel described Gertie to the gardener. The gardener squinted, nodded, and pointed down a leafy walkway.

"He said she went this way about two hours ago," Hansel said.

The walkway led away from the university buildings and back into the town. There was an outdoor coffee garden across the way, and people were drinking and eating on metal tables and chairs in the sunshine.

They asked one of the waiters about Miss Gertie. Someone matching her description had come and drunk five cups of tea and devoured three apple dumplings while poring over some sort of paper. Then she had left, going towards the university, not fifteen minutes earlier.

They hightailed it back down the leafy walkway.

"What business could she have at the university," Prue said, "once she got hold of that page? Unless. . . ."

"Unless Snow White is somewhere at the university?"

"That would be plum peculiar. There ain't any burials here, are there?"

"Not that I am aware of."

They were passing by a group of students, who were lolling on the grass in a courtyard. Hansel stopped and spoke to them briefly. The students laughed, and one of them pointed to a building across the courtyard.

Hansel thanked them. "They saw her," he said to Prue. "Hurry."

The building they had been directed to was ivy clad with mullioned windows.

"The philology building," Hansel said.

"What's that?"

"It is many things, but most significantly, it is the building that houses Professor Winkler's office."

"That horrible old fairy tale professor?" Prue balked at the door. "I'd rather meet up with a gouty grizzly bear."

"Winkler will not be here," Hansel said. "He is still in the midst of his study of the cottage. But there might be a reason Miss Darling wishes to visit his office."

Inside, the philology building smelled like mildew, and

the corridors were dark and creaking. They crept along. The first floor had lecture halls filled with desks. All of the halls were empty except one, where a man in a pulpit was droning to a pack of yawning students.

They went upstairs. It was even more murky than the first story, and it smelled of vinegar and something leathery. They went along the corridor, stopping at each closed door to read the nameplates.

The nameplate on the last door in the corridor said *Dr. Siegfried Winkler.*

The door was ajar. Large, sharp splinters speared up around the knob and lock.

Prue met Hansel's eyes. Someone had smashed their way in.

They tiptoed through.

Prue had expected maybe a desk and a bookshelf, some stacks of paper. There was a desk, sure, and piles of untidy books and papers. There was also a door on the far side of the office, gaping open. It led to some cavernous, dark room.

Hansel laid a finger to his lips, tipped his head.

Rustling. Coming from that big, dark room.

Inside the room, that vinegar-and-leather smell hung on the air. Shelves reached from floor to ceiling, filled with wooden crates. A long, cluttered counter stretched down the middle of the room. It was too dim to see what was on the counter, but it looked like boxes and glass cases and things. Maybe more of those gold-test fixings the professor had had at the castle.

Miss Gertie was nowhere to be seen.

"This don't look like a bookworm's hideout," Prue whispered. "Looks like a druggist's shop."

They had reached the middle counter when Gertie loomed up from behind it.

Prue shrieked. Hansel muttered something that didn't sound too gentlemanly.

"You pair." Gertie glared at them across the counter. Her pale eyes did not blink. "Why are you following me? Isn't it quite enough that you intruded upon my privacy at the sanatorium? Now you follow me all the way to Heidelberg?"

"Thought you was only keen on wee folk," Prue said. Her throat was scratchy from screaming. "Didn't know you fancied a college education to boot."

Gertie sniffed. "I have more education in my little toe than you've got in that silly head of yours. And, although it is none of your concern, it turns out that this laboratory houses vital additions to my research. Not that you two court jesters could comprehend that."

"Why did you stop here at Winkler's laboratory?" Prue asked. "Shouldn't you be making a beeline to wherever that ripped-out page says Snow White is buried?"

"How do you know"—Gertie's voice rose in pitch—"about the page?"

Prue shrugged. Hansel stayed silent.

"Of course I wish to locate Snow White's burial treasure," Gertie said.

*Treasure*?

Prue's jaw dropped, and she felt Hansel tense.

"How did you learn about the . . . treasure?" Hansel said.

He was bluffing.

"From that tapeworm Franz. When he had the indecency to wrangle with me over the manuscript at the library this morning, he let slip that it is not Snow White's remains that interest him, but the treasure that lies with her."

"So," Prue said, "you mean to swipe the treasure for yourself? It don't belong to you."

"Did the Rosetta Stone belong to the British troops who secured it? To the victor, you little dunce, go the spoils. Besides, I need the funds. I cannot bear another day of wiping spittle from that old biddy's mouth or listening to her eternal hacking. Have you any idea how much money my father invested in my education? And yet I've been playing nurse to Miss Upton for four years. Four! Paid companion? More like selling your soul to an archfiend in a wicker wheelchair." Gertie was rocking her weight from foot to foot. "This laboratory itself," she continued, "is a treasure. A treasure of scientific value. I had heard rumors of it for years. I could not pass up an opportunity to see it, since I happened to find myself in Heidelberg."

"*Happened* to?" Prue said. "I reckon you came straight here, once Franz told you about them old fairy tale books in the university library. I reckon you've been poking through these crates and things for days."

Gertie sniffed.

"I'll take that as a yes," Prue said.

"We merely want," Hansel said, "the stolen page from the manuscript. Then we shall leave you to snoop through Professor Winkler's rubbish to your heart's content."

"Rubbish?" Gertie sputtered. "*Rubbish?*" Her voice had reached a hysterical octave. She swung around, marched to the high window between two of the shelves, and snapped open the shade. Sunlight streamed across the counter.

Prue stared at the clutter, but she couldn't make heads or tails of it. Not straightaway. In front of her was a paperboard box filled with tiny shoes. Not baby shoes; shoes small enough to fit a newborn kitten, with curled-up pointy toes. There were also corked jars filled with dirt and rocks and brownish, shrively things. A vial of what seemed to be dried peas, another vial of thorns, and a larger glass vat filled with straw. Some delicate, winged things pinned in flat boxes, like butterflies. Except they weren't butterflies, because they had tiny, dried-up people faces and limbs, and they wore clothes the color and texture of dried leaves.

Could those be . . . *fairies?*

Then there was a box of sharp teeth, like a wolf's, and a bottle of dollhouse-size gold coins. There were a lot of gold odds and ends, actually: pocket watches, a gold-embroidered purse, a golden apple, a gold spindle. There was a pair of old-fashioned, red silk lady's shoes, a box of goose feathers, three spinning wheels in a corner, and, hanging on the wall, what appeared to be a big, dried fish's tail. Considering the state of affairs, Prue reckoned it must've been sawed off a mermaid.

Ugh.

The worst thing of all was the large, corked glass jar of brine in the middle of the table. Something that looked a lot like a gnome bobbed inside. Its little pointed hat floated at the surface of the liquid.

Every container had a label with a single word printed on it in blue, spidery ink: *Fictus*.

"What in tarnation is this stuff?" Prue said. She couldn't tear her eyes from the gnome. "And what does *fictus* mean?"

Hansel tried to reply, but he only emitted a scratchy croak. He cleared his throat. "Hoax," he said. "*Fictus* means hoax in Latin. Winkler is the famous fairy tale professor, recall."

"Fairy tale professor, my foot," Gertie said. She shoved something around in her copious bodice. "He labeled every last bit of scientific evidence in this laboratory a hoax. How is he capable of conducting proper fairy tale research if he believes it all to be humbug and chicanery? I believe *Winkler* is the hoax! Now, if you'll excuse me." She strode towards the door.

"Halt!" Hansel cried.

"Go to hell," Gertie said over her shoulder.

Prue ran over and leapt on Gertie's back. It was like mounting a dray horse attired in dun-colored linen. Gertie didn't collapse to the floor, as Prue had hoped. Instead, she spun around in circles, writhing, trying to fling Prue off.

Prue clung with tenacity. They went around and around. Prue's legs whirled out like a rag doll's. Gertie's satchel whirled out, too. Gertie staggered against one of the shelves, and a wooden crate slammed to the floor. Glass vials splintered across the floorboards. Filled with fake dragon's scales, maybe, or Sleeping Beauty's dried snot.

"It's in her bodice!" Prue shouted to Hansel, on the next spin around.

Hansel looked like a deer cornered by a steam tractor.

"Her bodice!" Prue yelled. "The missing page! Get it while I've still got her!"

"You haven't *got* me," Gertie snarled. She clawed at Prue's fingers, trying to peel her off. Prue dug in deep.

Hansel inched closer. He made a few lunges, but Gertie kept flailing out of his reach.

"Don't be such a—a *gentleman*, Hansel!" Prue shouted. "Get the page! Grab her right in the doorknobs!"

Hansel blanched.

Prue was going to have to take matters into her own hands. No way was Mister Chivalrous here going to leap on a lady.

Prue squeezed her eyes shut, reached around, and dug out the folded page, which was luckily sticking out from between a couple of buttons.

Gertie roared.

Prue hopped to her feet. She was soaked in sweat—*whose* sweat she didn't want to think about. She unfolded the page. Gertie was gearing up for another round; Prue saw her out of the corner of her eye, fists balled, shoulders rising and falling.

It truly was the last page from the library book. There was the black ink script that Prue couldn't decipher. But the picture was clear as day: Snow White, eyes shut, hands folded over her breast, lying in a glass coffin.

"What's she in?" Prue said. "Looks like an empty white chamber."

Gertie snatched at the page. Prue whisked it out of her grasp and passed it to Hansel.

Hansel scanned it while Prue blocked Gertie's path. "It says that Snow White lived to be very old," he said, "and when she died, she was, at her request, buried with the seven dwarf miners with whom she had spent the happiest days of her life."

"But where are the seven dwarf miners buried?" Prue said.

"You haven't," Gertie said, ripping the page from Hansel's fingers, "even a speck of a brain in that cranium of yours, have you? Just an empty dolly's head covered in yellow curls."

Prue planted her hands on her hips. "The gumption of you, Miss Gertie Darling. Why, you've got enough yellow hair—and enough *other* things, too, but I wasn't going to mention them—for two ladies put together."

"Is that an allusion," Gertie said through clenched teeth, "to my statuesque figure?"

"It's an allusion to them things some might mistake for steam-powered warships—"

Hansel stepped between them. "Do you mean to suggest," he said to Gertie, "that you know where the seven dwarves are buried?"

Gertie rolled her lashless eyes. "The location would be obvious to all but the haziest of intellects." She folded the page and stuffed it back in her bodice. "Good-bye." At the door, she paused, as though she'd just remembered something. She fished an item out of her leather satchel.

A revolver.

She turned and aimed it at Prue's head. She pulled the trigger.

Prue screamed. There was a bang and a smash. The bullet had exploded a jar of pickled golly-knew-what, on a shelf right next to Prue's ear. Brine and shattered glass and little brownish lumps puddled around Prue's feet. Brine dripped down her cheek. She was fair certain she was going to lose her breakfast. Just as soon as she finished having a hysterical crying fit.

Gertie puffed the smoke from the end of the revolver's barrel and snuggled it back inside her satchel. "Don't you dare follow me, or I *shall* kill you. I'm in just the mood."

# 30

~❧~

After Gertie left Professor Winkler's office, Hansel and Prue waited a couple of shaky minutes to make sure she wasn't coming back. Then they hurried out into the sunshine. Prue's ugly brown dress reeked of fairy tale brine and Gertie sweat. Ugh. How she hankered for a nice, hot bath, and then a big stack of waffles with honey.

"We must return to Schloss Grunewald," Hansel said. He glanced up at the clock on top of one of the university buildings. "We will catch the evening train back to Baden-Baden—it leaves in less than twenty minutes—and speak to Professor Penrose. He may have an idea of where to search next."

"Professor Penrose? But he said you was bent on putting him off the scent."

"I was. I detested the notion of him poking about on the cliff, on my own family's land. But now, well, we need his help."

"Treasure," Prue said. "That's what Franz and Miss Gertie are bent on finding." She glanced up at Hansel. "That's what your pa told you to find, in his letter, he just couldn't come right out and say it. That's what he was . . . what he died on account of. And Mr. Coop, too."

"Perhaps. The manuscript in the library noted something about the dwarves bringing Snow White jewelry, which they had crafted themselves from the gemstones and ore they mined. I wonder. . . ."

The comb felt heavy in Prue's bodice. She was going to have to tell him. She took a deep breath. "I know where Snow White is buried. And the dwarves." She dug into her bodice and pulled out the comb. She passed it to Hansel.

He stared at the comb. "Where did you get this?"

"I found it . . . outside." She swallowed. "Up on the cliff that night you took me along."

"You found it in the dirt?"

"That's right."

"But why did you not show it to me earlier?"

"I just wanted it to comb my hair with, up in the tower." She studied the toes of her banged-up boots. "I didn't tell you about it on account of I didn't want you to think I was . . . think I was vain."

She reckoned he was going to either tell her she *was* vain or accuse her of being a thief.

Instead, he smiled, crinkling up the corners of his eyes. "This is Snow White's comb."

"Yes, sir. Just like the one in the manuscript and the one in that painting of the girl at the Order's house."

"She must be buried on the cliff somewhere."

"Miss Gertie knows it," Prue said. "And so does Franz."

"Franz?"

"He saw the comb this morning and said something I didn't understand till now. He put the pieces together, see, and guessed that if I had that comb—"

"Which he would have recognized, like we do, from the manuscript and the portrait."

"Right. He must have guessed, since we were talking about the grave and the footprints, that I found the comb on the cliff. And he realized that if Snow White's comb came from up on the cliff, *she*'s probably buried up there, too. And so is her treasure."

Hansel placed the comb back in Prue's hand. "Keep it."

"Truly?"

"Yes." He grabbed Prue's hand, and they set off at a canter towards the railway station.

Ophelia and Professor Penrose rode into Baden-Baden and went directly to the *Conversationshaus*. Ophelia waited in the carriage while Penrose went inside. He wore his evening clothes and carried the brief note he'd jotted at the inn. It read,

> *Herr Ghent,*
>
> *Understanding that you are a gambling gentleman, I'd like to propose a game. If I win, you talk. If you win, I'll leave you in peace.*
>
> *Lord Harrington*

Penrose disappeared through the *Conversationshaus* doors.

Ophelia drummed her fingertips on the carriage seat. What would she do if this plan flopped? Smuggle Prue out of town in a traveling trunk? Join a band of gypsies, maybe? Or surely there were circuses here in Europe. Circus tricks and acting weren't the only things Ophelia knew how to do, anyway. She could garden, cook, and sew. Churn butter, lay up preserves, delouse cats. . . .

Three minutes went by. Seven.

It was only a matter of time before the police tracked her down. They'd find the revolver hidden in her chamber, of course—

Penrose emerged, strode down the steps. His expression was bleak.

"Ghent's accepted my offer," he said, climbing inside the

carriage. "I am to play roulette tonight at ten o'clock. But he's changed the terms. He sent a note down saying he'd talk if I win back my original stake seven times over—"

"Yes?"

"—but if I lose, he'll make certain we never talk again."

"This is mullet-headed. You can't!"

"He'll never get away with it."

"You didn't agree, did you?"

"It is possible that Ghent, for some reason, means to do away with us either way—recall the two thugs shooting at us in the wood. At least this way we might have a bit of a say in the matter. Now." Penrose eyed her rumpled woolen dress. "You must accompany me tonight. There's nowhere else for you to go, and I mean to be there when Schubert puts in an appearance. So we've got to get you something to wear."

Baden-Baden had an uncommonly great need for pawn-broker's shops, Ophelia soon learned. The back streets were crammed with them.

"Because of the gambling," Penrose said. "The wheel of fortune revolves rather quickly here, I'm afraid. That, and everyone here wishes to display their every thaler on their backs or in their equipage."

They chose an unassuming shop in a quiet court. The front of the shop was cluttered with the usual pawnbroker's shop fare—violins, candlesticks, books, china, and watches—but a back room held stacks of oil paintings, marble sculptures, wardrobes overflowing with opulent clothing, and a case of winking jewels.

The shopkeeper was an odd little chip with a pince-nez and a greasy waistcoat. He assisted them in finding an evening gown. It was a deep, shimmering, sea blue silk, with a gorgeous cream lace overskirt and an open neckline edged with another wide band of lace. The lady who'd been forced to pawn it off had also sold her crinoline, cream satin elbow gloves, a matching blue silk reticule, and dainty blue and white slippers with a high heel.

Ophelia sighed when she saw the slippers. Her toes throbbed already.

Penrose paid for the clothes, and they left.

They spent the rest of the day in a humble café in an unfashionable district. When evening fell, Ophelia changed into the gown in the washroom, fixing her hair as best she could in the cracked mirror. She stuffed her feet into the slippers. Ouch.

She emerged from the washroom.

Penrose, still at the table, looked up from his newspaper.

He didn't seem to notice the way she was hobbling like a lame pony.

"I hope it'll do," she said. "I've played grand ladies on the stage, but never . . . up close."

"I daresay," he said in a curiously gruff voice, "it'll do."

Ophelia and Professor Penrose swooped into the gaming rooms just before ten o'clock.

"You choose the table, Miss Flax," Penrose said in her ear. "You are luckier than I."

Ghent's two guards were watching them from the other side of the room. They stood like great black andirons, with their hands behind their backs.

Ophelia led Penrose to a table near the back. The table was less crowded than the others, with a grave cloud hanging over it. The green felt table was mounded with bank notes and coins.

Everyone held their breath as the croupier released the ivory ball into the spinning wheel, and everyone cheered when the ball fell home. The croupier raked money into eager hands.

Seemed a lucky enough table. If you believed in that sort of thing.

"This should do it," Ophelia said.

Penrose stepped up to the table.

"*Monsieur?*" the croupier murmured. He had oiled black hair and a narrow moustache.

Penrose placed a modest stack of gold Napoleons on black.

The wheel spun. The ball fell on black 15. Penrose swept half his winnings off the table, and left the remainder on black with his first stake.

The croupier spun the wheel again. This time the ball landed on red 7, and Penrose's stake was whisked away by the croupier's L-shaped stick.

Penrose placed a new modest sum on black.

Ophelia watched, standing just behind Penrose's elbow as he continued to place his stake on black. He was playing it safe. Since he was betting on all of the black numbers and keeping his wager fairly low, he never lost very much. But he didn't win much, either.

She frowned.

As the hour wore on, she observed another player at the table, a frazzled old dowager with a faded velvet reticule and curly white hair. She bet on only a few numbers at a time, and the payout when her numbers came up far exceeded Penrose's winnings.

After an hour and a half, Penrose had barely doubled his original stake.

Ophelia had never played roulette before, but the lads backstage at the theater had whiled away the time gambling on simple coin-toss games that had fifty-fifty odds. One fellow—he'd managed the footlights—often won big by always doubling his bet after a loss. That way, he'd boasted to the admiring circle around him, when he won again, he'd make up for all previous losses.

The ivory ball clicked and hopped onto red 9. There was a collective murmur and sigh around the table. But the frazzled old dowager took in several thousand francs.

"Could I have a few coins?" Ophelia whispered to Penrose.

He glanced back at her, his eyebrow lifted.

"Let me have a try," she said, "or we'll be here till doomsday."

"I'm insuring against catastrophic losses, Miss Flax."

"But also against large winnings."

He straightened his spectacles and plopped a fistful of gold Napoleons into her gloved hand.

Gabriel continued to employ his conservative strategy. Beside him, Miss Flax won four times in a row by placing her stake on only three numbers. Remarkable. A throng swelled round the table as people came to join their luck to hers or simply to admire the lucky young lady in blue.

And she *was* admirable—and very nearly beautiful, with the flush in her cheeks and that flash in her brown eyes. Her upswept hair shone amber in the chandelier light, and the lines of her shoulders and throat were worthy of a muse.

Something coiled darkly about Gabriel's heart. Miss Flax didn't cringe away from all those gazes as a proper young lady, used to quiet domestic scenes, would. What gnawed at him even more, however, was the simple fact that she seemed quite in her element gambling. Almost, in fact, as though she'd done it before.

She was an actress. A former circus performer and factory girl, for God's sake. He had no right—and, naturally, no need—to care one way or the other how she conducted herself. He'd been a fool, of course, trying to shield her virtue when that well had surely dried up long ago.

"Are you mad?" he whispered in her ear, as she nudged a pile of coins onto a single number—13.

"You said yourself that I'm lucky," she said.

The sparkle in her eye was diabolical.

The croupier spun the wheel, tossed the ball.

Gabriel stared in disbelief as the ball fell home on 13.

The crowd exploded into an uproar.

Ophelia laughed as the croupier pushed a tinkling mountain of gold towards her.

"You'll break the bank if you keep this up, miss," a British gentleman said, sucking on the stump of a cigar.

Gabriel felt a heavy tap on his shoulder. He turned. It was the guard with the enormous chin.

"Herr Ghent will see you now," he said.

Ophelia and Penrose followed the guard up the staircase they'd taken before and down the third-floor corridor with its hissing gas sconces.

Ophelia's reticule jangled with all the coins she'd won. She knew it rightly belonged to the professor—after all, he had put up the original stake—but still, it felt delicious to be lugging around all that gold. If it were hers to keep, well, just *think* what she could do with it. She'd buy herself and Prue first-class passage back to New York, buy her dairy farm and an entire herd of the best Brown Swiss cows—

"Gold gone to your head?" Penrose said.

His eyes were distant, but his lips curved upwards in what appeared, at least, to be good humor.

"It does seem to feel different than other things. Heavier and, I don't know, warmer, somehow."

Now his mouth was set. "Seductive, isn't it?"

The guard stopped at the door to Ghent's office. He thumped once with his huge fist.

The door opened a sliver.

It was the tiny, papery little secretary they'd seen before. In the crack of the door, his blue eye glittered like a shard of glass. "Ah," he said, fixing his eye on Ophelia. "Mademoiselle Luck." His eye swiveled to Penrose. "And the professor—or should I say earl?"

"We're here," Penrose said, "to see Herr Ghent."

"He is expecting you." The secretary opened the door. "That," he said to the guard, "will be all."

The guard bowed and left.

The secretary led them through the outer room, which was filled with velvet sofas, dusky oil paintings in gilt frames, and marble statuettes. He opened another door and, without announcing his arrival, led them in.

They found themselves in an office with polished mahogany shelves and cabinets, green leather chairs, and a massive desk, behind which was a high-backed chair, turned to face the other way.

Ophelia and Penrose stopped just inside the door.

Ophelia stared at the chair, expecting it to swivel around and reveal—what? A lion-headed patriarch, massive and threatening and—

Her jaw dropped.

The secretary had seated himself in the chair and turned it to face them. The chair dwarfed him; he looked like a marionette's puppet.

"I am enjoying the expressions on your faces," he said.

"You are," Penrose said, "Herr Ghent?"

"Yes. And you are the nuisances who have given my guards such a trying time of it." He tilted his head. "I thought they would have killed you by now—that is, after all, what I instructed them to do. But here you are." He studied Ophelia.

Even though Ophelia could probably lug Ghent around on her hip like a baby, she shrank back under his gaze.

"You," he said to her, "thought you would break my bank, did you?"

"I thought I'd try." She pretended boldness. "I didn't get a chance to finish."

"Well, close enough, close enough. When my messenger came up from the gaming rooms and said the young American lady was on a lucky streak, my curiosity got the better of me."

Ghent swung his legs to and fro beneath the desk. His feet didn't even reach the floor.

"I assume," Penrose said, "that even though you stopped the game short, you'll uphold your end of the bargain?"

"Of course. I am a gentleman."

"Then tell us, pray, what is Mr. George Smith's true name?"

"You cannot guess? I thought university professors were attentive."

Ophelia's breath caught. Ghent's eyes. She'd seen that shade of blue before. Recently. "Mr. Smith's real name," she said. "Is it . . . Ghent?"

"The maidservant outthinking the scholar!" Ghent smacked his small palms together. "Delightful."

Penrose's mouth was tight, but other than that his expression remained mild. "Mr. George Smith is, what? Your brother?"

"Cousin. My father's brother's son. He went off to seek his fortune in California during the gold rush of 1849. He left me to tend our family greengrocer's shop by myself." Ghent sniffed. "He told me he would not stay poor, like me, nor would he consent to sharing the profits of one small shop. He said that he would find gold and become a wealthy man. I stayed behind, scraping together enough to travel to Paris for a time and invest in speculative stocks. I earned enough money in Paris to purchase a small hotel in Baden-Baden, and it grew into a success. Over time, I saved and invested enough to buy this gaming establishment and make it into the triumph it is today."

The weight of all that gold in Ophelia's reticule no longer seemed delicious. It was a burden. Gold drove people to leave their families, to circle the globe, to sacrifice. To kill.

# 31

❧

"Princess Verushka," Penrose said to Ghent, "intimated that learning Smith's true name would reveal something important about the deaths of Mr. Coop and Count Grunewald. Yet I fail to see the connection between those crimes and the fact that the owner of the *Conversationshaus* happens to have an American cousin."

"No?" Ghent looked to Ophelia. "And you, Mademoiselle Luck? Have you any guesses?"

"Gold," she blurted. "You both want gold. There's gold hidden somewhere on the castle land, isn't there?"

"Very good. What a clever maidservant you are." Ghent sneered at Penrose.

Penrose shoved his hands in his trouser pockets.

"The gold is not precisely hidden, however," Ghent said. "There is a gold mine somewhere, said to be richer, deeper, than anything to be found in California. My cousin has been searching for it. But I shall have it."

"How did Smith—your cousin, that is," Penrose said, "know there was a mine on the estate?"

Ghent steepled his toy-like fingers. "Our family has

known there was a rich mine, somewhere in the *Schwarzwald*, for generations. We have been searching for it, without luck, as we grew poorer and poorer. But that mine by rights belongs to us. It is our inheritance."

"Are you. . . ." Ophelia furrowed her brow. "Are you Grunewalds, then?"

"*Ach*, perhaps you are not as clever as I thought. No. The Ghents are descendants of an ancient race of men who worked these mountains, bringing up gold."

"You are descended," Penrose said in a slow, wondering tone, "from Snow White's dwarves."

Ghent pounded his tiny fist on the desktop. "As though we belonged to that girl! As though we were her servants! No. The dwarves in that tale were my ancestors. But there is much more to the story than that. They had worked the mines since time immemorial, until somehow—no one is certain what happened—they lost access to their mines, and the knowledge of the mines' whereabouts was forgotten."

"Until Smith arrived," Penrose said.

"Yes. My cousin learned, I know not how, that the richest mine of all was located in the forest of Schloss Grunewald. He convinced Coop to purchase the castle, and he set to work searching for the entrance to the mine. When I learned he had returned to the *Schwarzwald*, and when my men reported that he had been sighted in the hills, making maps and testing the rocks, I knew at once what he was doing."

"Did you kill Mr. Coop?" Ophelia said.

"Of course not. I had no opportunity. When he died, however, I did send my men into the *schloss* to retrieve the skeleton and the rest of the contents of the house."

"Why?" Ophelia said.

"Would you want scholars poking and probing the remains of *your* ancestors?"

"Where are those relics now?" Penrose said.

"Relics, you say. As though they were meant to be in a museum. Or perhaps filed away in a crate on a university shelf."

Penrose flexed his jaw.

"The skeleton was buried," Ghent said.

"And the relics?"

Ghent smiled. "I sold them."

"Sold them!"

"You do not believe you are the only person in the world interested in folk relics? There are certain persons—collectors, properly speaking—who pay extravagantly for such things. And, as it turns out, it is fortunate that I sold them off quickly to the highest bidder, because I have, now, a deficit to make up in my gaming rooms." Ghent sighed. "I have revealed enough. Now listen. You, both of you, are to take the first morning train out of Baden-Baden—I care not where—and never return. If you do not leave, I shall make certain you are killed and buried so deeply in the *Schwarzwald*, no one but the wild beasts shall ever discover your remains. Go now. The thrill has worn off." He turned to some papers on his desktop.

"But who killed Mr. Coop and the count?" Ophelia said.

"*Miss Flax*," Penrose whispered.

Ghent lifted his vivid blue eyes. "Why, I thought that would be obvious. Once Coop and Count Grunewald became aware of the presence of the mines, my cousin killed them. He never did, you see, like to share."

"We must go directly to the police," Penrose told Ophelia, as they hurried down the corridor. "Smith told us in the cave yesterday that he planned to return to America, whether it was forbidden or not. We've got to tell Schubert about him before it's too late."

"Do you believe Herr Ghent?"

"He seemed forthright enough. Particularly when he got to the bit about having us killed."

"I mean the part about his ancestry, and Smith's ancestry. That they are descended from Snow White's dwarves. How are we going to tell *that* to Inspector Schubert with a straight face?"

"We'll tell Schubert exactly what Ghent told us. Prue shall be exonerated. Your goal shall be accomplished."

Why did he sound so chilly?

"What about *your* goal?" she said. "You haven't gotten an inch closer to it."

There was a pause. "Yes," he finally said. "Yes, I have."

"And?"

"I am well aware that you are a Yankee, and as such, you cannot extend your mind far enough to comprehend mysteries beyond your everyday scope of experience."

*What?* Ophelia scowled. "Why are you being so—so *sniffy* all of a sudden?"

"I believe—if that is even the correct word—in the truth of fairy tales, Miss Flax. I believe there are things that pass below our mundane routines, above our comprehension. I have committed my life to learning more of the mysteries contained within and alluded to in these pieces of folklore. They are based upon fact, not fiction."

"It seems you're most interested in relics," she said. "Not stories."

He stopped. They'd reached the top of the sweeping staircase that led to the foyer.

Ophelia stopped, too. "It's true, isn't it? You're one of those collectors, like Ghent sold those relics to. You pretend you've got a scholarly interest, but when it comes right down to it, you're just like any other rich fellow who reckons he ought to be able to buy whatever pretty bauble he wants. And if he can't buy it, why, he'll steal it!" She was panting.

His hair, always so neatly combed, was loose across his forehead, and his lips were parted in anger. "How dare you speak of things of which you know nothing?"

"How dare I? I reckon I'd never speak at *all* if you had your say! The fact is, professor, I kept thinking you were helping—not me, I guess—but I thought you were helping get to the bottom of these murders because it was the right thing to do. But it was staring me in the face all along that you were doing it out of greed. Out of—of an *obsession* with those relics. It's not wholesome—it's not right. They're just things! Aren't people more valuable than things? Well, you can take your relics, and welcome!" She took off down the stairs.

He was trotting down the steps beside her. "I'm aware you New Englanders adore staking out the moral high ground—"

"Why, I—"

"—but we mustn't overlook the fact that you, my dear, are a confidence trickster. And not as much of a new hand at it as you'd like me to believe. The way you positively soaked up the attention from the crowd at that roulette table—"

Wait. He almost sounded . . . *jealous.*

"—but, of course, it's really none of my concern. As soon as we relay this information to Schubert at the police station, you shall have no further need for me."

"Now wait a minute. You make it sound as though I just—just used you to get what I wanted!"

"That's what confidence sharks do, is it not?"

They rounded the last curve in the stairs.

Inspector Schubert lurked at the bottom of the stairs, flanked by policemen. "Miss Flax," he said, "you are under arrest for murder."

One of the other policemen grabbed her arm.

"Before you arrest her," Penrose said, "I've something to tell you."

He told Schubert all they had learned, about Princess Verushka, Mr. Smith, and Herr Ghent—even the part about Snow White's dwarves.

To Ophelia's surprise, Schubert didn't even smile at that part.

When Penrose had finished, Schubert was silent, thinking. At last, he said, "I am displeased that you both have meddled to this extent in my investigations. Nonetheless, the evidence that points to Mr. Smith as a possible suspect is compelling. I shall go with my men immediately to Schloss Grunewald. Miss Flax, return to the *schloss* as well, and await my further instructions."

Ophelia wrenched her arm free of the policeman's grip.

Penrose escorted Ophelia to the waiting carriage and helped her inside. But he didn't get in.

"I shall pay the driver and instruct him to return you to the castle," he said.

"Pay him? Oh! I nearly forgot!" Ophelia thrust her reticule towards him.

He waved a hand. "You keep it. You did quite a lot of hard work to earn that gold."

She narrowed her eyes. "You, Professor Penrose, are a sight too big for your breeches! You're a gullible, highfalutin stuffed shirt!"

"Gullible? Perhaps your superb acting abilities got the better of me." He moved to shut the carriage door.

"You think," she choked out, "you're too good for the likes of me." Just before the door closed, she flung the reticule to his feet. It burst open and gold coins flew out, sparkling yellow in the gaslight, falling to the gravel in a tinkling shower.

He hit the top of the carriage with unnecessary force, and the driver set his horses into motion.

Inside, Ophelia kicked off the pinching slippers, pressed her fist against her forehead, and, her breaths coming sharply, wished she could cry. Her carriage rolled off into the night.


Gabriel paced the streets of Baden-Baden for more than an hour, hands thrust in pockets and head hung low, before he decided to return to Schilltag.

Once in his chamber at the inn, he peeled off his evening jacket, loosened his tie, poured himself a large brandy, and sank down on the chair.

He took a first long swallow to dull the edge of his fury. The second swallow was to assuage his niggling conscience. Miss Flax was only a poor, young, uneducated lady trying to eke out a life. The third gulp was to blur the too-vivid memory of her lovely eyes.

From where he sat, he could see into the closet where his tweed jacket hung. His boots were on the floor, and beside the closet door was the chair with his leather valise. There was also a shelf at the top of the closet.

He stared hard. The shelf was empty. Yet—he lowered the brandy glass from his lips—yet that was where he'd stashed the two boxes from Horkheimer's shop.

The cuckoo clock and the dwarf figurine he'd purchased were gone.

He set his brandy aside and did a quick once-over of the chamber. The boxes were nowhere to be found.

When his chamber had been searched that night, he'd thought nothing had been taken.

He'd been wrong.

He slumped back down on the chair. It had to have been Ghent's guards.

A pity. That clock was the only thing Gabriel had left of the wondrous find in the wood to take with him back to Oxford.

Perhaps, before he went to the railway station in the morning, he'd stop and purchase another one.

He turned back to his brandy.


Ophelia stole back into the castle and hurried up to her bedchamber to change. Then she went down to the kitchen.

The kitchen was empty. Orange coals glowed in the grate. She paced and waited.

She would *not* think of the professor.

Fifteen minutes later, the police arrived.

By the time Schubert and his two men were at Mr. Smith's bedchamber door, in a remote wing of the castle, most of the household trailed in their wake.

Ophelia wanted to see Smith arrested and taken away with her own eyes. Then she'd demand that Prue be cleared of all suspicion.

"Miss Flax," Cook whispered to Ophelia, as they hovered behind the police, "I fancied I would never lay eyes on you again!"

"What do you mean?"

"Why, the police came here to arrest you and Prue, and they discovered you were both gone missing. Those naughty maids Katrina and Freda had been paid by Hansel to keep mum about Prue being gone. Prue went off with Hansel, to elope, I would judge. I never saw so much love-sick mooning in all my days."

"Prue is still gone?" Ophelia's blood chilled. Surely Prue should have returned from Heidelberg by now.

Cook nodded. "Mind you, I did not believe for a minute that you two were murderesses." She glanced at Ophelia. "Actresses, now *that* I could believe."

"Silence!" Schubert ordered.

Everyone clammed up.

Schubert knocked. No answer. He knocked again. Not a sound.

"This is the police, Smith! Open the door!" Schubert tried the door handle. To everyone's surprise, it opened easily.

It was soot dark inside.

"A light, Benjamin," Schubert said.

Benjamin lit a gas lamp, and the policemen ventured into the chamber. The servants hung back.

The chamber was in shambles. Tables and chairs were on their sides, the carpet was puckered, and one of the drapes dangled from the curtain rod. The oval mirror on the armoire was shattered and smeared with what was, unmistakably, blood.

Prue and Hansel sneaked into the shadowy castle gardens through the orchard door. They had ridden to Schilltag from the railway station on a hired mare and walked the rest of the way.

The castle windows were all lit up. Figures darted to and fro inside.

"Something is happening in there," Prue said. "And"—her breath caught—"ain't that someone standing up in that window, goggling down at us?"

Hansel squinted up at the tower. "We ought not go into the castle until after we have investigated the cliff for Snow White's tomb. We cannot afford any delays. The police might be searching for you in there, Prue."

Hansel dug out a lantern and shovel from the gardening shed. He grabbed Prue's hand, and they headed out into the forest.

Ophelia hurried along the battlement, towards the tower. Her hair flew behind her, and cold wind whipped and swirled down from the indigo sky. The tower loomed up. No light shone in its windows.

"Prue!" Ophelia yelled, as she neared the tower door. "Prue, wake up! It's me, Ophelia!"

Silence.

Her hands shook as she felt for the door handle. It was hard to see in the faded light. She should've brought a lamp.

The door was unlocked. She pushed it inwards. The hinges moaned.

"Prue?"

As her eyes adjusted to the deeper darkness, she saw a three-legged stool, a stack of books. In one corner, the ticking mattress. In another corner, the chamber pot.

It was true. Prue was gone.

Ophelia feared her heart would burst.

She turned and retraced her steps along the battlement. This time she was running.

# 32

~

She rushed to the kitchens, unable to think of where else to go.

"Prue's truly gone!" she cried, bursting in.

The servants were clustered around the hearth. They had been talking softly and were wide-eyed. They fell silent and stared at her.

Cook spoke first. "You look like a wild creature, Miss Flax."

"Prue's gone!" Ophelia repeated. "The tower is empty! Don't you care?"

"I told you," Cook said, "Prue has been missing since yesterday."

Katrina and Freda nodded. Freda crunched into a raspberry pastry.

"Oh, but she has returned," Wilhelm said.

Everyone turned to stare at him. "I saw Prue, and Hansel, too, not five minutes ago, going across the kitchen gardens hand in hand like two children."

Of course. *Hansel.*

"Why," Cook asked, "did you not tell us?"

Wilhelm shrugged. "I did not think it mattered anymore, since now the police are searching for Mr. Smith."

"You saw the blood in Mr. Smith's chamber!" Ophelia cried. "Something's happened to him, too, and the murderer—the *true* murderer—is still at large! Where were Prue and Hansel going?"

Wilhelm sipped his tea at what seemed an excruciatingly slow pace. "I do not know."

"Which direction were they headed?"

"Let me think." Wilhelm gazed into his teacup. "Towards the orchard, if I recall correctly. *Ja.* Towards the gate in the wall."

The forest. Hansel was taking her out to the *forest*.

No time for cogitating. Ophelia hotfooted across the kitchen to the door and out into the windswept, starry night.

She stumbled through the kitchen gardens and burst out into the top of the orchard.

Perhaps it was nothing. Perhaps Hansel and Prue *had* only been going for a stroll and a little fresh air.

But Ophelia couldn't forget the nasty gleam in Hansel's eyes, the grim set of his mouth, when he'd said Homer T. Coop had deserved to die. There was no telling what he was capable of.

She squinted down into the jagged black ring of trees. There was a flickering light, not far beyond the perimeter of the orchard. Someone was down there. Moving, step by step, deeper into the forest.

She hitched up her skirts and raced down the orchard slope, towards the light.


In the forest, Ophelia could no longer see the flickering light, but she rushed blindly forward. She stumbled on sharp stones, the thorny undergrowth tore at her clothes and cheeks, but she could think of nothing but Prue.

She'd let her down.

Ophelia's lungs wheezed and her heart thundered. She

stumbled and fell on a clump of ferns, and as she scrambled to her feet, she saw again, wavering in the trees ahead, the light.

"Prue!" she tried to yell. It came out as a croak. She scrabbled and clawed her way forward.

Above her in the canopy of trees, an owl hooted, and there were black, fanning wings. She recalled, dimly, the talk of bears in this wood and the furred boars with their pointed tusks. The wolves.

She didn't care. She'd fight them off with her bare hands. She'd—

Out of nowhere, an impossibly forceful blow hit her head.

The forest was, for a brief instant, lit up in a shower of stars. Then she was falling, and everything went black.

Hansel led the way up the steep path. The moon rode behind spiny, black treetops. Every last rustle and cheep in the thickets made Prue jump.

At the top, out on the cliff, cold wind whipped around in all directions. The landscape below and beyond the cliff was a vista of blurry grays. But a yellow light glowed and shuddered from behind one of the boulders on the cliff.

Prue glued herself to Hansel. "What's that scraping sound?" she whispered. It was grating and rhythmic, and it came from the direction of the light.

Hansel shook his head.

They picked their way over the rocks, towards the light. They came up to the boulder and peeked over.

There was a fizzing lantern balanced on a stone. There was also a man on his hands and knees. His face was averted, and he was scraping at a rock with some small tool. He turned his head.

"Franz!" Prue cried. "What, for land sakes, are you doing down there?"

Franz didn't stop scraping. "I found them," he said. "I found them all. All seven. See?" He lurched to his feet, lifted the lantern, and stumbling over rocks, illuminated a round stone. "Come closer." His voice was whipped away on a gust of wind.

Hansel and Prue came around the boulder.

Franz showed them seven stones carved with numerals: *I, II, III, IV, V, VI, VII*. There was the dug-up grave they'd found before, in front of the *IV* marker.

"Seven dwarves," Prue said. "Seven graves."

"But where in God's name is hers?" Franz said. "It must be here somewhere. It must!" It was tough to tell whether the wobble in Franz's voice was the start of laughter or tears. Maybe both. "I have been here, scraping, for hours. Yet look how many rocks there are still!" He swept a hand around the cliff. "It will take days. Days and days."

Prue gasped. She'd caught a flash of Franz's hand in the lantern light. His fingers were bloody, his nails clotted with black moss. And his eyes, beneath his wind-lashed hair, burned like those of a madman.

"Calm yourself," Hansel said.

"Calm myself!" Franz shrieked. Then he tipped back his throat and cackled up to the moon-glow clouds. "Calm? At a time like this? When a treasure beyond price lies in the balance? Hansel, Hansel. I would have thought you, of all people, would comprehend what a great difference it makes to one's life chances if one has treasure laid up in the bank."

Prue felt Hansel stiffen.

"Do you not think it a bit greedy," Franz said, "to attempt to steal this treasure out from under my nose?"

"He ain't stealing," Prue said. "The treasure belongs to Hansel, seeing as it's buried with *his* ancestress."

Franz squinched his eyes. "What did that missing manuscript page say? You saw it. You found that British bovine and saw the page." He prowled closer.

Prue's heart thumped.

"We are here," Hansel said, "because we realized, like you, that the comb in Miss Bright's possession belonged to Snow White. That it came from this cliff."

"I do not believe you," Franz said. "There is more." He bent and snatched something off the ground.

A sword. Long and thin, like those the students had been dueling with in Heidelberg.

He darted around Hansel, clutched Prue's elbow, and yanked her to his bony chest. He pressed the sword's edge to her throat.

"You know something I do not," Franz said. He dragged Prue, both of them staggering over rocks, to the cliff's edge. Cold, pine-scented wind gusted up from the abyss. "Tell me what the last page said or I shall slit her throat and toss her over."

He was trembling, and the sword's blade bit into Prue's skin.

Stinging pain blossomed. Blood tickled down Prue's neck, and tears blurred her vision.

Hansel inched towards them, speaking in lulling tones. "How did you know of the existence of a burial treasure?"

"Herr Ghent told me. He told all of us. All of his workers."

"Ghent? The owner of the gaming rooms?"

"How did you suppose I went from being a croupier to a student at university? Only gentlemen go to university. Ghent made a gentleman of me."

"But why?"

"He knew I could be of use to him. The evil little mite only uses people. Fancies the world is his chessboard. He caught me stealing from his casino, and he took an interest in me. Recognized another cunning spirit. He had long wished to learn about the Order of Blood and Ebony, suspecting they might possess knowledge about his ancestors."

"*His* ancestors?"

"The mining dwarves."

Prue squeezed away her tears, because another light had appeared behind Hansel, at the back of the cliff. It was a lantern carried by a bulky form in a skirt.

Gertie.

"In exchange for infiltrating the Order," Franz said to

Hansel, "Ghent paid for my education. And my clothing, and my boardinghouse, and so on. But as the year wore on, it became apparent that the Order of Blood and Ebony was nothing but a sorry excuse for young bucks to drink themselves into stupors and pester pretty black-haired barmaids. Ghent's patience was wearing thin when Homer T. Coop was killed."

"Then Ghent had further use for you, after all," Hansel said.

"Yes. He wished for me to discover more about the house in the wood and Coop's death. And this one"—Franz brought his lips close to Prue's cheek—"proved to be a font of knowledge."

"That is why we encountered you in Baden-Baden two days after Coop was murdered. Ghent summoned you."

Prue was watching Gertie's silhouette. Gertie had been bobbing around at the back of the cliff, shoving bushes and boulders. And then suddenly, Gertie and her lantern disappeared into some kind of black hole.

"This grows wearisome," Franz said. Keeping hold of Prue, he shoved her to the utmost edge of the cliff. One of her feet dangled in nothingness. The other was sliding on loose dirt, about to go over. She screamed. It echoed into the vast wilderness.

Hansel lunged forward. With one hand he reached out and grabbed a fistful of Prue's ugly brown dress. With his other hand he clobbered Franz square in the nose.

Franz made a noise that sounded like "Urgh." His fingers released Prue's wrist. Hansel dragged Prue to the safety of his arms. And Franz sagged like a sack of potatoes and pitched over the edge of the cliff.

"Holy mackerel!" Prue squirmed out from Hansel's arms and rushed to the cliff's edge. Franz had landed on a rocky ledge about six feet down. His jacket was hooked in a scraggly bush. His eyes were shut.

Hansel was next to her. "He appears to be breathing."

"Knocked out, though."

"That bush will most likely keep him from going over the precipice."

"He'll keep." Prue scrambled to her feet. "Let's see what Gertie's doing."

"Gertie? What about the wound on your neck?"

"Come on!"

Turned out, there was a cave back against the cliff, behind some rubble and bracken. The entrance was as big around as a barrel, glowing with light. Gertie must have rolled away the boulder that stood just to the side of the cave's entrance.

Inside, Prue was expecting more rubble, dirt, maybe a bear. But it was a chamber. It was paved all around—floor, walls, ceiling—in marble that might've been white as milk once. Now black lichen crept across everything.

A marble slab, also covered in lichen, sat in the middle of the chamber. On top of the slab was an oblong box. Gertie, disheveled and breathless, hunched over the box, holding her lantern high.

Prue and Hansel crept in. Pebbles skidded across the marble floor.

Gertie glanced up. Her eyes were round, her mouth slack. "She is here," she murmured. All her hostility seemed to be forgotten.

Prue and Hansel stole forward. Prue figured this was how visiting a shrine would feel, even though it smelled like earthworms and dirt.

The box was all clouded up with gray and black, made of some kind of glass.

"You going to open it?" Prue whispered. Her voice rebounded against all that marble. Goosebumps sprouted on her arms.

"It hasn't any hinges," Gertie said. "It will take several men to move the top." She set her lantern on the casket and started rubbing at the glass with her gloved hand.

A millipede squiggled past.

After a moment, Gertie had cleared a round patch.

"There she is." Gertie nudged the lantern closer. "Look."

Prue looked.

*Eek*.

A skull grimaced up at her. Strings of long gray hair

clung to the skull. Neck bones disappeared beneath the papery remains of a gown.

Prue edged away. "Well. No sign of treasure here. We'd best be going."

"Wait," Hansel said. "There is something in there. Yes, see? There is a bracelet about the bones of her wrist."

Gertie lunged forward. "So it is! And here! Ah! A breach in the casket."

There was a long crack along one side of the casket, and a small piece of glass had collapsed inward.

Gertie thrust her fist through and yanked the bracelet. It came out in her gloved fist, along with a couple of Snow White's finger bones. They tinkled to the floor.

Prue stared down at the finger bones. Then she stared up at Gertie, who was polishing the bracelet. It was made of the same tarnished gold as the ruby comb, a thick cuff deeply carved and inlaid with dirty green stones.

"Emeralds," Gertie said. "Gold." She rubbed frantically at the rest of the casket. "There ought to be more jewelry in there. Mounds and mounds of jewelry. I cannot wheel around that old battle axe any longer. One more consumptive cough into her hankie and I'll wring her bloody neck!" She scowled into the casket. "Where in blazing Hades is the rest of the treasure?" She raced around the perimeter of the marble room. There was nothing to be seen but twigs and leaves that critters had carted in.

Gertie let out a roar and gave the wall a ferocious kick with her walking boot. Then she kicked the wall in another place, and another. Suddenly, a big section of marble wall gave way, swinging back on slow hinges. Blackness yawned beyond. Gertie hesitated, but only for a second. She grabbed her lantern and brought it to the door. A tunnel curled steeply down into the earth. The dirt walls were held back by ancient beams.

"Do not go down there," Hansel called to Gertie. "The walls could collapse."

"Stuff it," Gertie said, and crawled through the hole on all fours.

Prue stared at Gertie's retreating rump. "We can't just let her go! She's crawling down into the belly of the mountain!"

"She is a woman grown," Hansel said. "We shall send men after her. But first, we must get help for Franz and bring him down to the castle. He must be looked after by a doctor—as should you. Your throat looks a sight. And there is no treasure here."

Gabriel rose at seven o'clock. He re-bandaged his shoulder wound, dressed, packed his valise and trunk, and left his chamber.

As he passed Winkler's door, he slowed. Ought he say good-bye? No. He'd see him soon enough back in Heidelberg.

He drank a cup of coffee in the empty dining room. He arranged for his luggage to be brought down from his chamber and for a carriage to take him to the Baden-Baden railway station at eight.

He made his way along the cobbled village lane, ignoring Schloss Grunewald towering up into the fresh morning sky.

There was no utility in thinking of Miss Flax, of her messy little confidence scheme, of the pained expression in her eyes, of her shoulders in that evening gown. He and Miss Flax came from different worlds. It was better this way.

Gabriel came to a stop before the window of Horkheimer's shop. Dark. He shaded his eyes and peered through the glass. The shop appeared somewhat . . . depleted. As though half of its stock was gone. Surely Horkheimer wasn't going out of business?

"*Kann Ich Sie helfen*?" a man called, somewhere above Gabriel's head.

Gabriel stepped back from the shop window and looked up. It was Horkheimer, leaning out of an upstairs window, a striped nightcap dangling from his head.

"Ah," Horkheimer said. "It is you. Enjoying your cuckoo clock?"

"I'm awfully sorry to have woken you," Gabriel said, "but as a matter of fact, I'd hoped to purchase another. The one I bought seems to have been . . . it was lost, I'm afraid."

"I would like to fulfill your request, sir, but I am afraid all of those particular clocks have been purchased."

"All of them? Those carved by Frau Herz, you understand."

"*Ja*. All of them are gone. And I would direct you to the shops in Baden-Baden where Frau Herz sometimes sells her clocks, but yesterday a tourist told me that all of her clocks have been purchased in Baden-Baden as well. We seem to have a collector in our midst."

"Who," Gabriel said, "purchased them all?"

Horkheimer told him.

"But *why*?"

"That I could not tell you."

"Martin?" a woman's voice said, somewhere behind Horkheimer.

"My wife," Horkheimer said to Gabriel. "Best of luck finding a clock." He let the window sash fall.

# 33

G abriel returned to the inn.
　　He pounded on Winkler's door. When there was
no response, he pushed it open.

The chamber was empty.

"Professor Winkler departed yesterday evening," the
innkeeper's wife said. She'd followed him upstairs.

Gabriel went back to his own chamber. He tore through
his trunk and dug up his revolver. He loaded it, rammed it
into his breast pocket, and headed up to the castle.

Miss Flax needed to be warned.

Gabriel arrived, breathless, at the castle, and pounded
with both fists on the huge front doors. He was met with
silence. Somewhere on the bluff, a lark twittered inanely.

He tried the door, but it was bolted fast. He strode across
the forecourt, around the castle's east side, and found the
doors that led into the kitchens. There were people moving
about in there, he saw through a window.

He burst in.

"Where is Miss Flax?" he said to no one in particular.

She wasn't in the kitchen.

The other servants were breakfasting at a long plank table. They stared at him as though he'd appeared from the ether.

"Miss Flax?" the cook said, her porridge spoon poised midair.

The two maidservants glanced at each other.

The footman—Gabriel recalled he was named Wilhelm—said, "Miss Flax has, ah—vanished."

"I beg your pardon?"

Wilhelm explained—with interjections from the two maids—that Smith, Miss Bright, Hansel, and Miss Flax had all disappeared during the night.

"Disappeared?" Gabriel said. "What do you mean by that?"

Wilhelm's soft cheeks trembled. "Simply gone." He described the scene of violence in Smith's bedchamber and how Miss Flax, searching for Prue, had disappeared as well.

"But there are mad people on the loose. Murderers."

"I am very sorry, sir," Wilhelm said.

Gabriel raked a hand through his hair. "Where's Schubert—is he still here?"

"Yes. He and his men began a thorough search of the *schloss* at daybreak—"

"At daybreak? Anything could have happened overnight."

"—and they are now, having failed to find any clues as to the whereabouts of the missing persons, conversing in the library."

"Conversing," Gabriel said. "Have they searched the wood?"

There was a screeching sound.

Gabriel noticed for the first time an old crone hunkered on her stool in the chimney corner. She was writing with a stub of chalk on a slate.

Surely the old countess. Matilda.

"What is she writing?" Gabriel said.

No one answered.

He rushed to Matilda's side, bent to read the slate. She had printed in German, in a shaking hand, *The gold mine*.

The gold mine!

How could he have been so bloody blind? It had *always* been about the gold. Every last detail.

Gabriel crouched and held out his palm, and Matilda dropped the chalk into his hand. *Where is it?* He wrote. He passed her the chalk.

*The dwarf's head.*

*I know there is a dwarf's head on the tapestry,* he scrawled, *but I could not find it in the wood.*

Matilda's eyes twinkled as she took the chalk.

How delightful to see the old dame was enjoying herself.

*The dwarf's face crumbled long ago*, she wrote.

Gabriel sucked in a breath.

*—and all that remains is the cliff on top of his head, and an outcrop by the stream.*

Gabriel kissed the lady's shrunken cheek and ran out of the kitchen.


The wood was peaceful. Birds chirruped, squirrels skittered up tree trunks, and sunlight sloped through the treetops in long, luminous shafts.

Gabriel found the path he'd taken twice before. Little had he known that the mouth of the cave he and Miss Flax had hidden in had been, quite literally, the mouth of the giant dwarf's head outcropping and the marker of the fabled gold mine. Perhaps the miners had carved it, long ago, as some fantastical monument to their industry. Or perhaps it was one of nature's poetic caprices.

The path began its curving ascent away from the valley. Gabriel was just about to plunge down into the fern-filled ravine, towards the cave, when he stopped in his tracks.

A few paces ahead, there was a large rock—a boulder, really—at the side of the path. It was pale gray and had patches of lichen here and there. But there was something else on it, too.

His belly clenched as he approached the rock. On it, at hip's height, was a two-fingered smear of blood. The blood had turned brown already.

He rushed further up the trail, scanning the loamy path and the rocks and tree trunks on either side. It was not long before he discovered another finger smear of blood, this time on the grooved bark of a tree.

Someone had left a deliberate trail.

He saw one last flash of Miss Flax's beautiful dark eyes, and his belly lurched one last time. Then he shuttered that part of his mind. It never paid to be sentimental.

He moved quickly and efficiently, scanning the trees and rocks and finding, spaced at varying intervals, smears of blood to mark the way. The blood led him high onto a mountainside, off the path, and deeper into the wood. He was so intent on his task that when he found himself in the clearing of the abandoned hunting lodge he did not, at first, realize where he was.

The lodge was smaller than he remembered. It was built of stone, with pointed gothic windows and crumbling gargoyles in the shape of—he smiled bitterly—dwarves.

He crept towards the lodge and peered through one of the windows. The diamond-shaped panes were so filthy he could make out nothing but a dull glow of light, a blur of motion.

Someone, then, was still alive in there.

He drew his revolver from inside his jacket, checked the cylinders. He mounted the steps of the lodge. He pushed the door open.


The sight that met his eyes was so strange he could not, for several dragging moments, comprehend it. There was the gaping fireplace, the mounted beasts' heads, the bronze and antler chandelier. But also, in the center of the chamber, a large cage, made of gnarled sticks tied together with twine.

There was a person inside the cage, curled on his side on the floor, his short, bare arms wrapped around naked knees.

"Smith?" Gabriel said.

Smith opened his eyes. They were as dull as rocks.

Gabriel rushed to the cage. Smith was unclothed, save a pair of drawers. There was a nasty-looking gash on his left arm.

"Are you all right?" Gabriel said. "Who put you in there?"

Smith only stared.

"I'm getting you out," Gabriel said. He started to circle round the cage. There appeared to be a door of sorts on the other side.

"Ah. Penrose. I was curious if you would turn up."

Gabriel stopped and turned to face Professor Winkler, who hulked in a doorway that led to another part of the lodge.

"I'm afraid," Gabriel said, "I must insist that you release this man."

"Man? He is hardly a *man*. As you have probably deduced by now—because I do, Penrose, despite everything, have the most reverential respect for your intellect—Mr. Smith here, or, shall we say, Mr. Ghent, is not a man at all. He is a dwarf."

"Is that why you've got him caged like an animal?"

"He is skittish, like most creatures, even the domesticated ones, and he would not allow me to study him. After he carelessly revealed to me yesterday that he'd been a California gold miner—a forty-niner, I believe he termed it—my suspicions were at last confirmed. I was forced to capture and cage him. Do not look at me like that, Penrose—I shall not *eat* him. I fully intend to release him when I am through."

Gabriel scanned the chamber. Winkler's black bag squatted on a table. Various unidentifiable items were arranged beside it. "I think, Winkler, that you're already quite through with him."

"Oh, but you are wrong. I have only just begun." Winkler's piggy eyes burned. "Do you not comprehend what an opportunity this is? I have waited and searched my whole life for a dwarf—a real dwarf! And at last I have succeeded."

"I was given to understand that you were a dyed-in-the-wool skeptic," Gabriel said. "As are all of our colleagues. As I am."

"As *you* are? Now, that is a laugh. You had me fooled, I confess, until we began to study Snow White's cottage. Your eyes were too bright, my dear professor. They held the gleam of the fanatic."

"Which, I take it, is what you are?"

"I am far older than you, Penrose. I have had decades to perfect the ruse. We both know what is at stake if our colleagues discover that we are not cold, disinterested scientists, but believers."

*We.* Gabriel looked at Winkler, at Smith huddled in his cage, at the scientific instruments arrayed on the tabletop. Was this what he'd become? A fanatic with a hot gleam in his eye? He'd always felt his belief in the inexplicable, in the possibility of enchantment, had been something beautiful. But Winkler made it seem, suddenly, diseased.

"You shall come round," Winkler said, studying his face. "If you truly believe, you will understand that, now and then, small sacrifices have to be made in the name of truth."

"Sacrifices. Is that how you'd describe your murders of Homer T. Coop and Count Grunewald?"

"Coop was greedy, as you doubtless noticed. It was clear that he purchased the *schloss* only to gain access to the gold mine. He planned to cut those trees in his search for the mine, and he sent for me because the dwarf—"

"Smith."

"—told him the cottage might contain clues to the location of the mine."

"And because Coop knew about the mine, you killed him."

"Well, yes. Of course. That, and because he had not the least respect for Snow White's cottage. Philistine. He intended to have it razed. Surely you are able to sympathize with me, Penrose. I saw the way you touched that dwarf's spoon. As though it were the Holy Grail."

"How did you pull it off?"

"It was simple, really. At least, it was for me. I have always been two paces ahead of everyone else. It is lonely—"

"You overheard, I assume, Coop speaking to the scullery maid, Miss Bright, and alluding to his suspicions regarding the virtue of his wife and to his newfound knowledge that Miss Amaryllis was his wife's daughter."

"Indeed. I overheard that exchange by chance. When the same maid arrived at the library with the washing powder, and looking like such a stupid little parcel, I saw that I had been presented with a valuable opportunity. I had noticed Coop eating green apples, and before tea, I simply asked him for one. He gave it to me from his own pocket! Then I went to the kitchens to find the scullery maid. Unseen, of course. Servants, being of peasant stock, have no powers of observation. I hid myself in a cupboard filled with dried herbs. When I saw her, I followed her up to her chamber door. I concealed myself, and when she came out again—she had gone in for only a few minutes for a new apron, it seemed—I went into her chamber, poisoned the apple, and left behind the incriminating objects. At teatime, I took the apple from my pocket and placed it in the urn. Elegant."

"What about the green-handled paring knife? The English book of fairy tales?"

"I took the knife when I was in the kitchens. The book came from the castle library." Winkler beamed, as though Gabriel ought to give him a gold star.

"Why did you kill Count Grunewald?" Gabriel said. "Because you discovered he knew of the gold mine?"

"I always did believe Oxford recruited England's best and brightest. Yes. When it came to my attention that the first footman was the disgraced count—"

"Who told you?"

"Miss Amaryllis. She was distraught that morning

when I arrived to call on Mrs. Coop. I feigned sympathy, and she confided to me the circumstances of the previous evening's masquerade ball. Both of those American ladies are credulous fools, you understand. Mrs. Coop accepted the laudanum I gave her without question."

"You gave it to her, then? Whatever for?"

"To keep her out of the way."

"Were those bottles not from America?"

"There was but one bottle, which belonged to Mrs. Coop, so I suppose she had indeed brought it from America—a quack cure, by all appearances. I refilled the bottle, twice, with something rather stronger that I had in my bag."

"No one could accuse you of being ill-prepared, could they?"

Winkler smiled again. "Well. I ascertained that Miss Amaryllis knew nothing of the mine. But I decided Count Grunewald, his son, and his mother must all die to keep the secret safe. I could not kill them all at once, however. Recalling the herb closet I had hidden myself in a few days earlier, I decided I would do well to find my next batch of poison there. The mushrooms presented themselves. Imagine my delight when, later, I learned that the herb closet belonged to the old countess and that suspicion would eventually fall on her. All that remained, then, was killing the son. Hansel."

"This gold mine," Gabriel said, "was worth killing for?"

"It was a sacrifice I was willing to make."

"Is that how you would describe tormenting Smith, here?"

"I am not tormenting him, Penrose—he knows, of course, that he shall get a smart thrashing if he resists, but dwarves have thick skins. They are different from us. No, it is not torment. I am merely measuring his cranium."

"Phrenology?"

"I *am* a scientist."

# 34

*◈*

"Why is Smith injured?" Gabriel demanded.

"Oh, he did that to himself," Winkler said, "when I captured him. Flailed about like a slippery little toad."

"If you are only measuring his cranium, then what are those?" Gabriel pointed to a pair of nasty-looking steel pinchers.

Winkler chuckled. "Do not be naïve, Penrose. Dwarves never willingly tell where they have hidden their gold. But I mean to find that mine. I shall not let him go until he tells me."

"Smith doesn't know where the mine is."

"Of course he does."

"He's been searching for it, just like so many others have, but he doesn't know where it is."

"He does!"

"No." Gabriel paused. "But *I* do."

Winkler flushed. "How?"

"The tapestry."

"Tapestry?" Winkler looked angry; he'd missed something.

"All those silly cuckoo clocks you bought up only

contained part of a design—clever, by the way, opening the window of my chamber at the inn the night you stole my clock, even though you'd entered through the door. At any rate, the entire design was to be found on an ancient tapestry in the *schloss*, which gives a clear indication of where the mine is located."

Winkler loomed forward. "Tell me where."

"Only if you tell me what you've done with the young ladies."

Winkler jerked his chins back. "I assure you, I have very little time for young ladies."

Gabriel frowned. Winkler seemed to be telling the truth. But, then, where was Miss Flax? Where was Miss Bright? And Hansel?

His thoughts flew to Ghent and his ogres, to Herz and his axe.

"Tell me where the mine is," Winkler said. Then he was upon Gabriel like a huge, whiskered animal, grabbing his throat and puffing his stale, sausagey breath into Gabriel's face. They collapsed to the stone floor.

"*Tell me!*" Winkler shrieked. His sweaty hands closed around Gabriel's throat.

Gabriel, choking, dug into his breast pocket, patting about for his revolver. His peripheral vision closed in.

He felt the cold handle of his gun, pulled it out, and thrust it against Winkler's temple.

Winkler released his hands.

"Kindly dismount," Gabriel said.

Winkler heaved himself off.

Gabriel leapt to his feet and pressed the barrel of the revolver into Winkler's back. He nudged him towards the cage. "Unlock it."

Winkler unlocked it.

"Smith," Gabriel said, "Come on."

Smith stared, motionless.

"Come on," Gabriel repeated.

At last, Smith rose stiffly to his feet and hobbled out of the cage.

Gabriel pushed Winkler inside and locked it. "The cage," he said, "rather suits you, you beast."

There was blackness. It had been there for ages. Heavy and honey thick, seductive yet headachey, too. She only wished to keep still, in that blackness, until the throbbing in her temples went away.

But light pressed through her eyelids. And there was all that giggling.

Ophelia cracked open her eyes and winced. Golden light flooded her vision, blinded her. She saw fluttering silhouettes up above. Tree leaves. Then a fat little face appeared above her. It was grubby, with sparkling green eyes and an impish grin.

"Who are you?" Ophelia mumbled.

The creature only laughed.

Another chubby face popped into her vision, and another and another, until she was lying there on the forest floor with a total of seven little faces giggling and staring down at her, wearing expressions that ranged from diabolical to—in the case of the smallest one—cherubic.

"Mama!" one of them called over its shoulder. *"Hier!"*

Ophelia squeezed her eyes shut. Did fairy tale dwarves have mothers?

"Good heavens," someone else was saying.

A gentleman's voice, with a British accent. Warm, familiar. Yet there was something irksome about it, too.

"Miss Flax."

Then there were warm lips pressed against her forehead. Another torrent of giggles. She opened her eyes again and found herself staring up into Professor Penrose's shining hazel eyes. She boosted herself on her elbows.

"Thank God you're all right," Penrose murmured. "I've been worried sick."

"Where—where's Prue?" Memories flooded back.

"She's fine. She's at the castle, resting. Come, let's see if you can stand—Frau Herz has brought a horse for you."

Ophelia looked blearily around. They were in a mossy clearing. She saw a plump, smiling woman surrounded by seven urchins.

Then she noticed her feet, poking up from the muddy hem of her dress. On her left foot, she wore her boot. From her right toes dangled a dainty, yellow silk slipper.

"Where did that come from?" she said.

Penrose smiled. "Miss Amaryllis's slipper, which you dropped in the orchard. Herz picked it up, it seems, and gave it to his children as a plaything. They decided it was Cinderella's slipper, I believe, and when they found you out here this morning, they thought they'd see if you were its missing princess."

"Not this time, I'm afraid," Ophelia said, and sighed. "It's at least two inches too small."

"They found her," Hansel said to Prue.

Prue jerked her chin up from her chest. She'd been snoozing upright in an armchair in the castle's blue salon, too worried about Ophelia to think of going to bed, and too spent to care that she wasn't supposed to loiter in velvet chairs. "Where?" She staggered to her feet.

"In the wood."

"And she is—"

"She suffered a blow to the head, but it does not appear to be serious. The doctor is going to look her over."

Prue sank back into the chair. "I thought maybe. . . ."

"I know." Hansel crossed the carpet and took her hand. "But she is not. And you two shall return to America, safe and sound. Well, almost sound." He motioned towards Prue's neck.

She touched her throat, where a linen bandage covered the cut from Franz's sword. It stung a little, but it was nothing to write home about.

"What about Franz? Oh, crackers—what about Miss Gertie? She ain't still in that tunnel, is she?"

"Franz is at Gasthaus Schatz, in the village, resting. He

shall be fine. But Miss Darling is . . . there has been an accident."

"Oh no."

"Yes. The tunnel collapsed. The village men are still searching for her, but I believe she is . . . she shall not be found."

"Buried in the mountain with her treasure." Prue shuddered.

"The tunnel Miss Darling discovered seems to have been one of the shafts of a gold mine."

"Gold mine! Then your pa was right."

"Yes. Grandmother told me that Father read about an ancient mine in the Grunewald forest once, in a volume of *Schwarzwald* history somewhere in the castle library, but he could never find the passage again amid all those thousands of books. Yet, recalling the suggestion of the gold mine, he guessed that was what Coop and Smith were searching for."

"Why didn't he just come right out and tell you instead of sending you on a wild-goose chase after Snow White's tomb?"

"Father did not feel it was safe to put it in writing in the event that he was mistaken in his suspicions. He confided in grandmother about the mine—fortuitously, it turns out, since grandmother provided Professor Penrose with the clue he needed to lead him to the murderer."

Prue's eyes grew wide. "Who?"

"Professor Winkler."

"Ugh. I should've known. He set me up, too?"

Hansel nodded. "At any rate, the mine, as it is on castle land, now belongs to Mrs. Coop."

That was that, then. Hansel was still a poor fellow. Only Prue didn't give a monkey's peanut.

She stared down at their entangled fingers, his strong and brown, hers small, chapped, with a border of grime under the nails. Ashamed, she tugged her hand, but he didn't let go.

"Prue," he said gently. "I also wish to tell you that. . . ."

She swallowed. She couldn't lift her eyes to his.

"I wish to tell you," he said, "that Professor Penrose has offered me a substantial sum for an old tapestry belonging to my grandmother. It seems he collects such things. Antiquities and relics and so forth. With that money, I shall be able to establish my grandmother in a cottage with a servant to care for her. And I shall be able to return to university and complete my medical studies."

"You'll be a doctor," Prue said. "A doctor *and* a count." She tried to smile, but her face wouldn't move. "And I'll just be a—" What would she be? An out-of-work actress who, at the grand old age of nineteen, had already lost her looks? Who everyone said was simple and ill-spoken?

"It seems, Prue, that you have been taught to view yourself as no more than a beauty. And I have been, for most of my life, regarded as a landed and wealthy aristocrat. You knew me at first as only a gardener, yet still, you . . . you *saw* me. As I, perhaps, have truly seen you. Not simply your outward beauty." His voice was husky now. "If you are able to—willing, I should say—willing to wait a few years and carry out a correspondence with me, until I have completed my studies, perhaps you would consent, at a later date, of course, for I do not wish to burden one so young with weighty promises, well. . . ." He cleared his throat.

Prue lifted her eyes to his. "What sort of promise you angling at?"

"The promise to consider the possibility of, one day, becoming a doctor's wife."

Prue bit down on her lower lip to keep it from wobbling. "Sure," she said, her throat tight. "Sure I'll consider it."

Hansel smiled, but his brown eyes were grave, and he lifted her chapped hand to his lips and kissed it.


The doctor from Schilltag set to work on Ophelia's head wound in the castle kitchen. While the doctor worked, Penrose sat with her and told her how Professor Winkler had murdered both Coop and Count Grunewald, kidnapped Mr. Smith, and caged him in the hunting lodge.

Cook was bustling around in the kitchen, baking.

"Winkler struck me in the head?" Ophelia said to Penrose, wincing under the doctor's ministrations.

"Yes. He heard you following him—this was when he was taking Smith out to the lodge—and he came round behind you and hit you with a rock. He's been hauled off to jail in Baden-Baden."

"I'd have guessed it was Herz who struck me."

"Herz was working for Coop and, after Coop died, for Smith. He was merely protecting the estate from interlopers as Smith searched for the mine. Although he did kidnap us that night, I don't think, now, that he would've done us any real harm. Evidently, Smith told him to leave us in peace, because Smith suspected we might lead him to the gold mine. Which, as a matter of fact, I did."

"Tea, Miss Flax?" Cook said, proffering a cup.

"Please, Miss Flax," the doctor said, snipping a length of gauze with tiny scissors. "Stay still."

Ophelia took the tea and tried not to move her head. Cook trundled back to her oven.

"You found the gold mine?" Ophelia said to Penrose. "It really exists?"

"Yes, I believe it does. Only time will tell whether it contains the riches Ghent claimed it does. The main entrance, inside the very cave where you and I hid, has fallen in. Another shaft was discovered, too, on a cliff higher up, but it collapsed last night as well. And also. . . ."

"You have such a peculiar look on your face."

"What appears to be Snow White's tomb was discovered."

"Oh." Probably wisest not to make a detour into any more fairy tale business. "Will Smith work in the gold mine?"

"No. He wishes to return to America."

"Does Mrs. Coop know about the mine?"

"She's been informed, yes. She shall have to contend

with Ghent, of course. Perhaps she'll agree to sell him the mountain. But I understand her time shall be taken up with a still more pressing piece of business."

"Oh?"

"Mr. Hunt!" Cook called over her shoulder, as she pulled a cake pan from the oven. "He arrived at the castle yesterday evening—he said he wished to return a handkerchief—and Mrs. Coop was gussied up like Snow White when he arrived. Black hair, red lips, skin like chalk, and a gown suited to a girl of twelve. She said he was her prince, come at last. Says she means to marry him."

"Marry him!" Ophelia said. "Someone ought to warn her that he's pretty keen on her fortune."

"I suspect she knows," Penrose said, "and that she doesn't mind."

"That hankie," Ophelia said, "belongs to Miss Amaryllis. Why did Hunt have it? And why was he returning it to Mrs. Coop?"

"Hunt is ever so fond of sugared almonds," Cook said. "Madam had bundled up a few of them for him. As a token of her regard."

"But why in Miss Amaryllis's hankie?"

Cook tipped the cake pan onto a rack. "Did not wish to spoil her own, I fancy. Probably demanded Miss Amaryllis hand hers over."

"Poor Miss Amaryllis." Ophelia toyed with her teacup. "I know she's not the sweetest posy in the garden, but what'll become of her?"

"She means to return to New York," Cook said. "She says she has friends there, and she cannot sit idly by while her mother weds another monster."

They fell silent. Ophelia became aware that Penrose wore traveling clothes and that there was a leather bag near his feet.

He was leaving.

She pondered the wooden grain of the tabletop.

Penrose drew a watch out of his waistcoat pocket. His

expression was veiled. "Well, Miss Flax, I must be going." He stood. "I meant to ask you. . . ."

Her belly fluttered unaccountably. "Yes?"

"Would you accept the sum that you won in the gaming rooms last night? To assist you in your return to America, perhaps?"

"No! I couldn't. It was your money to begin with." Ophelia's ears burned. Was she some kind of charity case to him?

Penrose was frowning. "Are you certain?"

"Yes."

He paused. "I've a train to catch," he said at last. "But I must say, it was a pleasure to—to meet you. And I . . ." His voice trailed away, yet his eyes glowed strangely.

"Professor," Ophelia began. But she didn't know what it was she wished to tell him. That he couldn't go just yet, not till the indistinct, yet somehow urgent, thought welling in her throat came unstuck? That there was an awful twisting feeling where her heart was supposed to be?

"Ophelia!" Prue cried from the doorway. She was as pretty as ever, though a little worse for wear. She seemed to have some sort of bandage around her throat.

Penrose lifted his hat. "Good-bye, Miss Flax."

"Good-bye, Professor," Ophelia said. Then Prue was clinging around her neck, and he was gone.

Ophelia's throat ached with that unspoken thought. The twisting feeling in her chest went cold and still.

"I've been having forty fits about you!" Prue said. "I don't even hold it against you that you thought Hansel was a murderer and even went looking for, I don't know, my dead body in the forest, and—" She stopped, noticing the tears in Ophelia's eyes. "Oh, it doesn't matter. I'm just awful glad to see you."

"What has happened to your neck?"

Prue touched the bandage at her throat. "Just a scratch."

Ophelia saw Hansel. "I'm sorry," Ophelia said to him. "For—for suspecting you, and—"

"Please do not apologize, Miss Flax. You were only looking after Miss Bright."

"I know," Prue said to Ophelia, "you must be chomping at the bit to get back to New York, but I've had the most tip-top news."

Ophelia looked at Hansel. He blushed.

Oh no.

"Not that, silly." Prue laughed. "Hansel's going back to Heidelberg to study medicine. No, the news is ever so much more exciting than you could ever think up. Mr. Hunt's upstairs, calling on Mrs. Coop—my, what a bat she is—and I told him how my ma run off with someone, and you'll never guess."

"Mr. Hunt knows your mother?"

"Nope. But he knows where she is. Who'd have thought it? Ophelia, Ma married a baron or something, and she's in France. In Paris! Mr. Hunt wrote down exactly where."

"You've got your mother's address?" Ophelia had gotten used to the idea of Henrietta Bright being gone forever.

"You bet I do." Prue waved a piece of paper. "Say you'll come with me to find her."

Ophelia hesitated. She thought of misty green fields, a white barn, sweet-eyed dairy cows.

They would have to wait.

Ophelia squared her shoulders. "All right," she said to Prue. "I'll help you find your mother under one condition."

"What's that?"

Ophelia smiled. "No more hocus-pocus. No more fairy tales. And positively no more murders."

Turn the page for a preview of
Maia Chance's next Fairy Tale Fatal Mystery . . .

# Cinderella Six Feet Under

Coming soon from Berkley Prime Crime!

*Shams and delusions are esteemed for soundest
truths, while reality is fabulous. If men would steadily
observe realities only, and not allow themselves to be
deluded, life . . . would be like a fairy tale.*

—Henry David Thoreau (1854)

November, 1867
Oxford, England

The murdered girl, grainy in black-and-gray newsprint,
stared up at him. Her eyes were mournful and blank.

Gabriel placed the chipped Blue Willow teacup beside
the picture. His hand shook, and tea sloshed onto the newspaper. Ink bled.

Gabriel Augustus Penrose, despite being a bespectacled
professor, hadn't—not yet, at least—developed round shoulders or a nearsighted scowl. Although, such shoulders and
such a scowl *would* have suited the oaken desk, swaybacked
sofa, towers of books, and swirling dust motes in his study at
St. Remigius's College, Oxford. And Gabriel, at four-and-
thirty years of age, was certainly not given to fits of trembling.

But *this*.

He tore his eyes from the girl's. Was it today's newspaper? He glanced at the upper margin—yes. Perhaps
there was still time.

Time for . . . what?

He didn't customarily peruse the papers during his four o'clock cup of tea, but a student had come to see him, and he'd happened to leave *The Times* behind. The morgue drawing was on the fourth page, tucked between a report about a Piccadilly thief and an advertisement for stereoscopic slides. A familiar, lovely, and—according to the report—dead face.

SENSATIONAL MURDER IN PARIS: In the Marais district, a young woman was found dead as the result of two gunshot wounds in the garden of the mansion of the Marquis de la Roque-Fabliau, 15 Rue Garenne. She is thought to be the daughter of American actress Henrietta Bright, who wed the Marquis in January. The family solicitor said that it is not known how the tragic affair arose and that the family was unaware of the daughter's presence in Paris. The commissaire de police of that quarter has undertaken an assiduous search for her murderer.

Gabriel removed his spectacles, leaned forward on his knees, and laid his forehead in his palm. The murdered girl, Miss Prudence Bright, was a mere acquaintance. Perhaps the same might be said of Miss Ophelia Flax, the young American actress who had been traveling with Miss Bright when he'd encountered them in the Black Forest two months ago.

Mere acquaintance. The term could not account for the ripping sensation in his lungs. Fear for Miss Flax's safety, Gabriel could admit. But the underpinning of desire that spread below each and every memory of Miss Flax, well, that was simply inadmissible.

Bother.

Gabriel replaced his spectacles, stood, and strode to the jumbled bookcase behind his desk. He drew an antique volume from the shelf: *Histoires ou contes du temps passé* (*Stories or Fairy Tales from Past Times*) by Charles Perrault. He flipped through the pages, making certain a loose sheet of paper was still wedged inside.

He stuffed the volume in his leather satchel, along with

a few notebooks, yanked on his tweed jacket, clamped on his hat, and made for the door.

Two Days Earlier
Paris

The mansion's door knocker was shaped like a snarling mouse's head. Its bared teeth glinted in the gloom. Raindrops dribbled off the tip of its nose. It *ought* to have been enough of a warning. But Miss Ophelia Flax was in no position to skedaddle. She'd come too far, she had too little money left in her purse, and chill rainwater was making inroads into her left boot.

"Ready?" she said to Prue, the nineteen-year-old girl dripping like an unwrung mop next to her.

"Can't believe Ma would take up residence in a pit like this," Prue said. Her tone was all bluster, but her china doll's face was taut beneath her bonnet, and her yellow curls drooped. "You sure you got the address right?"

"Certain." The inked address had long since run, and the paper was as soggy as bread pudding by now. However, Ophelia had committed the address—15 Rue Garenne—to memory, and she'd studied the *Baedeker*'s Paris map in the railway car all the way from Germany, where she and Prue had lately been employed as maids in the household of an American millionaire. "It's hardly a pit, either. More like a palace." The mansion's stones, true, were streaked with soot, and the neighborhood was shabby. But Henrietta's mansion would dwarf every building in Littleton, New Hampshire, where Ophelia had been born and raised. It was grander than most buildings in New York City, too. "It's past its prime, that's all."

"I reckon Ma, of all people, wouldn't marry a poor feller."

"Likely not."

"But what if she ain't here? What if she went back to New York?"

"She'll be here. And she'll be ever so pleased to see you. It's been how long? Near a twelvemonth since she. . . ." Ophelia's voice trailed off. It was a chore to keep up the chipper song and dance.

"This is cork-brained," Prue said.

"We've come all this way, and we're not turning back now." Ophelia didn't mention that she had just enough maid's wages saved up for one—and *only* one—railway ticket to Cherbourg, one passage back to New York.

Prue's mother, Henrietta Bright, had been the star actress of Howard DeLuxe's Varieties, back in Manhattan, up until she'd figured out that walking down the aisle with a French marquis was a sight easier than treading the boards. She'd abandoned Prue, since ambitious brides have scant use for blossoming daughters.

But Prue and Ophelia had recently discovered Henrietta's whereabouts, so Ophelia fully intended to put her Continental misadventures behind her, just as soon as she installed Prue in the arms of her long-lost mother. If that installation was unsuccessful, well, they'd be in the suds all right. Again.

Before Ophelia could lose her nerve, she hefted the mouse-head door knocker and let it crash.

Prue eyed Ophelia's disguise. "Think she'll buy that getup?"

"Once we're safe inside, I'll take it off."

The door squeaked open.

A grizzle-headed gent loomed. His spine was shaped like a question mark, and his eyelids were studded with flesh-colored bumps. A steward, judging by his drab togs and stately wattle.

"Good evening," Ophelia said in her best matron's warble. "I wish to speak to Madame la Marquise de la Roque-Fabliau." What a mouthful. Like sucking on marbles.

"Regrettably, that shall not be possible," the steward said.

He spoke English. Lucky.

His gaze drifted southward.

Ophelia was five-and-twenty years of age, tall, and beanstalk straight as far as figures went. However, at present she appeared to be a pillowy-hipped, deep-bosomed dame in a black bombazine gown and woolen cloak. Her light brown hair was concealed beneath a steel gray wig and a black taffeta traveling bonnet, and her oval face was crinkly with cosmetics. All for the sake of practicality. Beautiful flibbertigibbets like Prue needed chaperones when traveling, so Ophelia had dug into her theatrical case and transformed herself into the sort of daunting chaperone that made even the most shameless lotharios turn tail and pike off.

"Now see here!" Ophelia said. "We shan't be turned out into the night like beggars. My charge and I have traveled hundreds of miles in order to visit the marquise, and we mean to see her. This young lady is her daughter."

The steward took in Prue's muddy skirts, her cheap cloak and crunched straw bonnet, the two large carpetbags slumped at their feet. He didn't budge.

Stuffed shirt.

"Baldewyn," a woman's voice called behind him. "Baldewyn, *qui est cette personne la*?" There was a *tick-tick* of heels, and a young lady appeared beside the steward. She was perhaps twenty years of age, with a pointed snout of a face like a mongoose and beady little animal eyes to match. Her gown had more ruffles than a flustered goose. Her shiny dark hair was bedecked with a lace headdress, and gems sparkled at her throat.

"*Pardonnez-moi* Mademoiselle Eglantine," Baldewyn said, "this young lady—an American, clearly—claims to be a kinswoman of the marquise."

"Kinswoman?" Eglantine said. "How do you mean, kinswoman? Of my *belle-mère*? Oh. Well. She is . . . absent."

Ophelia had picked up enough French from a fortuneteller, during her stint in P. Q. Putnam's Traveling Circus a few years back, to know what *belle-mère* meant: stepmother.

"No matter," Ophelia said. "Mademoiselle, may I present to you your stepsister, Miss Prudence Deliverance Bright?"

"I assure you," Eglantine said, "I have but one sister, and she is inside. I do not know who you are, or what sort of little amusement you are playing at, but I have guests to attend to. Now, *s'il vous plaît*, go away!" She spun around and disappeared, the *tick-tick* of her heels receding.

Baldewyn's dour mouth twitched upwards. Then he slammed the door in their noses.

"Well, I never!" Ophelia huffed. "They didn't even ask for proof!"

"I *told* you Ma don't want me."

"For the thousandth time, humbug." Ophelia hoisted her carpetbag and trotted down the steps, into the rain. "She doesn't even know you're on the European continent, let alone on her doorstep. That Miss Eglantine—"

"Fancies she's the Queen of Sheba!" Prue came down the steps behind her, hauling her own bag.

"—said your Ma's absent. So all we need to do is wait. The question is, where?" They stood on the sidewalk and looked up and down the street. It was lined with monumental old buildings and shivering black trees. A carriage splashed by, its driver bent into the slanting rain. "We can't stay out of doors. May as well be standing under Niagara Falls. I'm afraid my greasepaint's starting to run, and this padding is like a big sponge." Ophelia shoved her soaked pillow-bosom into line. "Come on. Surely we'll find someplace to huddle for an hour or so. Your sister—"

"Don't *call* her that!"

"Very well, Miss Eglantine, said they've got guests. So I figure your ma will be home soon."

The mansion's foundation stones went right to the pavement. No front garden. But further along they found a carriageway arch. Its huge iron gates stood open.

"Now see?" Ophelia said. "Nice and dry under there."

"Awful dark."

"Not . . . terribly."

More hoof clopping. Was it—Ophelia squinted—was it the same carriage that had passed by only a minute ago? Yes. It was. The same bent driver, the same splashing horses. And—

Her heart went lickety-split.

—and a pale smudge of a face peering out the window. Right at her.

Then it had gone.

On the other side of the carriageway arch was a big, dark courtyard. It was bordered on two sides by the wings of Henrietta's mansion. The third side was an ivy-covered carriage house and stables, and the fourth side was a tall stone wall. The garden seemed neglected. Shrubs were shaggy. Flower beds were tangled with weeds. The air stank of decay.

"Look," Prue said, pointing. "A party."

Light shone from tall windows. Figures moved about inside a chamber, and piano music tinkled.

"Let's have a look." Ophelia abandoned her carpetbag under the arch and set off down a path. Wet twigs and leaves dragged at her skirts.

"You mean spy on them?"

"Miss Eglantine didn't seem the most honest little fish."

"And that Baldy-win feller was a troll."

"So maybe your ma is really in there after all."

Up close to the high windows, it was like peeping into a jewel box: cream paneled walls with gold leaf flowers and swags, and enough mirrors and crystal chandeliers to make your eyes sting. Ophelia counted five richly dressed ladies and gentlemen loitering about. A plump, dour woman in a gray bun—a servant—stood against a wall. A frail young lady in owlish spectacles crashed away at the piano.

"There's Eggy," Prue said. "Maybe that's the sister she mentioned." A young lady in a lavish green tent of a gown sat next to Eglantine.

"Same dark hair," Ophelia said.

"Same mean little eyes."

"A good deal taller, however, and somewhat . . . wider."

"Spit it out. She looks like a prizefighter in a wig."

"Prue! That might be your own sister you're going on about."

"*Step*sister. Look—they're having words, I reckon. Eggy don't seem too pleased."

The young ladies' heads were bent close together, and they appeared to be bickering. The larger lady in green had her eyes stuck on something across the room.

Ah. A gentleman. Fair-haired, flushed, and strapping, crammed into a white evening jacket with gold buttons, medals and ribbons, and epaulets on the shoulders. He conversed with a burly fellow in black evening clothes, with a lion's mane of dark gold hair flowing to his shoulders.

"Ladies quarreling about a fellow," Ophelia said. "How very tiresome."

"*Some* fellers are worth talking of."

"If you are hinting I care to discuss any gentleman, least of all Professor Penrose, then—well, I do not, I *sincerely* do not, feel a whit of sentiment for that man." Well, maybe Ophelia felt a smidge of vexation and a trifle of fury. But nothing else.

"Oh, sure," Prue said.

Ophelia longed for things, certainly. But not for *him*. She longed for a home. She longed, with that gritted-molars sort of longing, to be snug in a third-class berth in the guts of a steamship barging towards America. She'd throw over acting, head up north to New Hampshire or Vermont, get work on a farmstead. Merciful heavens! She knew how to scour pots, tend goats, hoe beans, darn socks, weave rush chair seats, and cure a rash with apple cider vinegar. So why was she gallivanting across Europe, penniless, half-starved, shivering, in this preposterous disguise?

Her eyes slid sideways.

Prue. She was doing it for Prue.

"*Duck!*" Prue whispered.

There was a clatter above, voices coming closer; someone was pushing a window open.

Ophelia and Prue stumbled off to the side until they were safely in shadow once more. They'd come to the second wing of the mansion. All of the windows were black except two on the main floor.

"Let's look," Ophelia whispered. "Could be your ma."

"Sure. Could be a wolf, too."

"A wolf? In Paris? Indoors?"

They picked their way towards the windows, into what seemed to be a marshy vegetable patch.

Ophelia stepped around some sort of half-rotten squash and wedged the toe of her boot between two building stones. She gripped the sill and pulled herself up. Her waterlogged rump padding threatened to pull her backwards. She squinted through the glass. "Most peculiar," she whispered. "Looks like some sort of workshop. Tables heaped with knickknacks."

"A tinker's shop?" Prue clambered up. "Oh. Look at all them gears and cogs and things."

"Why would there be a tinker's shop in this grand house? Your Ma married a nobleman. Yet it's on the main floor of the house, not down where the servants' workplaces must be. And it looks like a library. A fancy one." The chamber was walled with bookshelves. A fire burned in a carved fireplace, and thousands of gold-embossed book spines glimmered.

"Crackers," Prue whispered. "Someone's in there."

Sure enough, a round, bald man was hunched over a table. One of his hands held a cube-shaped box. The other twisted a screwdriver. Ophelia couldn't see his face because he wore brass jeweler's goggles.

"What in tarnation is he doing?" Prue spoke too emphatically and bumped her bonnet brim on the windowpane.

The man glanced up. His goggles lenses shone.

Holy Moses. He looked like something crawled out of a nightmare.

The man stood so abruptly that his chair collapsed behind him. He lurched towards them.

Ophelia hopped down into the vegetable patch.

Prue recoiled. For a few seconds she seemed suspended, twirling her arms in the air like a graceless hummingbird. Then she pitched backwards and thumped into the garden, a few steps from Ophelia.

"Hurry!" Ophelia whispered to Prue. "Get up! He's opening the window!"

Prue didn't get up. She screamed. The kind of long, shrill scream you'd use when, say, falling off a cliff.

The man flung open the window. He yelled down at them in French.

"Get me off of it!" Prue yelled. "Oh golly, get me *off* of it!"

Ophelia crouched, hooked her hands under Prue's arms, and dragged her to her feet. They both stared, speechless, down into the dark vegetation. Raindrops smacked Ophelia's cheeks. Prue panted and whimpered at the same time.

Then—the man must've turned on a lamp—light flared up.

A gorgeous gown of ivory tulle and silk sprawled at Ophelia and Prue's feet, embroidered with gold and silver thread that shone like spider's webbing in the gaslight.

A gown. That was all. That had to be all.

But there was a foot—mercy, a *foot*—protruding from the hem of the gown. Bare, white, slick with rainwater. Toes bruised and blood raw, the big toenail purple.

Ophelia's tongue went sour.

There was hair. Long, wet, curled hair, tangled with a leaf and clotted with blood. A face. Eyes stretched open. Dead as a doornail.

Ophelia stopped breathing.

The thing was, the dead girl was the spitting image of . . . Prue.